Philip Roth

THE COUNTERLIFE

VINTAGE

TO MY FATHER AT EIGHTY-FIVE

Published by Vintage 2005

2 4 6 8 10 9 7 5 3

Copyright © Philip Roth 1986

First published in Great Britain in 1987 by
Jonathan Cape

The selection on page 43 is reprinted with permission from *Fodor's Switzerland 1986*, copyright © 1985 by Fodor's Travel Guides. Published by Fodor's Travel Guides. Lyrics from 'Lay, Lady, Lay' by Bob Dylan, copyright © 1969 by Big Sky Music. Used by permission. All rights reserved. The selection on page 190 from *The Short Novels of Tolstoy*, selected, with an introduction by Philip Rahv, translated by Aylmer Maude, Dial Press, 1946

Vintage
Random House, 20 Vauxhall Bridge Road, London SW1V 2SA

Addresses for companies within The Random House Group Limited can be found at: www.randomhouse.co.uk/offices.htm

The Random House Group Limited Reg. No. 954009

A CIP catalogue record for this book
is available from the British Library

ISBN 9780099481355

The Random House Group Limited makes every effort to ensure that the papers used in its books are made from trees that have been legally sourced from well-managed and credibly certified forests. Our paper procurement policy can be found at: www.randomhouse.co.uk/paper.htm

Printed in

The Counterlife

1. Basel

Ever since the family doctor, during a routine checkup, discovered an abnormality on his EKG and he went in overnight for the coronary catheterization that revealed the dimensions of the disease, Henry's condition had been successfully treated with drugs, enabling him to work and to carry on his life at home exactly as before. He didn't even complain of chest pain or of the breathlessness that his doctor might well have expected to find in a patient with advanced arterial obstruction. He was asymptomatic before the routine examination that revealed the abnormality and remained that way during the year before he decided on surgery—without symptoms but for a single terrible side effect from the very medication that stabilized his condition and substantially reduced the risk of a heart attack.

The trouble began after two weeks on the drug. "I've heard this a thousand times," the cardiologist said when Henry telephoned to report what was happening to him. The cardiologist, like Henry a successful, vigorous professional man not yet into his forties, couldn't have been more sympathetic. He would try to reduce the dose to a point where the medicine, a beta-blocker, continued to control the coronary disease and to blunt the hypertension without interfering with Henry's sexual function. Through a fine-tuning of the medication, he said, you could sometimes achieve "a compromise."

They experimented for six months, first with the dosage and, when that didn't work, with other brands of the drug, but nothing helped: he no longer awakened with his morning erection or had sufficient potency for intercourse with his wife, Carol, or with his assistant, Wendy, who was sure that it was she, and not the medication, that was responsible for this startling change. At the end of the day, with the outer-office door locked and the blinds down, she worked with all her finesse to arouse him, but work it was, hard labor for both of them, and when he told her it was no use and begged her to stop, had finally to pry open her jaws to make her stop, she was even more convinced that the fault was hers. One evening, when she had burst into tears and told him that she knew it was only a matter of time before he went out and found somebody new, Henry struck her across the face. If it had been the act of a rhino, of a wild man in an orgasmic frenzy, Wendy would have been characteristically accommodating; this, however, was a manifestation, not of ecstasy, but of utter exhaustion with her blindness. She didn't understand, the stupid girl! But of course he didn't either, failed as yet to comprehend the confusion that this loss might elicit in somebody who happened to adore him.

Immediately afterward, he was overcome with remorse. Holding her to him, he assured Wendy, who was still weeping, that she was virtually all he thought about now every day—indeed (though he could not say as much) if Wendy would only let him find work for her in another dental office, he wouldn't have to be reminded every five minutes of what he could no longer have. There were still moments during office hours when he surreptitiously caressed her or watched with the old yearning as she moved about in her formfitting white tunic and trousers, but then he remembered his little pink heart pills and was plummeted into despair. Soon Henry began to have the most demonic fantasies of the adoring young woman who would have done any-

8

thing to restore his potency being overwhelmed before his eyes by three, four, and five other men.

He couldn't control his fantasies of Wendy and her five face-less men, and yet at the movies with Carol he preferred now to lower his lids and rest his eyes till the love scenes were over. He couldn't stand the sight of the girlie magazines piled up in his barbershop. He had all he could do not to get up and leave the table when, at a dinner party, one of their friends began to joke about sex. He began to feel the emotions of a deeply unattractive person, an impatient, resentful, puritan disdain for the virile men and appetizing women engrossed by their erotic games. The cardiologist, after putting him on the drug, had said, "Forget your heart now and live," but he couldn't, because five days a week from nine to five he couldn't forget Wendy.

He returned to the doctor to have a serious talk about surgery. The cardiologist had heard that a thousand times too. Patiently he explained that they did not like to operate on people who were asymptomatic and in whom the disease showed every sign of being stabilized by medication. If Henry did finally choose the surgical option, he wouldn't be the first patient to find that preferable to an indefinite number of years of sexual inactivity; nonetheless, the doctor strongly advised him to wait and see how the passage of time affected his "adjustment." Though Henry wasn't the worst candidate for bypass surgery, the location of the grafts he'd need didn't make him the ideal candidate either. "What does that mean?" Henry asked. "It means that this operation is no picnic in the best of circumstances, and yours aren't the best. We even lose people, Henry. Live with it."

Those words frightened him so that on the drive home he sternly reminded himself of all those who live of necessity without women, and in far more harrowing circumstances than his own—men in prison, men at war . . . yet soon enough he was remembering Wendy again, conjuring up every position in which she could be entered by the erection he no longer had, envision-ing her just as hungrily as any daydreaming convict, only without recourse to the savage quick fix that keeps a lonely man half-sane

*in his cell. He reminded himself of how he'd happily lived with-
out women as a prepubescent boy—had he ever been more
content than back in the forties during those summers at the
shore? Imagine that you're eleven again . . . but that worked no
better than pretending to be serving a sentence at Sing Sing.
He reminded himself of the terrible unruliness spawned by un-
constrainable desire—the plotting, the longing, the crazily im-
petuous act, the dreaming relentlessly of the other, and when
one of these bewitching others at last becomes the clandestine
mistress, the intrigue and anxiety and deception. He could now
be a faithful husband to Carol. He would never have to lie
to Carol—he'd never have anything to lie about. They could
once more enjoy that simple, honest, trusting marriage that had
been theirs before Maria had appeared in his office ten years
earlier to have a crown repaired.*

*He'd at first been so thrown by the green silk jersey dress and
the turquoise eyes and the European sophistication that he could
hardly manage the small talk at which he was ordinarily so pro-
ficient, let alone make a pass while Maria sat in the chair obediently opening her mouth. From the punctiliousness with which
they treated each other during her four visits, Henry could never
have imagined that on the eve of her return to Basel ten months
later, she would be saying to him, "I never thought I could love
two men," and that their parting would be so horrendous—it
had all been so new to both of them that they had made adultery positively virginal. It had never occurred to Henry, until
Maria came along to tell him so, that a man who looked like
him could probably sleep with every attractive woman in town.
He was without sexual vanity and deeply shy, a young man still
largely propelled by feelings of decorum that he had imbibed and
internalized and never seriously questioned. Usually the more
appealing the woman, the more withdrawn Henry was; with the
appearance of an unknown woman whom he found particularly
desirable, he would become hopelessly, rigidly formal, lose all
spontaneity, and often couldn't even introduce himself without
flushing. That was the man he'd been as a faithful husband—*

that's why *he'd been a faithful husband. And now he was doomed to be faithful again.*

The worst of adjusting to the drug turned out to be adjusting to the drug. It shocked him that he was able to live without sex. It could be done, he was doing it, and that killed him—just as once being unable *to live without it was what killed him. Adjusting meant resigning himself to being this way, and he refused to be this way, and was further demoralized by stooping to the euphemism "this way." And yet, so well did the adjustment proceed, that some eight or nine months after the cardiologist had urged him not to rush into surgery before testing the effect of the passage of time, Henry could no longer remember what an erection was. Trying to, he came up with images out of the old pornographic funnies, the blasphemous "hotbooks" that had disclosed to kids of his generation the underside of Dixie Dugan's career. He was plagued by mental images of outlandish cocks and by the fantasies of Wendy with all those other men. He imagined her sucking them off. He imagined himself sucking them off. He began secretly to idolize all the potent men as though he no longer mattered as a man himself. Despite his dark good looks and tall, athletic physique, he seemed to have passed overnight from his thirties to his eighties.*

One Saturday morning, after telling Carol that he was going for a walk up in the Reservation hills—"to be by myself," he explained to her somberly—he drove into New York to see Nathan. He didn't phone ahead because he wanted to be able to turn around and come home if he decided at the last minute it was a bad idea. They weren't exactly teenagers anymore, up in the bedroom trading hilarious secrets—since the death of their parents, they weren't even like brothers. Yet he desperately needed someone to hear him out. All Carol could say was that he must not even begin to think of surgery if that meant running the slightest risk of rendering fatherless their three children. The illness was under control and at thirty-nine he remained a tremendous success in every imaginable way. How could all this suddenly matter so when for years now they'd rarely made love with any real passion? She wasn't complaining, it happened to everyone—there wasn't a marriage she knew of that was any different. "But I am only thirty-nine," Henry replied. "So am I," she said, trying to help by being sensible and firm, "but after eighteen years I don't expect marriage to be a torrid love affair."

It was the cruelest thing he could imagine a wife saying to a husband—What do we need sex for anyway? He despised her for saying it, hated her so that then and there he'd made up his mind to talk to Nathan. He hated Carol, he hated Wendy, if Maria were around he would have hated her too. And he hated men, men with their enormous hard-ons from just looking at Playboy magazine.

He found a garage in the East 80s and from a street-corner box nearby dialed Nathan's apartment, reading, while the phone rang, what had been scribbled across the remains of a Manhattan directory chained to the cubicle: Want to come in my mouth? Melissa 879-0074. Hanging up before Nathan could answer, he dialed 879-0074. A man answered. "For Melissa," said Henry, and hung up again. This time after dialing Nathan, he let the phone ring twenty times.

You can't leave them fatherless.

At Nathan's brownstone, standing alone in the downstairs hallway, he wrote him a note that he immediately tore up. Inside a hotel on the corner of Fifth he found a pay phone and dialed 879-0074. Despite the beta-blocker, which he'd thought was supposed to prevent adrenaline from overcharging the heart, his was pounding like the heart of something wild on a rampage—the doctor wouldn't need a stethoscope to hear it now. Henry grabbed at his chest, counting down to the final boom, even as a voice sounding like a child's answered the phone. "Hullo?"

"Melissa?"

"Yes."

"How old are you?"

"Who is this?"

He hung up just in time. Five, ten, fifteen more of those resounding strokes and the coronary would have settled every-

thing. Gradually his breathing evened out and his heart felt more like a wheel, stuck and spinning vainly in the mud.

He knew he should telephone Carol so that she wouldn't worry, but instead he crossed the street to Central Park. He'd give Nathan an hour; if Nathan wasn't back by then, he'd forget about the operation and go home. He could not leave them fatherless.

Entering the underpass back of the museum, he saw at the other end a big kid, white, about seventeen, balancing a large portable radio on one shoulder and drifting lazily into the tunnel on roller skates. The volume was on full blast—Bob Dylan singing, "Lay, lady, lay . . . lay across my big brass bed . . ." Just what Henry needed to hear. As though he'd come inadvertently upon a dear old pal, the grinning kid raised a fist in the air, and gliding up beside Henry he shouted, "Bring back the sixties, man!" His voice reverberated dully in the shadowy tunnel, and amiably enough Henry replied, "I'm with you, friend," but when the boy had skated by him he couldn't hold everything inside any longer and finally began to cry. Bring it all back, he thought, the sixties, the fifties, the forties—bring back those summers at the Jersey Shore, the fresh rolls perfuming the basement grocery in the Lorraine Hotel, the beach where they sold the bluefish off the morning boats . . . He stood in that tunnel behind the museum bringing back all by himself the most innocent memories out of the most innocent months of his most innocent years, memories of no real consequence rapturously recalled—and bonded to him like the organic silt stopping up the arteries to his heart. The bungalow two blocks up from the boardwalk with the faucet at the side to wash the sand off your feet. The guess-your-weight stall in the arcade at Asbury Park. His mother leaning over the windowsill as the rain starts to fall and pulling the clothes in off the line. Waiting at dusk for the bus home from the Saturday afternoon movie. Yes, the man to whom this was happening had been that boy waiting with his older brother for the Number 14 bus. He couldn't grasp it—he could as well have been trying to understand particle physics. But then he couldn't believe that the man to whom it was happening was himself and that, whatever this man must undergo, he must undergo too. Bring the past back, the future, bring me back the present—I am only thirty-nine!

He didn't return to Nathan's that afternoon to pretend that nothing of consequence had transpired between them since they were their parents' little boys. On the way over he had been thinking that he had to see him because Nathan was the only family he had left, when all along he had known that there was no family anymore, the family was finished, torn asunder—Nathan had seen to that by the ridicule he'd heaped upon them all in that book, and Henry had done the rest by the wild charges he'd leveled after their ailing father's death from a coronary in Florida. "You killed him, Nathan. Nobody will tell you—they're too frightened of you to say it. But you killed him with that book." No, confessing to Nathan what had been going on in the office for three years with Wendy would only make the bastard happy, prove him right—I'll provide him with a sequel to Carnovsky! It had been idiotic enough ten years earlier telling him everything about Maria, about the money I gave her and the black underwear and the stuff of hers that I had in my safe, but bursting as I was I had to tell someone—and how could I possibly understand back then that exploiting and distorting family secrets was my brother's livelihood? He won't sympathize with what I'm going through—he won't even listen. "Don't want to know," he'll tell me from behind the peephole, and won't even bother to open the door. "I'd only put it in a book and you wouldn't like that at all." And there'll be a woman there—either some wife he's bored with on the way out or some literary groupie on the way in. Maybe both. I couldn't bear it.

Instead of going directly home, back in Jersey he drove to Wendy's apartment and made her pretend to be a black twelve-year-old girl named Melissa. But though she was willing—to be black, twelve, ten, to be anything he asked—it made no difference to the medication. He told her to strip and crawl to him on her knees across the floor, and when she obeyed he struck her.

14

That didn't do much good either. His ridiculous cruelty, far from goading him into a state of arousal, reduced him to tears for the second time that day. Wendy, looking awfully helpless, stroked his hand while Henry sobbed, "This isn't me! I'm not this kind of man!" "Oh, darling," she said, sitting at his feet in her garter belt and beginning now to cry herself, "you must have the operation, you must—otherwise you're going to go mad."

He'd left the house just after nine in the morning and didn't get home until close to seven that evening. Fearing that he was alone somewhere dying—or already dead—at six Carol had called the police and asked them to look for the car; she'd told them that he'd gone for a walk in the Reservation hills that morning and they said that they would go up and check the trails. It alarmed Henry to hear that she had called the police—he had been depending upon Carol not to crack and give way like Wendy, and now his behavior had shattered her too.

He remained himself still too stunned and mortified to grasp the nature of the loss to all the interested parties.

When Carol asked why he hadn't phoned to say he wouldn't be home until dinner, he answered accusingly, "Because I'm impotent!" as though it was she and not the drug that had done it.

It was she. He was sure of it. It was having to stay with her and be responsible to the children that had done it. Had they divorced ten years earlier, had he left Carol and their three kids to begin a new life in Switzerland, he would never have fallen ill. Stress, the doctors told him, was a major factor in heart disease, and giving up Maria was the unendurable stress that had brought it on in him. There was no other explanation for such an illness in a man otherwise so young and fit. It was the consequence of failing to find the ruthlessness to take what he wanted instead of capitulating to what he should do. The disease was the reward for the dutiful father, husband, and son. You find yourself in the same place after such a long time, without the possibility of escape, along comes a woman like Maria, and instead of being strong and selfish, you are, of all things, good.

The cardiologist gave him a serious talking-to the next time Henry came for a checkup. He reminded him that since he'd been on the medication his EKG had shown a marked diminution of the abnormality that had first signaled his trouble. His blood pressure was safely under control, and unlike some of the cardiologist's patients, who couldn't brush their teeth without the effort causing severe angina, he was able to work all day standing on his feet without discomfort or shortness of breath. He was again reassured that if there was any deterioration in his condition, it would almost certainly occur gradually and show up first on the EKG or with a change of symptoms. Were that to happen, they would then reevaluate the surgical option. The cardiologist reminded him that he could continue safely along on this regimen for as long as fifteen or twenty years, by which time the bypass operation would more than likely be an outmoded technique; he predicted that by the 1990s they would almost certainly be correcting arterial blockage by other than surgical means. The beta-blocker might itself soon come to be replaced by a drug that did not affect the central nervous system and cause this unfortunate consequence—that sort of progress was inevitable. In the meantime, as he'd advised him already and could only repeat, Henry must simply forget his heart and go out and live. "You must see the medication in context," the cardiologist said, lightly striking his desk.

And was that the last there was to say? Was he now expected to get up and go home? Dully Henry told him, "But I can't accept the sexual blow." The cardiologist's wife was someone Carol knew and so of course he couldn't explain about Maria or Wendy or the two women in between, and what each of them had meant to him. Henry said, "This is the most difficult thing I've ever had to face."

"You haven't had a very difficult life then, have you?"

He was stunned by the cruelty of the reply—to say such a thing to a man as vulnerable as himself! Now he hated the doctor too.

That night, from his study, he again phoned Nathan, his last remaining consolation, and this time found him home. He was barely able to prevent himself from dissolving in tears when he *told his brother that he was seriously ill and asked if he could come to see him. It was impossible living alone any longer with his staggering loss.*

Needless to say, these were not the three thousand words that Carol had been expecting when she'd phoned the evening before the funeral and, despite all that had driven the two brothers apart, asked if Zuckerman would deliver a eulogy. Nor was the writer ignorant of what was seemly, or indifferent to the conventions that ruled these occasions; nonetheless, once he'd started there was no stopping, and he was at his desk most of the night piecing Henry's story together from the little he knew.

When he got over to Jersey the next morning, he told Carol more or less the truth about what had happened. "I'm sorry if you were counting on me," he said, "but everything I put down was wrong. It just didn't work." He supposed that she would now suppose that if a professional writer finds himself stymied by what to say at his own brother's funeral, it's either hopelessly mixed emotions or an old-fashioned bad conscience that's doing it. Well, less harm in what Carol happened to think of him than in delivering to the assembled mourners this grossly inappropriate text.

All Carol said was what she usually said: she understood; she even kissed him, she who had never been his greatest fan. "It's all right. Please don't worry. We just didn't want to leave you out. The quarrels no longer matter. That's all over. What matters today is that you were brothers."

Fine, fine. But what *about* the three thousand words? The trouble was that words that were morally inappropriate for a funeral were just the sort of words that engaged him. Henry wasn't dead twenty-four hours when the narrative began to burn a hole in Zuckerman's pocket. He was now going to have a very hard time getting through the day without seeing everything that happened as *more*, a continuation not of life but of his work or work-to-be. Already, by failing to use his head and discreetly cobbling together some childhood memories with a few conventionally consoling sentiments, he'd made it impossible for himself to take his place with everyone else, a decent man of mature years mourning a brother who'd died before his time—instead he was again the family outsider. Entering the synagogue with Carol and the kids, he thought, "This profession even fucks up grief."

Though the synagogue was large, every seat was occupied, and clustered at the rear and along the side aisles were some twenty or thirty adolescents, local youngsters whose teeth Henry had been taking care of since they were children. The boys looked stoically at the floor and some of the girls were already crying. A few rows from the back, unobtrusive in a gray sweater and skirt, sat a slight, girlishly young blonde whom Zuckerman wouldn't even have noticed if he hadn't been looking for her—whom he wouldn't have been able to recognize if not for the photograph that Henry had brought along on his second visit. "The picture," Henry warned, "doesn't do her justice." Zuckerman was admiring nonetheless: "Very pretty. You make me envious." A little immodest little-brother smirk of self-admiration could not be entirely suppressed, even as Henry replied, "No, no, she doesn't photograph well. You can't really see from this what it is she has." "Oh yes I can," said Nathan, who was and wasn't surprised by Wendy's plainness. Maria, if not as astonishingly beautiful in *her* picture as she'd first been described by Henry, had been attractive enough in a sternly Teutonic, symmetrical way. However, *this* bland little twat—why, Carol with her curly black hair and long dark lashes looked erotically more promising. It was, of course, with Wendy's picture still in his hand that Zuckerman should have laid into Henry with all he had—that might even have been *why* Henry had brought the picture, to give him the opening, to hear Nathan tell him, "Idiot! Ass! Absolutely not! If you wouldn't leave Carol to run off with Maria, a woman whom you actually *loved*, you are not going into the hospital for dangerous surgery just because some broad at the office blows you every night before you go home for dinner! I have heard your case for that operation and up till now haven't said a word—but my verdict, which is law, is *no!*"

18

But inasmuch as Henry wasn't dead then but alive—alive and outraged that a man with his moral credentials should be thwarted in this single, small, harmless transgression—inasmuch as he had already accepted the compromise of Wendy when what he had dreamed of and denied himself was to be remade in Europe with a European wife, to become in Basel an unfettered, robust, fully grown-up American expatriate dentist, Zuckerman had found his thoughts moving more along these lines: "This is his rebellion against the deal he's made, the outlet for what's survived of brutish passion. He surely hasn't come to me to be told that life obstructs and life denies and there's nothing to do but accept it. He's here to argue it out in my presence because my strong point isn't *supposed* to be a talent for self-denial—I, in their lore, am the reckless, freewheeling impulsive, to me they've assigned the role of family id, and he is the exemplary brother. No, a certified irresponsible spirit can't now come on in fatherly tones, gently telling him, 'You don't need what you want, my boy—relinquish your Wendy and you'll suffer less.' No, Wendy is his freedom and his manhood, even if she happens to look to me a little like boredom incarnate. She's a nice kid with an oral hang-up who he's pretty sure will never phone the house—so why *shouldn't* he have her? The more I look at this picture, the more I understand his point. How much is the poor guy asking for?"

But you reason differently so close to the coffin of your only brother that you can practically rest your cheek on the shining mahogany wood. When Nathan made the inevitable effort to imagine Henry laid out inside, he did not see, silenced, the unmanned, overheated adulterer who had refused to be resigned to losing his potency—he saw the boy of ten, lying there wearing flannel pajamas. One Halloween when they were children, hours after Nathan had brought Henry home from trick-or-treating in the neighborhood, after the whole family had long been in bed, Henry had wandered out of his room, down the stairs, out the door, and into the street, heading for the intersection at Chancellor Avenue without even his slippers on and still in his sleep. Miraculously, a friend of the family who lived over in Hillside happened to be driving by their corner as Henry was about to step off the curb against the light. He pulled over, recognized the child under the street lamp as Victor Zuckerman's little son, and Henry was safely home and back beneath the covers only minutes later. It was thrilling for him to learn the next morning of what he'd done while still fast asleep and to hear of the bizarre coincidence that had led to his rescue; until adolescence, when he began to develop more spectacular ideas of personal heroism as a hurdler for the high-school track team, he must have repeated to a hundred people the story of the daring midnight excursion to which he himself had been completely tuned out.

But now he was in his coffin, the sleepwalking boy. This time nobody had taken him home and tucked him back into bed when he went wandering off alone in the dark, unable to forswear his Halloween kicks. Equally possessed, in a Herculean trance, carried along by an exciting infusion of Wild West bravado—that's how he'd struck Nathan on the afternoon he arrived at his apartment fresh from a consultation with the cardiac surgeon. Zuckerman was surprised: it wasn't the way he would have imagined walking out of one of those guys' offices after he'd told you his plans for carving you up.

Henry unfolded on Nathan's desk what looked like the design for a big cloverleaf highway. It was the sketch that the surgeon had made to show him where the grafts would go. The operation sounded, as Henry described it, no trickier than a root-canal job. He replaces this one and this one and hooks them up here, bypasses three tiny ones feeding into the one back there—and that's the whole shmeer. The surgeon, a leading Manhattan specialist whose qualifications Zuckerman had double-checked, told Henry that he had been through quintuple bypass surgery dozens of times and wasn't worried about holding up his end; it was Henry who now had to squelch all his doubts and approach the operation with every confidence that it was going to be a hundred percent success. He would emerge from the surgery with a brand-new system of unclogged vessels supplying blood to a heart that was itself as strong still as an athlete's and completely unimpaired. "And no medication afterwards?" Henry asked him. "Up to your cardiologist," he was told; "probably something for a little mild hypertension, but nothing like the knockout drops you're on now." Zuckerman wondered if, upon hearing the marvelous prognosis, Henry's euphoria had prompted him to present the cardiac surgeon with a personally signed $8\frac{1}{2} \times 11$ glossy of Wendy in her garter belt. He seemed loopy enough for it when he arrived, but probably that was how you had to be to steel yourself for such a frightening ordeal. When Henry had finally mustered the courage to stop asking for reassurance and get up and go, the confident surgeon had accompanied him to the door. "If the two of us are working together," he told him, shaking Henry by the hand, "I can't foresee any problems. In a week, ten days, you'll be out of the hospital and back with your family, a new man."

Well, from where Zuckerman was sitting it looked as though on the operating table Henry hadn't been pulling his weight. Whatever he was supposed to do to assist the surgeon had apparently slipped his mind. This can happen when you're unconscious. My sleepwalking brother! Dead! Is that you in there, really, an obedient and proper little boy like you? All for twenty minutes with Wendy before hurrying home to the household you loved? Or were you showing off for me? It cannot be that your refusal to make do with a desexed life was what you thought of as your heroism—because if anything it was your *repression* that was your claim to fame. I mean this. Contrary to what you thought, I was never so disdainful of the restrictions under which you flourished and the boundaries you observed as you were of the excessive liberties you imagined me taking. You confided in me because you believed I would understand Wendy's mouth—and you were right. It went way beyond the juicy pleasure. It was your drop of theatrical existence, your disorder, your escapade, your risk, your little daily insurrection against all your overwhelming virtues—debauching Wendy for twenty minutes a day, then home at night for the temporal satisfactions of ordinary family life. Slavish Wendy's mouth was your taste of reckless fun. Old as the hills, the whole world operates this way . . . and yet there must be more, there *has* to be more! How could a genuinely good kid like you, with your ferocious sense of correctness, wind up in this box for the sake of that mouth? And why didn't I stop you?

Zuckerman had taken a seat in the first row, on the aisle, next to Bill and Bea Goff, Carol's parents. Carol sat at the center of the row, beside her mother; on her other side she had placed the children—her eleven-year-old daughter, Ellen, her fourteen-year-old son, Leslie, and nearest the far aisle, Ruth, the thirteen-year-old. Ruth was holding her violin on her knee and looking steadily at the coffin. The other two children, nodding silently while Carol spoke to them, preferred looking into their laps. Ruth was to play a piece on the violin that her father had always liked, and at the conclusion of the service, Carol would speak. "I asked Uncle Nathan if he wanted to say anything, but he says he's a little too shaken up right now. He says he's too stunned, and I understand. And what I'm going to say," she explained to them, "isn't going to be a eulogy, really. Just a few words about Daddy that I want everyone to hear. Nothing flowery, but words that are important for me. Then we're going to take him up to the cemetery by ourselves, just Grandma and Grandpa, Uncle Nathan, and the four of us. We're going to say goodbye to him at the cemetery, as a family, and then we're going to come back here and be with all our relatives and friends."

The boy wore a blazer with gold buttons and a pair of new tan boots, and though it was the end of September and the sun had been in and out all morning, the girls were in thin pastel dresses. They were tall, dark children, Sephardic-looking like their father, with rather prepossessing eyebrows for such innocent, coddled kids. They all had beautiful caramel eyes, a shade lighter and less intense than Henry's—six eyes, exactly alike, liquidly shining with amazement and fear. They looked like little startled does who'd been trapped and tamed and shod and clothed. Zuckerman was particularly drawn to Ruth, the middle child, diligently at work emulating her mother's calm despite the scale of the loss. Leslie, the boy, seemed the softest, the most girlish, the closest to collapsing really, though when, a few minutes

22

before they left for the synagogue, he took his mother aside, Zuckerman overheard him ask, "I've got a game at five, Mom—can I play? If you don't think I should . . ." "Let's wait, Les," Carol said, one hand lightly brushing down the back of his hair, "let's see if you still want to then."

While people were still crowding into the back of the synagogue and bridge chairs were found to seat some elderly late-comers, while there was nothing to do but sit in silence only feet from the coffin deciding whether to keep looking at it or not, Bill Goff began rhythmically to make a fist and then undo it, opening and closing his right hand as though it were a pump with which to work up courage or to drain off fear. He barely resembled any longer the agile, sharp-dressing, spirited golfer that Zuckerman had first seen some eighteen years before, dancing with all the bridesmaids at Henry's wedding. Earlier that morning, when Goff had opened the door to let him in, Nathan hadn't even realized at first whose hand he was shaking. The only thing about him that looked undiminished was the full head of wavy hair. Inside the house, turning sadly to his wife—and sounding just a bit affronted—Goff had said to her, "How do you like that? He didn't even recognize me. That's how much I changed."

Carol's mother went off with the girls to help Ellen settle for a second time on which of her good dresses was right to wear, Leslie returned to his room to buff his new boots again, and the two men walked out back for some fresh air. They looked on from the patio while Carol clipped the last of the chrysanthemums for the children to take with them to the cemetery.

Goff began telling Nathan why he'd had to sell his shoe store up in Albany. "Colored people started to come in. How could I turn them away? That's not my nature. But my Christian customers of twenty and twenty-five years, they didn't like it. They told me right out, no bones about it, 'Look, Goff, I'm not going to sit here and wait while you try ten pairs of shoes on some nigger. I don't want his rejects either.' So one by one they left me, my wonderful Christian friends. That's when I had the first attack. I sold and got out, figuring the worst was over. Get out from under the pressure, the doctor told me, so I cut my losses, and a year and a half later, on my holiday, down in Boca playing golf, I had the second attack. Whatever the doctor said, I did, and the second attack was worse than the first. And now this. Carol has been a fortress: one hundred pounds soaking wet and she has the strength of a giant. She was like that when her brother died. We lost Carol's twin brother his second year in law school. First Eugene at twenty-three, now Henry at thirty-nine." Suddenly he said, "What'd I do?" and took from his pocket a small plastic prescription vial. "Angina pills," he said. "My nitroglycerin. I knocked the goddamn top off again."

All the while he'd been mourning the loss of the store, his health, the son, and the son-in-law, deep in his trouser pockets his hands had been nervously jingling his change and his keys. Now he emptied his pocket and began to pick the tiny white pills out from among the coins, the keys, and a pack of Rolaids. When he tried dropping them back into the little vial, however, half of them fell to the flagstone floor. Zuckerman picked them up, but each time Mr. Goff tried to get them into the vial again he dropped a few more. Finally he gave up and held everything in his two cupped hands while Nathan picked the pills out one by one and deposited them in the vial for him.

They were still at this when Carol came up from the garden with the flowers and said it was time to leave. She looked maternally at her father, a gentle smile to try to calm him down. The same operation from which Henry had died at thirty-nine was in the offing for him at sixty-four if his angina got any worse. "You all right?" she asked him. "I'm fine, cookie," he replied, but when she wasn't looking, he slipped a nitroglycerin pill under his tongue.

The little violin piece that Ruth played was introduced by the rabbi, who came across as amiable and unpretentious, a large man, square-faced, red-haired, wearing heavy tortoise-shell glasses and speaking in a mild, mellifluous voice. "Henry and Carol's daughter, thirteen-year-old Ruth, is going to play the Largo from Handel's opera *Xerxes*," he said. "Talking with her up at the house last night, Ruthie told me that her father called it 'the most soothing music in all the world' whenever he heard her practicing. She wants to play it now in his memory."

At the center of the altar, Ruth placed the violin under her chin, sharply cranked up her spine, and stared out at the mourners with what looked almost like defiance. In the second before she lifted the bow she allowed herself a glance down at the coffin and seemed to her uncle like a woman in her thirties—suddenly he saw the expression she would wear all her life, the grave adult face that prevents the helpless child's face from crumbling with angry tears.

Though not every note was flawlessly extracted, the playing was tuneful and quiet, slow and solemnly phrased, and when Ruthie was finished, you expected to turn around and see sitting there the earnest young musician's father smiling proudly away.

Carol got up and stepped past the children into the aisle. Her only concession to convention was a black cotton skirt. The hem, however, was banded in some gaily embroidered American Indian motif of scarlet, green, and orange, and the blouse was a light lime color with a wide yoked neck that revealed the prominence of the collarbone in her delicate torso. Around her neck she wore a coral necklace that Henry had surreptitiously bought for her in Paris, after she'd admired it in a shop window but had thought the price ridiculously high. The skirt he'd bought for her in an open-air market in Albuquerque, when he'd been there for a conference.

Though gray hairs had begun cropping up along her temple, she was so slight and so peppy that climbing the stairs to the altar she looked as though she were the family's oldest adolescent girl. With Ruth he believed that he had caught a glimpse of the woman she'd be—in Carol, Zuckerman saw the plucky, crisply pretty college coed before she'd fully come of age, the ambitious, determined scholarship student her friends had called admiringly by her two first initials until Henry had put a stop to it and made people use her given name. At the time, Henry half-jokingly had confided to Nathan, "I really couldn't get myself worked up with somebody called C.J." But then even with somebody called Carol, the lust was never to be what it was with a Maria or a Wendy.

Just as Carol reached the altar lectern, her father took his nitroglycerin pills out of his pocket and accidentally spilled them all over the floor. Handel's Largo hadn't soothed him the way it used to soothe Henry. Nathan was able to get his arm under the seat and fish around with his hand until he found a few pills that he could reach and pick up. He gave one to Mr. Goff, and the others he decided to keep in his pocket for the cemetery.

While Carol spoke, Zuckerman again imagined Henry in his flannel pajamas decorated with the clowns and the trumpets, saw him mischievously eavesdropping from within the dark box as he would from his bed when there was a card party at the house and he left the door to his room ajar so as to hear the adults kibitz downstairs. Zuckerman was remembering back to when absolutely nothing was known in the boys' bedrooms of erotic temptation or death-defying choice, when life had been the most innocent pastime and family happiness had seemed eternal. Harmless Henry. If he could hear what Carol was saying, would he laugh, would he weep, or would he think with relief, "Now nobody will ever know!"

But of course Zuckerman knew, Zuckerman who was not so harmless. What *was* he to do with those three thousand words? Betray his brother's final confidence, strike a blow against the family of the very sort that had alienated him from them in the first place? The evening before, after thanking Carol for her graciousness and telling her that he would sit down at once to compose a eulogy, he'd located, among the loose-leaf journals stacked atop his file cabinets, the volume in which he'd kept his account of Henry's affair with the Swiss patient. Must he really go in now and plunder these notes that he'd mercifully all but forgotten—had they been waiting there all these years for an inspiration as unforeseen as this?

Scattered throughout the handwritten pages were dozens of shortish entries about Henry and Maria and Carol. Some were no more than a line or two long, others ran to almost a page, and before trying to figure out what to say at the funeral, Zuckerman, seated at his desk, had read them all slowly through, thinking as he heavily underscored the promising lines, "Here the ending began, with as commonplace and unoriginal an adventure as this—with the ancient experience of carnal revelation."

H. at midnight. "I have to phone somebody. I have to tell somebody that I love her. Do you mind—at this hour?" "No. Go ahead." "I at least have you to tell. She has nobody. I'm bursting to tell everyone. I'm actually dying to tell Carol. I want her to know how terrifically happy I am." "She can live without it." "I realize that. But I keep wanting to say, 'Do you know what Maria said today? Do you know what little Krystyna said last night when Maria was bathing her?' "

"She seems far off in the distance, the way the bedposts looked when I was a kid in our room. Remember the knobs on the top of the maple bedposts? I used to put myself to sleep by imagining them to be far far away, until actually they were, and I had to stop because I was scaring myself. Well, she seemed far away just like that, as though I couldn't possibly reach a hand out and touch her. She was on top of me, far far away, and each time she came, I said, 'More, do you want *more*?' And she nodded her head, like a child playing bouncy-horsy she nodded yes and started off again, red in the face and riding me, and all I wanted was for her to have *more* and *more* and *more*—and all the time I kept seeing her so very far away."

"You should see what she looks like, you should see this beautiful blond girl, with those eyes, up on top of me in her black silk camisole." Maria thought she'd have to go over to New York to buy the black underwear but then she found some down in the village. H. wonders if she oughtn't to have gone to New York to get it anyway.

Saturday H. saw her husband in the street. Looks like a nice fellow. Big and handsome. Bigger even than H. Very jolly with his kids. "Will you show him the underwear?" "No." "Will you wear it when you're with him?" "No." "Only for me." "Only for you." H. feels sorry for him. Looked so trusting.

In their motel room, while he watches her dressing to go home.
　　H. "You really are my whore, aren't you?" Maria laughs: "No. I'm not. Whores get money."
　　H. has cash in his wallet—a wad to pay motel, etc., without using

credit card. Peels off two crisp hundred-dollar bills and presents them to her.

She doesn't at first know what to say. Then apparently she does. "You're supposed to throw them on the floor," she tells him. "I think that's the way it's done."

H. lets them flutter to the floor. In the black silk camisole she bends to pick them up and puts them into her purse. "Thanks."

H., to me. "I thought, 'My God, I'm out two hundred bucks. That's a lot of dough.' But I didn't say a word. I thought, 'It's worth two hundred, just to see what it's like.'"

"What is it like?"

"I don't know yet."

"She still has the money?"

"She does—she has it. She says, 'You are a crazy man.'"

"Sounds like she wants to see what it's like too."

"I guess we both do. I want to give her more."

Maria confides that a woman who'd had an affair with her husband before she married him once told a friend of hers, "I was never so bored in my life." But he is a wonderful man with the children. And he holds her together. "I am the impulsive one," she says.

Maria says that whenever she can't believe that H. is real and their affair is really happening, she goes upstairs and looks at the two hundred-dollar bills hidden away in her underwear drawer. That convinces her.

H. amazed that he is not in any way guilty or tormented by being so joyously unfaithful to Carol. He wonders how someone who tries so hard to be so good, who *is* good, can be doing this so easily.

Carol spoke without notes, though as soon as she began it was clear to Zuckerman that every word had been thought through beforehand and nothing left to chance. If Carol had ever held any mystery for her brother-in-law, it had to do with what if anything lay behind her superagreeable nature; he had never been able to figure out precisely how naïve she was, and what she now had to say didn't help. The story Carol had chosen to tell wasn't the one that he had pieced together (and had decided—for now —to keep to himself); Henry's misery lived in Zuckerman's recollection with a significance and meaning entirely different. Hers was the story that was intended to stand as the officially authorized version, and he wondered while she recounted it if she believed it herself.

"There's something about Henry's death," she began, "that I want all of you gathered here today to know. I want Henry's children to know. I want his brother to know. I want everyone who ever loved him or cared about him to know. I think it may help to soften the force of this stupendous blow, if not this morning, then sometime in the future, when we're all less stunned.

"If he had chosen to, Henry could have gone on living without that horrible operation. And if he hadn't had that operation he'd be working away in his office right now and, in a few hours, would be coming home to me and the kids. It isn't true that the surgery was imperative. The medication that the doctors had given him when the disease was first diagnosed was effectively controlling his heart problem. He was in no pain and in no immediate danger. But the medication had drastically affected him as a man and put an end to our physical relationship. And this Henry couldn't accept.

"When he began seriously considering surgery, I begged him not to risk his life just to preserve that side of our marriage, much as I missed it myself. Of course I missed the warmth and tenderness and intimate affection, but I was coming to terms with it. And we were otherwise so fortunate in our lives together and with our children that it was unthinkable to me that he should undergo an operation that could destroy everything. But Henry was so dedicated to the completeness of our marriage that he wouldn't be deterred, not by anything.

"As you all know—as so many of you have been telling me during these last twenty-four hours—Henry was a perfectionist, not just in his work, where everyone knows he was the most meticulous craftsman, but in all his relationships with people. He held nothing back, not from his patients, not from his children, and never from me. It was unthinkable to a man so outgoing, so full of life, that still in his thirties he should be so cruelly disabled. I have to admit to you all, as I never did to him, that however much I opposed the surgery because of the risk, I did sometimes wonder if I could carry on as a loving and useful wife feeling so cut off from him. Over the course of our last year together, when he was so withdrawn and brutally depressed, so tormented by the damage that he felt the marriage to be suffering because of this bewildering thing that had happened, I thought 'If there could only be some miracle.' But I'm not someone who makes miracles happen; I'm someone who tends to make do with what's at hand—even, I'm afraid, with her own imperfections. But Henry would no more accept imperfection in himself than in his work. If I didn't have the courage to try for a miracle, Henry did—he had the courage, we now know, for everything life could demand of a man.

"I'm not going to tell you that going on without Henry is going to be easy for us. The children are frightened about the future with no loving father to protect them, and so am I frightened of no Henry by my side. I'd grown used to him, you know. However, I *am* strengthened by remembering that his life did not come to a senseless end. Dear friends, dear family, my dear, dear, dear children, Henry died to recover the fullness and richness of married love. He was a strong and brave and loving man who desperately wanted the bond of passion between a husband and a wife to continue to live and flourish. And, dearest Henry, dearest, sweetest man of them all, it will—the passionate bond between this husband and this wife will live as long as I do."

Just the intimate family, along with Rabbi Geller, followed the hearse to the cemetery. Carol didn't want the children riding out in one of those funeral-procession black limousines and so drove them herself—the kids, the Goffs, and Nathan—in the family station wagon. The interment lasted no time at all. Geller recited the mourner's prayer, and the children laid the chrysanthemums from the garden on the coffin lid. Carol asked if anyone wanted to say anything. No one answered. Carol said to her son, "Leslie?" He took a moment to prepare himself. "I just wanted to say . . ." but afraid of breaking down, he went no further. "Ellen?" Carol said, but Ellen, in tears and clinging to her grandmother's hand, shook her head no. "Ruth?" Carol asked. "He was the best father," said Ruth in a loud, clear voice, "the *best*." "All right," said Carol, and the two burly attendants lowered the coffin. "I'll be a few minutes," Carol told the family, and she remained alone by the graveside while the rest of them walked down to the parking lot.

Carol and the kids to Albany to celebrate her parents' anniversary. Heavy backlog of lab work prevents H. from going along. Maria parks three blocks away and walks from there to the house. Appears as requested in silk jersey dress and black underwear. Has brought her favorite record to play. She waters plants in back hallway that Carol forgot before she left—also plucks out the dead leaves. Then in bed, anal love. After initial difficulties both ecstatic. H.: "This is how I marry you, this is how I make you my wife!" "Yes, and nobody knows, Henry! I am a virgin there no longer and nobody knows! They all think I'm so good and responsible. Nobody knows!" In the bathroom with him afterwards, while arranging her hair with his brush, she sees his pajamas hanging on the back of the door and reaches over to touch them. ("I didn't realize what she'd done until that night. Then I went in and did it myself, stroked my own pajamas— to see what she'd felt." Also combed her hairs out of his brush so Carol wouldn't find them.) Sitting with her in the family room—no lights on—H., famished, ate a quart of ice cream right out of the carton while she played her record for him. Maria: "This is the most beautiful slow movement of the eighteenth century." H. doesn't remember what it was. Haydn? Mozart? "I don't know," he told me. "I don't know anything about that kind of music. But it was beautiful, just watching her listen." Maria: "This makes me think of university, sitting here like this, full of you in every way, and nothing else in the world." "You are my wife now," says H., "my other wife." Played his Mel Tormé record for her—had to dance with her while they had the chance. Glued loin to loin the way he danced in high school with Linda Mandel. Sleeps alone that night in sheets spotted with baby oil, the vibrator, unwashed, on the pillow beside his head. Took it to work with him the next day. Hidden in the office with copy of Fodor's *Switzerland* that he's bought to read, and her photograph. Also took with him the hair of hers that he combed out of the brush. All in the safe. The sheets he stuffed into a black plastic bag and dumped in a trash can at the Millburn Mall five miles from the scene of their marriage. Fodor's *Dostoevsky*.

It was early in the afternoon at the end of September; from the cold touch of the breeze and the light heat of the sun and the dry unsummery whish of the trees you could easily have guessed the month with your eyes closed—perhaps have even guessed the week. Should it matter to a man, however young and virile, to be sentenced to a lifetime of celibacy when, every year for as long as he lives, there will be autumn days like this to enjoy? Well, that was a question for an old guy with a beard and a gift for impossible riddles, and amiable Mark Geller struck Zuckerman as a rabbi of another kind entirely—consequently he declined the invitation to drive back to the house in Geller's car, and waited with the children and their grandparents down by the cemetery gate where the station wagon was parked.

Ruth, looking quite drained, came over and took her uncle's hand.

"What is it?" he asked her. "Are you okay?"

"I just keep thinking that when kids at school talk about their parents, I'll only be able to say 'my mother.' "

"You'll be able to say your parents, plural, whenever you talk about the past. You had thirteen years of that. Nothing you did with Henry is ever going to go away. He'll always be your father."

"Dad would take us alone, two times a year, without Mom, shopping in New York. It was his treat. Just him and us kids. We went shopping first and then we went to the Plaza Hotel and had lunch in the Palm Court—where they play the violin. Not very well, either. Once in the fall and once in the spring, every year. Now Mom will have to do all the things our dad did. She'll have to do both their jobs."

"Don't you think she can?"

"I do, sure I do. Maybe someday she'll remarry. She really likes to be married. I hope she does do it too." Then, very gravely, she rushed to add, "But only if she can find somebody who'll be good to us children as well as herself."

They waited there close to half an hour before Carol, walking briskly, emerged from the cemetery to drive everyone home.

. . .

Food had been laid out by a local caterer under the patio awning while the mourners were still at the synagogue, and scattered around the downstairs rooms were folding chairs rented from the funeral parlor. The girls from Ruth's softball team, who had taken the afternoon off from school to help out the Zuckermans, were clearing away the used paper plates and replenishing the serving platters from the reserves in the kitchen. And Zuckerman went looking for Wendy.

It was Wendy actually—when she'd become frightened that Henry was beginning to lose his mind—who had first suggested Nathan as a confidant. Carol, assuming that Nathan hadn't the slightest authority over his brother any longer, had urged Henry to talk to a psychotherapist in town. And for an hour each Saturday morning—until that horrendous Saturday expedition to New York—he had done it, gone off and spoken with great candor about his passion for Wendy, pretending to the therapist, however, that the passion was for Carol, that it was she whom he was describing as the most playful, inventive sexual partner any man could ever hope to have. This resulted in long, thoughtful discussions of a marriage that seemed to interest the therapist enormously but depressed Henry even further because it was such a cruel parody of his own. As far as Carol knew, not until she'd phoned to tell Nathan that Henry was dead had he even been aware of his brother's illness. Scrupulously following Henry's wishes, Zuckerman played dumb on the telephone, an absurd act that only compounded the shock and made clear to him how incapable Henry had been of reaching *any* decision rationally once the ordeal had begun. Out at the cemetery, while Henry's children stood at the graveside struggling to speak, Zuckerman had finally understood that the reason to have stopped him was that he had wanted to be stopped. The last thing Henry must have imagined was that Nathan would sit there and accept with a straight face, as justification for such a dangerous operation, the single-minded urging of that maniac-making lust that he had himself depicted so farcically in *Carnovsky*. Henry had expected Nathan to *laugh*. Of course! He had driven over from Jersey to confess to the mocking author the ridiculous absurdity of his dilemma, and instead he had been indulged by a solicitous brother who was unable any longer to give either advice or offense. He had come over to Nathan's apartment to be told how utterly meaningless was Wendy's mouth beside the ordered enterprise of a mature man's life, and instead the sexual satirist had sat there and seriously listened. Impotence, Zuckerman had been thinking, has cut him off from the simplest form of distance from his predictable life. As long as he was potent he could challenge and threaten, if only in sport, the solidity of the domestic relationship; as long as he was potent there was some give in his life between what was routine and what is taboo. But without the potency he feels condemned to an ironclad life wherein all issues are settled.

Nothing could have made this clearer than how Henry had described to him becoming Wendy's lover. Apparently from the instant she'd come into the office for the interview and he'd closed the door behind her, virtually every word they exchanged had goaded him on. "Hi," he'd said, shaking her hand, "I heard such marvelous things about you from Dr. Wexler. And now that I look at you, I think you're almost too good. You're going to be so distracting, you're so pretty."

"Uh-oh," she said, laughing. "Maybe I should go then."

What had delighted Henry was not only the speed with which he'd put her at her ease but having put himself at ease as well. It wasn't always like that. Despite his well-known rapport with his patients, he could still be ridiculously formal with people he didn't know, men no less than women, and sometimes, say, when interviewing someone for a job in his own office, seem to himself as though *he* were the person being interviewed. But something vulnerable in this young woman's appearance—something particularly tempting about her tiny breasts—had emboldened him, though precisely at a moment when being emboldened might not be such a great idea. Both at home and in the office everything was going so well that an extraneous adventure with a woman was the *last* thing he needed. And yet, because everything *was* going well, he could not rein in that robust, manly confidence that he could tell was knocking her for a loop already. It was just one of those days when he felt like a movie star, acting out some grandiose whatever-it-was. Why suppress it? There were enough days when he felt like a twerp.

"Sit down," he said. "Tell me about yourself and what you want to do."

"What I want to do?" Someone must have advised her to repeat the doctor's question if she needed time to think up the right answer or to remember the one she'd prepared. "I want to do a lot of things. My first exposure to a dental practice was with Dr. Wexler. And he's wonderful—a true gentleman."

"He's a nice guy," Henry said, thinking, altogether involuntarily, out of this damn excess of confidence and strength, that before it was over he'd show her what wonderful was.

"I learned a lot in his office of what's going on in dentistry."

He encouraged her gently. "Tell me what you know."

"What do I know? I know that a dentist has to make a choice of what kind of practice he wants. It's a business, you have to choose a market, and yet you're dealing with something that's very intimate. People's mouths, how they feel about them, how they feel about their smiles."

Mouths *were* his business, of course—hers too—and yet talking about them like this—at the end of the day, with the door closed, and the slight, young blonde petitioning for a job—was turning out to be awfully stimulating. He remembered the sound of Maria's voice telling him all about how wonderful his cock was— "I put my hand into your trousers, and it astonishes me, it's so big and round and hard." "Your control," she would say to him, "the way you make it last, there's no one like you, Henry." If Wendy were to get up and come over to the desk and put her hand in his pants, she'd find out what Maria was talking about.

"The mouth," Wendy was saying, "is really the most personal thing that a doctor can deal with."

"You're one of the few people who's ever said that," Henry told her. "Do you realize that?"

When he saw the flattery raise the color in her face, he pushed the conversation in a more ambiguous direction, knowing, however, that no one overhearing them could legitimately have charged him with talking to her about anything other than her qualifications for the job. Not that anyone could possibly overhear them.

"Did you take *your* mouth for granted a year ago?" he asked.

"Compared to what I think of it now, yes. Of course, I always cared for my teeth, cared about my smile—"

"You cared about *yourself*," Henry put in approvingly.

Smiling—and it *was* a good smile, the badge of utterly innocent, childish abandon—she happily picked up the cue. "I care about me, yes, sure, but I didn't realize that there was so much psychology involved in dentistry."

Was she saying that to get him to slow down, was she asking him politely to please back off about *her* mouth? Maybe she wasn't as innocent as she looked—but that was even *more* exciting. "Tell me a bit about that," Henry said.

"Well, what I said before—how you feel about your smile is a reflection of how you feel about yourself and what you present to other people. I think that whole personalities may develop, not only about your teeth, but everything else that goes with it. You're dealing in a dental office with the whole person, even if it just looks like you're dealing with the mouth. How do I satisfy the whole person, including the mouth? And when you talk about cosmetic dentistry, that's *real* psychology. We had some problems in Dr. Wexler's office with people who were having crowns done, and they wanted white-white teeth, which didn't go with their own teeth, with their coloring. You have to get them to understand what natural-looking teeth are. You tell them, 'You're going to have the smile that's perfect for you, but you can't go through and just pick out *the* perfect smile and have it put in your mouth.' "

"And have the mouth," Henry added, helping her out, "that looks like it belongs to you."

"Absolutely."

"I want you to work with me."

"Oh, great."

"I think we can make it," Henry said, but before *that* took on too much meaning, he moved quickly to present to his new assistant his own ideas, as though by being dead serious about dentistry he could somehow stop himself before he got grossly suggestive. He was wrong. "Most people, as you must know by now, don't even think that their mouth is part of the body. Or teeth are part of the body. Not consciously they don't. The mouth is a hollow, the mouth is nothing. Most people, unlike you, will never tell you what their mouth means. If they're frightened of dental work it's sometimes because of some frightening experience early on, but primarily it's because of what the mouth means. Anyone touching it is either an invader or a helper. To get them from thinking that someone working on them is invading them, to the idea that you are helping them on to something good, is almost like having a sexual experience. For most people, the mouth is secret, it's their hiding place. Just *like* the genitals. You have to remember that embryologically the mouth is related to the genitals."

"I studied that."

"Did you? Good. Then you realize that people want you to be very tender with their mouths. Gentleness is the most important consideration. With all types. And surprisingly enough, men are more vulnerable, particularly if they've lost teeth. Because losing teeth for a man is a strong experience. A tooth for a man is a mini-penis."

"I hadn't realized that," she said, but didn't seem affronted in any way.

"Well, what do *you* think of the sexual prowess of a toothless man? What do you think he thinks? I had a guy here who was very prominent. He had lost all his teeth and he had a young girlfriend. He didn't want her to know he had dentures, because that would mean he was an old man, and she was a young girl. About your age. Twenty-one?"

"Twenty-two."

"She was twenty-one. So I did implants for him, instead of dentures, and he was happy, and she was happy."

"Dr. Wexler always says that the most satisfaction comes from the greatest challenge, which is usually a disaster case."

Had Wexler fucked her? Henry had never as yet gone beyond

the usual flirtation with any assistant of any age—it wasn't only unprofessional but hopelessly distracting in a busy practice, and could well lead to the *dentist's* becoming the disaster case. He realized then that he ought never to have hired her; he had been entirely too impulsive, and was now making things even worse by all this talk about mini-penises that was giving him an enormous hard-on. Yet with everything that was combining these days to make him feel so bold, he couldn't stop. What's the worst that could happen to him? Feeling so bold, he had no idea. "The mouth, you mustn't forget, is the primary organ of experience . . ." On he went, looking unblinkingly and boldly at hers.

Nonetheless, a full six weeks passed before he overcame his doubts, not only about crossing the line further than he had at the interview but about keeping her on in the office at all, despite the excellent job she was doing. Everything he'd been saying about her to Carol happened to be true, even if to him it sounded like the most transparent rationalization for why she was there. "She's bright and alert, she's cute and people like her, she can relate to them, and she helps me enormously—because of her, when I walk in, I can get right to it. This girl," he told Carol, and more often than he needed to during those early weeks, "is saving me two, three hours a day."

Then one evening after work, as Wendy was cleaning his tray and he was routinely washing up, he turned to her and, because there simply seemed no way around it any longer, he began to laugh. "Look," he said, "let's pretend. You're the assistant and I'm the dentist." "But I *am* the assistant," Wendy said. "I know," he replied, "and I'm the dentist—but pretend anyway." "And so," Henry had told Nathan, "that's what we did." "You played Dentist," Zuckerman said. "I guess so," Henry said, "—she pretended she was called 'Wendy,' and I pretended I was called 'Dr. Zuckerman,' and we pretended we were in my dental office. And then we pretended to fuck—and we fucked." "Sounds interesting," Zuckerman said. "It was, it was wild, it made us crazy—it was the strangest thing I'd ever done. We did it for weeks, pretended like that, and she kept saying, 'Why is

38

it so exciting when all we're pretending to be is what we are?' God, was it great! Was she hot!"

Well, that larky, hot stuff was over now, no more mischievously turning what-was into what-wasn't or what-might-be into what-was—there was only the deadly earnest this-is-it of what-is. Nothing a successful, busy, energetic man likes more than a little Wendy on the side, and nothing a Wendy could more enjoy than calling her lover "Doctor Z."—she's young, she's game, she's in his office, he's the boss, she sees him in his white coat being adored by everyone, sees his wife chauffeuring the children and turning gray while she doesn't think twice about her twenty-inch waist . . . heavenly all around. Yes, his sessions with Wendy had been Henry's art; his dental office, after hours, his atelier; and his impotence, thought Zuckerman, like an artist's artistic life drying up for good. He'd been reassigned the art of the responsible—unfortunately by then precisely the hackwork from which he needed longer and longer vacations in order to survive. He'd been thrown back on his talent for the prosaic, precisely what he'd been boxed in by all his life. Zuckerman had felt for him terribly, and so, stupidly, stupidly, did nothing to stop him.

Down in the living room, he worked his way through the clan, accepting their sympathies, listening to their memories, answering questions about where he was living and what he was writing, until he had made his way to Cousin Essie, his favorite relative and once upon a time the family powerhouse. She was sitting in a club chair by the fireplace with a cane across her knees. Six years back, when he'd seen her last at his father's funeral in Florida, there'd been a new husband—an elderly bridge player named Metz—now dead, easily thirty pounds less of Essie, and no cane. She was always, as Zuckerman remembered her, large and old, and now she was even larger and older, though seemingly still indestructible.

"So, you lost your brother," she said, while he was leaning over to kiss her. "I once took you kids to Olympic Park. Took you on all the rides with my boys. At six Henry was the image of Wendell Willkie with that shock of black hair. That little boy adored you then."

They must return to Basel—Jurgen transferred home. Maria can't stop crying. "I'm going back to be a good wife and a good mother!" In six weeks Switzerland, where she'll have *only* the money to make it real.

"Did he?"

"Christ, he wouldn't let go of your hand."

"Well, he has now. We're all here at his house and Henry's up at the cemetery."

"Don't tell me about the dead," said Essie. "I look in the mirror in the morning and I see the whole family looking back at me. I see my mother's face, I see my sister, I see my brother, I see the dead from all the way back, all of them right in my own ugly kisser. Look, let's you and me talk," and after he'd helped her up from the chair, she led him out of the living room, struggling forward like some large vehicle plunging ahead on a broken axle.

"What is it?" he asked when they were in the front hallway.

"If your brother died to sleep with his wife, then he's already up with the angels, Nathan."

"But he was always the best boy, Esther. Son to end all sons, father to end all fathers—well, from the sound of it, the husband to end all husbands too."

"From the sound of it the shmuck to end all shmucks."

"But the kids, the folks—Dad would have a fit. How do I practice dentistry in Basel?" "Why would you have to live in Basel?" "Because she loves it, that's why—she says the only thing that made South Orange endurable was me. Switzerland is her *home*." "There are worse places than Switzerland." "That's easy for you to say." So I say no more, just remember her astride him in the black silk camisole, far far away, like the bedposts on his schoolboy bed.

"It's not so shmucky when you're impotent at thirty-nine," said Zuckerman, "and have reason to think it might never end."

"Being up at the cemetery isn't going to end either."

"He expected to live, Essie. Otherwise he wouldn't have done it."

"And all for the little wife."

"That's the story."

"I like better the ones you write."

Maria tells him that the person who stays behind suffers even more than the one who goes away. Because of all the familiar places.

Coming down the staircase just behind them were two elderly men he had not seen for a very long while: Herbert Grossman, the Zuckermans' only European refugee, and Shimmy Kirsch, designated years ago by Nathan's father as the brother-in-law Neanderthal, and arguably the family's stupidest relative. But as he was the wealthiest in the family as well, one had to wonder if Shimmy's stupidity wasn't something of an asset; watching him one wondered if in fact the passion to live and the strength to prevail might not be, at their core, *quite stupid*. Though the mountainous build had been eroded by age, and his deeply furrowed face bore all the insignia of his lifelong exertion, he was still more or less the person Nathan remembered from childhood—a huge unassailable nothing in the wholesale produce line, one of those rapacious sons of the old greenhorn families who will not shrink from anything even while, fortunately for society, enslaved by every last primitive taboo. For Zuckerman's father, the responsible chiropodist, life had been a dogged climb up from the abyss of his immigrant father's poverty, and not merely so as to improve his personal lot but eventually to rescue everyone as the family messiah. Shimmy had never seen any need to so assiduously cleanse his behind. Not that he wished necessarily to debase himself. All his steadfastness had gone into being what he'd been born and brought up to be— Shimmy Kirsch. No questions, no excuses, none of this who-am-I, what-am-I, where-am-I crap, not a grain of self-mistrust or the slightest impulse toward spiritual distinction; rather, like so many of his generation out of Newark's old Jewish slums, a man who breathed the spirit of opposition while remaining completely in accord with the ways and means of the earth.

Back when Nathan had first fallen in love with the alphabet and was spelling his way to stardom at school, these Shimmys had already begun to make him uncertain as to whether the real oddball wasn't going to be him, particularly when he heard of the notoriously unbrainy ways in which they successfully beat back their competitors. Unlike the admirable father who had taken the night-school path to professional dignity, these drearily banal and conventional Shimmys displayed all the ruthlessness of the renegade, their teeth ripping a chunk out of life's raw rump, then dragging that around with them everywhere, all else paling in significance beside the bleeding flesh between their jaws. They had absolutely no wisdom; wholly self-saturated, entirely self-oblivious, they had nothing to go on but the most elemental manhood, yet on that alone they came pretty damn far. They too had tragic experiences and suffered losses they were by no means too brutish to feel: being bludgeoned almost to death was as much their specialty as bludgeoning. The point was that pain and suffering did not deter them for half an hour from their intention of living. Their lack of all nuance or doubt, of an ordinary mortal's sense of futility or despair, made it tempting sometimes to consider them inhuman, and yet they were men about whom it was impossible to say that they were anything *other* than human: they were what human really is. While his own father aspired relentlessly to embody the best in mankind, these Shimmys were simply the backbone of the human race.

Shimmy and Grossman were discussing Israel's foreign policy. "Bomb 'em," Shimmy said flatly, "bomb the Arab bastards till they cry uncle. They want to pull our beards again? We'll die instead!"

Essie, cunning, shrewd, self-aware, another sort of survivor entirely, said to him, "You know why I give to Israel?"

Shimmy was indignant. "*You*? You never parted with a dime in your life."

"You know why?" she asked, turning to Grossman, a far better straight man.

"Why?" Grossman said.

"Because in Israel you hear the best anti-Semitic jokes. You hear even better anti-Semitic jokes in Tel Aviv than on Collins Avenue."

After dinner H. returns to the office—lab work, he tells Carol—and sits there all evening reading Fodor's *Switzerland*, trying to make up his mind. "Basel is a city with an atmosphere entirely of its own, in which elements of tradition and medievalism are unexpectedly mingled with the modern . . . behind and around its splendid old buildings and fine modern ones, a maze of quaint old lanes and busy streets . . . the old merging imperceptibly with the new . . ." He thinks: "What a terrific victory if I could pull it off!"

"I was there three years ago with Metz," Essie was saying. "We're driving from the airport to the hotel. The taxi driver, an Israeli, turns to us, and in English he says, 'Why do Jews have big noses?' 'Why?' I ask him. 'Because the air is free,' he says. On the spot I wrote a check for a thousand bucks to the UJA."

"Come on," Shimmy told her, "who ever pried a *nickel* out of you?"

"I asked her if she would leave Jurgen. She asked me to tell her first if I would leave Carol."

Herbert Grossman, whose obstinately lachrymose view of life was the only unyielding thing about him, had meanwhile begun to tell Zuckerman the latest bad news. Grossman's melancholia had at one time driven Zuckerman's father almost as crazy as Shimmy's stupidity; he was probably the only person about whom Dr. Zuckerman had finally to admit, "The poor man can't help it." Alcoholics could help it, adulterers could help it, insomniacs, murderers, even stammerers, could help it—according to Dr. Zuckerman, anyone could change *anything* in himself through the diligent exercise of his will; but because Grossman had had to flee from Hitler, he seemed to *have* no will. Not that Sunday after Sunday Dr. Zuckerman hadn't tried to get the damn thing going. Optimistically he would rise from the table after their hearty breakfast and announce to the family, "Time to phone Herbert!" but ten minutes later he'd be back in the kitchen, utterly defeated, muttering to himself, "The poor man can't help it." Hitler had done it—there was no other explanation. Dr. Zuckerman could not otherwise understand someone who simply was not there.

To Nathan, Herbert Grossman seemed now, as he did then, a delicate, vulnerable refugee, a Jew, to recast Isaac Babel's formula and bring it up to date, with a pacemaker in his heart and spectacles on his nose. "Everyone worries about Israel," Grossman was saying to him, "but you know what I worry about? Right here. America. Something terrible is happening right here. I feel it like in Poland in 1935. No, not anti-Semitism. That will come anyway. No, it's the crime, the lawlessness, people afraid. The money—everything's for sale and that's all that counts. The young people are full of despair. The drugs are only despair. Nobody wants to feel that good if they aren't in deep despair."

H. phones and for half an hour speaks of nothing but Carol's virtues. Carol is someone whose qualities you can only really know if you've lived with the woman as long as he has. "She's interesting, dynamic, curious, perceptive . . ." A long and very impressive list. A *startling* list.

"I feel it on the streets," Grossman said. "You can't even walk to the store. You go out to the supermarket in broad daylight and blacks come up and rob you blind."

Maria has left. Terrible tearful exchange of farewell presents. After consultation with cultivated older brother, H. gave her a boxed set of Haydn's *London Symphonies*. Maria gave him her black silk camisole.

When Herbert Grossman excused himself to go get something to eat, Essie confided to Zuckerman, "His last wife had diabetes. She made his life a misery. They took her legs off, she went blind, and she still didn't stop bossing him around."

So the surviving Zuckerman brother passed the long afternoon —waiting to see if Wendy would show up while he listened to the lore of the tribal elders and remembered the journal entries that had not seemed, when he'd written them, to be the doomladen notes for *Tristan and Isolde*.

Maria phoned H. at the office the day before Christmas. His heart began pounding the moment he was told he had an overseas call and didn't stop until long after she'd said goodbye. She wanted to wish him a Merry American Christmas. She told him that it had been very hard for these six months but that Christmas was helping. There was the children's excitement, and Jurgen's family was all there, and they would be sixteen for dinner the next day. She found that even the snow helped some. Was it snowing yet in New Jersey? Did he mind her phoning him like this at the office? Were his children okay? His wife? Was he? Did Christmas make it any easier for him, or wasn't it that hard anymore? "What did you say to that?" I asked. H.: "I was afraid to say anything. I was afraid somebody in the office would hear. I fucked up, I suppose. I said we didn't observe Christmas."

And could *that* be why he'd let her go, because Maria observed Christmas and we do not? One would have imagined that among secular, college-educated atheists of Henry's generation running away with shiksas had gone out as a felony years ago and was perceived, if at all, as a fictitious issue in a love affair. But then Henry's problem may have been that having passed so long for a paragon, he had got himself ridiculously entangled in this brilliant disguise at just the moment he was destined to burst forth as less admirable and more desperate than anyone ever imagined. How absurd, how awful, if the woman who'd awakened in him the desire to live differently, who meant to him a break with the past, a revolution against an old way of life that had reached an emotional standstill—against the belief that life is a series of duties to be perfectly performed—if that woman was to be nothing more or less than the humiliating memory of his first (and last) great fling *because she observed Christmas and we do not.* If Henry had been right about the origins of his disease, if it did indeed result from the stress of that onerous defeat and those arduous feelings of self-contempt that dogged him long after her return to Basel, then, curiously enough, it was being a Jew that had killed him.

If/then. As the afternoon wore on, he began to feel himself straining more and more after an idea that would release those

45

old notes from their raw factuality and transform them into a puzzle for his imagination to solve. While peeing in the upstairs bathroom, he thought, "Suppose on that afternoon she'd secretly come to the house, after they married each other by performing anal love, he watched her, right in this room, pinning up her hair before getting in with him to take a shower. Seeing him adoring her—seeing his eyes marvel at this strange European woman who embodies simultaneously both innocent domesticity and lurid eroticism—she says, confidently smiling, 'I really look extremely Aryan with my hair up and my jaw exposed.' 'What's wrong with that?' he asks. 'Well, there's a quality in Aryans that isn't very attractive—as history has shown.' 'Look,' he tells her, 'let's not hold the century against you . . .' "

No, that's not them, thought Zuckerman, and came down the stairs into the living room, where Wendy was still nowhere to be seen. But then it needn't be "them"—could be me, he thought. Us. What if instead of the brother whose obverse existence mine inferred—and who himself untwinnishly inferred me—*I* had been the Zuckerman boy in that agony? What is the real wisdom of that predicament? Could it be simple for anyone? If that is indeed how those drugs incapacitate most of the men who must take them to live, then there's a bizarre epidemic of impotence in this country whose personal implications nobody's scrutinizing, not in the press or even on Donahue, let alone in fiction . . .

In the living room someone was saying to him, "You know, I tried to interest your brother in cryonics—not that that's any consolation now."

"Did you?"

"I didn't even know he was sick. I'm Barry Shuskin. I'm trying to get a cryonics facility going here in New Jersey and when I came to Henry he laughed. A guy with a bad heart, he can't fuck anymore, and he wouldn't even read the literature I gave him. It was too bizarre for a rationalist like him. In his position I wouldn't have been so sure. Thirty-nine and it's all over—*that's* bizarre."

Shuskin was a youthful fifty—very tall, bald, with a dark chin-beard and a staccato delivery, a vigorous man with plenty to say, whom Zuckerman at first took to be a lawyer, a litigator, maybe some sort of hard-driving executive. He turned out to be an associate of Henry's, a dentist in the same office complex whose specialty was implanting teeth, anchoring custom-built teeth in the jawbone rather than fitting bridges or dentures. When implant work was too involved or too time-consuming for Henry to handle in his general family practice, he referred it to Shuskin, who also specialized in reconstructing the mouths of accident and cancer victims. "You know about cryonics?" Shuskin asked, after identifying himself as Henry's colleague. "You should. You ought to be on the mailing list. Newsletters, magazines, books—everything documented. They have figured out how to freeze now without damage to the cells. Suspended animation. You don't die, you're put on hold, hopefully for a couple of hundred years. Until science has solved the problem of thawing out. It's possible to be frozen, suspended, and then revitalized, all of the broken parts repaired or replaced, and you're as good if not better than new. You know you're going to die, you've got cancer, it's about to strike the vital organs. Well, you've got an option. You contact the cryonics people, you say I want to be awakened in the twenty-second century, give me an overdose of morphine, at the same time drain me, profuse me, and suspend me. You're not dead. You just go from life to being shut down. No intermediary stage. The cryonic solution replaces the blood and prevents ice crystallization damaging the cells. They encase the body in a plastic bag, store the bag in a stainless-steel container, and fill it with liquid nitrogen. Minus 273 degrees. Fifty thousand bucks for the freezing, and then you set up a trust fund to pay the maintenance. That's peanuts, a thousand, fifteen hundred a year. The problem is that there is a facility only in California and Florida—and speed is everything. This is why I want to seriously explore setting up a nonprofit organization right here in

Jersey, a cryonics facility for those men like myself who don't want to die. Nobody would make any dough out of it, except a few salaried people, who are on the up and up, to run the facility. A lot of guys would say, 'Shit, Barry, let's do it—we'll make a buck out of this and fuck everybody who thinks that there's something to it.' But I don't want to muddy it up with that kind of shit. The idea is to get a membership group together of men who want to be preserved for the future, guys who are committed to the principle and not to making a buck. Maybe fifty. You probably could get five thousand. There are a lot of high-powered guys who are enjoying life and have a lot of power and a lot of know-how, and they feel that it's a crock of shit to get burned or buried—why not frozen?"

Just then a woman took hold of Zuckerman's hand, a tiny, elderly woman with exceptionally pretty blue eyes, a large bust, and a full, round, merry-looking face. "I'm Carol's aunt from Albany. Bill Goff's sister. I want to extend my sympathies."

Indicating that he understood the sentimental obligations of the brother of the deceased, quietly, in an aside, Shuskin muttered to Zuckerman, "I want your home address—before you go."

"Later," said Zuckerman, and Shuskin, who was enjoying life, had a lot of power and a lot of know-how and no intention of being buried or burned—who would lie there like a lamb chop till the twenty-second century and then wake up, defrosted, to a billion more years of being himself—left Zuckerman to commiserate with Carol's aunt, who was still tightly holding his hand. Forever Shuskin. *Is* that the future, once the freezer has replaced the grave?

"This is a loss," she said to Zuckerman, "that no one will ever understand."

"It is."

"Some people are amazed by what she said, you know."

"By Carol? Are they?"

"Well, to get up at your husband's funeral and talk like that? I'm of the generation that didn't even say such things privately. Many people wouldn't have felt the same need that she did to be

48

open and honest about something so personal. But Carol has always been an astonishing girl and she didn't disappoint me today. The truth to her has always been the truth and nothing she has to hide."

"I thought what she said was just fine."

"Of course. You're an educated man. You know about life. Do me a favor," she whispered. "When you have a minute, tell her father."

"Why?"

"Because if he keeps on the way he's going, he'll give himself another heart attack."

He waited one more hour, till almost five, not so as to sedate Mr. Goff, whose confusion was Carol's business, but on the remote chance that Wendy might yet appear. A decent girl, he thought—she doesn't want to force herself on the wife and the children, even if they're innocent of her great role in all this. He had thought at first that she would want terribly to talk to the only other person who knew why this had happened and what she must be going through, but maybe it was precisely because Henry had told Nathan everything that she was staying away— because she didn't know whether to expect to be castigated by him, or cross-examined for a fictional exposé, or perhaps even wickedly seduced by the twisted brother, à la Richard the Third. As the minutes passed, he realized that waiting around for Wendy went further than wanting to find out how she'd behave with Carol, or seeing for himself at close range if there was anything there that the photograph hadn't disclosed; it was more like hanging around to meet a movie star or to catch a glimpse of the Pope.

Shuskin caught him just as he was heading for his coat in what was now the widow's bedroom. They walked up the stairs together, Zuckerman thinking, Strange Henry never mentioned his visionary colleague, the implantologist—that in his wild state he hadn't even been tempted. But probably he hadn't even heard him. Henry's delusions didn't run to living thawed out in the second millennium. Even a life in Basel with Maria was too much like science fiction for him. By comparison he had asked for so very little—willing to be wholly content, for the rest of his natural days, with the modest miracle of Carol, Wendy, and the kids. Either that, or to be an eleven-year-old boy in the cottage at the Jersey Shore with the faucet at the side to wash the sand off your feet. If Shuskin had told him that science was working on making it the summer of 1948 again, 'he might have had himself a customer.

"There's a group in L.A.," Shuskin was saying, "I'm going to send you their newsletter. Some very bright guys. Philosophers. Scientists. Engineers. A lot of writers too. What they're doing on the West Coast, because of their feeling that the body is not what's important, that your identity is all up here, so they separate the head from the body. They know they'll be able to reconnect heads to bodies, reconnect the arteries, the brain stem, and everything else all to a new body. They'll have solved the immunological problems, or they may be able to clone new bodies. Anything is possible. So they're just freezing the heads. It's cheaper than freezing and storing the whole body. Faster. Cuts storage costs. They find that appealing in intellectual circles. Maybe you will too, if you ever find yourself in Henry's shoes. I don't go for it myself. I want my whole body frozen. Why? Because I personally believe your experience is very much connected to your memories that every cell in your body has. You don't separate the mind from the body. The body and the mind are one. The body *is* the mind."

No disputing that, not here today, thought Zuckerman, and after locating his coat on the king-sized bed that Henry had exchanged for a coffin, he wrote out his address. "If I wind up in Henry's shoes," he said, handing it to Shuskin.

"I said 'if'? Pardon my delicacy. I meant when."

Though Henry had been a slightly heavier, more muscular man than his older brother, they were still more or less the same size and build, and that perhaps explained why Carol held on to him so very long when he came downstairs to leave. It was, for both of them, such a strongly emotional moment that Zuckerman wondered if he wasn't about to hear her say, "I know about her, Nathan. I've known all along. But he would have gone crazy if I told him. Years ago I found out about a patient. I couldn't believe my ears—the kids were small, I was younger, and it mattered terribly to me then. When I told him that I knew, he went berserk. He had a hysterical fit. He wept for days, every time he came home from the office begging me to forgive him, begging me from down on his knees not to make him move out of the house —calling himself the most awful names and begging me not to throw him out. I never wanted to see him like that again. I've known about them all, every one, but I let him be, let him have what he wanted so long as at home he was a good father to the kids and a decent husband to me."

But in Zuckerman's arms, pressing herself up against his chest, all she said, in a breaking voice, was "It helped me enormously, your being here."

Consequently he had no reason to reply, "So that's why you made up that story," but said nothing more than what was called for. "It helped *me*, being with you all."

Carol did not then respond, "Of course that's why I said what I did. Those bitches all weeping their hearts out—sitting there weeping for *their man*. The hell with that!" Instead she said to him, "It meant a lot to the children to see you. They needed you today. You were lovely to Ruth."

Nathan did not ask, "And you let him go ahead with the surgery, knowing who it was for?" He said, "Ruth's a terrific girl."

Carol replied, "She's going to be all right—we all are," and bravely kissed him goodbye, instead of saying, "If I had stopped him, he would never have forgiven me, it would have been a nightmare for the rest of our lives"; instead of, "If he wanted to risk his life for that stupid, slavish, skinny little slut, that was his business, not mine"; instead of, "It served him right, dying like that after what he put me through. Poetic justice. May he rot in hell for his nightly blow job!"

Either what she'd told everyone from the altar was what she truly believed, either she was a good-hearted, courageous, blind, loyal mate whom Henry had fiendishly deceived to the last, or she was a more interesting woman than he'd ever thought, a subtle and persuasive writer of domestic fiction, who had cunningly reimagined a decent, ordinary, adulterous humanist as a heroic martyr to the connubial bed.

He didn't really know what to think until at home that evening, before sitting down at his desk to reread those three thousand words written in his notebook the night before—and to record his observations of the funeral—he again got out the journal from ten years back and turned the pages until he found his very last entry about Henry's great thwarted passion. It was pages on in the notebook, buried amid notes about something else entirely; that's why the evening before it had eluded his search.

The entry was dated several months after Maria's Christmas call from Basel, when Henry was beginning to think that if there was any satisfaction to be derived from his crushing sense of loss, it was that at least he had never been discovered—back when the inchoate, debilitating depression had at last begun to lift and to be replaced by the humbling realization of what the affair with Maria had so painfully exposed: the fact that he was somehow not quite coarse enough to bow to his desires, and yet not quite fine enough to transcend them.

Carol picks him up at Newark Airport, after Cleveland orthodontic conference. He gets in behind the wheel at the airport parking lot. Night and a late-winter gale on the way. Carol, all at once in tears, undoes her alpaca-lined storm coat and flips on the car light. Naked beneath but for black bra, panties, stockings, garter belt. For a flickering moment he is even aroused, but then he spots the price tag stapled to the garter belt, and sees in that all the desperateness of this startling display. What he sees is not some wealth of passion in Carol, undiscovered by him till then, that he might suddenly begin to plumb, but the pathos of these purchases obviously made earlier that day by the predictable, sexually unadventurous wife to whom he would be married for the rest of his life. Her desperation left him limp—then angry: never had he ached more for Maria! How could he have let that woman go! "Fuck me!" Carol cries, and not in the incomprehensible Swiss-German that used to make him so excited, but in plain, understandable English. "Fuck me before I die! You haven't fucked me like a woman in years!"

2. *Judea*

WHEN I located him at his newspaper, Shuki couldn't at first understand who I said was calling—when he did, he pretended to be stupefied. "What's a nice Jewish boy like you doing in a place like this?"

"I come regularly every twenty years to be sure everything's okay."

"Well, things are great," Shuki replied. "We're going down the drain six different ways. It's too awful even to joke about."

We'd met eighteen years earlier, in 1960, during my only previous visit to Israel. Because *Higher Education*, my first book, had been deemed "controversial"—garnering both a Jewish prize and the ire of a lot of rabbis—I'd been invited to Tel Aviv to participate in a public dialogue: Jewish-American and Israeli writers on the subject "The Jew in Literature."

Though only a few years older than I, Shuki back in 1960 had already completed a ten-year stint as an army colonel and just been appointed Ben-Gurion's press attaché. One day he'd taken me up to the Prime Minister's office to shake the hand of "the Old Man," an event that, however special, turned out to be nowhere near so instructive as our lunch beforehand with Shuki's father in the Knesset dining room. "You might learn something meeting an ordinary Israeli working man," Shuki said; "and as for him, he loves coming down here to eat with the big shots." Of course why he especially liked coming to eat at the Knesset was because his son was now working there for his political idol.

Mr. Elchanan was in his mid-sixties then and still employed as a welder in Haifa. He'd emigrated to mandate Palestine from Odessa in 1920, when the Soviet revolution was proving to be more hostile to Jews than its Russian-Jewish supporters had foreseen. "I came," he told me, in the good if heavily accented English that he'd learned as a Palestinian Jew under the British, "and I was already an old man for the Zionist movement—I was twenty-five." He was not strong, but his hands were strong—his hands were the center of him, the truly exceptional thing in his whole appearance. He had kind, very mild, soft brown eyes, but otherwise plain, ungraspable features set in a perfectly round and gentle face. He was not tall like Shuki but short, his chin was not protruding heroically but slightly receding, and he was a little stooped from a lifetime of physical work forming joints and connections. His hair was grayish. More than likely you wouldn't even see him if he sat down across from you on a bus. How intelligent was he, this unprepossessing welder? Intelligent enough, I thought, to raise a very good family, intelligent enough to bring up Shuki and his younger brother, an architect in Tel Aviv, and of course intelligent enough to understand in 1920 that he had better leave Russia if he was intent upon remaining a socialist and a Jew. In conversation, he displayed his share of forceful wit, and even a playful, poetic imagination of sorts when it came time to put me through my paces. I myself couldn't see him as a worker who was nothing more than "ordinary," but then I wasn't his offspring. In fact, it wasn't at all difficult to think of him as an Israeli counterpart to my own father, who was then still practicing chiropody in New Jersey. Despite the difference in professional status, they would have got on well, I thought. That may even be why Shuki and I got on so well.

We were just beginning our soup when Mr. Elchanan said to me, "So you're going to stay."

"Am I? Who said so?"

"Well, you're not going back there, are you?"

Shuki kept spooning the soup—this was obviously a question he wasn't startled to hear.

I figured at first that Mr. Elchanan was joking with me. "To America?" I said, smiling. "Going next week."

"Don't be ridiculous. You'll stay." Here he put down his spoon and came over to my side of the table. With one of those extraordinary hands of his he lifted me by the arm and steered me over to a window of the dining room that looked out across modern Jerusalem to the old walled city. "See that tree?" he said. "That's a Jewish tree. See that bird? That's a Jewish bird. See, up there? A Jewish cloud. There is no country for a Jew but here." Then he set me back down where I could resume eating.

Shuki said to his father, once he was over his plate again. "I think that Nathan's experience makes him see things differently."

"What experience?" The voice was brusque as it hadn't been with me. "He needs us," Mr. Elchanan pointed out to his son, "—and even more than we need him."

"Is that so," Shuki said softly, and continued eating.

However earnest I may have been at twenty-seven, however dutifully, obstinately sincere, I really didn't want to tell my friend's well-meaning, stoop-shouldered old father just how wrong he was, and in response to their exchange I merely shrugged.

"He lives in a museum!" Mr. Elchanan said angrily. Shuki half-nodded—this too he seemed to have heard before—and so Mr. Elchanan turned to say it again directly to me. "You are. We are living in a Jewish theater and you are living in a Jewish museum!"

"Tell him, Nathan," said Shuki, "about your museum. Don't worry, he's been debating with me since I was five—he can take it."

So I did as Shuki said and, for the remainder of the lunch, I told him—as was my style in my twenties (with fathers particularly), told him overpassionately and at enormous length. I wasn't improvising, either: these were conclusions I'd been reaching on my own in the last few days, the result of traveling for three weeks through a Jewish homeland that couldn't have seemed to me more remote.

To be the Jew that I was, I told Shuki's father, which was neither more nor less than the Jew I wished to be, I didn't need to live in a Jewish nation any more than he, from what I understood, felt obliged to pray in a synagogue three times a day. My landscape wasn't the Negev wilderness, or the Galilean hills, or the coastal plain of ancient Philistia; it was industrial, immigrant America—Newark where I'd been raised, Chicago where I'd been educated, and New York where I was living in a basement apartment on a Lower East Side street among poor Ukrainians and Puerto Ricans. My sacred text wasn't the Bible but novels translated from Russian, German, and French into the language in which I was beginning to write and publish my own fiction—not the semantic range of classical Hebrew but the jumpy beat of American English was what excited me. I was not a Jewish survivor of a Nazi death camp in search of a safe and welcoming refuge, or a Jewish socialist for whom the primary source of injustice was the evil of capital, or a nationalist for whom cohesiveness was a Jewish political necessity, nor was I a believing Jew, a scholarly Jew, or a Jewish xenophobe who couldn't bear the proximity of goyim. I was the American-born grandson of simple Galician tradesmen who, at the end of the last century, had on their own reached the same prophetic conclusion as Theodor Herzl—that there was no future for them in Christian Europe, that they couldn't go on being themselves there without inciting to violence ominous forces against which they hadn't the slightest means of defense. But instead of struggling to save the Jewish people from destruction by founding a homeland in the remote corner of the Ottoman Empire that had once been biblical Palestine, they simply set out to save their own Jewish skins. Insomuch as Zionism meant taking upon oneself, rather than leaving to others, responsibility for one's survival as a Jew, this was their brand of Zionism. And it worked. Unlike them, I had not grown up hedged in by an unnerving Catholic peasantry that could be whipped into a Jew-hating fervor by the village priest or the local landowner; even more to the point, my grandparents' claim to legitimate political entitlement had not been staked in the midst of an alien, indigenous population that had no commitment to Jewish biblical rights and no sympathy for what a Jewish God said in a Jewish book about what constitutes Jewish territory in perpetuity. In the long run I might even be far more secure as a Jew in my homeland than Mr. Elchanan, Shuki, and their descendants could ever be in theirs.

I insisted that America simply did not boil down to Jew and Gentile, nor were anti-Semites the American Jew's biggest problem. To say, Let's face it, for the Jews the problem is always the goyim, may have a ring of truth about it for a moment—"How can anyone dismiss that statement out of hand in this century? And if America should prove to be a place of intolerance, shallowness, indecency, and brutality, where all American values are flushed into the gutter, it could have more than just the ring of truth—it could turn out to be so." But, I went on, the fact of it was that I could not think of any historical society that had achieved the level of tolerance institutionalized in America or that had placed pluralism smack at the center of its publicly advertised dream of itself. I could only hope that Yacov Elchanan's solution to the problem of Jewish survival and independence turned out to be no less successful than the unpolitical, unideological "family Zionism" enacted by my immigrant grandparents in coming, at the turn of the century, to America, a country that did not have at its center the idea of exclusion.

"Though I don't admit this back in New York," I said, "I'm a little idealistic about America—maybe the way that Shuki's a little idealistic about Israel."

I wasn't sure if the smile I saw wasn't perhaps a sign of how impressed he was. He ought to be, I thought—he certainly doesn't hear stuff like this from the other welders. I was even, afterwards, a little chagrined that I had said quite so much, fearing that I might have demolished too thoroughly the aging Zionist and his simplifications.

But he merely continued smiling away, even as he rose to his feet, came around the table, and once again lifted me by my arm and led me back to where I could look out on his Jewish trees and streets and birds and clouds. "So many words," he finally said to me, and with just a trace of that mockery that was more recognizably Jewish to me than the clouds—"such brilliant explanations. Such deep thoughts, Nathan. I never in my life saw a better argument than you for our never leaving Jerusalem again."

His words were our last words, for before we could even eat dessert Shuki rushed me upstairs for my scheduled minute with another stocky little gentleman in a short-sleeve shirt who, in person, also looked to me deceptively inconsequential, as though the model of a tank that I spotted among the papers and family photos on his desk could have been nothing more than a toy constructed for a grandchild in his little workshop.

Shuki told the Prime Minister that we'd just come up from lunch with his father.

This amused Ben-Gurion. "So you're staying," he said to me. "Good. We'll make room."

A photographer was already there, poised to take a picture of Israel's Founding Father shaking hands with Nathan Zuckerman. I am laughing in the photograph because just as it was to be snapped, Ben-Gurion whispered, "Remember, this isn't yours—it's for your parents, to give them a reason to be proud of you."

He wasn't wrong—my father couldn't have been happier if it had been a picture of me in my Scout uniform helping Moses down from Mount Sinai. This picture wasn't merely beautiful, it was also ammunition, to be used primarily, however, in his struggle to prove to *himself* that what leading rabbis were telling their congregations from the pulpit about my Jewish self-hatred couldn't possibly be true.

Framed, the photograph was exhibited for the remaining years of my parents' lives atop the TV console in the living room, alongside the picture of my brother receiving his dental diploma. These to my father were our greatest achievements. And his.

· · ·

After a shower and something to eat, I walked out back of my hotel to a bench on the wide promenade overlooking the sea where Shuki and I had arranged to meet. Christmas trees were already stacked on the pavement outside of our London greengrocer's, and a few evenings back, Maria and I had taken her little daughter, Phoebe, to see the Oxford Street lights, but in Tel Aviv it was a blue, bright, windless day, and on the beach below, female flesh was toasting in the sun and a handful of bathers were bobbing about in the waves. I remembered how, driving to the West End with Phoebe, Maria and I had talked about my first English Christmas and all the holiday celebrations to come. "I'm not one of those Jews for whom Christmas is an awful trial," I said, "but I have to tell you that I don't actually participate so much as look on anthropologically from a distance." "That's fine with me," she said; "you do the next-best thing. Which is to write large checks. That's really all the participating that's necessary."

As I sat there with my jacket in my lap and my sleeves rolled up, watching the elderly men and women on the nearby benches reading their papers, and eating ice cream, and some, with their eyes shut, just pleasantly warming their bones, I was reminded of the journeys I used to make to Florida after my father's retirement, when he had given up the Newark practice and was devoting his attention entirely to the daily *Times* and Walter Cronkite. There couldn't have been any more ardent Israeli patriots welding away in the Haifa shipyards than were gathered in those lounge chairs around the condominium pool after the triumph of the Six-Day War. "Now," said my father, "they'll think twice before they pull our beards!" Militant, triumphant Israel was to his aging circle of Jewish friends their avenger for the centuries and centuries of humiliating oppression; the state created by Jews in the aftermath of the Holocaust had become for them the belated answer *to* the Holocaust, not only the embodiment of intrepid Jewish strength but the instrument of justifiable wrath and swift reprisal. Had it been Dr. Victor Zuckerman rather than General Moshe Dayan who'd been the Israeli Minister of Defense in May 1967—had it been any one of my father's Miami Beach cohorts rather than Moshe Dayan—tanks emblazoned with the white Mogen David would have rolled right on through the cease-fire lines to Cairo, Amman, and Damascus, where the Arabs would then have proceeded to surrender like the Germans in 1945, unconditionally, as though they *were* the Germans of 1945.

Three years after the '67 victory, my father died and so he's missed Menachem Begin. That's too bad, for not even Ben-Gurion's fortitude, Golda's pride, and Dayan's valor taken all together could have provided him with that profound sense of personal vindication that so many of his generation have found in an Israeli Prime Minister who could pass, from his appearance, for the owner of a downtown clothing store. Even Begin's English is right, sounding more like the speech of their own impoverished immigrant parents than what emanates, say, from Abba Eban, cunning Jewish central casting's spokesman to the Gentile world. After all, who better than the Jew caricatured by generation upon generation of pitiless enemies, the Jew ridiculed and despised for his funny accent and his ugly looks and his alien ways, to make it perfectly clear to everyone that what matters now isn't what goyim think but what Jews do? The only person who might conceivably have delighted my father even more by issuing the general warning that Jewish helplessness in the face of violence is a thing of the past would have been, as commander in chief of the Israeli Army and Air Force, a little peddler with a long beard.

Until his trip to Israel eight months after the bypass surgery, my brother, Henry, had never shown any interest at all in the country's existence or in its possible meaning for him as a Jewish homeland, and even that visit arose from neither an awakening of Jewish consciousness nor out of curiosity about the archaeological traces of Jewish history but strictly as a therapeutic measure. Though his physical rehabilitation had by then been successfully completed, at home after work he was succumbing still to fits of terrible despair, and many nights would drag himself away from the dinner table midway through the family meal to fall asleep on the couch in the study.

Beforehand, the doctor had warned the patient and his wife about these depressions, and Carol had prepared the children. Even men like Henry who were young and healthy enough to make a rapid physical recovery from bypass surgery often suffered emotional repercussions lasting sometimes as long as a year. In his case it had been clear from the beginning that he wasn't to escape the worst aftereffects. Twice during the week following the operation, he had to be moved from his private room into intensive care because of chest pains and arrhythmia, and when, after nineteen days, he was able to return home, he was twenty pounds lighter and barely strong enough to stand in front of the mirror and shave. He wouldn't read or watch television, he ate practically nothing, and when Ruth, his favorite child, came in after school and offered to play for him the little tunes that he liked on her violin, he sent her away. He even refused to begin the exercise course at the cardiac rehab clinic, but lay instead under a blanket in the lounge chair on the back patio, looking out at Carol's garden and weeping. Tearfulness, the doctor assured everyone, was common among patients after serious surgery, but Henry's tears did not abate and after a while no one knew what he was crying about. If, when asked, he even bothered to reply, it was blankly, with the words "It's staring me right in the face." "What is?" Carol said. "Tell me, darling, and we'll talk about it. What is staring you right in the face?" "The words," he angrily told her, "the words 'it's staring you right in the face'!"

At dinner one night, when Carol, trying still to be perky, suggested that now that he was physically himself again he might enjoy going along on the two-week snorkeling trip that Barry Shuskin was planning, he replied that she knew damn well that he couldn't stand Shuskin, and headed for the studio couch. That was when she telephoned me. Although Carol was right to think that our rift had all but healed, she mistakenly believed that the reconciliation resulted from the visits I'd paid to the hospital while he was moving in and out of intensive care; she still knew nothing about the times he'd called on me in New York before the operation, when he found himself without anyone else to whom he dared confide what, in reality, was making the treatment of his disease unbearable.

I reached him at his office the morning after Carol's call.

"The sun, the sea, the reefs—you deserve it," I said, "after what you've been through. Let snorkeling wash away all the old debris."

"Yeah, and then what?"

"You'll come back. You'll begin your new life."

"What'll be new about it?"

"It'll pass, Henry, the depression will pass. Sooner rather than later, if you push yourself a little."

His voice sounded disembodied when he told me, "I don't have the guts to change."

I wondered if he was talking about women again. "What sort of change do you have in mind?"

"The one that's staring me right in the face."

"Which is?"

"How would I know? I'm not only too gutless to do it, I'm too stupid to know what it is."

"You had the guts for the operation. You had the guts to say no to the medication and take your chances on the block."

"And what's it got me?"

"I take it you're off the drugs now—that you're yourself again sexually."

"So what?"

That night, while he was back brooding in the study, Carol phoned to say how much talking to me had meant to Henry and begged me to stay in touch with him. Though the call had hardly seemed to me successful, I nonetheless phoned him again a few days later and, in fact, spoke to him more over the next few weeks than I had since college, each conversation as hopelessly circular as the one before—until all at once he relented about the trip and, along with Shuskin and two other friends, set off one Sunday on TWA with his face mask and fins. Though Carol told me gratefully how it was my concern that had turned him around, I wondered if Henry hadn't simply caved in, knuckled under to me the way he used to give in on the phone to our father back when he was a student at Cornell.

One of the stops on their itinerary was Eilat, the coastal town at the southern end of the Negev. After snorkeling for three days in the coral grottoes, the others flew on to Crete; Henry, however, remained in Israel, and only in part because of Shuskin's unbearable egomaniacal monologues. On a day tour of Jerusalem, he had broken away from the other four after lunch and wandered back by himself into the Orthodox quarter, Mea She'arim, where they had all been that morning with the guide. It was there, alone outside the classroom window of a religious school, that he had the experience that changed everything.

"I was sitting in the sunshine on the stone sill of this broken-down old cheder. Inside was a class, a room full of kids, little eight-, nine-, ten-year-old kids with skullcaps and *payess*, screaming the lesson out for their teacher, all of them reciting in unison at the top of their voices. And when I heard them, there was a surge inside me, a realization—at the root of my life, the very *root* of it, *I was them*. I always *had* been them. Children chanting away in Hebrew, I couldn't understand a word of it, couldn't recognize a single sound, and yet I was listening as though something I didn't even know I'd been searching for was suddenly reaching out for me. I stayed all week in Jerusalem. Every morning around eleven I went back to that school and sat on the windowsill and listened. You have to understand that the place isn't picturesque. The surroundings are hideous. Rubble dumped between the buildings, old appliances piled on the porches, piled in the yards—everything clean enough, but dilapidated, crumbling, rusty, everything coming apart wherever you looked. And not a color, a flower, a leaf, not a blade of grass or fresh coat of paint, nothing bright or attractive anywhere, nothing trying to please you in any way. Everything superficial had been cleared away, burned away, didn't matter—*was trivial*. In the courtyards there were all their underclothes strung on the line, big ugly underwear having nothing to do with sex, underwear from a hundred years ago. And the women, the married women—

kerchiefs wrapped around their heads, underneath shaved to the bone, and no matter how young, absolutely unappealing women. I looked for a pretty woman and I couldn't find *one*. The children too—gawky, awkward, drained and pale, utterly colorless little kids. Half the old people looked like dwarfs to me, little men in long black coats with noses right out of an anti-Semitic cartoon. I can't describe it any other way. Only the uglier and more barren everything looked, the more it held me—the clearer everything became. I hung around there all one Friday, watching them get ready for the Sabbath. I watched the men going to the bathhouse with their towels under their arms and to me the towels looked like prayer shawls. I watched those bloodless little kids hurrying home, coming out of the bathhouse twisting their wet earlocks and then hurrying home for the Sabbath. Across from a barbershop, I watched the Orthodox men in those hats and coats going in to get their hair cut. The place was jammed, hair piling up around everyone's shoes, nobody bothering to sweep it away—and I couldn't move. Only a barbershop, yet I couldn't move. I bought a challah in some little dungeon bakery—stood in the crush and bought a challah and carried it all day in a bag under my arm. When I got back to the hotel, I took it out of the bag and put it on the bureau. I didn't eat it. I left it there the whole week—left it on the bureau and looked at it, as though it were a piece of sculpture, something precious I'd stolen from a museum. Everything was like this, Nathan. I couldn't stop looking, over and over again going back to stare at the same places. And that's when I began to realize that of all that I am, I am nothing, I have never been *anything*, the way that I am this Jew. I didn't know this, had no idea of it, all of my life I was swimming *against* it—then sitting and listening to those kids outside that cheder window, suddenly it *belonged* to me. Everything else *was* superficial, everything else *was* burned away. Can you understand? I may not be expressing it right, but I actually don't care how it sounds to you or to anyone. I am not *just* a Jew, I'm not *also* a Jew—*I'm a Jew as deep as those Jews*. Everything else *is* nothing. And it's that, *that*, that all these months has been staring me right in the face! The fact that that is the root of my life!"

He told me all this on the phone his first night back, talking at a terrific, almost incomprehensible clip, as though he could not otherwise communicate what had happened to make his life important again, to make life suddenly of the *greatest* importance. By the end of the first week, however, when nobody to whom he repeated the story seemed to warm to his identification with those cheder kids, when he couldn't get anyone to take seriously that the more hideous the surroundings looked, the more purified he felt, when nobody at all seemed able to appreciate that it's the sheer *perversity* of these conversions that is their transforming power, his fervent excitement turned to bitter disappointment and he began to feel even more depressed than before he'd left.

Worn down, and by now pretty depressed herself, Carol telephoned the cardiologist to tell him that the trip had failed and that Henry was worse. He in turn told her that she was forgetting what he'd warned her at the outset—for some patients the emotional upheaval afterwards could be even more trying than the surgery. "He's back working every day," he reminded her— "despite the irrational episodes he's able to get himself to do his job, and that means that sooner or later, he's going to come completely around and be himself."

And maybe that's what happened three weeks later when, halfway through the day, after telling Wendy to cancel his afternoon appointments, he took off his white coat and walked out of the office. He hired a taxi to drive him from Jersey all the way over to Kennedy, and from there he phoned Carol to tell her his decision and to say goodbye to the kids. Aside from his passport, which he'd been carrying with him for days, he flew off to Israel on the El Al night flight with nothing but the suit on his back and his credit cards.

Five months had passed and he hadn't returned.

Shuki now lectured in contemporary European history at the university and wrote a weekly column for one of the left-wing

66

papers, but compared to the days when he was in government he saw relatively few people, kept mostly to himself, and taught abroad as often as he could. He was as tired of politics, he said, as of all his old amusements. "I'm not even a great sinner anymore," he confessed. As a reserve military officer in Sinai during the Yom Kippur War, he'd lost his hearing in one ear and most of the sight in one eye when an exploding Egyptian shell threw him fifteen feet from his position. His brother, a reserve paratroop officer who in civilian life had been the architect, was taken prisoner when the Golan Heights were overrun. After the Syrian retreat, they found him and the rest of his captured platoon with their hands tied behind them to stakes in the ground; they had been castrated, decapitated, and their penises stuffed in their mouths. Strewn around the abandoned battlefield were necklaces made of their ears. A month after he'd received this news, Shuki's father, the welder, died of a stroke.

Shuki told me all of this, matter-of-factly, while he maneuvered through the heavy traffic and circled the side streets to find a space within walking distance of the downtown cafés. Eventually he was able to squeeze his VW in at an angle between two cars, half up on the sidewalk in front of an apartment building. "We could have sat like two nice old fellows beside the tranquil sea, but I remember that last time you preferred sitting on Dizengoff Street. I remember you devouring the girls with your eyes as though you thought they were shiksas."

"Is that right? Well, I was probably never much good at telling the difference."

"I don't go in for it any more myself," Shuki said. "It isn't that the girls aren't interested in me—I'm so big now they don't even see me."

Years back, after taking me to Jaffa and around the Tel Aviv sights, Shuki had entertained me one evening at a noisy café frequented by his journalist friends, where we'd wound up playing chess for several hours before moving on to the red-light district and my special sociological treat, a Rumanian prostitute on Yarkon Street. Now he led me into a barren colorless little place with some pinball machines in the back and nobody at any of the streetside tables except a couple of soldiers and their girls. At our table he said, "No, sit on this side, so I can hear you."

Though he hadn't become quite the behemoth of his own self-caricature, he bore little resemblance to the dark, slim, mischievous hedonist who'd guided me to Yarkon Street eighteen years earlier—the hair that used to spring from his forehead in tenacious black tiers had thinned down to just a few gray wisps combed across his scalp, and because the face had considerably puffed out, the features seemed larger and less refined. But the biggest change was in the grin, a grin having nothing to do with amusement, though clearly he liked still to be amused and knew how to be amusing. Thinking about his brother's death—and his father's fatal stroke—I found myself equating that grin of his with the dressing over a wound.

"How's New York?" he asked.

"I'm not living in New York anymore. I'm married to an English woman. I've moved to London."

"You in England? The Jersey boy with the dirty mouth who writes the books Jews love to hate—how do you survive there? How can you stand the silence? I was invited a couple of years ago to lecture at Oxford. I was there six months. At dinner, whatever I said, somebody next to me always replied, 'Oh, really?' "

"You didn't like the small talk."

"Truthfully? I didn't mind it. I needed a vacation from this place. Every Jewish dilemma there ever was is encapsulated in this country. In Israel it's enough to live—you don't have to do anything else and you go to bed exhausted. Have you ever noticed that Jews shout? Even one ear is more than you need. Here everything is black and white, everybody is shouting, and everybody is always right. Here the extremes are too great for a country so small. Oxford was a relief. 'Tell me, Mr. Elchanan, how is your dog?' 'I don't have a dog.' 'Oh, really?' My problem began when I got back. My wife's family would meet at our house on Friday nights to argue about politics, and I couldn't get a word in. During six months at Oxford I had learned civility and the rules of civilized discourse, and this turned out to be absolutely crippling in an Israeli discussion."

"Well," I said, "that hasn't changed—you still hear the best anti-Semitic cracks in a Dizengoff Street café."

"The only reason left to live here," Shuki said. "Tell me about your English wife."

I told him how I had met Maria in New York a little over a year before, when she and the husband from whom she was already hopelessly estranged had moved into the duplex upstairs from my apartment. "They were divorced four months back and we married and moved to England. Life is fine there. If it wasn't for Israel, everything in London would be wonderful."

"Yes? Israel's also to blame for living conditions in London? I'm not surprised."

"Last night, at a dinner party, when Maria mentioned where I was off to today, I wasn't the most popular boy at the table. You might have thought from the skiing holidays in Switzerland and the summer houses in Tuscany and the BMWs in the garage that all these nice, liberal, privileged Englishmen would have been a little leery of revolutionary socialism. But no, when it comes to Israel, it's the Sayings of Chairman Arafat right down the line."

"Of course. In Paris as well. Israel is one of those places you know so much better before you wind up there."

"They were all friends of Maria's, younger than I, in their thirties, television people, in publishing, a couple of journalists— all bright and successful. I was put right in the dock: how long can the Israelis keep importing cheap Jewish labor from North Africa to do their dirty work? It's well known in W11 that Oriental Jews are brought to Israel to be exploited as an industrial proletariat. Imperialist colonization, capitalist exploitation— all carried on from behind the facade of Israeli democracy and the fiction of Jewish national unity. And that was only the beginning."

"And you championed our wickedness?"

"I didn't have to. Maria did."

He looked alarmed. "You haven't married a Jew, Nathan."

"No, my record's intact. She just finds the moral posturing of the fashionable left very very depressing. But mostly what she resented was that defending Israel should appear to everyone to fall automatically upon her new husband. Maria isn't someone who relishes a fight, so her vehemence surprised me. So did theirs. I asked her on the way home how strong this Israel-hatred is in England. She says that the press thinks it is, and thinks it should be, but, in her words, 'it just bloody well isn't.' "

"I'm not sure she's right," Shuki said. "In England I myself sensed a certain, shall we say, *distaste* for Jews—a willingness to not always, in every circumstance, think the very best of us. I was interviewed one morning on BBC radio. We'd been on the air two minutes when the interviewer said to me, 'You Jews learned a lot from Auschwitz.' 'What's that?' I asked. 'How to be Nazis to the Arabs,' he said."

"What did you say?"

"I couldn't speak. On the Continent I just grit my teeth—there the anti-Semitism is so pervasive and ingrained, it's positively Byzantine. But in civilized England, with people so well-spoken, so well-bred, even I was caught off guard. I'm not known around here as this country's leading P.R. man, but if I'd had a gun I would have shot him."

At dinner the evening before, Maria had looked about ready to reach for a weapon herself. I'd never seen her so combative or incensed, not even during the divorce negotiations, when her husband seemed out to wreck our marriage before it began by forcing her to sign a legal document guaranteeing that Phoebe would be domiciled in London and not in New York. If Maria refused, he threatened to go to court and sue for custody, citing our adulterous liaison as grounds for claiming that she was an unfit mother. Assuming that I might be reluctant to be exiled from America until the turn of the century for the sake of his visitation rights, Maria immediately began to imagine herself returning to London unmarried, alone with Phoebe, and being plagued there by his bullying. "Nobody, but nobody, would ever want to get into a serious recrimination with him. If I'm on my own and he starts in, it'll be worse than just lonely and hard." She was equally as frightened of my resentment if, after accepting his conditions and agreeing to move to England, I found that cutting myself off from familiar sources had begun to damage my work. She lived in dread of yet another husband suddenly becoming estranged after she had taken the irrevocable step of becoming pregnant.

It bewildered her still to recall her ex-husband's coldness to her after she'd had Phoebe. "At any point up to then," she explained, "he could have said, with perfect justice, this isn't working for me. And *had* he said that, I would have said, absolutely, it just isn't, and however painful that is, that's it, and we will do other things with our lives. But why he couldn't perceive that clearly until after I had my baby—I mean I *had* accepted all the limitations of our relationship, otherwise I wouldn't have had a child. I *do* accept limitations. I expect them. Everybody tells me I'm submissive just because I happen to recognize the utter ridiculousness of railing against the kinds of disappointment that are simply inevitable. There's something every woman wants, and that's a man to blame. I refused to do it. To me the shortcomings of our marriage were no shock. I mean he had some dreadful qualities, but so many wonderful ones as well. No, what was a shock to me, after the baby came, was overt, relentless bad behavior—mistreatment, which is what happened as soon as my child was born and which I had never encountered before. I had encountered many, many things I didn't like, but they were things one can look at one way or another. But not misbehavior. There it is—that's what's happened. And if it were ever to happen to me again, I don't know what I'd do."

I assured her it wouldn't and told her to sign the agreement. I wasn't going to let him get away with this kind of shit, and I certainly wasn't going to give her up and, with her, my desire, at forty-four, after three childless marriages, to have a house, if not exactly full of babies, with a child in it of my own, and a young wife whom, though she described herself to me more than once as "mentally very lazy" and "intellectually very reclusive" and "sexually rather shy," I hadn't tired of in any way through our several hundred secret afternoons. I'd waited months before asking her to leave him, even though I was already thinking about it the first time we arranged to meet in my apartment. When she stubbornly resisted my proposal, I couldn't tell if it was because she took me to be another male bully simply wanting his way or whether she truly believed that I was dangerously self-deluded.

"I've fallen in love with you," I told her. "You're too self-aware to 'fall in love.' You know," she said, looking at me across my bed, "if you were really so convinced of the comic absurdity that you're so good at showing, you wouldn't be taking any of this seriously. Why can't you think of this as strictly a business meeting?" When I said I wanted a child, she replied, "Do you really want to spend a lot of time dealing with the melodrama of family life?" When I said that I couldn't get enough of her, she replied, "No, no, I've read your books—you need a lionlike temptress in here to give your libido a good thrashing. You need a woman who goes around organizing herself into the right kind of highly stylized erotic postures whenever she sits down—and that is definitely not me. You want a new experience and I'll only be the same old thing. It won't be dramatic at all. It'll be a long dull English evening in front of the fire with a very sensible, responsible, respectable woman. In time you'll need all sorts of polymorphous perversity to keep up your interest, and I'm really quite content, as you see, with simple penetration. I know that it's not on anymore, but I'm not interested in sucking elbows and all those things, truly I'm not. Just because I'm free in the afternoons for certain immoral purposes, you may have got the wrong idea. I don't want six men at a time, outdated as that sounds. Sometimes in the past, when I was younger, I had fantasies about that sort of thing, but real men, they're rarely nice enough to want *one* at a time. I don't want to dress like a chambermaid and indulge anyone's apron fetishism. I don't have the desire to be tied up and whipped, and as for buggery, it's never given me much pleasure. The idea is exciting but I'm afraid it hurts, so we can't found a marriage on that. If the truth be known, I really just like to arrange flowers and do a little bit of writing here and there—and that's it." "Then why do I have erotic thoughts about you?" "Really? What are they? Tell me." "I had them all morning." "What were we doing?" "You were assiduously performing fellatio." "Oh, I thought it was going to be something more unusual. That I wouldn't really do." "Maria, how can I be so hooked if you're as ordinary as you say?" "I think you like me because I don't have the usual feminine vices. I think a lot of those women who seem bright also seem very ferocious. What you like is that I seem bright without being ferocious, somebody who *is* really rather ordinary and is not determined to kick you in the teeth. But why carry it further—why marry me and have a child and settle down like everyone else to an impostor's life?" "Because I've decided to give up the artificial fiction of being myself for the genuine, satisfying falseness of being somebody else. *Marry me.*" "God, when you want something, you look at me so *scarily.*" "Because I'm conspiring with you *to escape.* I love you! I want to live with you! I want to have a child!" "Please," she replied, "do try to confine your fantasies in my presence. I really thought you were more worldly than this."

But I continued to confine nothing that I felt and in time she came to believe me, or collapsed in the face of my insistence— or both—and after that, the next thing I knew I was advising her to sign a document that would effectively sever me from my American life until tiny Phoebe was old enough to vote. Of course it wasn't what I had been anticipating and I did worry what effect moving abroad might have on my writing, but a courtroom custody battle would have been horrible for every reason, and I also believed that two or three years on, when everyone's divorce-delirium had abated, when Phoebe was older and beginning school and Maria's ex-husband was himself remarried and perhaps even a father again, it would be possible to renegotiate the custody stipulations. "And if it's not possible?" "It will be," I told her; "we'll live two or three years in London, he'll calm down, and it will all work out." "Will it? Can it? Does it ever? I dread thinking what happens when things start going wrong in England with your fantasy of family life."

When Maria had begun defending Israel against our fellow dinner-party guests, who'd been arguing as though the alleged crimes of what they called "appalling Zionism" were somehow mine to answer for, I wondered if what was driving her on weren't perhaps fears she continued to have about things going wrong for us in England rather than the reputation of the Jewish state. It was difficult otherwise to understand why someone who considered head-on confrontations hell, who despised *any* situation that required raising her voice, should place herself at the center of an argument she'd never seemed at all concerned with before. The closest I'd seen her get to entangling herself in the problems of Jews, and Jewish problems with Gentiles, was in a far more subdued, secluded setting, the bedroom of my Manhattan apartment when she'd told me what it was like for her living in a "Jewish city."

"I rather like it, actually," she'd said. "Life is sort of fizzy here, isn't it? A seemingly higher proportion of interesting people around. I like the way they talk. Gentiles have their little pale moments of exuberance, but nothing like this. It's the way one talks when one's been drinking. It's like Virgil. Whenever he tries any of that epic stuff, you knew you were in for twenty-five lines of seriously difficult Latin, all beside the point. 'And then the good Antaeus begged his son to put him down, saying, "My son, think first of our family, as when . . ."' This manic asidedness—well, that's New York and the Jews. Heady stuff. The only thing I don't like is that they all seem a bit too quick to find fault with Gentiles in their attitudes toward Jews. You have a touch of it too—finding things horrendously anti-Semitic, or even mildly so, when they really aren't. I know it's not entirely unjustified for Jews to be thin-skinned on that score—nonetheless, it's irritating. Uh-oh," she said, "I shouldn't be telling you these things." "No," I said, "go on—telling me what you know you shouldn't be telling is one of your endearing strategies." "Then I'll tell you something else that irritates me. About Jewish men." "Do." "All the shiksa-fancying. I don't like that. I don't like it at all. I don't feel it with you. Probably I'm deluding myself and you're the man

74

who invented it. I mean, I know there's an element of strangeness here, but I like to think all that doesn't operate *too* much." "So other Jewish men fancy you too—is that what you're saying?" "Are attracted to me because I'm not? In New York? Absolutely. Yes. That happens frequently when my husband and I go out." "But why should it irritate you?" "Because there are enough politics in sex without racial politics coming into it." I corrected her: "We're not a race." "It *is* a racial matter," she insisted. "No, we're the same race. You're thinking of Eskimos." "We are *not* the same race. Not according to anthropologists, or whoever measures these things. There's Caucasian, Semitic—there are about five different racial groups. Don't look at me like that." "I can't help it. Some nasty superstitions always tend to crop up when people talk about a Jewish 'race.'" "See, you're about to get angry at a Gentile for saying the wrong thing about Jews—proving my thesis. But all I can tell you is that you *are* a different race. We're supposed to be closer to Indians than to Jews, actually. I'm talking about Caucasians." "But I am Caucasian, kiddo. In the U.S. census I am, for good or bad, counted as Caucasian." "*Are* you? *Am* I wrong? Oh, you're not going to speak to me after this. It's always a mistake to be frank." "I'm nuts about you for being frank." "That won't last." "Nothing lasts, but right now it's true." "Well then, all I *am* saying—and I am not talking now about you *or* race—is that I don't feel with a lot of men in New York who do seem to want to chat me up that this is a personal thing, that they find me an interesting person who just happens not to be Jewish. On the contrary, this is a type that they had met before and that they quite liked having lunch with, or perhaps doing other things with, only because she *was* that type."

As it turned out, if anyone at that dinner party had been overly quick to find fault with Gentiles in their attitude toward Jews, it had been Maria herself. And in the car driving home, when she wouldn't let up about their hypocritical line on the Middle East, I began to wonder once again whether all this indignation might not have something to do with her anxiety about our English

75

future. I might even be seeing signs of that tendency toward self-annihilating accommodation that had been exploited so cruelly by her former husband once he'd begun losing interest in her.

The car door had barely shut behind her when she said to me, "I assure you, people in this country who have any sense at all, who are people of any kind of discrimination and judgment, are *not* anti-Israel. I mean, these people bat on about Israel in terms of great disgust, but the man who runs Libya thinks he can *fly*. It's just unreal, isn't it, their selective disapproval? These people disapprove selectively and most strongly of the least reprehensible parties." "You're really stirred up by all this." "Well, there comes a time when even nicely brought-up females lose their self-control. It's true I have trouble shouting at people, and I don't necessarily always say what I think, but even I don't have trouble being angry when people are being insulting and stupid."

After I'd repeated to Shuki the gist of the London dinner-table argument of the night before, he asked, "And she's beautiful too, your foolhardy Christian defender of our incorrigible state?"

"She considers herself Gentile, not Christian." In my billfold I found the Polaroid snapshot taken at Phoebe's second birthday party only a few weeks before. It showed Maria bending over the party table, helping the child cut the cake, both of them with the same dark curls, oval face, and feline eyes.

Shuki asked, examining the picture, "She has a job?"

"She used to work for a magazine; now she's writing fiction."

"So, gifted as well. Very attractive. Only an English girl can have that expression on her face. Observing everything and giving away nothing. She is surrounded by a large serenity, Maria Zuckerman. Effortless tranquillity—not a trait we're renowned for. Our great contribution is effortless anxiety." He turned the photograph over and read aloud the words written there by me. " 'Maria, five months pregnant.' "

"A father finally at forty-five," I said.

"I see. By marrying this woman and having a child you will be mixing at last in the everyday world."

"That may be part of it."

"The only problem is that in the everyday world girls don't look like this. And if it's a boy," Shuki asked, "your English rose will consent to circumcision?"

"Who says circumcision's required?"

"Genesis, chapter 17."

"Shuki, I've never been completely sold on biblical injunctions."

"Who is? Still, it's been a unifying custom among Jews for rather a long time now. I think it would be difficult for you to have a son who wasn't circumcised. I think you would resent a woman who insisted otherwise."

"We'll see."

Laughing, he handed back the picture. "Why do you pretend to be so detached from your Jewish feelings? In the books all you seem to be worrying about is what on earth a Jew is, while in life you pretend that you're content to be the last link in the Jewish chain of being."

"Chalk it up to Diaspora abnormality."

"Yes? You think in the *Diaspora* it's abnormal? Come live here. This is the *homeland* of Jewish abnormality. Worse: now *we* are the dependent Jews, on your money, your lobby, on our big allowance from Uncle Sam, while *you* are the Jews living interesting lives, comfortable lives, without apology, without shame, and perfectly *independent*. As for the condemnation of Israel in London W11, it may upset your lovely wife, but, really, it shouldn't bother you out there. Left-wing virtue-hounds are nothing new. Feeling morally superior to Iraqis and Syrians isn't really much fun, so let them feel superior to the Jews, if that's all it takes to make life beautiful. Frankly I think the English distaste for Jews is nine-tenths snobbery anyway. The fact remains that in the Diaspora a Jew like you lives securely, without real fear of persecution or violence, while we are living just the kind of imperiled Jewish existence that we came here to replace. Whenever I meet you American-Jewish intellectuals with your non-Jewish wives and your good Jewish brains, well-bred, smooth, soft-spoken men, educated men who know how to order in a good restaurant, and to appreciate good wine, and to listen courteously to another point of view, I think exactly that: we are the excitable, ghettoized, jittery little Jews of the Diaspora, and you are the Jews with all the confidence and cultivation that comes of feeling at home where you are."

"Only to an Israeli," I said, "could an American-Jewish intellectual look like a charming Frenchman."

"What the hell *are* you doing in a place like this?" Shuki asked.

"I'm here to see my brother. He's made aliyah."

"You've got a brother who's emigrated to Israel? What is he, a religious nut?"

"No, a successful dentist. Or he was. He's living in a little frontier settlement on the West Bank. He's learning Hebrew there."

"You're making this up. Carnovsky's brother on the West Bank? This is another of your hilarious ideas."

"My sister-in-law wishes it were. No, Henry's made it up. Henry appears to have left his wife, his kids, and his mistress to come to Israel to become an authentic Jew."

"Why would he want to be something like that?"

"That's what I'm here to find out."

"Which settlement is it?"

"Not far from Hebron, in the Judean hills. It's called Agor. His wife says he's found a hero there—a man named Mordecai Lippman."

"Oh, has he?"

"You know Lippman?"

"Nathan, I can't talk about these things. It's too painful for me. I mean this. Your brother is a follower of Lippman's?"

"Carol says that when Henry calls to speak to the kids, Lippman's all he talks about."

"Yes? He's so impressed? Well, when you see Henry, tell him all he has to do is go to the jail and he can meet plenty of little gangsters just as impressive."

"He intends to stay on, to live at Agor after he's finished his Hebrew course, *because* of Lippman."

"Well, that's wonderful. Lippman drives into Hebron with his pistol and tells the Arabs in the market how the Jews and Arabs can live happily side by side as long as the Jews are on top. He's dying for somebody to throw a Molotov cocktail. Then his thugs can really go to town."

"Carol mentioned Lippman's pistol. Henry told the kids all about it."

"Of course. Henry must find it very romantic," Shuki said. "The American Jews get a big thrill from the guns. They see Jews walking around with guns and they think they're in paradise. Reasonable people with a civilized repugnance for violence and blood, they come on tour from America, and they see the guns and they see the beards, and they take leave of their senses. The beards to remind them of saintly Yiddish weakness and the guns to reassure them of heroic Hebrew force. Jews ignorant of history, Hebrew, Bible, ignorant of Islam and the Middle East, they see the guns and they see the beards, and out of them flows every sentimental emotion that wish fulfillment can produce. A regular pudding of emotions. The fantasies about this place make me sick. And what *about* the beards? Is your brother as thrilled by the religion as by the explosives? These settlers, you know, are our great believing messianic Jews. The Bible is their *bible*— these idiots take it seriously. I tell you, all the madness of the human race is in the sanctification of that book. Everything going wrong with this country is in the first five books of the Old Testament. Smite the enemy, sacrifice your son, the desert is yours and nobody else's all the way to the Euphrates. A body count of dead Philistines on every other page—that's the wisdom of their wonderful Torah. If you're going out there, go tomorrow for the Friday night service and watch them sitting around kissing God's ass, telling him how big and wonderful he is—telling the rest of us how wonderful *they* are, bravely doing his work as courageous pioneers in biblical Judea. Pioneers! They work all day in government jobs in Jerusalem and drive home to biblical Judea for dinner at night. Only eating chopped chicken liver at the biblical source, only going to bed on the biblical sites, can a Jew find true Judaism. Well, if they want so much to sleep at the biblical source because that is where Abraham tied his shoelaces, then they can sleep there under Arab rule! Please, don't talk to me about what these people are up to. It makes me too crazy. I'll need a *year* at Oxford."

"Tell me more about my brother's hero."

"Lippman? I smell fascism on people like Lippman."

"What's that smell like here?"

"It smells the same here as it does everywhere. The situation gets so complicated that it seems to require a simple solution, and that's where Lippman comes in. His racket is to play upon Jewish insecurity—he says to the Jews, 'I have the solution to our problem of fear.' Of course there's a long history of these people. Mordecai Lippman doesn't come from nowhere. In every Jewish community there was always such a person. What could the rabbi do for their fears? The rabbi looks like you, Nathan—the rabbi is tall, he is thin, he is introverted and ascetic, always over his books, and usually he's also ill. He is not a person who can deal with the goyim. So in every community there is a butcher, a teamster, a porter, he is big, he is healthy—you sleep with one, two, maybe three women, he sleeps with twenty-seven, and all at the same time. *He* deals with the fear. He marches off at night with the other butcher and when he comes back there are a hundred goyim you don't ever have to worry about again. There was even a name for him: the *shlayger*. The whipper. The only difference between the Old Country *shlayger* and Mordecai Lippman is that on a superficial level Mr. Lippman is very deep. He hasn't only a Jewish gun, he has a Jewish mouth—remnants even of a Jewish brain. There is now so much antagonism between Arab and Jew that even a child would understand that the best thing is to keep them apart—so Mr. Lippman drives into Arab Hebron wearing his pistol. Hebron! This state was not established for Jews to police Nablus and Hebron! This was not the Zionist idea! Look, I have no illusions about Arabs and I have no illusions about Jews. I just don't want to live in a country that's *completely* crazy. It excites you to hear me going on like this—I can see it.

You envy me—you think, 'Craziness and dangerousness—that sounds like fun!' But believe me, when you have so much of it over so many years that even craziness and dangerousness become tedious and boring, then it's *really* dangerous. People are frightened here for thirty-five years—when will there be another war? The Arabs can lose and lose and lose, and we can lose only once. All that is true. But what is the result? Onto the stage comes Menachem Begin—and the logical step after Begin, a gangster like Mordecai Lippman, who tells them, 'I have the solution to our Jewish problem of fear.' And the worse Lippman is, the better. He's right, they say, that's the kind of world we live in. If the humane approach fails, try brutality."

"And yet my little brother likes him."

"Ask your little brother, then, 'What are the consequences of this delightful man?' The destruction of the country! Who comes to this country now to settle and live? The intellectual Jew? The humane Jew? The beautiful Jew? No, not the Jew from Buenos Aires, or Rio, or Manhattan. The ones who come from America are either religious or crazy or both. This place has become the American-Jewish Australia. Now who we get is the Oriental Jew and the Russian Jew and the social misfits like your brother, roughnecks in yarmulkes from Brooklyn."

"My brother's from suburban New Jersey. You couldn't possibly describe him as a misfit. The problem that brought him here may have been the opposite: he fit all too well into his comfortable existence."

"So what did he come for? The pressure? The tensions? The problems? The danger? Then he's really meshugge. You're the only smart one—you, of all people, are the only normal Jew, living in London with an English Gentile wife and thinking you won't even bother to circumcise your son. You, who say, I live in this time, I live in this world, and out of that I form my life. This, you understand, was supposed to be the place where to become a normal Jew was the *goal*. Instead we have become the Jewish obsessional prison par excellence! Instead it has become the breeding ground for every brand of madness that Jewish genius can devise!"

It was dusk when we started back to the car. Waiting there with his wife and his little child was a darkish, strongly built man in his early thirties, crisply dressed in pale slacks and a white short-sleeve shirt. It seemed that Shuki, by angling the VW half onto the sidewalk, had inadvertently made it impossible for this other driver to back his car out of the space in front. At the sight of us approaching the VW, he started shouting and shaking his fist, and I wondered if he might not be an Israeli Arab. His fury was amazing. Shuki raised his voice to reply, but there wasn't really much fury in him, and while the angry man screamed away, menacing him up close with a clenched fist, Shuki unlocked the car and let me in.

I asked, once we were driving off, in what language the fellow had been berating him, Arabic or Hebrew.

"Hebrew." Shuki laughed. "The man is like you, Nathan, a Jew. Hebrew, of course. He was telling me, 'I can't believe it— another Ashkenazi donkey! Every Ashkenazi I meet is another donkey!'"

"Where's he from?"

"I don't know—Tunis, Algiers, Casablanca. Have you heard who is now coming to live here? Jews from Ethiopia. So desperate are these bastards like Begin to perpetuate the old mythology that they're beginning to drag *black* Jews here. Pleasant, affectionate, good-natured people, most of them peasants, they come here speaking the Ethiopian language. Some are so sick when they arrive they have to be taken by stretcher and rushed to the hospital. Most are unable to read or write. They have to be taught how to turn on the tap and turn off the tap and how to use a toilet and what stairs are. Technologically they live in the thirteenth century. But within a year, I assure you, they'll already be Israelis, shouting about their rights and staging sitdown strikes, and soon enough they will be calling me an Ashkenazi donkey because of how I park my car."

At my hotel, Shuki apologized for being unable to have dinner with me, but he didn't like leaving his wife alone at night and she wasn't up to socializing. It was a bad time for her. Their eighteen-year-old son, who had emerged through competition as one of the outstanding young musicians in the country, had been drafted into the army for his three years of service and as a result would be unable to practice his piano regularly, if at all. Daniel Barenboim had listened to Mati play and offered to help arrange for him to study in America, but the boy had decided that he couldn't leave the country to pursue his own ambitions while his friends were doing their military service. Once he had finished his basic training, allowances were supposed to be made for him to practice several times a week, but Shuki doubted that even this would happen. "Maybe he doesn't need our approbation anymore, but he still needs theirs. Mati's not so obstinate out of the house. If they tell him to go and hose down the tanks at the hour reserved for his practice, Mati is not going to take his note out of his pocket and say, 'Daniel Barenboim suggests I play the piano instead.'"

"Your wife wanted him to go to America."

"She tells him his responsibility is to music and not to the stupid infantry. In his nice loud voice, he says, 'Israel has given me plenty! I've had a good time here! I have to do my duty!' and she goes completely crazy. I try to intervene but I am as effective as one of the fathers in your books. I even thought about you while it was happening. I thought it really didn't require all the agonies of creating a Jewish state where our people could shed their ghetto behavior, for me to wind up like a helpless father out of a Zuckerman novel, a real old-fashioned Jewish father who's either kissing the children or shouting at them. Another powerless Jewish father against whom the poor Jewish son has nevertheless to stage his ridiculous rebellion."

"Goodbye, Shuki," I said, taking his hand.

"Goodbye, Nathan. And don't forget to come again in another twenty years. I'm sure if Begin is still in power I'll have even more good news."

I decided, after Shuki left, that rather than stay in Tel Aviv that evening, I'd have the front desk phone ahead to Jerusalem to arrange a room for the night. From there I'd get in touch with

Henry and try to get him to meet me for dinner. If Shuki hadn't exaggerated, and Lippman was anything like the *shlayger* he'd described, then it was possible that Henry was as much captive as disciple, and, in fact, something like what might have been in Carol's mind when she'd indicated that dealing with a suburban husband who'd turned himself into a born-again Jew was like having a child become a Moonie. How could she go ahead, she asked, and institute separation proceedings leading to a divorce if the man had really lost his mind? When she'd phoned me in London it was because she'd begun to feel as though she might be losing her mind herself—and because she didn't know whom else to turn to.

"I don't want to match his irrationality with my own, I don't want to act prematurely, but he couldn't have gone any farther from me if he *had* died in surgery. If he's cast me off for good, *and* the practice, *and* everything else, I *have* to act, I can't wait here like an idiot for him to come to his senses. But I'm paralyzed—I cannot grasp it—I don't understand what has happened *at all*. Do you? You've known him all his life. In a way brothers probably know each other better than they ever know anyone else."

"How they know each other, in my experience, is as a kind of deformation of themselves."

"Nathan, he can't put you off the way he can me. Before I do anything that's going to destroy it for good, I have to know if he's completely flipped out."

I thought I ought to know too. The relationship to Henry was the most elemental connection I had left, and however vexing its surface had become after the long years of our estrangement, what was evoked in me by Carol's call was the need to be responsible not so much to the disapproving brother with whom I'd already come to blows but to the little boy in the flannel pajamas who was known to sleepwalk when he was overexcited.

Not that it was filial duty alone that was goading me on. I was also deeply curious about this swift and simple conversion of a kind that isn't readily allowed to writers unless they wish to commit the professional blunder of being uninquiring. Henry's

84

life was no longer coming true in its most pedestrian form, and I had to ask if it all *had* been as mindlessly gained as Carol meant by suggesting he'd "flipped out." Wasn't there possibly more genius than madness in this escape? However unprecedented in the annals of suffocating domesticity, wasn't this escape somehow incontestable in a way that it never would have been had he run off with an alluring patient? Certainly the rebellious script that he had tried following ten years back could hardly touch this one for originality.

Within half an hour I'd settled my bill, and my bag was beside me in the taxi heading away from the sea. The industrial outskirts of Tel Aviv were already disappearing in the winter darkness when we turned onto the thruway and eastward across the citrus groves to the Jerusalem hills. As soon as I had a room at the hotel, I called Agor. The woman who answered seemed at first to be quite convinced that nobody named Henry Zuckerman lived at Agor. "The American," I said loudly, "the American— the dentist from New Jersey!" Here she disappeared and I didn't know quite what was up.

While waiting for someone to come back on the phone, I recalled in detail the message I'd got from Henry's thirteen-year-old daughter, Ruth, during dinner in London the evening before. It was a collect person-to-person call, placed in New Jersey after school from the house of a friend. Her mother had told her that I was going down to see her father, and though she wasn't sure she was right even to be phoning me—for a week now she'd been putting it off from one day to the next—she wondered if she could ask me to tell him something "confidentially," something she herself was not able to say on Sundays what with her older brother, Leslie, and her younger sister, Ellen, and sometimes even her mother hovering over the phone. But first she wanted me to know that she didn't happen to agree with her mother that her father was behaving "childishly." "She keeps saying," Ruthie told me, "that he's not reliable anymore, that she doesn't trust his motives, and that if he wants to see us it's going to have to be here. We were supposed to fly over for the school holiday and travel with him around the country, but now I'm not really sure she's going to let us. She's very down on him right now—very. She's hurting terribly and I can sympathize. But what I would like you to tell my dad for me is that I think I understand better than Leslie and Ellen. Leave out Leslie and Ellen—just tell him that I understand." "You understand what?" "He's out there to learn something—he's trying to find something out. I don't say I understand *everything*, but I do think he's not too old to learn—and I think he has the right." "I'll tell him that," I said. "Don't you think it's so?' she asked. "What do *you* think about all this, Uncle Nathan? Do you mind my asking?" "Well," I said, "I don't know if it's where I'd go, but I suppose I've done similar things myself." "Have you really?" "Things that look childish to other people? I have. And perhaps for the reason you suggest—trying to find something out." "In a way," said Ruth, "I even admire him. It's awfully brave to go so far—isn't it? I mean he's giving up an awful lot." "It looks that way. Are you afraid that he's given you up?" "No, Ellen is, I'm not. Ellen's the one who's in a bad way. She's a mess right now, though don't tell him—he shouldn't have to worry about that too." "And your brother?" "He's just bossier than ever—he's now the man around here, you see." "You sound okay, Ruth." "Well, I'm not great, frankly. I miss him. I'm confused without my father." "Do you want me to tell him that too, that you're confused without him?" "If you think it's a good idea, I guess so."

Henry must have been at the other end of the settlement—maybe, I thought, attending evening prayers—because it was a full ten minutes before they found him and he finally came to the phone. I wondered if he was wearing his prayer shawl. I really didn't know what to expect.

"It's me," I announced, "Cain to your Abel, Esau to your Jacob, here in the Land of Canaan. I'm calling from the King David Hotel. I just arrived from London."

"My, my." Sardonic words, just two of them, and then the long pause. "Here for Chanukah?" he finally asked.

"Chanukah first and to see you second."

A longer pause. "Where's Carol?"

"I'm alone."

"What do you want?"

"I thought you might come in to have dinner with me in Jerusalem. They could probably find a bed for you here in the hotel if you wanted to stay over."

As he was now an even longer time replying, I figured he was about to hang up. "I have a class tonight," he eventually said.

"How about tomorrow? I'll drive out to you."

"You do have to admit it's a little bizarre that you're the one Carol deputized to fly in to remind me of my family obligations."

"I didn't come down here to bring you back alive."

"You couldn't," he snapped, "if you wanted to. I know what I'm doing and there's nothing to say—the decision's irrevocable."

"Then what harm can I do? I'd like to see Agor."

"This is rich," he said. "You in Jerusalem."

"Well, neither of us was renowned in New Jersey for his pious devotion."

"What *do* you want, Nathan?"

"To visit you. To find out how you're doing."

"And Carol's not with you?"

"I don't play those games. Neither Carol nor the cops. I flew from London by myself."

"On the spur of the moment."

"Why not?"

"And what if I tell you to go back to London on the spur of the moment?"

"Why should you?"

"Because I don't need anyone to come out here and decide if I'm deranged. Because I've made the appropriate explanations already. Because—"

Once Henry got going like that I knew he'd have to see me.

When I'd visited Israel back in 1960, the Old City was still on the other side of the border. Across the narrow valley opening out behind this same hotel, I'd been able to watch the armed Jordanian soldiers posted as guards atop the Wall but of course I'd never got to visit the Temple remnant known as the Western or Wailing Wall. I was curious now to see if anything like what had happened to my brother in Mea She'arim would surprise and overtake me while standing at this, the most hallowed of all Jewish places. When I asked at the desk, the hotel clerk had assured me that I wouldn't find myself alone there, not at any hour. "Every Jew should go at night," he told me, "you'll remember it for the rest of your life." With nothing to do until I left the next morning for Agor, I got a cab to drive me over.

It *was* more impressive than I'd anticipated, perhaps because the floodlights dramatizing the massive weight of the ancient stones seemed simultaneously to be illuminating the most poignant of history's themes: Transience, Endurance, Destruction, Hope. The Wall was asymmetrically framed by a pair of minarets jutting up from the holy Arab compound just beyond, and by two mosque domes there, the grand one of gold and a smaller one of silver, placed as though subtly to unbalance the picturesque composition. Even the full moon, hoisted to an unobtrusive height so as to avoid the suggestion of superfluous kitsch, seemed, beside those domes silhouetting the sky, decorative ingenuity in a very minor mode. This gorgeous Oriental nighttime backdrop made of the Wailing Wall square an enormous outdoor theater, the stage for some lavish, epic, operatic production whose extras one could watch walking casually about, a handful already got up in their religious costumes and the rest, unbearded, still in street clothes.

Approaching the Wall from the old Jewish quarter, I had to pass through a security barrier at the top of a long flight of stairs. A middle-aged Sephardic soldier, scruffily dressed in army fatigues, fumbled through the tourists' shopping bags and purses before letting them pass on. At the foot of the stairs, lounging back on their elbows, as oblivious to the Divine Presence as to the crowd milling about, were four more Israeli soldiers, all quite young, any one of whom, I thought, could have been Shuki's son, out not practicing his piano. Like the guard up by the barrier, each appeared to have improvised a uniform from a heap of old clothes at an army surplus store. They reminded me of the hippies I used to see around Bethesda Fountain in

Central Park during the Vietnam War years, except that slung across these Israeli khaki rags were automatic weapons.

A stone divider insulated those who'd come to pray piously at the Wall from the people circulating in the square. There was a small table at one end of the barrier and on it a box of cardboard yarmulkes for hatless male visitors—women prayed by themselves down at their own partitioned segment of the Wall. Two of the Orthodox were stationed—or had decided to situate themselves—just beside the table. The older one, a slight, bent figure with a storybook white beard and a cane, was seated on the stone bench running parallel to the Wall; the other, who was probably younger than I, was a bulky man in a long black coat, with a heavy face and a stiff beard shaped like a coal scoop or a shovel. He stood above the man with the cane, talking with great intensity; however, no sooner had I placed a yarmulke on my head than abruptly he turned his attention on me. "Shalom. Shalom aleichem."

"Shalom," I replied.

"I collect. Charity."

"Me too," the old man chimed in.

"Yes? Charity for what?"

"Poor families," answered the one with the black shovel beard.

I reached into my pocket and came up with all my change, Israeli and English. To me this seemed a generous enough donation given the nebulous quality of the philanthropy he claimed to represent. He offered in return, however, a just perceptible look that I had to admire for its fine expressive blend of incredulity and contempt. "You don't have paper money?" he asked. "A couple of dollars?"

Because my meticulous concern for his "credentials" suddenly struck me as pretty funny in the circumstances, and also because old-fashioned shnorring is so much more humanly appealing than authorized, respectable, humanitarian "fund-raising," I began to laugh. "Gentlemen," I said, "fellows—" but the shovel-beard was already showing me, rather like a curtain dropping when the act is over, the back of his extensive black coat, and had already resumed firing his Yiddish at the seated old man. It hadn't taken all day for him to decide not to waste time on a cheap Jew like me.

Standing singly at the Wall, some rapidly swaying and rhythmically bobbing as they recited their prayers, others motionless but for the lightning flutter of their mouths, were seventeen of the world's twelve million Jews communing with the King of the Universe. To me it looked as though they were communing solely with the stones in whose crevices pigeons were roosting some twenty feet above their heads. I thought (as I am predisposed to think), "If there is a God who plays a role in our world, I will eat every hat in this town"—nonetheless, I couldn't help but be gripped by the sight of this rock-worship, exemplifying as it did to me the most awesomely retarded aspect of the human mind. Rock is just right, I thought: what on earth could be less responsive? Even the cloud drifting by overhead, Shuki's late father's "Jewish cloud," appeared less indifferent to our encompassed and uncertain existence. I think that I would have felt less detached from seventeen Jews who openly admitted that they *were* talking to rock than from these seventeen who imagined themselves telexing the Creator directly; had I known for sure it was rock and rock alone that they knew they were addressing, I might even have joined in. Kissing God's ass, Shuki had called it, with more distaste than I could muster. I was simply reminded of my lifelong disaffection from such rites.

I edged up to the Wall to get a better look, and from only a few feet away watched a man in an ordinary business suit, a middle-aged man with a monogrammed briefcase at his feet, conclude his prayers by placing two soft kisses upon the stone, kisses such as my own mother would lay upon my brow when I was a child home in bed with a fever. The fingertips of one hand remained in gentlest conjunction with the Wall even after he had lifted his lips from the last lingering kiss.

Of course, to be as tenderized by a block of stone as a mother is by her ailing child needn't really mean a thing. You can go around kissing all the walls in the world, and all the crosses, and the femurs and tibias of all the holy blessed martyrs ever butchered by the infidel, and back in your office be a son of a bitch to the staff and at home a perfect prick to your family. Local history hardly argued that transcendence over ordinary human failings, let alone the really vicious proclivities, is likely to be expedited by pious deeds committed in Jerusalem. Nonetheless, at that moment, even I got a little carried away, and would have been willing to concede that what had just been enacted before me with such affecting sweetness might not be *entirely* inane. Then again I could have been wrong.

Nearby, an archway opened into a large cavernous vault where, through a floodlit grate in the stone floor, you could see that there was even more Wailing Wall below the ground than above —way back then was way down there. A hundred or so square feet, the entry to this chamber, were partitioned off into a smallish makeshift room that, except for the fire-blackened, roughly vaulted ceiling and the stones of the Second Temple Wall, looked something like the unprepossessing neighborhood synagogue where I had been enrolled for late-afternoon Hebrew classes at the age of ten. The large Torah ark might have been built as a woodwork project by a first-year shop class in vocational school—it was as unholy-looking as it could possibly be. Rows of storage shelves along the wall facing the ark were piled unevenly with a couple of hundred worn prayer books, and, randomly scattered about, were a dozen battered plastic chairs. But what reminded me most of my old Talmud Torah wasn't so much the similarity of the decor as the congregation. A chazan stood off in one corner, flanked by two very thin teenagers in Chasidic garb who chanted intermittently with great fervor while he intoned in a rough baritone wail—otherwise the worshippers seemed only marginally engaged by the liturgy. It was very much as I remembered things back on Schley Street in Newark: some of them kept turning around to see if anything of more piquancy might be developing elsewhere, while others looked every which way, as though for friends they were expecting to arrive. The remaining few, in a desultory way, seemed to be counting the house.

I was just easing myself in beside the bookshelves—so as to look on unobtrusively from the sidelines—when I was approached by a young Chasid, distinguished in this assemblage by the elegant fit of his long satin coat and the unblemished black sheen of a new velvet hat with a low crown and an imposing brim. His pallor was alarming, however, a skin tone a breath away from the morgue. The elongated fingers with which he was tapping my shoulder suggested something erotically creepy at one extreme and excruciatingly delicate at the other, the hand of the helpless maiden *and* of the lurid ghoul. He was inviting me, worldlessly, to take a book and join the minyan. When I whispered no, he replied, in hollow, accented English, "Come. We need you, mister."

I shook my head again just as the chazan, with a raw, wrenching wail that could well have been some terrible reprimand, pronounced "Adonoi," the name of the Lord.

Unfazed, the young Chasid repeated, "Come," and pointed beyond the partition to what looked more like an empty warehouse than a house of prayer, the sort of space that a smart New York entrepreneur would jump to convert to sauna, tennis courts, steam room, and swimming pool: The Wailing Wall Health and Racquet Club.

In there too were pious worshippers, seated with their prayer books only inches from the Wall. Leaning forward, their elbows on their knees, they reminded me of poor souls who'd been waiting all day in a welfare office or on an unemployment line. Low lozenge-like floodlights did not serve to make the place any cozier or more congenial. Religion couldn't come less adorned than this. These Jews needed nothing but that wall.

Collectively they emitted a faint murmur that sounded like bees at work—the bees genetically commandeered to pray for the hive.

Still patiently waiting at my side was the elegant young Chasid.

"I can't help you out," I whispered.

"Only a minute, mister."

You couldn't say he was insisting. In a way he didn't even seem to care. From the fixed look in his eye and the flat, forceless voice, I might even have concluded, in another context, that he was mentally a little deficient, but I was trying hard here to be a generous, tolerant cultural relativist—trying a hell of a lot harder than he was.

"Sorry," I said. "That's it."

"Where are you from? The States? You were bar mitzvah?"

I looked away.

"Come," he said.

"Please—enough."

"But you are a Jew who was bar mitzvah."

Here we go. One Jew is about to explain to another Jew that he is not the same kind of Jew that the first Jew is—the source, this situation, of several hundred thousand jokes, not to mention all the works of fiction. "I am not observant," I said. "I don't participate in prayer."

"Why do you come here?" But it was again as though he wasn't asking because he really cared. I was beginning to doubt that he fully understood his own English, let alone mine.

"To see the Old Temple Wall," I replied. "To see Jews who *do* participate in prayer. I'm a tourist."

"You had religious education?"

"None that you could take seriously."

"I pity you." So flatly stated that he might as well have been telling me the time.

"Yes, you feel sorry for me?"

"Secular don't know what they are living for."

"I can see how to you it might look that way."

"Secular are coming back. Jews worse than you."

"Really? How much worse?"

"I don't like to say even."

"What is it? Drugs? Sex? Money?"

"Worse. Come, mister. It'll be mitzvah, mister."

If I was correctly reading his persistence, my secularism represented to him nothing more than a slightly ridiculous mistake. It wasn't even worth getting excited about. That I wasn't pious was the result of some misunderstanding.

Even while I was making a stab at surmising what he thought, I realized that of course I could have no more idea of what was going on in his mind than he could have of what was going on in mine. I doubt that he even tried to figure out what was in mine.

"Leave me alone, okay?"

"Come," he said.

"Please, what's it to you whether I pray or not?" I didn't bother to tell him—because I didn't think it was my place to—that frankly I consider praying beneath my dignity. "Let me just stand quietly out of the way here and watch."

"Where in the States? Brooklyn? California?"

"Where are *you* from?"

"From? I am a Jew. Come."

"Look, I'm not criticizing your observance or your outfit or your appearance, I don't even mind your insinuations about my short-comings—so why are you so offended by me?" Not that he appeared in the least offended, but I was trying to place our discussion on a higher plane.

"Mister, you are circumcised?"

"Do you want me to draw you a picture?"

"Your wife is a shiksa," he suddenly announced.

"That wasn't as hard to figure out as you like to make it seem," I said, but in the bloodless face there was neither amusement nor fellow-feeling—only a pair of unfazed eyes focused blandly on my ridiculous resistance. "All four of my wives have been shiksas," I told him.

"Why, mister?"

"That's the sort of Jew I am, Mac."

"Come," he said, motioning to indicate that it was time for me to stop being silly and to do as I was told.

"Look, get yourself another boy, all right?"

But because he couldn't completely follow what I was saying, or because he wanted to harass me and drive my sinfulness from this holy place, or because he wished to correct the little mistake of my having left the fold, or maybe because he simply needed another pious Jew in the world the way someone who is thirsty needs a glass of water, he wouldn't let me be. He just stood there saying "Come," and just as stubbornly I remained where I was. I wasn't committing any infraction of religious law, and refused either to do as he wished or to take flight as an intruder. I wondered if, in fact, I hadn't been right at the outset, and if he wasn't perhaps a little defective, though on further reflection, I saw it could well appear that the man without all his marbles had to be the one with four Gentile wives.

I was out of the cavern no more than a minute, taking a last look around the square at the minarets, the moon, the domes, the Wall, when someone was shouting at me, "It's you!"

Standing in my path was a tall young man with a thin, scraggly growth of beard who looked as though he had all he could do not to give me an enormous hug. He was panting hard, whether from excitement or from having run to catch me, I couldn't tell. And he was laughing, gusts of jubilant, euphoric laughter. I don't think I've ever before come across anyone so tickled to see me.

"It's really you! Here! Great! I've read all your books! You wrote about my family! The Lustigs of West Orange! In *Higher Education*! That's them! I'm your biggest admirer in the world! *Mixed Emotions* is your best book, better than *Carnovsky*! How come you're wearing a cardboard yarmulke? You should be wearing a beautiful, embroidered *kipa* like mine!"

He showed me the skullcap—held by a hair-clip to the top of his head—as though it had been designed for him by a Paris milliner. He was in his mid-twenties, a very tall, dark-haired, boyishly handsome young American in a gray cotton jogging suit, red running shoes, and the embroidered *kipa*. He danced in place even as he spoke, bouncing up on his toes, his arms jiggling like a boxer's before the bell to round one. I didn't know what to make of him.

"So you're a West Orange Lustig," I said.

"I'm Jimmy Ben-Joseph, Nathan! You look great! Those pictures on your books don't do you justice! You're a good-looking guy! You just got married! You have a new wife! Numero four! Let's hope this time it works!"

I began laughing myself. "Why do you know all this?"

"I'm your greatest fan. I know everything about you. I write too. I wrote the Five Books of Jimmy!"

"Haven't read them."

"They haven't been published yet. What are you doing here, Nathan?"

"Seeing the sights. What are *you* doing?"

"I was praying for you to come! I've been here at the Wailing Wall praying for you to come—and you came!"

"Okay, calm down, Jim."

I still couldn't tell whether he was half-crazy or completely crazy or just seething with energy, a manicky kid far away from home clowning around and having a good time. But since I was beginning to suspect that he might be a little of all three, I started back toward the low stone barrier and the table where I'd picked up my yarmulke. Beyond a gate across the square I could see several taxis waiting. I'd catch one back to the hotel. Intriguing as people like Jimmy can sometimes be, you usually get the best of them in the first three minutes. I've attracted them before.

He didn't exactly walk *with* me as I started off but, springing on the toes of his running shoes, proceeded backwards away from the Wall a couple of steps in front of me. "I'm a student at the Diaspora Yeshivah," he explained.

"Is there such a place?"

"You never heard of the Diaspora Yeshivah? It's over there on top of Mount Zion! On top of King David's mountain! You should come and visit! You should come and stay! The Diaspora Yeshivah is made for guys like you! You've been away from the Jewish people too long!"

"So they tell me. And how long do you plan to stay?"

"In Eretz Yisrael? The rest of my life!"

"And how long have you been here?"

"Twelve days!"

In the setting of his surprisingly small, delicately boned face, which was miniaturized further by a narrow frame of new whiskers, his eyes looked to be still in the throes of creation, precariously trembling bubbles at the tip of a fiery eruption.

"You're in quite a hyped-up state, Jimmy."

"You bet! I'm high as a kite on Jewish commitment!"

"Jimmy the Luftyid, the High-Flying Jew."

"And you? What are you, Nathan? Do you even know?"

"Me? From the look of things, a grounded Jew. Where'd you go to college, Jim?"

"Lafayette College. Easton, PA. Habitat of Larry Holmes. I studied acting and journalism. But now I'm back with the Jewish people! You shouldn't be estranged, Nathan! You'd make a great Jew!"

I was laughing again—so was he. "Tell me," I said, "are you here alone or with a girlfriend?"

"No, no girlfriend—Rabbi Greenspan is going to find me a wife. I want eight kids. Only a girl here will understand. I want a religious girl. Multiply and be fruitful!"

"Well, you've got a new name, a start on a new beard, Rabbi Greenspan is out looking for the right girl—and you're even living on top of King David's mountain. Sounds like you've got it made."

At the table by the barrier, where there was nobody any longer collecting for the poor, if there ever had been, I placed my yarmulke on top of the others piled in the box. When I extended my hand Jimmy took it, not to shake but to hold affectionately between the two of his.

"But where are you going? I'll walk you. I'll show you Mount Zion, Nathan. You can meet Rabbi Greenspan."

"I've already got my wife—numero four. I have to be off," I said, breaking away from him. "Shalom."

"But," he called after me, having resumed that vigorous, athletic bounding about on his toes, "do you even understand why I love and respect you the way I do?"

"Not really."

"Because of the way you write about baseball! Because of all you feel about baseball! That's the thing that's missing here.

How can there be Jews without baseball? I ask Rabbi Greenspan but he don't comprendo. Not until there is baseball in Israel will Messiah come! Nathan, I want to play center field for the Jerusalem Giants!"

Waving goodbye—and thinking how relieved the Lustigs must be back in West Orange now that Jimmy is here in Eretz Yisrael and Rabbi Greenspan's to worry about—I called, "Go right ahead!"

"I will, I will if you say so, Nate!" and beneath the bright floodlights, he suddenly broke away and began to run—back-pedaling first, then turning to his right, and with his delicate, freshly bearded face cocked as though to follow the flight of a ball struck off a Louisville Slugger from somewhere up in the old Jewish quarter, he was racing back toward the Wailing Wall without any regard for who or what might be in his way. And in a piercing voice that must have made him something of a find for the Lafayette College Drama Society, he began to shout, "Ben-Joseph is going back, back—it could be gone, it may be gone, this could be curtains for Jerusalem!" Then, with no more than three feet between him and the stones of the Wall—and the worshippers at the Wall—Jimmy leaped, sailing recklessly into the air, his long left arm extended high across his body and far above his embroidered *kipa*. "Ben-Joseph catches it!" he screamed, as along the length of the Wall a few of the worshippers turned indignantly to see what the disturbance was. Most, however, were so rapt in prayer that they didn't even bother looking up. "Ben-Joseph catches it!" he cried again, holding the imaginary ball in the pocket of his imaginary glove and jumping up and down in the very spot where he had marvelously brought it in. "The game is over!" Jimmy was shouting. "The season is over! The Jerusalem Giants win the pennant! The Jerusalem Giants win the pennant! Messiah is on his way!"

Friday morning after breakfast a taxi took me out to Agor, a forty-five-minute trip through the rock-clogged white hills south-east of Jerusalem. The driver, a Yemenite Jew who understood hardly any English, listened to the radio while he drove. Some twenty minutes beyond the city we passed an army roadblock manned by a couple of soldiers with rifles; it consisted of no more than a wooden sawhorse, and the taxi simply swerved around it in order to continue on. The soldiers didn't appear to be interested in stopping anyone, not even the Arabs with West Bank plates. One shirtless soldier was lying on the ground at the shoulder of the road taking the sun, while the other shirtless soldier tapped his feet in time to a portable radio playing under his roadside chair. Thinking back to the soldiers lolling in the square by the Wailing Wall, I said, for no reason, really, other than to hear my voice, "Easygoing army you have here."

The taxi driver nodded and took a billfold out of his back pocket. Fumbling with one hand, he found a picture to show me, a snapshot of a young soldier, kneeling and looking up at the camera, an intense-looking boy with large dark eyes and, from the evidence of his fresh and neatly pressed fatigues, the best-dressed member of the Israeli Defense Forces. He was holding his weapon like somebody who knew how to use it. "My son," the driver said.

"Very nice," I said.

"Dead."

"Oh. I'm sorry to hear that."

"Someone is shooting a bomb. He is no more there. No shoes, nothing."

"How old?" I asked, handing back the picture. "How old a boy was he?"

"Killed," he replied. "No good. I never see my son no more."

Farther on, a hundred yards back from the winding road, there was a Bedouin encampment tucked into the valley between two rocky hills. The long, dark, brown tent, patched with black squares, looked from that distance less like a habitation than like the wash, like a collection of large old rags draped on poles to dry in the sun. Up ahead we had to stop to let a little man with a mustache and a stick guide his sheep across the road. He was a Bedouin herdsman wearing an old brown suit, and if he reminded me of Charlie Chaplin, it wasn't only because of his appearance

99

but because of the seeming hopelessness of his pursuit—what his sheep would find to eat in those dry hills was a mystery to me.

The taxi driver pointed to a settlement on the next hilltop. It was Agor, Henry's home. Though there was a high wire fence topped with curling barbed wire fronting the road, the gate was wide open and the guard booth empty. The taxi turned sharply in and drove up a dirt incline to a low corrugated-metal shed. A man with a blowtorch was working at a long table in the open air and from inside the shed I heard a hammer pounding.

I got out of the car. "I'm looking for Henry Zuckerman."

He waited to hear more.

"Henry Zuckerman," I repeated. "The American dentist."

"Hanoch?"

"Henry," I said. Then, "Sure—Hanoch."

I thought, "Hanoch Zuckerman, Maria Zuckerman—the world is suddenly full of brand-new Zuckermans."

He pointed farther up the dirt road to a row of small, block-like concrete buildings. That was all there was up there—a raw, dry, dusty hill with nothing growing anywhere. The only person to be seen about was this man with a blowtorch, a short muscular fellow wearing wire-rimmed glasses and a little knitted skullcap pinned to his crew cut. "There," he said brusquely. "School is there."

A stout young woman in a pair of overalls and wearing a large brown beret came bounding out of the shed. "Hi," she called, smiling at me. "I'm Daphna. Who you looking for?"

She spoke with a New York accent and reminded me of the hearty girls I used to see dancing to Hebrew folk songs at the Hillel House when I was a freshman new to Chicago and went around there at night, during the first lonely weeks, trying to get laid. That was as close as I ever came to Zionism and constituted the whole of my "Jewish commitment" at college. As for Henry, his commitment consisted of playing basketball at Cornell for his Jewish fraternity.

"Hanoch Zuckerman," I said to her.

"Hanoch is at the ulpan. The Hebrew school."

"Are you American?"

The question affronted her. "I'm Jewish," she replied.

"I understand. I was just guessing from your speech that you were born in New York."

"I'm Jewish by *birth*," she said and, clearly having had her fill of me, went back into the shed, where I heard the pounding of the hammer resume.

Henry/Hanoch was one of fifteen students gathered in a half-circle around their teacher's chair. The students were either seated or sprawled on the grassless ground and, like Henry, most of them were writing in exercise books while the teacher spoke in Hebrew. Henry was the oldest by at least fifteen years—probably a few years older even than his teacher. Except for him it looked like any collection of summer-school kids enjoying their lesson in the warm sun. The boys, half of whom were growing beards, were all in old jeans; most of the girls wore jeans too, except for two or three in cotton skirts and sleeveless blouses that showed how tan they were and that they'd stopped shaving under their arms. The minaret of an Arab village was clearly visible at the foot of the hill, yet Agor's ulpan in December could as easily have been Middlebury or Yale, a college language center in July.

Where the topmost buttons of Henry's work shirt were undone I could see the scar from his bypass surgery neatly dividing his strong chest. After nearly five months in the hot desert hills he looked not unlike the dead soldier son of my Yemenite taxi driver—more like that boy's brother now than mine. Seeing him so fit and darkly tanned and wearing shorts and sandals, I found myself recalling our boyhood summers at the rented cottage on the Jersey Shore, and how he used to follow after me, down to the beach, along the boardwalk at night—wherever I went with my friends, Henry would come tagging along as our adoring mascot. Strange to find the second-born son, whose sustaining passion was always to be the equal of those already grown up, back in school at the age of forty. Even stranger to come upon his classroom atop a hill from which you could see off to the Dead Sea, and beyond that to the creviced mountains of a desert kingdom.

I thought, "His daughter Ruthie's right—he's here to learn something and it isn't just Hebrew. I *have* done similar things, but he hasn't. Never before, and this is his chance. His first and maybe his last. Don't be his older brother—don't pick on him where he's vulnerable and where he'll always be vulnerable." "I admire him," Ruth had said, and right then so did I—in part because it all did seem a little bizarre, just as childish, probably, as Carol thought it was. Looking at him sitting, in his short pants, with all those kids and writing in his exercise book, I thought I really ought to turn around and go home. Ruthie was right about everything: he was giving up an awful lot to become this *tabula rasa*. Let him.

The teacher came over to shake my hand. "I'm Ronit." Like the woman called Daphna up at the shed, she wore a dark beret and spoke American English—a slender, rangy, good-looking woman in her early thirties, with a prominent, finely chiseled nose, a heavily freckled face, and intelligent dark eyes still confidently sparkling with the light of childhood precocity. I didn't this time make the mistake of saying to her that her accent was obviously that of a native-born American raised in New York City. I simply said hello.

"Hanoch told us last night that you were coming. You must stay and celebrate Shabbat. We have a room for you to sleep," Ronit said. "It won't be the King David Hotel, but I think you'll be comfortable. Take a chair, join us—it would be wonderful if you would talk to the class."

"I just want Henry to know I'm here. Don't let me interrupt. I'll wander around until the class is over."

From where he was seated in the semicircle of students, Henry thrust a hand up in the air. Smiling broadly, though still with a touch of that embarrassed shyness he could never quite outgrow, he said, "Hi," and that too reminded me of our childhood, of the times when as an upper-grade monitor in the hallways of the grammar school, I'd see him passing along with the other little kids to gym class or shop or the music room. "Hey," they'd whisper, "it's your brother," and Henry would sort of bark to me beneath his breath, "Hi," and then submerge instantaneously into the body of his class like a little animal dropping down a hole. He'd succeeded brilliantly, at his studies, at sports, eventually at his profession, and yet there was always this hobbling aversion to being nakedly conspicuous that thwarted an unquenchable dream, dating back to the bedtime reveries of earliest boyhood, not merely to excel but to be uniquely heroic. The admiration that had once made him so worshipful of my every utterance, and the resentment that came to discolor, even before I published *Carnovsky*, the natural and intimate affection springing from our childhood bond, seemed to have been nourished by a belief he continued to hold long after he was old enough to know better, that I was among the narcissistic elite blessed by an unambiguous capacity to preen in public and guiltlessly adore it.

"Please," Ronit said, laughing, "how often do we ensnare someone like you on a hilltop in Judea?" She motioned for one of the boys to pick up a wooden folding chair from the ground and set it up for me. "Anybody crazy enough to come to Agor," she told the students, "we put him right to work."

Taking my cue from her bantering tone, I looked at Henry and feigned a helpless shrug; he got the idea, and kiddingly called back, "We can take it if you can." For "we" I substituted "I," and so with the permission of the brother whose refuge this was —as much perhaps from his history with me as from everything else purged from his life—I took a seat facing the class.

The first question came from a boy whose accent was also American. Maybe they were all American-born Jews. "Do you know Hebrew?" he asked.

"All the Hebrew I know are the two words we began with in the Talmud Torah in 1943."

"What were the words?" Ronit asked.

" 'Yeled' was one."

" 'Boy.' Very good," she said. "And the other?"

" 'Yaldaw,' " I said.

The class laughed.

" 'Yaldaw,' " said Ronit, amused by me as well. "You say it like my Lithuanian grandfather. 'Yal*da*,' " she said, 'Girl.' 'Yalda.' "

" 'Yalda,' " I said.

"Now," she told the class, "that he says 'yalda' correctly, maybe he can begin to have a good time here."

They laughed again.

"Excuse me," said a boy upon whose chin were the first faint beginnings of a little beard, "but who are you? Who is this guy?" he asked Ronit. He was not in any way amused by the proceedings—a big boy, probably no more than seventeen, with a very young and unformed face but a body already as large and imposing as a construction worker's. From the evidence of his accent, he too was a New Yorker. He wore a yarmulke pinned to a head of heavy, dark, unruly hair.

"Tell him, please," Ronit said to me, "who you are."

I pointed to the one they called Hanoch. "His brother."

"So?" the boy said, implacable and getting angry. "Why should we be taking a break to hear him?"

A theatrical moan rose from the back of the class, while close by me a girl who was stretched on the ground with her pretty round face propped up between her hands said in a voice comically calculated to suggest that they'd all been together long enough for certain people to begin to drive others nuts, "He's a writer, Jerry, that's why."

"What are your impressions of Israel?" I was asked this by a girl with an English accent. If not all American, they were obviously all English-speaking.

Though I had been in the country less than twenty-four hours, strong first impressions had of course been formed, beginning with Shuki, impressions fostered by what little I'd heard from him about his massacred brother, his disheartened wife, and that patriotic young pianist of his serving in the army. And of course I hadn't forgotten the argument on the street with the Sephardi to whom Shuki Elchanan was nothing more than an Ashkenazi donkey; nor could I forget the Yemenite father who'd driven me to Agor, who, without any common language to express to me the depths of his grief, nonetheless, with Sacco-Vanzettian eloquence, had cryptically described the extinction of his soldier-son; nor had I forgotten the center fielder for the Jerusalem Giants haul-

ing in a home-run blast up against the Wailing Wall—is Jimmy
Ben-Joseph of West Orange, New Jersey, just a freakish anomaly
or *was* this place becoming, as Shuki claimed, something of an
American-Jewish Australia? In short, dozens of conflicting, trun-
cated impressions were already teasing to be understood, but
the wisest course seemed to me to keep them to myself so long
as I didn't begin to know what they added up to. I certainly
saw no reason to affront anybody at Agor by telling of my un-
spiritual adventures at the Wailing Wall. That the Wailing Wall
is what it is was of course clear even to me. I wouldn't think to
deny the reality of that enigma of silent stoniness—but my en-
counters of the night before had left me feeling as though I'd
had a walk-on role—as Diaspora straight man—in some local
production of Jewish street theater, and I wasn't sure that such a
description would be understood here in the spirit with which
it was meant. "Impressions?" I said. "Just arrived really—don't
have any yet."

"Were you a Zionist when you were young?"

"I never had enough Hebrew, Yiddish, or anti-Semitism to
make me a Zionist when I was young."

"Is this your first trip?"

"No. I was here twenty years ago."

"And you never came back?"

The way that a couple of the students laughed at that question
made me wonder if they might not themselves be considering
packing up and going home.

"Things didn't lead me back."

" 'Things.' " It was the large boy who'd indignantly asked
why the class was listening to me. "You didn't want to come
back."

"Israel wasn't at the center of my thoughts, no."

"But you must have gone to other countries that weren't at the
center quote unquote."

I saw how this could become, if it hadn't already, an exchange
even less satisfactory than my colloquy with the young Chasid at
the Wailing Wall.

"How can a Jew," he asked, "make a single visit to the home-land of his people, and then never, not in twenty *years*—"

I cut him off before he really got going. "It's easy. I'm not the only one."

"I just wonder what's wrong with such a person, Zionist or not."

"Nothing," I said flatly.

"And it's of no concern to you that the whole world would as soon see this country obliterated?"

Though a few of the girls began to shift about, ill at ease with his aggressive questioning, Ronit leaned forward in her chair, eager to hear my answer. I wondered if there might not be a conspiracy operating here—between the boy and Ronit, and even perhaps including Hanoch.

"Is that what the world would like?" I asked, meanwhile think-ing that even if there was no preconceived plot, should I agree to stay the night this could well turn out to be one of the least restful Sabbaths of my life.

"Who would shed a tear?" the boy replied. "Certainly not a Jew who in twenty years, despite the persistent danger to the Jewish people—"

"Look," I said, "admittedly I've never had the right caste spirit—I take your point about people like me. I'm not un-familiar with such fanaticism."

This brought him to his feet, furiously pointing a finger. "Excuse *me*! What is *fanatical*? To put egoism before Zionism is what is fanatical! To put personal gain and personal pleasure before the survival of the Jewish people! *Who* is fanatical? The Diaspora Jew! All the evidence that the goyim give him and give him that the survival of the Jews couldn't matter to them less, and the Diaspora Jew believes they are friends! Believes that in their country he is safe and secure—an equal! What is fanatical is the Jew who never learns! The Jew oblivious to the Jewish state and the Jewish land and the survival of the Jewish people! *That* is the fanatic—fanatically ignorant, fanatically self-deluded, fanatically full of shame!"

I stood too, putting my back to Jerry and the class. "Henry and I are going for a walk," I said to Ronit. "I came out really to talk to him."

Her eyes remained just as bright as before with passionate curiosity. "But Jerry has had his say—you're entitled now to yours."

Was it overly suspicious to believe that the naïveté was feigned and she was having me on? "I'll relinquish my rights," I said.

"He's young," she explained.

"Yes, but I'm not."

"But to the class your thoughts would be fascinating. Many are children of deeply assimilationist families. The egregious failure of American Jews, of most Jews of the world, to seize the opportunity to return to Zion is something that all of them are grappling with. If you—"

"I'd rather not."

"But just a few words about assimilation—"

I shook my head.

"But assimilation and intermarriage," she said, turning quite grave, "in America they are bringing about a second Holocaust—truly, a spiritual Holocaust is taking place there, and it is as deadly as any threat posed by the Arabs to the State of Israel. What Hitler couldn't achieve with Auschwitz, American Jews are doing to themselves in the bedroom. Sixty-five percent of American Jewish college students marry non-Jews—*sixty-five percent* lost forever to the Jewish people! First there was the hard extermination, now there is the soft extermination. And this is why young people are learning Hebrew at Agor—to escape the Jewish oblivion, the extinction of Jews that is coming in America, to escape those communities in your country where Jews are committing spiritual suicide."

"I see," was all I replied.

"You won't talk to them about this, for just a few minutes, just till it's time for their lunch?"

"I don't think my credentials qualify me to talk about this. I happen to be married to a non-Jew myself."

"All the better," she said, smiling warmly. "They can talk to *you*."

"No, no thanks. It's Henry who I'm here to talk to. I haven't seen him for months."

Ronit took hold of my arm as I started away, rather like a friend who hates to see you go. She seemed to like me, despite my faulty credentials; probably my brother acted as my advocate. "But you will stay for Shabbat," Ronit said. "My husband had to be in Bethlehem today, but he's looking forward to meeting you tonight. You and Hanoch are coming for dinner."

"We'll see how things go."

"No, no, you're coming. Henry must have told you—they have become great friends, your brother and my husband. They're very alike, two strong and dedicated men."

Her husband was Mordecai Lippman.

From the moment that we started along the path that sloped down the hill toward the two long unpaved streets that constituted Agor's residential quarter, Henry began making it clear that we weren't going to sit in the shade somewhere having a deep discussion about whether or not *he'd* done the right thing by seizing the opportunity to return to Zion. He was now nothing like as friendly as he'd seemed when I'd showed up in front of his class. Instead, as soon as we two were alone, he immediately turned querulous. He had no intention, he told me, of being reproved by me and wouldn't tolerate any attempt to investigate or challenge his motives. He'd talk about Agor, if I wanted to know what this place stood for, he'd talk about the settlement movement, its roots and ideology and what the settlers were determined to achieve, he'd talk about the changes in the country since Begin's coalition had taken charge, but as for the American-style psychiatric soul-searching in which my own heroes could wallow for pages on end, that was a form of exhibitionistic indulgence and childish self-dramatization that blessedly belonged to the "narcissistic past." The old life of nonhistorical personal problems seemed to him now embarrassingly, disgustingly, unspeakably puny.

Telling me all this, he had worked up more emotion than anything I'd said could possibly have inspired, especially as I had as yet said nothing. It was one of those speeches that people spend hours preparing and delivering while lying in bed unable to sleep. The smiles up at the ulpan had been for the crowd. This was the distrustful fellow I'd talked to on the phone the night before.

"Fine," I said. "No psychiatry."

Still on the offense, he said, "And don't condescend to me."

"Well, don't knock my wallowing heroes. Besides, I wouldn't say condescension has been my strong suit, not so far today. I myself wasn't even condescended to by that kid up in your class. I was mugged by the little prick in broad daylight."

"Forthright is the style out here—take it or leave it. And no shit, please, about my name."

"Relax. Anybody can call you anything you want, as far as I'm concerned."

"You *still* don't get it. The hell with *me*, forget *me*. *Me* is somebody I have forgotten. *Me* no longer exists out here. There isn't time for *me*, there isn't need of *me*—here Judea counts, not *me*!"

His plan was to ride over to Arab Hebron for lunch, only a twenty-minute drive if we followed the shortcut through the hills. We could use Lippman's car. Mordecai and four other settlers had gone off by truck to Bethlehem early that morning. In the last several weeks, disturbances had erupted there between some local Arabs and the Jews of a little settlement newly erected on a hillside outside the city. Two days earlier rocks had been thrown through the windshield of a passing school bus carrying the Jewish settlement's children, and settlement members from all over Judea and Samaria, organized and led by Mordecai Lippman, had gone to distribute leaflets in the Bethlehem market. If I hadn't been visiting, Henry was to have skipped his class and gone with them.

"What do the leaflets say?" I asked.

"They say, 'Why don't you people try living in peace with us, since we mean you no harm. Only a few among you are violent extremists. The rest are peace-loving people who believe, as we do, that Jew and Arab can live in harmony.' That's the general idea."

"The general idea sounds benign enough. What's it supposed to mean to the Arabs?"

"What it says—we intend them no harm."

Not me—we. That's where Henry's me had gone.

"We'll drive through the village—it's right down there. You'll see how the Arabs who want to can live in peace, side by side, only a couple of hundred yards away. They come up here and buy our eggs. The chickens that are too old to lay, we sell to them for pennies. This place could be a home for everybody. But if violence against Jewish schoolchildren continues, then steps will be taken to stop it. The army could move in there tomorrow, weed out the troublemakers, and the stone throwing would be over in five minutes. But they don't. They even throw stones at the soldiers. And when the soldier does nothing, you know what the Arabs think? They think you are a shmuck—and you *are* a shmuck. Any place else in the Middle East, you throw a stone at a soldier, and what does he do? He shoots you. But suddenly they discover in Bethlehem that you throw a stone at an Israeli soldier and he doesn't shoot you. He doesn't do anything. And that's where the trouble begins. Not because we are cruel, but because they have found out we are weak. There are things you have to do here that are not so nice. They don't respect niceness and they don't respect weakness. What the Arab respects is power."

Not me but we, not niceness but power.

I waited by the battered Ford that was parked on the dirt street outside the Lippman house, one of the cinder-block structures that had looked from the entry road like pillboxes or bunkers. Up close you couldn't quite believe that life within was very far from the embryonic stage of human development. Everything, including the load of topsoil deposited in a corner of each of the dry, stony yards, proclaimed a world of bare beginnings.

Two, maybe even three of these little settlement dwellings could have been stored without difficulty in the basement of the sprawling house of cedar and glass built by Henry some years back on a wooded hillside in South Orange.

When he came out of Lippman's, it was with car keys in one hand and a pistol in the other. He tossed the pistol into the glove compartment and started the engine.

"I'm trying," I told him, "to take things in stride, but it's going to entail almost superhuman restraint not to make the sort of comment that's going to piss you off. Nonetheless, it's a little astonishing to be going off for a drive with you and a gun."

"I know. It's not how we were raised. But a gun isn't a bad idea driving down to Hebron. If you run into a demonstration, if they surround the car and start heaving rocks, at least you have some bargaining power. Look, you're going to see a lot of things that are going to astonish you. They astonish me. You know what astonishes me even more than what I've learned to do in five months here? What I learned to do in forty years there. To do and to be. I shudder when I remember everything I was. I look back and I can't believe it. It fills me with revulsion. It makes me want to hide my head when I think how I wound up."

"How was that?"

"You saw it, you were there. You *heard* it. What I risked my life for. What I had that operation for. *Who* I had it for. That skinny little kid in my office. That's what I was willing to die for. That's what I was *living* for."

"No, it was a part of living. Why not? Losing your potency at thirty-nine isn't an ordinary little experience. Life came down very hard on you."

"You don't understand. I'm talking about how *small* I was. I'm talking about my grotesque apology for a life."

It was several hours on, after we'd been through the alleyways of the Hebron market and up to the ancient olive trees by the graves of Hebron's Jewish martyrs, and then on to the burial ground of the Patriarchs, that I got him to expand a little on that grotesque life he'd abandoned. We were eating lunch on the open terrace of a small restaurant on the main road out of Hebron. The Arab family who ran the place couldn't have been more welcoming; indeed, the owner, who took our order in English, called Henry "Doctor" with considerable esteem. It was late by then and aside from a young Arab couple and their small child eating at a corner table nearby, the place was empty.

Henry, to make himself comfortable, draped his field jacket over the back of his chair, the pistol still in one pocket. That's where he'd been carrying it during our tour of Hebron. Shepherding me through the crowded market, he pointed out the abundance of fruits, vegetables, chickens, sweets, even while my mind remained on his pistol, and on Chekhov's famous dictum that a pistol hanging on the wall in Act One must eventually go off in Act Three. I wondered what act we were in, not to mention which play—domestic tragedy, historical epic, or just straight farce? I wasn't sure whether the pistol was strictly necessary or whether he was simply displaying, as drastically as he could, the distance he'd traveled from the powerless nice Jew that he'd been in America, this pistol his astounding symbol of the whole complex of choices with which he was ridding himself of that shame. "Here are the Arabs," he'd said in the marketplace, "and where is the yoke? Do you see a yoke across anyone's back? Do you see a soldier threatening anyone? You don't see a soldier here at all. No, just a thriving Oriental bazaar. And why is that? Because of the brutal military occupation?"

The only sign of the military I'd seen was a small installation about a hundred yards down from the market, where Henry had left the car. Inside the gates some Israeli soldiers were kicking a soccer ball around an open area where their trucks were parked, but as Henry said, there was no military presence within the market, only Arab stallkeepers, Arab shoppers, scores of small Arab children, some very unamicable-looking Arab adolescents, lots of dust, several mules, some beggars, and Dr. Victor Zuckerman's two sons, Nathan and Hanoch, the latter packing a gun whose implications had begun obsessively to engage the former. What if who he shoots is me? What if that was to be Act Three's awful surprise, the Zuckerman differences ending in blood, as though our family were Agamemnon's?

At lunch I began with what couldn't be taken right off as a remonstrance or a challenge, given his enthusiasm about the antiquity of a wall that he'd wanted me to see at the Cave of Machpelah. How holy, I asked, was that wall to him? "Suppose it's all as you tell me," I said. "In Hebron Abraham pitched his tent. In the cave of Machpelah he and Sarah were buried, and after them Isaac, Jacob, and their wives. It's here that King David reigned before he entered Jerusalem. What's any of it got to do with you?"

"That's where the claim rests," he said. "That's *it*. It's no accident, you know, that we're called Jews and this place is called Judea—there may even be some relation between those two things. We are Jews, this is Judea, and the heart of Judea is Abraham's city, Hebron."

"That still leaves unexplained the riddle of Henry Zuckerman's identification with Abraham's city."

"You don't get it—this is where the Jews *began,* not in Tel Aviv but here. If anything is territorialism, if anything is colonialism, it's Tel Aviv, it's Haifa. *This* is Judaism, *this* is Zionism, *right here* where we are eating our lunch!"

"In other words, it didn't all begin up that outside flight of wooden stairs where Grandma and Grandpa lived on Hunterdon Street. It didn't begin with Grandma on her knees washing the floors and Grandpa stinking of old cigars. Jews didn't begin in Newark, after all."

"The famous gift for reductive satire."

"Is it? It might be that what you've developed over the last five months is something of a gift for exaggeration."

"I don't think that the part that the Jewish Bible has played in the history of the world owes much to me and my illusions."

"I was thinking more about the part you seem to have assigned yourself in the tribal epic. Do you pray too?"

"The subject's not under discussion."

"You do pray then."

Riled by my insistence, he asked, "What's wrong with prayer, is there something wrong with prayer?"

"When do you pray?"

"Before I go to sleep."

"What do you say?"

"What Jews have said for thousands of years. I say the Shema Yisrael."

"And in the morning you lay tefillin?"

"Maybe one day. I don't yet."

"And you observe the Sabbath."

"Look, I understand that this is all outside your element. I understand that hearing all this you feel nothing but the disdainful amusement of the fashionably 'objective,' postassimilated Jew. I realize that you're too 'enlightened' for God and that to you it's clearly all a joke."

"Don't be so sure what to me is a joke. If I happen to have questions I wouldn't mind answered, it's because six months ago I had a different brother."

"Living the life of Riley in New Jersey."

"Come on, Henry—there's no such thing as the life of Riley, in New Jersey or anywhere else. America is also a place where people die, where people fail, where life is interesting and tense, and hardly without conflict."

"But Riley's life was still whose mine was. In America the massacre of your brother's Judaism couldn't have been more complete."

" 'Massacre'? Where'd you pick up *that* word? You lived like everybody you knew. You accepted the social arrangement that existed."

"Only the arrangement that existed was completely abnormal."

Normal and abnormal—twenty-four hours in Israel and there was that distinction again.

"How did I even get that disease?" he asked me. "Five occluded coronary arteries in a man not even forty years old. What sort of stress do you think caused it? The stresses of a 'normal' life?"

"Carol for a wife, dentistry for a livelihood, South Orange for a home, well-behaved kids in good private schools—even the girlfriend on the side. If that's not normalcy, what is?"

"Only all for the goyim. Camouflaging behind goyish respectability every last Jewish marking. All of it from them, for them."

"Henry, I walk in Hebron and I see *them*—them with a vengeance. All I remember seeing around your place were other prosperous Jews like you, and none of them packing a gun."

"You bet: prosperous, comfortable, Hellenized Jews—galut Jews, bereft of any sort of context in which actually to be Jewish."

"And you think this is what made you sick? 'Hellenization'? It didn't seem to ruin Aristotle's life. What the hell does it even *mean*?"

"Hellenized—hedonized—egomaniazed. My whole *existence* was the sickness. I got off easy with just my heart. Diseased with self-distortion, self-contortion, diseased with self-disguise—up to my eyeballs in meaninglessness."

First it was the life of Riley, now it was nothing but a disease. "You felt all that?"

"Me? I was so conventionalized I never felt anything. Wendy. Perfect. Shtupping the dental assistant. My office blow job, the great overwhelming passion of a completely superficial life. Before that, even better—Basel. Classic. The Jewish male's idolatry —worship of the shiksa; dreaming of Switzerland with the beloved shiksa. The original Jewish dream of escape."

And as he spoke I was thinking, *the kind of stories that people turn life into, the kind of lives that people turn stories into.* Back in Jersey, he ascribes the stress that he was convinced had culminated in the coronary artery disease to the humiliating failure of nerve that had *prevented* him from leaving South Orange for Basel; in Judea his diagnosis is just the opposite— here he attributes the disease to the insidious strain of Diaspora abnormality manifested most blatantly by "the original Jewish dream of escape . . . Switzerland with the beloved shiksa."

As we headed back to Agor to be there in time to prepare for Shabbat, I tried to figure out if Henry, who had hardly grown up in some New World Vienna, could actually have swallowed a self-analysis that to me seemed mostly platitudes gleaned from a turn-of-the-century handbook of Zionist ideology and having nothing whatsoever to do with him. When had Henry

Zuckerman, raised securely among Newark's ambitious Jewish middle class, educated with hundreds of other smart Jewish kids at Cornell, married to a loyal and understanding woman just as secular a Jew as himself, ensconced in the sort of affluent, attractive Jewish suburb that he'd aspired to all his life, a Jew whose history of intimidation by anti-Semitism was simply nonexistent, when had he given a moment's serious consideration to the expectations of those he now derisively referred to as the "goyim"? If every project of importance in his former life had been undertaken to prove himself to someone dismayingly strong or subtly menacing, it certainly didn't look to me to have been to the omnipotent goy. Wasn't what he described as a revolt against the grotesque contortions of the spirit suffered by the galut, or exiled Jew, more likely an extremely belated rebellion against the idea of manhood imposed upon a dutiful and acquiescent child by a dogmatic, superconventional father? If so, then to overthrow all those long-standing paternal expectations, he had enslaved himself to a powerful Jewish authority far more rigidly subjugating than even the omnipresent Victor Zuckerman could ever have had the heart to be.

Though maybe the key to understanding his pistol was simpler than that. Of all he'd said over lunch, the only word that sounded to me with any real conviction was "Wendy." It was the second time in the few hours we'd been together that he'd alluded to his dental assistant, and in the same tone of disbelief, outraged that it was she for whom he'd risked his life. Maybe, I thought, he's doing penance. To be sure, learning Hebrew at an ulpan in the desert hills of Judea constituted a rather novel form of absolution from the sin of adultery, but then hadn't he also chosen to undergo the most hazardous surgery in order to keep Wendy in his life half an hour a day? Maybe this was no more than the appropriately preposterous denouement to their bizarrely overburdened drama. He seemed now to look upon his little dental assistant as some girl he'd known in Nineveh.

Or was the whole thing a cover-up for the act of abandonment? There's hardly a husband around anymore who is unable to say to his wife, when the end has come, "I'm afraid this is over, I've found true love." Only for my brother—and our father's best son —is there no possible way to walk out on a marriage in 1978 other than in the name of Judaism. I thought, "What's Jewish isn't coming here and becoming a Jew, Henry. What's Jewish is thinking that, in order to leave Carol, your only justification can be coming here." But I didn't say it, not with him packing that gun.

I was totally obsessed by that gun.

At the crest of the hill outside Agor, Henry pulled the car to the side of the road and we got out to take in the view. In the falling shadows, the little Arab village at the foot of the Jewish settlement looked nothing like so grim and barren as it had a few minutes before when we'd driven down its deserted main street. A desert sunset lent a little picturesqueness even to that cluster of faceless hovels. As for the larger landscape, you could see, particularly in this light, how someone might get the impression that it had been created in only seven days, unlike England, say, whose countryside appeared to be the creation of a God who'd had four or five chances to come back to perfect it and smooth it out, to tame and retame it until it was utterly habitable by every last man and beast. Judea was something that had been left just as it had been made; this could have passed for a piece of the moon to which the Jews had been sadistically exiled by their worst enemies rather than the place they passionately maintained was theirs and no one else's from time immemorial. What he finds in this landscape, I thought, is a correlative for the sense of himself he would now prefer to effect, the harsh and rugged pioneer with that pistol in his pocket.

Of course he could have been thinking much the same of me, living now where everything is in its place, where the landscape has been cultivated so long and the density of people is so great that nature will never reclaim either again, the ideal setting for a man in search of domestic order and of renewing his life at the midpoint on a satisfying scale. But in this unfinished, otherterrestrial landscape, attesting theatrically at sunset to Timeless Significance, one might well imagine self-renewal on the grandest scale of all, the legendary scale, the scale of mythic heroism.

I was about to say something conciliatory to him, something about the spectacular austerity of this swelling sea of low rocky hills and the transforming influence it must exert on the soul of a newcomer, when Henry announced, "They laugh, the Arabs, because we build up here. In winter we're exposed to the wind and the cold, in summer to the heat and the sun, while down there they're protected from the worst of the weather. But," he said, gesturing toward the south, "whoever controls this hill controls the Negev." Then he was directing me to look west, to where the hills were now seventeen shades of blue and the sun was slipping away. "You can shell Jerusalem from here," Henry told me, while I thought, Wendy, Carol, our father, the kids.

Lippman's very looks seemed to be making a point about colliding forces. His wide-set, almond-shaped, slightly protuberant eyes, though a gentle milky blue, proclaimed, unmistakably, STOP; his nose had been smashed at the bridge by something that—more likely, someone who—had tried and failed to stop *him*. Then there was the leg, mangled during the '67 war when, as a paratroop commander, he'd lost two-thirds of his company in the big battle to break into Jordanian Jerusalem. (Henry had described to me, in impressive military detail, the logistics of the "Ammunition Hill" assault as we'd driven together back from Hebron.) Because of his injury Lippman walked as though intending with each step to take wing and fly at your head—then the torso slowly sank into the imperfect leg and he looked like a man who was melting. I thought of a circus tent about to cave in after the center pole has been withdrawn. I waited for the thud, but there he was again, advancing. He was a couple of inches under six feet, shorter than both Henry and me, yet his face had the sardonic mobility that comes of peering nobly down upon self-deceiving mankind from the high elevation of Hard Truth. When he'd returned in dusty combat boots and a filthy old field jacket from where the Jewish settlers organized by him had been distributing leaflets in the Bethlehem market, he looked as though he'd been under fire. A deliberate front-line appearance, I thought, except that he wore no battered helmet—or rather, the helmet protecting him was a skullcap, a little knitted *kipa* riding his hair like a tiny lifeboat. The hair was yet another drama, the kind of hair that your enemy uses to hold up your head after severing it from your carcass—a bunchy cabbage of disarranged plumage that was already a waxy, patriarchal white, though Lippman couldn't have been much over fifty. To me he looked, from the first moment I saw him, like some majestic Harpo Marx—Harpo as Hannibal, and as I was to discover, hardly mute.

The Sabbath table was prettily set with a lace-trimmed white cloth. It was at the kitchen end of a tiny living room lined to the ceiling with book-crammed shelves. There would be eight of us for dinner—Lippman's wife (and Henry's Hebrew teacher), Ronit, and the two Lippman children, a daughter eight and a son fifteen. The boy, already an ace marksman, was doing hundreds of push-ups twice a day in order to qualify for commando training when he entered the army in three years. Visiting from next door was the couple I'd already met up by the shed on my arrival, the metalworker, called Buki, and his wife, Daphna, the woman who'd informed me she was a Jew "by birth." Lastly, there were the two Zuckermans.

Lippman, having showered, was dressed for the occasion exactly like Henry and the metalworker, in a light, freshly laundered shirt whose lapels were ironed flat and a pair of dark cotton trousers. Ronit and Daphna, who'd been wearing berets earlier in the day, now had their hair bound up in white kerchiefs, and they too had gotten into fresh clothes for the Sabbath evening celebration. The men wore velvet skullcaps, mine presented to me ceremoniously by Lippman as I was stepping into the house.

While we were waiting for the guests from next door, and while Henry played like a kindly uncle with the Lippman kids, Lippman found for me, among his books, the German translations of Dante, Shakespeare, and Cervantes that they'd carried out of Berlin in the mid-thirties when his parents had fled with him to Palestine. Even for an audience of one he held nothing back, as shameless as some legendary courtroom litigator cunning in the use of booming crescendo and insinuating diminuendo to sway the emotions of the jury.

"When I was in a Nazi high school in Germany, could I dream that I would sit one day with my family in my own house in Judea and celebrate with them the Shabbat? Who could have believed such a thing under the Nazis? Jews in Judea? Jews once again in Hebron? They say the same in Tel Aviv today. If Jews dare to go and settle in Judea, the earth will stop rotating on its axis. But has the world stopped rotating on its axis? Has it stopped revolving around the sun because Jews have returned to live in their biblical homeland? *Nothing is impossible*. All the Jew must decide is what he wants—then he can act and achieve it. He cannot be weary, he cannot be tired, he cannot go around crying, 'Give the Arab anything, everything, as long as there is no trouble.' Because the Arab will take what is given and then continue the war, and instead of less trouble there will be *more*. Hanoch tells me that you were in Tel Aviv. Did you get a chance to talk to all the niceys and the goodies there who want to be humane? Humane! They are embarrassed by the necessities of survival in a jungle. This is a jungle with wolves all around! We have weak people here, soft people here, who like to call their cowardice Jewish morality. Well, only let them practice their Jewish morality and it will lead to their destruction. And afterwards, I can assure you, the world will decide that the Jews brought it on themselves *again*, are guilty *again*—responsible for a second Holocaust the way they were for the first. But there will be no more Holocausts. We didn't come here to make graveyards. We have had enough graveyards. We came here to live, not to die. Who did you talk to in Tel Aviv?"

"A friend. Shuki Elchanan."

"Our great intellectual journalist. Of course. All for Western consumption, every word this hack utters. Every word he writes is poison. Whatever he writes, it's with one eye on Paris and the other on New York. You know what my hope is, my dream of dreams? That in this settlement, when we will have the resources, we will create, like Madame Tussaud's waxworks, a Museum of Jewish Self-Hatred. I'm only afraid we wouldn't have room for the statues of all the Shuki Elchanans who know only how to condemn the Israelis and to bleed for the Arab. They feel every pain, these people, they feel every pain and then they give in—not only do they want *not* to win, not only do they *prefer* to lose, above all they want to lose *the right way*, like Jews! A Jew who argues the Arab cause! Do you know what the Arab thinks of such people? They think, 'Is he crazy or is he a traitor? What's wrong with that man?' They think it is a sign of treachery, of betrayal—they think, 'Why should he argue our case, we don't argue his.' In Damascus not even a lunatic would dream of entertaining the Jewish position. Islam is not a civilization of doubt like the civilization of the Hellenized Jew. The Jew is always blaming himself for what happens in Cairo. He is blaming himself for what happens in Baghdad. But in Baghdad, believe me, they do not blame themselves for what is happening in Jerusalem. Theirs is not a civilization of doubt—theirs is a civilization of *certainty*. Islam is not plagued by niceys and goodies who want to be sure they don't do the wrong thing. Islam wants one thing only: to *win*, to *triumph*, to obliterate the cancer of Israel from the body of the Islamic world. Mr. Shuki Elchanan is a man who lives in a Middle East that, most unfortunately, does not exist. Mr. Shuki Elchanan wants us to sign a piece of paper with the Arabs and give it *back*? No! History and reality will make the future and not pieces of paper! This is the Middle East, these are Arabs—paper is worthless. There is no paper deal to be made with the Arabs. Today in Bethlehem an Arab tells me that he dreams of Jaffa and how one day he will return. The Syrians have convinced him, just hang on, keep throwing stones at the Jewish school buses, and it'll *all* be yours someday—you'll go back to your village near Jaffa, and have everything else besides. That's what this man was telling me—he will go back, even if it takes him the two thousand years that it took the Jews. And you know what I tell *him*? I tell him, 'I respect the Arab who wants Jaffa.' I tell him, 'Don't give up your dream, dream of Jaffa, go ahead; and someday, if you have the power, even if there are a *hundred* pieces of paper, you will take it from me by force.' Because he is not so humane, this Arab who throws stones in Bethlehem, as your Mr. Shuki Elchanan who writes his columns in Tel Aviv for Western consumption. The Arab waits until he thinks you're weak, and then he tears up his paper and attacks. I'm sorry if I disappoint you, but I do not have such nice thoughts as Mr. Shuki Elchanan and all the Hellenized Jews in Tel Aviv with their European ideas. Mr. Shuki Elchanan is afraid to rule and to be a master. Why? Because he wants the approval of the goy. But I'm not interested in the goy's approval —I am interested in Jewish survival. And if the price I pay is a bad name, fine. We pay that anyway, and it's better than the price we usually pay in addition."

All this merely as appetizer to my Sabbath meal, and while proudly exhibiting to me, one by one, the treasured leather-bound masterpieces collected in Berlin by his grandfather, a celebrated philologist gassed at Auschwitz.

At the dinner table, in a resonant cantorial baritone, a rich pleasing voice that sounded trained and whose excellence wasn't entirely a surprise, Lippman began the little song to welcome the Sabbath queen, and then everyone joined in, except me. Vaguely I remembered the melody but found that thirty-five years on, the words had simply vanished. Henry seemed to have a special fondness for the Lippman boy, Yehuda; they grinned at each other while they sang, as though between them there were some joke about the song, the occasion, or even about my presence at the table. Many years back I had exchanged just such grins with Henry myself. As for the Lippmans' eight-year-old girl, she was so fascinated by the fact that I wasn't singing that her father had to wave a finger to get her to stop mumbling and make herself heard with everyone else.

My silence must, of course, have been inexplicable to her; but if she was wondering how Hanoch could have a brother like me, you can be sure that I was now even more confused by having a brother like Hanoch. I could not grasp this overnight change so against the grain of what I and everyone took to be the very essence of Henry's Henryness. Is there really something irreducibly Jewish that he's discovered in his own bedrock, or has he only developed, postoperatively, a taste for the ersatz in life? He undergoes a terrible operation to restore his potency and becomes as a result a full-fledged Jew; this guy has his chest ripped apart, and in a seven-hour operation, hooked up to a machine that does his breathing for him and pumps his blood, he has the vital lines to his heart replaced by veins drawn out of his leg, and subsequently he winds up in Israel. I don't get it. This all seems to give new meaning to the old Tin Pan Alley idea of recklessly toying with somebody's heart. What purpose is hidden in what he now calls "Jew"—or is "Jew" just something he now hides behind? He tells me that here he is essential, he belongs, he fits in—but isn't it more likely that what he has finally found is the unchallengeable means to escape his hedged-in life? Who hasn't been driven crazy by that temptation—yet how many pull it off like this? Not even Henry could, so long as he called his flight plan "Basel"—it's designating it "Judea" that's done the trick. If so, what inspirational nomenclature! Moses against the Egyptians, Judah Maccabee against the Greeks, Bar Kochba against the Romans, and now, in our era, Hanoch of Judea against Henry of Jersey!

And still not a word of remorse—not any word *at all*—about Carol or the kids. Amazing. Though he phones the children every Sunday, and expects them to fly over to visit him at Passover, he's given not a single sign to me that he's still in any way fettered by the sentiments of a husband and father. And about my new life in London, *my* renovation, of more than passing interest even to Shuki Elchanan, Henry has nothing to ask. He appears to have totally repudiated his life, all of us, and all he's been through, and anybody who does that, I thought, *must* be taken seriously. Not only do such people qualify as true converts but, for a while at least, they become criminals of a kind—to those they've abandoned, even to themselves, even perhaps to those with whom they've formed their new pact—and this true conversion can't be dismissed any more easily than it can be comprehended. Listening to his mentor's professional voice rising in song above the rest, I thought, "Whatever the tangle of motive in him, he certainly hasn't been drawn to nothing."

There was a second song, a melody more lyrical and poignant than the first, and the voice that dominated now was Ronit's, leading with her folksingerish, fervent soprano. Singing in the Sabbath, Ronit looked as contented with her lot as any woman could be, her eyes shining with love for a life free of Jewish cringing, deference, diplomacy, apprehension, alienation, self-pity, self-satire, self-mistrust, depression, clowning, bitterness, nervousness, inwardness, hypercriticalness, hypertouchiness, social anxiety, social assimilation—a way of life absolved, in short, of all the Jewish "abnormalities," those peculiarities of self-division whose traces remained imprinted in just about every engaging Jew I knew.

Lippman blessed the wine with Hebrew words familiar even to me, and as I sipped from my glass along with everyone else, I thought, "Can it be a *conscious* ploy? What if it isn't still more of that passionate, driving naïveté for which he has always shown such talent but a calculated and devilishly cynical act? What if Henry has signed on with the Jewish cause without believing a word? Could he have become that interesting?"

"And," Lippman said, lowering his glass and speaking in the smallest, soothing, most delicate voice, "that's it—the whole thing." He was addressing me. "There it is. The meaning of this country in a nutshell. This is a place where nobody has to apologize for wearing a little hat on his head and singing a couple of songs with his family and friends before he eats his Friday night meal. It's as simple as that."

Smiling at his smile, I said, "Is it?"

He pointed proudly to his handsome young wife. "Ask her. Ask Ronit. Her parents weren't even religious Jews. They were ethnic Jews and no more—probably, from what Hanoch tells me, like your family in New Jersey. Hers was in Pelham, but the same thing, I'm sure. Ronit didn't even know what religion was. But still nowhere she lived in America did she feel right. Pelham, Ann Arbor, Boston—it made no difference, she never felt right. Then, in '67, she heard on the radio there was a war, she got on a plane and she came to help. She worked in a hospital. She saw everything. The worst of it. When it was over she stayed. She came here and she felt right and she stayed. That's the whole story. They come and they see that there is no need to apologize anymore and they stay. Only the goody-goods need to be approved of by the goy, only the niceys who want people to say nice things about them in Paris and London and New York. To me it is incredible that there are still Jews, even here, even in the country where they are masters, who live for the goy to smile at them and tell them that they are right. Sadat came here a little while back, you remember, and he was smiling, and they screamed with joy in the streets, those Jews. My enemy is smiling at me! Our enemy loves us after all! Oh, the Jew, the Jew, how he rushes to forgive! How he wants the goy to throw him just a little smile! How desperately he wants that smile! Only the Arab is very good at smiling and lying at the same time. He is also good at throwing stones—so long as nobody stops him. But I will tell you something, Mr. Nathan Zuckerman: if nobody else will stop him, I will. And if the army doesn't like me to do it, let the army come and fire on me. I have read Mr. Mahatma Gandhi and Mr. Henry David Thoreau, and if the Jewish army wants to fire upon a Jewish settler in biblical Judea while the Arab is looking on, let him—let the Arab witness such Jewish craziness. If the government wants to act like the British, then we will act like the Jews! We will practice civil disobedience and proceed by illegal settlement, and let their Jewish army come and stop us! I dare this Jewish government, I dare *any* Jewish government, to try to evict us by force! As for the Arabs, I will go back to Bethlehem every day—and I told this to their leader, I told them *all*, and in their own tongue so they would not fail to understand, so there will not be any doubt what my intentions are: I will come here with my people, and I will stand here with my people, *until the Arab stops throwing stones at the Jew*. Because do not comfort yourself, Mr. Nathan Zuckerman from London, Newark, New York, and points west—they are not throwing stones at Israelis. They are not throwing stones at 'West Bank' lunatics. They are throwing stones at *Jews. Every stone is an anti-Semitic stone.* That is why it must stop!"

He paused dramatically for a response. I said only, "Good luck," but those two syllables were enough to inspire an even more impassioned aria.

"We don't *need* luck! God protects us! All we need is never to give ground and God will see to the rest! We are God's instrument! We are building the Land of Israel! See this man?" he said, pointing to the metalworker. "Buki lived in Haifa like a king. Look at the car he drives—it's a Lancia! And yet he comes with his wife to live with us. To build Israel! For the love of the Land of Israel! We are not Jewish losers in love with loss. We are people of hope! Tell me, when have Jews been so well off, even *with* all our problems? All we need is not to give ground, and if the army wants to fire on us, let them! We are not delicate roses—we are here to stay! Sure, in Tel Aviv, in the café, in the university, in the newspaper office, the nice, humane Jew can't *stand* it. Shall I tell you why? I think he is actually jealous of the losers. Look at how sad he looks, the loser, look at him sitting there losing, how helpless he looks, how *moving. I* should be the one who is moving because *I* am sad and hopeless and lost, not him—I am the one who loses, not him—how *dare* he steal my touching melancholy, my Jewish softness! But if this is a game that only one can win—and those are rules the Arabs have set, those are the rules established not by us but by *them—then somebody must lose.* And when he loses, it is not pretty—he loses *bitterly.* It is not *loss* if it is not bitter! Just ask us, we are the experts on the subject. The loser hates and is the virtuous one, and the winner wins and is wicked. Okay," he said lightly, a thoroughly reasonable man, "I accept it. Let us be wicked winners for the next two thousand years, and when the two thousand years are over, when it is 3978, we will take a vote on which we prefer. The Jew will democratically decide whether he wants to bear the injustice of winning or whether he prefers living again with the honor of losing. And whatever the majority wants, I too will agree, in 3978. But in the meantime, *we do not give ground!*"

"I am in Norway," the metalworker, Buki, said to me. "I go there on business. I am in Norway on business for my product and written on a wall I read, 'Down with Israel.' I think, 'What did Israel ever do to Norway?' I know Israel is a terrible country, but after all, there are countries even more terrible. There are so many terrible countries—why is this country the most terrible? Why don't you read on Norwegian walls, 'Down with Russia,' 'Down with Chile,' 'Down with Libya'? Because Hitler didn't murder six million Libyans? I am walking in Norway and I am thinking, 'If only he had.' Because then they would write on Norwegian walls, 'Down with Libya,' and leave Israel alone." His dark brown eyes, fixed upon mine, appeared to be set in his head crookedly because of a long jagged scar on his forehead. His English came haltingly, but with forceful fluency all the same, as though he had mastered the language in one large gulp just the day before. "Sir, why all over the world do they hate Menachem Begin?" he asked me. "Because of politics? In Bolivia, in China, in Scandinavia, what do they care about Begin's politics? They hate him because of his nose!"

Lippman cut in. "The demonization," he told me, "will never end. It started in the Middle Ages as the demonization of the Jew and now in our age it is the demonization of the Jewish state. But it is always the same, the Jew is always committing the crime. We don't accept Christ, we reject Mohammed, we commit ritual murder, we control white slavery, we wish through sexual intercourse to poison the Aryan bloodstream, and now we have really ruined everything, now we have perpetrated truly monstrous evil, the worst the world press has ever known, upon the innocent, peaceful, blameless Arab. The Jew is a problem. How wonderful for everybody it would be without us."

"And in America that will happen," Buki said to me. "Don't think it won't."

"What will happen?" I asked.

"In America there will be a great invasion—of Latinos, of Puerto Ricans, people fleeing poverty and the revolutions. And the white Christians will not like it. The white Christians will turn against the dirty foreigner. And when the white Christian turns against the dirty foreigner, the dirty foreigner he turns against first will be the Jew."

"We have no desire for such a catastrophe," Lippman explained. "We have seen enough catastrophe. But unless something momentous is done to stop it, this catastrophe too will occur: between the hammer of the pious white American Christian and the anvil of the dirty foreigner, the Jew in America will be crushed—if he is not slaughtered first by the blacks, the blacks in the ghettos who are already sharpening their knives."

I interrupted him. "And how do the blacks accomplish this slaughter?" I asked. "With or without the help of the federal government?"

"Don't worry," Lippman said, "the American goy will let them loose when the time is ripe. There is nothing the American goy would like better than a *Judenrein* United States. First," Lippman informed me, "they permit the resentful blacks to take all their hatred out on the Jews, and afterward they take care of the blacks. And without the nosy Jews around to complain that they are violating black civil rights. Thus will come the Great American Pogrom out of which American white purity will be restored. You think this is ludicrous, the ridiculous nightmare of a paranoid Jew? But I am not *only* a paranoid Jew. Remember: *Ich bin ein Berliner* as well. And not out of run-of-the-mill opportunism—not like your handsome, heroic, young President when he announced that he was one with them to all the jubilant ex-Nazis, before, unfortunately, he succumbed to *his* paranoid nightmare. I was born there, Mr. Nathan Zuckerman, born and educated among all the sane, precise, reasonable, logical, unparanoid German Jews who are now a mountain of ashes."

"I only pray," said Buki, "that the Jew senses in time that such a catastrophe is on its way. Because if he does, then the ships will come again. In America there are young religious people, even secular people like your brother, who are tired of purposeless living. Here in Judea there is a purpose and a meaning, so they come. Here there is a God who is present in our lives. But the mass of Jews in America, they will not come, never, unless there is a crisis. But whatever the crisis, however it begins, the ships will sail again, and we will not just be three million. Then we will be ten million and the situation will be a little corrected. Three million the Arabs think they can kill. But they cannot kill ten million so easily."

"And where," I asked all of them, "will you put ten million?" Lippman's answer was ecstatic. "Judea! Samaria! Gaza! In the Land of Israel given by God to the Jewish people!"

"You really believe," I asked, "that this will happen? American Jews sailing by the millions to escape persecution resulting from a Hispanic invasion of the U.S.A.? Because of a black uprising, urged on and abetted by the white officials, to eliminate the Jews?"

"Not today," said Buki, "not tomorrow, but yes, I am afraid it will happen. If not for Hitler we would be ten million already. We would have the offspring of the six million. But Hitler succeeded. I only pray that the Jews will leave America before a second Hitler succeeds."

I turned to Henry, eating as silently as the two Lippman children. "Is that what you felt living in America? That such a catastrophe is in the offing?"

"Well, no," he said shyly. "Not really . . . But what did I know? What did I see?"

"You weren't born in a bomb shelter," I replied impatiently. "You didn't make your life in a hole in the ground."

"Didn't I?" he said, flushing, "—don't be so sure," but then would say no more.

I realized that he was leaving me to them. I thought, Is this the role he has decided to play—the good Jew to my bad Jew? Well, if so, he's found the right supporting cast.

I said to Buki, "You describe the situation of the Jew in America as though we were living under a volcano. To me it seems you feel so strongly the need for so many million more Jews that you're inclined to imagine this mass emigration pretty unrealistically. When were you last in America?"

"Daphna was raised in New Rochelle," he said, motioning to his wife.

"And when you looked up in New Rochelle," I asked her, "you saw a volcano?"

Unlike Henry, she wasn't reluctant to have her say; she'd been waiting her turn, her eyes on me, ever since I'd silently sat there while they'd sung in the Sabbath. Hers was the only animus I felt. The others were educating a fool—she was confronting an enemy, like young Jerry, who'd given it to me at the ulpan that morning.

"Let me ask you a question," said Daphna, replying to mine. "You are a friend of Norman Mailer?"

"Both of us write books."

"Let me ask you a question about your colleague Mailer. Why is he so interested in murder and criminals and killing? When I was at Barnard, our English professor assigned those books to read—books by a Jew who cannot stop thinking about murder and criminals and killing. Sometimes when I think back to the innocence of that class and the idiotic nonsense that they said there, I think, Why didn't I ask, 'If this Jew is so exhilarated by violence, why doesn't he go to Israel?' Why doesn't he, Mr. Zuzkerman? If he wants to understand the experience of killing, why doesn't he come here and be like my husband? My husband has killed people in four wars, but not because he thinks murder is an exciting idea. He thinks it is a horrible idea. It is not even an *idea*. He kills to protect a tiny country, to defend an embattled nation—he kills so that perhaps his children may grow up one day to lead a peaceful life. He does not have a brilliant genius's intellectually wicked adventures of killing imaginary people inside his head—he has a decent man's dreadful experience of killing real people in Sinai and in the Golan and on the Jordanian border! Not to gain personal fame by writing bestselling books but to prevent the destruction of Jewish people!"

"And what do you want to ask me?" I said.

"I am asking you why is this genius's sick Diaspora rage celebrated in *Time* magazine while our refusal to be obliterated by our enemies in our own homeland is called in the same magazine monstrous Jewish aggression! That's what I'm asking!"

"I'm not here on behalf of *Time* or anyone else. I'm visiting Henry."

"But you are not nobody," she sarcastically replied. "You are a famous novelist, too—a novelist, what's more, who has written *about* Jews."

"It would be hard to believe, sitting at this table, in this settlement, that there's anything else a novelist *could* write about," I said. "Look, imagining violence and the release of the brute, imagining the individuals engaged in it, doesn't necessitate embracing it. There's no retreat or hypocrisy in a writer who doesn't go out and do what he may have thought about doing in every gory, horrifying detail. The only retreat is retreating from what you know."

"So," said Lippman, "what you are telling us is that we are not so nice as you American-Jewish writers."

"That's not at all what I'm telling you."

"But it's true," he said, smiling.

"I'm telling you that to see fiction as Daphna does is to see it from a highly specialized point of view. I'm telling you that it isn't obligatory for a novelist to go around personally exhibiting his themes. I'm not talking about who's nicer—niceness is even more deadly in writers than it is in other people. I'm only responding to a very crude observation."

"Crude? Yes, that is true. We are not like the intellectual goodies and the humane niceys who have the galut mentality. We are not polished people and we are terrible at the polite smile. All Daphna is saying is that we do not have the luxury you American-Jewish writers have of indulging in fantasies of violence and force. The Jew who drives the school bus past the Arabs throwing stones at his windscreen, he does not *dream* of violence—he *faces* violence, he *fights* violence. We do not *dream* about force—we *are* force. We are not afraid to rule in order to survive, and to put it again as unpalatably as possible, *we are not afraid to be masters*. We do not wish to crush the Arab—we simply will not allow him to crush *us*. Unlike the niceys and the goodies who live in Tel Aviv, I have no phobia of Arabs. I can live alongside him, and I do. I can even speak to him in his own tongue. But if he rolls a hand grenade into the house where my child is sleeping, I do not retaliate with a *fantasy* of violence of the kind everybody loves in the novels and the movies. I am not someone sitting in a cozy cinema; I am not someone playing a role in a Hollywood movie; I am not an American-Jewish novelist who steps back and from a distance appropriates the reality for his literary purposes. No! I am somebody who meets the enemy's real violence with my real violence, and I don't worry about the approval of *Time* magazine. The journalists, you know, got tired of the Jew making the desert bloom; it became *boring* to them. They got *tired* of the Jews being attacked by surprise and still winning all the wars. That too became *boring*. They prefer now the greedy, grasping Jew who oversteps his bounds—the Arab as Noble Savage versus the degenerate, colonialist, capitalist Jew. Now the journalist gets excited when the Arab terrorist takes him to his refugee camp and, displaying the gracious Arab hospitality, graciously pours him a cup of coffee with all the freedom fighters looking on—he thinks he is living dangerously drinking coffee with a gracious revolutionary who flashes his black eyes at him, and drinks his coffee with him, and assures him that his brave guerrilla heroes will drive the thieving Zionists into the sea. Much more thrilling than drinking borscht with a big-nosed Jew."

"Bad Jews," said Daphna, "make better copy. But I don't have to tell that to Nathan Zuckerman and Norman Mailer. Bad Jews sell newspapers just the way they sell books."

She's a honey, I thought, but ignored her, leaving Mailer to protect Mailer and figuring that I'd already sufficiently defended myself on that issue elsewhere.

"Tell me," Lippman said, "can the Jew do *anything* that doesn't stink to high heaven of his Jewishness? There are the goyim to whom we stink because they look down on us, and there are the goyim to whom we stink because they look up to us. Then there are the goyim who look both down *and* up at us—they are *really* angry. There is no end to it. First it was Jewish clannishness that was repellent, then what was preposterous was the ridiculous phenomenon of Jewish assimilation, now it is Jewish independence that is unacceptable and unjustified. First it was Jewish passivity that was disgusting, the meek Jew, the accommodating Jew, the Jew who walked like a sheep to his own slaughter—now what is worse than disgusting, outright *wicked*, is Jewish strength and militancy. First it was the Jewish sickliness that was abhorrent to all the robust Aryans, frail Jewish men with weak Jewish bodies lending money and studying books—now what is disgusting are strong Jewish men who know how to use force and are not afraid of power. First it was homeless Jewish cosmopolites that were strange and alien and not to be trusted—now what is alien are Jews with the arrogance to believe that they can determine their destiny like anybody else in a homeland of their own. Look, the Arab can remain here and I can remain here and together we can live in harmony. He can have any experience he likes, live here however he chooses and have everything he desires—except for the experience of statehood. If he wants that, if he cannot endure without that, then he can move to an Arab state and have the experience of statehood there. There are fifteen Arab states for him to pick from, most of them not even an hour away by car. The Arab homeland is vast, it is enormous, while the State of Israel is no more than a speck on the map of the world. You can put the State of Israel *seven times* into the state of Illinois, but it is the only place on this entire planet where a *Jew* can have the experience of statehood, and that is why *we do not give ground!*"

Dinner was over.

Henry guided me along one of their two long residential streets to where I was to sleep, the house of a settlement couple who had gone to spend the Sabbath in Jerusalem with family. Down in the Arab village a few lights were still burning, and on a distant hill, like an unblinking red eye, something that would once have been understood here as auguring the wrath of Almighty God, was the steady radar beacon of a missile-launching site. One of the missiles, heroically angled in firing position, was undisguised and plainly visible when we'd driven by on our way to Hebron. "The next war," Henry had said, pointing to the base up on the hilltop, "will take five minutes." The Israeli missile we saw was aimed at downtown Damascus to dissuade the Syrians, he told me, from launching their missile targeted for downtown Haifa. Except for that red omen, the distant blackness was so vast that I thought of Agor as a minute, floodlit earth-colony, the vanguard of a brave new Jewish civilization evolving in outer space, with Tel Aviv and all the decadent niceys and goodies as far off as the dimmest star.

If I had nothing to say to Henry right off it was because, following Lippman's seminar, language didn't really seem my domain any longer. I wasn't exactly a stranger to disputation, but never in my life had I felt so enclosed by a world so contentious, where the argument is enormous and constant and everything turns out to be pro or con, positions taken, positions argued, and everything italicized by indignation and rage.

Nor had my word-whipping ended with dinner. For two hours more, while I sat squeezed in beside Lippman's German editions of the European masterpieces and was graciously served tea and cake by contented Ronit, Lippman continued to flog away. I tried to ascertain whether his rhetoric wasn't perhaps being fomented a little by my questionable position among the Jews—by my reputedly equivocal position *about* Jews, which Daphna had indignantly alluded to—or whether he was deliberately playing it a bit broader at this performance to give me a taste of what had confounded my brother, particularly if I had any idea of abducting back into the Diaspora his prize dental surgeon, a paragon of worldly, assimilationist success, for whom he and the Deity had other plans. From time to time I'd thought, "Fuck it, Zuckerman, why don't you say what you think—all these bastards are saying what *they* think." But my way of handling Lippman had been by being practically mute. If that's handling. After dinner I may have looked to him as though I was sitting there in his living room saving myself up like some noble silent person, but the simple truth is I was outclassed.

Henry had nothing to say either. At first I thought it was because Lippman, along with Buki and Daphna, had left him
feeling vindicated and without any inclination to soften the
blow. But then I wondered if my presence might not have forced
him, maybe for the first time since succumbing to Lippman's
conviction, to evaluate his bulldozing mentor from a perspective
somewhat alien to Agor's ethos. That might even have been why
he'd clammed up like a child when I'd turned to ask if *he* had
been living under a volcano in the U.S.A. Perhaps by then he
was quietly wondering about what Muhammad Ali confessed had
crossed the mind of even a man as courageous as he in the
thirteenth round of that terrible third fight with Frazier: "What
am I doing here?"

While we walked the unpaved settlement street, as alone
together as Neil Armstrong and Buzz Aldrin up there planting
their toy flag in the lunar dust, it occurred to me that Henry
might have been wanting me to take him home from the
moment I'd phoned from Jerusalem, that he had seriously lost
his way but couldn't face the humiliation of admitting that to
someone whose admiration had meant nearly as much to him
once as the blessing he'd struggled to extract from our father.
Instead (perhaps) he'd had to buck himself up by bravely thinking something along these lines: "Let it be this way then, the
lost way. Life is the adventure of losing your way—and it's about
time I found out!"

Not that I thought of that as contemplating one's burden over-
dramatically; certainly a life of writing books is a trying adventure
in which you cannot find out where you *are* unless you lose your
way. Losing his way may actually have been the vital need that
Henry had been fumbling toward during his recuperation, when
he'd spoken tearfully of something unnameable, some unmistakable choice to which he was maddeningly blind, an act both
wrenching and utterly self-apparent that, once he'd discovered it,
would deliver him from his baffling depression. If so, then it
wasn't *roots* that he had unearthed sitting on the sunlit windowsill of that cheder in Mea She'arim; it wasn't his unbreakable

bond to a traditional European Jewish life that he'd heard in the chanting of those Orthodox children clamorously memorizing their lessons—it was his opportunity to be *uprooted*, to depart from the path that had been posted with his name the day he was born, and in the disguise of a Jew to cunningly defect. Israel instead of Jersey, Zionism instead of Wendy, assuring that he'd never again be bound to the actual in the old, suffocating, self-strangulating way.

What if Carol had it right and Henry was crazy? No crazier than Ben-Joseph, the author of the Five Books of Jimmy, but not significantly less so either. If his decision was to be seen from all sides, then the possibility that he had, in Carol's phrase, "flipped out" also had to be considered. Perhaps he'd never entirely recovered from the hysterical collapse precipitated by the prospect of a lifetime of drug-induced impotence. It might even be the resuscitated potency that he was really escaping, fearful of some punishing new calamity that might succeed this time in destroying him completely were he to dare ever again to look for salvation in something so antisocial as his own erection. He's in crazy flight, I thought, from the folly of sex, from the intolerable disorder of virile pursuits and the indignities of secrecy and betrayal, from the enlivening anarchy that overtakes anyone who even sparingly abandons himself to uncensored desire. Here in Abraham's bosom, far away from his wife and kids, he can be a model husband again, or maybe just a model boy.

The truth is that despite my persistent effort I still didn't know, at the end of the day, how to understand my brother's relationship to Agor and to his friends there, ideologically wired to see every Jew not merely as a potential Israeli but as the foreordained victim of a horrendous, impending anti-Semitic catastrophe should they try living normally anywhere else. Momentarily I gave up searching for some appropriate set of motives that would make this metamorphosis look to me less implausible and like something other than self-travesty. Instead, I began to remember the last time that we had been alone together in a place as black as Agor was at eleven o'clock at night—I was remembering way back to the early forties, before my father bought the one-family house up from the park, when we were still small boys sharing a bedroom at the back of the Lyons Avenue flat, and would lie in the dark, our bodies no farther apart than they were descending this settlement street, our only light shining from behind the dial of the Emerson radio on the small night table between the beds. I was remembering how, whenever the door creaked open at the beginning of another ghoulish episode of "Inner Sanctum," Henry would fly out from beneath his blanket and beg to be allowed to come over with me. And when, after feigning indifference to his childish cowardice, I lifted my covers and invited him to jump in, could two kids have been closer or any more contented? "Lippman," I should have said, when we'd shaken hands for the night at his door, "even if everything you've told me is a hundred percent true, the fact remains that in our family the collective memory doesn't go back to the golden calf and the burning bush, but to 'Duffy's Tavern' and 'Can You Top This?' Maybe the Jews begin with Judea, but Henry doesn't and he never will. He begins with WJZ and WOR, with double features at the Roosevelt on Saturday afternoons and Sunday doubleheaders at Ruppert Stadium watching the Newark Bears. Not nearly as epical, but there you are. Why don't you let my brother go?"

Only what if he genuinely didn't want to go? And did I even want him to want to? Wasn't it just liberal sentimentality—wasn't I really the *worst* nicey and goody—to prefer that I had a rational brother who had emigrated to Israel for the right reasons, and met the right people, and that I had come away from our meeting having seen him doing and thinking all the right things? If not sentimental, it was surely unprofessional. For observed solely from the novelist's point of view, this was far and away Henry's most provocative incarnation, if not exactly the most convincing—that is, it was the most eminently exploitable by me. My motives too must be taken into account. I wasn't there *just* as his brother.

"You haven't mentioned the children," I said as we were nearing the last house on the road.

His reply was quick and defensive. "What about them?"

"Well, you seem to have adopted a cavalier attitude toward them that's more appropriate to my reputation than to yours."

"Look, don't pull that on me—you certainly *aren't* the one who's going to talk to me about my children. They're coming here Passover—that's all arranged. They're going to see this place and they're going to love it—and then we'll go from there."

"You think they'll decide to live here too?"

"I told you to get off my ass. You've had three marriages and as far as I know flushed all your children down the toilet."

"Maybe I did and maybe I didn't, but you don't have to be a father to ask the right question. When did your children cease having any meaning to you?"

This made him still angrier. "Who said they had?"

"You told me in Hebron about your old life—'up to my eyeballs in meaninglessness.' I started wondering about your kids—about how three children can be left out of the account when a father is talking about whether life is meaningful. I'm not trying to make you feel guilty—I'm only trying to find out if you really have thought this whole thing through."

"Of course I have—a thousand times a day! Of *course* I miss them! But they're coming at Passover, and they're going to see what I'm doing here and what it's all about, and yes, who knows, they may even see where they belong!"

"Ruthie phoned me before I left London," I said.

"She did?"

"She knew I was coming to see you. She wanted me to tell you something."

"I speak to her every Sunday—what's the matter?"

"Her mother's there when you speak to her on Sunday, and she feels she can't say everything. She's a smart girl, Henry—at thirteen she's a grown-up and not a child. She said, 'He's out there to learn. He's trying to find something out. He's not too old to learn and I think he has the right.'"

Henry didn't reply at first, and when he did he was crying. "Is that what she said?"

"She said, 'I'm confused without my father.'"

"Well," he replied, desperate suddenly, and like a boy of ten, "I'm confused without *them*."

"I thought you might be. I just wanted to give you the message."

"Well, thanks," he said, "thanks."

Henry pushed open the unlocked door and turned on the lights of a small, square, cinder-block building laid out exactly like the Lippmans', though done up with far more religio-nationalistic verve. The living room of this house was dominated not by books but by a pair of outsized expressionistic paintings, portraits of two aged and, to me, unidentifiable biblical figures, either prophets or patriarchs. There was a large fabric-hanging pinned to one wall, and rows of shelves along another, jammed with tiny clay pots and bits of stone. The ancient earthenware had been collected by the husband, an archaeologist at Hebrew University, and the fabric stamped with the Oriental motif was designed by the wife, who worked for a small textile printing company in an older settlement nearby. The paintings, thickly encrusted with bright oranges and bloody reds and executed with violent brushstrokes, were the work of a well-known settlement artist, one of whose watercolors of the Jerusalem camel market Henry had bought to send home to the kids. For Henry's sake I stood in front of the paintings for several minutes demonstrating more enthusiasm than I felt. His own enthusiasm may well have been genuine and yet the art-appreciation talk about the circular composition struck me as entirely artificial. He seemed all at once to be working much too hard to convince me that I was absolutely wrong if I suspected that the euphoria of the adventure had begun to flag.

Only a few feet of corridor separated the living room from a bedroom smaller even than the one we'd shared as small boys. Two beds were squeezed into it, though not a "set" fitted out like ours with maple headboards and footboards whose notches and curves we used to pretend were the defensive walls of a cavalry fort besieged by Apaches—these were more like folding cots drawn up side by side. He flipped a light on to show me the toilet and then said he'd see me in the morning. He would be sleeping up the hill in a dormitory room with the young men who were his fellow students.

"Why not a night away from the delights of communal living? Sleep here."

"I'll be going back," he replied.

In the living room I said, "Henry, sit down."

"For a second," but when he dropped onto the sofa beneath the paintings he looked as though he were a lost child—one of his own, in fact—a child waiting on a police-station bench for somebody he loved to come and claim him, while at the same time feeling four times as old and, if it was possible, twice as tormented as the impastoed sage above his head, whose own hopes for Jewish renewal and ethical transformation appeared to have been smashed by something the size of a train.

Since I am not without affection for him, and never will be, the effect of this melancholy sight was to make me want to rush to assure him that he *hadn't* made a stupid mistake—if anything the stupid mistake had been mine, thinking this was any of my business and making him vulnerable to every uncertainty. The last thing he needs, I thought, is to be dwarfed by yet another personality bigger than his own. That's been the story of his life. Why not lay off and give him the benefit of the doubt? He left what he couldn't stand anymore. He understood, "The imperative is now—do it now!" and came here. That's all there is to it. Let him call it a high moral mission if he likes the sound of that. He wants out of nowhere to have an elevated goal—so let him. Russian literature is replete with just such avid souls and their bizarre, heroic longings, probably more of them in Russian literature than in life. Fine—let him be full to the brim with Myshkin motives: And if it *is* all only a wild-goose chase, that's the pathos of his situation and has nothing to do with me . . . Yet what if he desperately wants out of Agor and to be back with the kids, and yes, even back with his wife? What if he wants this tremendous aggression of his, released by Agor, once again walled in by the old pieties and habits? What if he realizes that Ruthie alone is probably more "meaningful" than anything he'll ever find in Israel—what if he's seen how hopelessly overcommitted he is to what he can't begin to be? Even assertive, even packing that pistol, even with the best of Lippman bled into his veins, he seemed to me far more trapped than he did in New Jersey, someone utterly swamped and overcome.

I'd begun my visit telling myself, "Don't pick on him where he's vulnerable and where he'll always be vulnerable." But when vulnerability was everywhere, what was I to do? It was awfully late in the day to try to start shutting up. These boys are brothers, I thought, about as unlike as brothers come, but each has taken the other's measure and been measured against the other for so long that it's unthinkable that either could even learn to remain unconcerned by the judgment his counterpart embodies. These two men are boys who are brothers—these two boys are brothers who are men—these brothers are men who are boys—therefore the discrepancies are irreconcilable: the challenge is there merely in their being.

"So that was your crowd," I said, sitting down across from him.

He answered solemnly, already protecting himself from what I might say. "Those are some of the people here, yes."

"His opponents must find Lippman a formidable foe."

"They do."

"What draws you to him?" I asked, wondering if he might not answer, "The man is the embodiment of potency." Because wasn't it precisely that?

"What's wrong with him?" he replied.

"I didn't say anything was. The question isn't what I think of Lippman—it's what I think of your fascination with him. I'm only asking about his hold on you."

"Why do I admire him? Because I believe he's right."

"About what?"

"Right in what he advocates for Israel and right in the assessment he makes of how to achieve it."

"That may be, for all I know, but tell me, who does he remind you of?" I asked. "Anyone we know?"

"Oh, no, please, no—save the psychoanalysis for the great American public." Wearily he said, "Spare me."

"Well, that's the way it sticks in *my* mind. Strip away the aggressive bully, strip away the hambone actor and the compulsive talker, and we could have been back at the kitchen table in Newark, with Dad lecturing us on the historical struggle between the goy and the Jew."

"Tell me something, is it at all possible, at least outside of those books, for you to have a frame of reference slightly larger than the kitchen table in Newark?"

"The kitchen table in Newark happens to be the source of your Jewish memories, Henry—this is the stuff we were raised on. It *is* Dad—though this time round without the doubts, without the hidden deference to the goy and the fear of goyish mockery. It's Dad, but the dream-Dad, supersized, raised to the hundredth power. Best of all is the permission Lippman gives not to be so nice. That must come as a relief after all these years—to be a good Jewish son and *not* nice, to be a roughneck *and* a Jew. Now that's having everything. We didn't have Jews quite like that in our neighborhood. The tough Jews we used to meet at weddings and bar mitzvahs were mostly fat guys in the produce line, so I can see the appeal, but aren't you overdoing just a bit all the justifiable aggression?"

"Why is it that all my life you've trivialized everything I do? Why don't you psychoanalyze that? I wonder why my aspirations can't ever be as valid as yours."

"I'm sorry, but being skeptical of revolvers is in my nature—as skeptical of revolvers as of the ideologues who wield them."

"Lucky you. Fortunate you. Righteous you. *Humane* you. You're skeptical of just about everything."

"Henry, when are you going to stop being an apprentice fanatic and start practicing dentistry again?"

"I ought to punch you in the fucking nose for that."

"Why don't you blow my brains out with your gun?" I asked, now that he was unarmed. "That shouldn't be too hard, seeing that you're conflict-free and untainted by doubt. Look, I'm all for authenticity, but it can't begin to hold a candle to the human gift for playacting. That may be the only authentic thing that we *ever* do."

"I always have the sensation speaking to you that I'm becoming progressively sillier and more ridiculous—why do you think that is, Nathan?"

"Is that so? Well, it's fortunate then that we haven't had to speak very often and were able to go our different ways."

"It would simply never occur to you, *never*, to praise or appreciate anything I've done. Why do you think that is, Nathan?"

"But it's not the case. I think what you've done is colossal. I'm not sweeping that aside. An exchange of existences like this—it's like after a great war, the exchange of prisoners. I don't minimize the scale of this thing. I wouldn't be here if I did. You've tried like hell not to let on, but I also see what it's costing you—of course you're paying a steep price, particularly where the kids are concerned. It's indisputable that you've registered a powerful objection against the way you once lived. I don't make light of that, it's all I've thought about since I laid eyes on you. I've only been asking if in order to change some things, you had to change *everything*. I'm talking about what the missile engineers call 'escape velocity'—the trick is to manage to leave the atmosphere without overshooting your target."

"Look—" he said, and jumped up suddenly as though to go for my throat, "—you're a very intelligent man, Nathan, you're very subtle, but you have one large defect—the only world that exists for you is the world of psychology. That's *your* revolver. Aim and fire—and you've been firing it at me all my life. Henry is doing *this* because he wants to please Momma and Poppa, Henry is doing *this* because he wants to please Carol—or displease Carol, or displease Momma, or displease Poppa. On and on and on it goes. It's never Henry as an autonomous being, it's always Henry on the brink of being a cliché—my brother the stereotype. And maybe that was once even so, maybe I *was* a man who kept dropping into the stereotype, maybe that accounts for a lot of the unhappiness that I felt back home. Probably you think that the ways I choose to 'rebel' are only stereotypical. But unfortunately for you I'm *not* someone who's only his simple, silly motives. All my life you've been right on top, like a guy guarding me in a basketball game. Won't let me take one lousy shot. Everything I throw up you block. There's always the explanation that winds up belittling me. Crawling all over me with your fucking thoughts. Everything I do is predictable, everything I do *lacks depth*, certainly compared to what *you* do. 'You're only taking that shot, Henry, because you want to score.' Ingenious! But let me tell you something—you can't explain away what I've done by motives any more than I can explain away what you've done. Beyond all your profundities, beyond the Freudian lock you put on every single person's life, there is another world, a larger world, a world of ideology, of politics, of history—a world of things larger than the kitchen table! You were in it tonight: a world defined by *action*, by *power*, where how you wanted to please Momma and Poppa *simply doesn't matter*! All you see is escaping Momma, escaping Poppa—why don't you see what I've escaped *into*? *Everybody* escapes—our grandparents came to America, were they escaping their mothers and fathers? They were escaping history! Here they're *making* history! There's a world outside the Oedipal swamp, Nathan, where what matters isn't what made you do it *but what it is you do*—not what decadent Jews like you think but what committed Jews like the people here *do*! Jews who aren't in it for laughs, Jews that have something more to go on than their hilarious inner landscape! Here they have an *outer* landscape, a nation, a world! This isn't a hollow intellectual game! This isn't some exercise for the brain divorced from reality! This isn't writing a novel, Nathan! Here people don't jerk around like your fucking heroes worrying twenty-four hours a day about what's going on inside their heads and whether they should see their psychiatrists —here you fight, you struggle, here you worry about what's going on in *Damascus*! What matters isn't Momma and Poppa and the kitchen table, it isn't *any* of that crap you write about—*it's who runs Judea!*"

And out the door he went, furious, and before he could be talked into going home.

3. *Aloft*

SHORTLY AFTER the seat-belt sign went off a group of religious Jews formed a minyan up by the bulkhead. I couldn't hear them over the noise of the engines, but in the sunlight streaming through the safety-exit window I could see the terrific clip at which they were praying. Off and running faster than a Paganini Caprice, they looked like their objective was to pray at supersonic speed—praying itself they made to seem a feat of physical endurance. It was hard to imagine another human drama as intimate and frenzied being enacted so shamelessly in a public conveyance. Had a pair of passengers thrown off their clothes and, in a fit of equally unabashed fervor, begun making love out in the aisle, watching them wouldn't have seemed to me any more voyeuristic.

Though numbers of Orthodox Jews were seated throughout the tourist cabin, at my side was an ordinary American Jew like myself, a smallish man in his middle thirties, clean-shaven and wearing horn-rimmed glasses, who was alternately leafing through that morning's *Jerusalem Post*—the Israeli English-language paper—and looking with curiosity at the covered heads bobbing and jerking in that square blaze of sunlight up by the bulkhead.

Some fifteen minutes out of Tel Aviv he turned and asked in a friendly voice, "Visiting Israel or on business?"

"Just a visit."

"Well," he said, putting aside his paper, "what are your feelings about what you saw?"

"Sorry?"

"Your feelings. Were you moved? Were you proud?"

Henry was still very much on my mind, and so rather than indulge my neighbor—what he was fishing for was pretty clear— I said, "Don't follow you," and reached into my briefcase for a pen and a notebook. I had the urge to write my brother.

"You're Jewish," he said, smiling.

"I am."

"Well, didn't you have any feelings when you saw what they've done?"

"Don't have feelings."

"But did you see the citrus farms? Here are the Jews, who aren't supposed to be able to farm—and there are those miles and miles of farms. You can't imagine my feelings when I saw those farms. And the Jewish farmers! They took me out to an Air Force base—I couldn't believe my eyes. Weren't you moved by *anything*?"

I thought, while listening to him, that if his Galician grandfather were able to drop in on a tour from the realm of the dead upon Chicago, Los Angeles, or New York, he might well express just such sentiments, and with no less amazement: "We aren't supposed to be Americans—and there are those millions and millions of American Jews! You can't imagine my feelings when I saw how American they looked!" How do you explain this American-Jewish inferiority complex when faced with the bold claims of militant Zionism that they have the patent on Jewish self-transformation, if not on boldness itself? "Look," I said to him, "I can't answer these kinds of questions."

"Know what *I* couldn't answer? They kept wanting me to explain why American Jews persist in living in the Diaspora—and I couldn't answer. After everything I'd seen, I didn't know what to say. Does anybody know? Can *anyone* answer?"

Poor guy. Sounds like he must have been plagued by this thing —probably been on the defensive night and day about his artificial identity and totally alienated position. They said to him, "Where is Jewish survival, where is Jewish security, where is Jewish history? If you were really a good Jew you'd be in Israel, a Jew in a Jewish society." They said to him, "The one place in the world that's really Jewish and only Jewish is Israel"—and he was too cowed by the moral one-upmanship even to recognize, let alone admit, that that was one of the reasons he didn't want to live there.

"Why *is* it?" he was asking, his helplessness in the face of the question now rather touching. "Why *do* Jews persist in living in the Diaspora?"

I didn't feel like writing off with one line a man obviously in a state of serious confusion, but I didn't want this conversation either, and wasn't in the mood to answer in detail. That I would save for Henry. The best I could try to do was to leave him with something to think about. "Because they like it," I replied, and got up and moved to an empty aisle seat a few rows back where I could concentrate undisturbed on what more, if anything, to say to Henry about the wonder of his new existence.

Now in the window seat to my left was a thickly bearded young man in a dark suit and a tieless white shirt buttoned up to the neck. He was reading a Hebrew prayer book and eating a candy bar. His doing both struck me as strange, but then an unsympathetic secular mind is hardly a fit arbiter of what distinguishes piety from irreverence.

I placed my briefcase on the floor—his was open on the seat between us—and began my letter to Henry. It didn't just drift up on the page any more than anything ever does. It was more like using an eyedropper to extinguish a fire. I wrote and revised for nearly two hours, working consciously to constrain the big-brother caviling that persisted in coloring the early drafts. "All you want me to see are the political realities. I see them. But I also see you. You're a reality too." I crossed this out, and more like it, working and reworking what I'd written till finally I came as close as I could to looking at things more or less his way, not

147

so much to achieve a reconciliation, which was both out of the question and nothing either of us needed any longer, but so that we might be able to part without my hurting his feelings and causing more damage than I had already in that final face-off. Though personally I couldn't believe that he was there for good —the kids were to fly out to visit him at Passover, and seeing them, I thought, might well change everything—I wrote as though I assumed that his decision was irrevocable. If that's what he wants to think, that's what I'll think too.

Aloft/El Al
Dec. 11, 1978

Dear Henry,
Having sifted mistrustfully through each other's motives, having been stripped of our worth in each other's eyes, where does this leave you and me? I've been wondering ever since I boarded Flight 315. You've become a Jewish activist, a man of political commitment, driven by ideological conviction, studying the ancient tribal tongue and living sternly apart from your family, your possessions, and your practice on a rocky hillside in biblical Judea. I've become (in case you're interested) a bourgeois husband, a London homeowner, and, at forty-five, a father-to-be, married this time to a country-reared, Oxford-educated English woman, born into a superfluous caste that decreed for her an upbringing not in the remotest way like ours—as she'd tell you herself, resembling hardly anyone's in recent centuries. You have a land, a people, a heritage, a cause, a gun, an enemy, a mentor—a powerhouse mentor. I have none of these things. I have a pregnant English wife. Traveling in opposite directions, we've managed in middle age to position ourselves equidistantly from where we began. The moral I derive from this, confirmed by Friday night's conversational duel when I stupidly asked why you didn't shoot me, is that the family is finally finished. Our little nation is torn asunder. I didn't think I'd live to see the day.

As much, admittedly, from writerly curiosity as from tottering old genetic obligation, I have been racking my brain for forty-eight hours, trying to understand the reason for your overturning your life, when it's really not hard to figure out. Tired of the expectations of others, the opinions of others, as sick of being respectable as of your necessarily more hidden side, at a time of life when the old stuff is dry, there comes this rage from abroad, the color, the power, the passion of it, as well as issues that are shaking the world. All the dissension in the Jewish soul there on display every day in the Knesset. Why *should* you resist it? Who are you to be restrained? I agree. As for Lippman, I have a terrific weakness for these showmen too. They certainly take things out of the realm of the introspective. Lippman seems to me someone for whom centuries of distrust and antipathy and oppression and misery have become a Stradivarius on which he savagely plays like a virtuoso Jewish violinist. His tirades have an eerie reality and even while rejecting him one has to wonder if it's because what he says is wrong or because what he says is just unsayable. I asked, with excessive impatience, if your identity was to be formed by the terrifying power of an imagination richer with reality than your own, and should have known the answer myself. *How else does it happen?* The treacherous imagination is everybody's maker—we are all the invention of each other, everybody a conjuration conjuring up everyone else. We are all each other's authors.

Look at the place you now want to call home: a whole *country* imagining itself, asking itself, "What the hell is this business of being a Jew?"—people losing sons, losing limbs, losing this, losing that, in the act of answering. "What is a Jew in the first place?" It's a question that's always had to be answered: the sound "Jew" was not made like a rock in the world—some human voice once said "Djoo," pointed to somebody, and that was the beginning of what hasn't stopped since.

Another place famous for inventing (or reinventing) the Jew was Germany under Hitler. Fortunately for the two of us, earlier on there'd been our grandfathers—as you rightly reminded me Friday night—incongruously wondering beneath their beards if a Jew was somebody who had necessarily to be destined for destruction in Galicia. Think of all they unpinned from our tails, in addition to saving our skin—think of the audacious, inventive genius of the un-knowing greenhorns who came to America to settle. And now, marked by the dread of another Hitler and a second great Jewish slaughter, comes the virtuoso violinist of Agor, and with him a vision, ignited by the Nazi crematoria, of sweeping aside every disadvantageous moral taboo in order to restore Jewish spiritual preeminence. I have to tell you that there were moments on Friday night when it seemed to me that it was the Jews out at Agor who are really ashamed of Jewish history, who cannot abide what Jews have been, are embarrassed by what they've become, and display the sort of revulsion for Diaspora "abnormalities" that you can also find in the classic anti-Semite they abhor. I wonder what you would call the waxworks representing those of your friends who scornfully disparage every introspective Jew of pacific inclinations and humanistic ideals as either a coward or a traitor or an idiot, if not the Museum of Jewish Self-Hatred. Henry, do you really believe that in the struggle for the imagination of the Jews the Lippmans are the people who should win?

I still find it hard to believe, despite what you told me, that your blossoming Zionism is the result of a *Jewish* emergency that befell you in America. I would never dare decry any Zionist whose decision to go to Israel arose out of the strong sense that he was escaping dangerous or disabling anti-Semitism. Were the real critical questions, in your case, anti-Semitism, or cultural isolation, or even a sense, no matter how irrational, of personal guilt about the Holocaust, there would be little to question. But I happen to be convinced that if you were repelled or deformed by anything, it wasn't by a ghetto situation, the ghetto mentality, or the goy and the menace he posed.

You know better than to swallow uncritically the big cliché they seem to cherish at Agor of American Jews eating greedily from the shopping-center fleshpots, with one wary eye out for the Gentile mob —or, worse, blindly oblivious to the impending threat—and all the while inwardly seething with their self-hatred and shame. Seething with self-love is more like it, seething with confidence and success. And maybe that's a world-historical event on a par with the history you are making in Israel. History doesn't have to be made the way a mechanic makes a car—one can play a role in history without its having to be obvious, even to oneself. It may be that flourishing mundanely in the civility and security of South Orange, more or less forgetful from one day to the next of your Jewish origins but remaining identifiably (and voluntarily) a Jew, you were making Jewish history no less astonishing than theirs, though without quite knowing it every moment, and without having to say it. You too were standing in time and culture, whether you happened to realize it or not. Self-hating *Jews*? Henry, America is full of self-hating *Gentiles*, as far as I can see—it's a country that's full of Chicanos who want to look like Texans, and Texans who want to look like New Yorkers, and any number of Middle Western Wasps who, believe it or not, want to talk and act and think like Jews. To say Jew and goy about America is to miss the point, because America simply is not that, other than in Agor's ideology. Nor does the big cliché metaphor of the fleshpot in any way describe your responsible life there, Jewish or otherwise; it was as conflicted and tense and valuable as anyone else's, and to me looked nothing like the life of Riley but like *life*, period. Think again about how much "meaninglessness" you're willing to concede to their dogmatic Zionist challenge. By the way, I really can't remember ever before hearing *you* use the word goy with such an air of intellectual authority. It reminds me of how I used to go around during my freshman year at Chicago talking about the lumpenproletariat as though that testified to a tremendous extension of my understanding of American society. When I saw the creeps outside the Clark Street saloons, I thrilled myself by muttering, "Lumpenproletariat." I thought I knew something. Frankly I think you learned more about "the goy" from your Swiss girlfriend than you'll ever learn at Agor. The truth is that you could teach *them*. Try it some Friday night. Tell them at dinner about everything you reveled in during that affair. It should be an education for everyone and make the goy a little less abstract.

Your connection to Zionism seems to me to have little to do with feeling more profoundly Jewish or finding yourself endangered, enraged, or psychologically straitjacketed by anti-Semitism in New Jersey—which doesn't make the enterprise any less "authentic." It makes it absolutely classical. Zionism, as I understand it, originated not only in the deep Jewish dream of escaping the danger of insularity and the cruelties of social injustice and persecution but out of a highly conscious desire to be divested of virtually everything that had come to seem, to the Zionists as much as to the Christian Europeans, distinctively Jewish behavior—to reverse the very form of Jewish existence. The construction of a counterlife that is one's own anti-myth was at its very core. It was a species of fabulous utopianism, a manifesto for human transformation as extreme—and, at the outset, as implausible—as any ever conceived. A Jew could be a new person if he wanted to. In the early days of the state the idea appealed to almost everyone except the Arabs. All over the world people were rooting for the Jews to go ahead and un-Jew themselves in their own little homeland. I think that's why the place was once universally so popular—no more Jewy Jews, great!

At any rate, that you should be mesmerized by the Zionist laboratory in Jewish self-experiment that calls itself "Israel" isn't such a mystery when I think about it this way. The power of the will to remake reality is embodied for you in Mordecai Lippman. Needless to say, the power of the pistol to remake reality also has its appeal.

My dear Hanoch (to invoke the name of that anti-Henry you are determined to unearth in the Judean hills), I hope that you don't get killed trying. If it was weakness you considered the enemy while exiled in South Orange, in the homeland it may be an·excess of strength. It isn't to be minimized—not everybody has the courage at forty to treat himself like raw material, to abandon a comfortable, familiar life when it's become hopelessly alien to him, and to take upon himself voluntarily the hardships of displacement. Nobody travels as far as you have and, to all appearances, fares so well so quickly on audacity or obstinacy or madness alone. A massive urge to self-renovation (or, as Carol sees it, to self-sabotage) can't be assuaged delicately; it requires muscular defiance. Despite the un-nerving devotion to Lippman's charismatic vitality, you in fact seem freer and more independent than I would have imagined possible. If it's true that you were enduring intolerable limitations and living in agonizing opposition to yourself, then for all I know you have used your strength wisely and everything I say is irrelevant. Maybe it's appropriate that you've wound up there; it may be what you needed all your life—a combative métier where you feel guilt-free.

And who knows, in a year or two things may well change for you, and you'll have reasons for living there that will sound more congenial to me—if you're still talking to me—and that will in fact be more like what I imagine to be the reasons that most people live there, or anywhere, reasons that I don't happen to think are any less serious or meaningful than the ones you have right now. Surely Zionism is more subtle than just Jewish boldness since, after all, Jews who act boldly aren't just Israelis or Zionists. Normal/abnormal, strong/weak, we-ness/me-ness, not-so-nice/niceness—there's one dichotomy missing about which you said little, or nothing: Hebrew/English. Out at Agor anti-Semitism comes up, Jewish pride comes up, Jewish power comes up, but nothing that I heard all night from you or your friends about the Hebrew aspect and the large, overwhelming cultural reality of *that*. Perhaps this only occurs to me because I'm a writer, though I frankly can't imagine how it wouldn't occur to anyone, since it's finally Hebrew more than heroism with which you have surrounded yourself, just as if you went to live forever in Paris it would be French with which you constructed your experience and thought. In present-ing your reasons for staying there, I'm surprised you don't harp as much on the culture you're acquiring as on the manliness flowing out of the pride and the action and the power. Or maybe you'll only come to that when you begin feeling the loss of the language and the society that you look to me to be so blindly giving up.

To tell you the truth, had I run into you on a Tel Aviv street with a girl on your arm, and you told me, "I love the sun and smell and the falafel and the Hebrew language and living as a dentist in the middle of a Hebrew world," I wouldn't have felt like challenging you in any way. All that—which corresponds to *my* ideas of normalcy—I could have understood far more easily than your trying to lock yourself into a piece of history that you're simply not locked into, into an idea and a commitment that may have been cogent for the people who came up with it, who built a country when they had no hope, no future, and everything was only difficulty for them—an idea that was, without a doubt, brilliant, ingenious, courageous, and vigorous in its historical time—but that doesn't really look to me to be so very cogent to you.

In the meantime, at the risk of sounding like Mother when you used to go off to practice the hurdles in high school, for God's sake, be careful. I don't want to come out next time to collect your remains.

Your only brother,

Nathan

P.S. You will see from the signature that I haven't bothered about changing my own name, but in England embark upon the search for *my* anti-self carrying my old identity papers and disguised as N.Z.

Next I recorded in my notebook all I could remember of my conversation the previous evening with Carol; it was seven hours earlier in Jersey and she was about to begin preparing supper for the children when I phoned in as my brother's deprogrammer before going to sleep at the hotel. Since Henry's disappearance five months back Carol had undergone a transformation remarkably like his: she too was finished with being nice. That relentlessly accommodating personality that to me had always seemed little more than a bland enigma was armed now with the necessary cynicism to ride out this bizarre low blow, as well as with the hatred required to begin to heal the wound. The result was that for the first time in my life I felt some sort of power in her (as well as some womanly appeal) and wondered what I could possibly achieve persisting on playing the domestic peacemaker. Wasn't everyone happier enraged? They were certainly more interesting. People are unjust to anger—it can be enlivening and a lot of fun.

"I spent Friday with him at his settlement and then stayed overnight. I couldn't use the phone to order a taxi the next day because they're all religious people—nobody enters and nobody leaves on the Sabbath, and nobody could drive me, so I was there Saturday as well. I've never seen him healthier, Carol—he looks fine, and, well, you ask me."

"And is he doing all that Jewish stuff, too?"

"Some of it. Mostly he's learning Hebrew. He's devoted to that. He says his decision's irrevocable and he's not coming back. He's in a very rebellious state of mind. I don't see an ounce of remorse or any real yearning for home. No wavering at all, frankly. That may just be euphoria. He's still pretty much in the euphoric stage."

"Euphoria you call it? Some little Israeli bitch has taken him away from me—isn't that the real story? There's a little soldier there, sure as hell, with her tits and her tommy gun."

"I wondered about that myself. But no, there's no woman."

"Doesn't this Lippman have a wife he's screwing?"

"Lippman's a giant to Henry—I don't think that's in the cards. Sex is a 'superficiality,' and he's burned all superficiality away. He's discovered the aggressive spirit in himself, assisted by Lippman. He's seen power. He's discovered dynamism. He's discovered nobler considerations, purer intentions. I'm afraid it's Henry who's taken over as the headstrong, unconventional son. He needs a bigger stage for his soul."

"And this jerkwater settlement, this absolute nowhere, he considers *bigger*? It's the desert—it's the *wilds*."

"But the biblical wilds."

"You're telling me it's God then?"

"It's bizarre to me, too. Where that came from, I have no idea."

"Oh, I know where. Living in that little ghetto when you

were kids, from your crazy father—he's gone right back to the roots of that madness. It's that craziness gone in another direction."

"You never found him crazy before."

"I always thought he was crazy. If you want the truth, I thought you were all a little nuts. You got off best. You never bothered with it in life—you poured that stuff into books and made yourself a fortune. You turned the madness to profit, but it's still all part of the family insanity on the subject of Jews. Henry's just a late-blooming Zuckerman nut."

"Explain it any way you like, but he doesn't look insane or sound insane, nor has he completely lost touch with his life. He's looking forward tremendously to seeing the kids at Passover."

"Only I don't want my kids involved in all this. I never did. If I had I would have married a rabbi. I don't want it, it doesn't interest me, and I didn't think it interested him."

"I think Henry *assumes* the kids are coming at Passover."

"Is he inviting me, or just the kids?"

"I thought he was inviting the children. The way I understood it, the visit's already set."

"I'm not letting them go by themselves. If he was crazy enough to do what he's done to himself, he's crazy enough to keep them there and try to turn Leslie into a little thing with squiggle curls and a dead-white face, a little monstrous religious creature. I'm certainly not sending my girls, not so he can throw them in a bath and shave their heads and marry them to the butcher."

"I think it may have communicated the wrong idea, my being unable to use the phone there on Saturday. It's not the Orthodoxy that's inspired him, it's the place—Judea. It seems to give him a more serious sense of himself having the roots of his religion all around him."

"What roots? He left those roots two thousand years ago. As far as I know he's been in New Jersey for two thousand years. It's all nonsense."

"Well, do what you like, of course. But if the kids could get over for Passover, it might open up communication between you two. Right now he's pouring all his responsibility into the Jewish cause, but that may change when he sees them again. So far he's fenced us all off with this Jewish idealism, but when they show up we might begin to find out if this really is a revolutionary change or just some upheaval he's passing through. The last great outburst of youth. Maybe the last great outburst of middle age. It comes to more or less the same thing: the desire to deepen his life. The desire looks genuine enough, but the means, I admit, seem awfully vicarious. Right now it's a little as though he's out to take vengeance on everything that he wants to believe was once holding him back. He's still very much caught up in the solidarity of it. But once the euphoria starts dwindling away, seeing the children could even lead to a reconciliation with you. If you want that, Carol."

"My kids would loathe it there. They've been brought up by me, by *him*, not to want to have anything to do with religion of any kind. If he wants to go over there and wail and moan and hit his head on the floor, let him, but the kids are staying here, and if he wants to see them, he'll have to see them right here."

"But if his determination does start to give way, would you take him back?"

"If he were to come to his senses? Of course I would take him back. The kids are holding up, but this isn't great fun for them, either. They're upset. They miss him. I wouldn't say they were confused, because they're extremely intelligent. They know precisely what's going on."

"Yes? What is that?"

"They think he's having a nervous breakdown. They're only scared that I will."

"Will you?"

"If he kidnaps my children, I will. If this madness goes on very much longer, yes, I may well have one."

"My guess is that this could all be so much fallout from that ghastly operation."

"Mine too, of course. I think it's clutching at God, or straws, or whatever, out of dread of dying. Some kind of magic charm, some form of placation to make sure it never happens again. Penance. Oh, it's too awful. It makes no sense at all. Who could have dreamed of this happening?"

"May I suggest then that if at Passover you *could* bring yourself—"

"When *is* Passover? I don't even know when Passover *is*, Nathan. We don't *do* any of that. We never did, not even when I was at home with my parents. Even my father, who owned a shoe store, was free of all that. He didn't care about Passover, he cared about golf, which now appears to put him three thousand rungs up the evolutionary scale from his stupid son-in-law. Religion! A lot of fanaticism and superstition and wars and death! Stupid, medieval nonsense! If they tore down all the churches and all the synagogues to make way for more golf courses, the world would be a better place!"

"I'm only telling you that if you do want him back some time in the future, I wouldn't cross him on the Passover business."

"But I *don't* want him back if he's crazy like this. I do not want to live my life with a crazy Jew. That was okay for your mother but it isn't for me."

"What you could say is, 'Look, you can be a Jew in Essex County, too.' "

"Not with me he can't."

"But you did after all marry a Jew. So did he."

"No. I married a very handsome, tall, athletic, very sweet, very sincere, very successful, responsible dentist. I didn't marry a Jew."

"I didn't know you had these feelings."

"I doubt that you've known anything about me. I was just Henry's dull little wife. Sure I was perfunctorily Jewish—who ever even thought about it? That's the only decent way to be any of those things. But Henry has more than scratched the surface with what he's gone out and done. I simply will not be connected with all that narrow-minded, bigoted, superstitious, and totally unnecessary crap. I certainly don't want my children connected with it."

"So to come home Henry has to be just as un-Jewish as you."

"That's right. Without his little curls and his little beanie. Is that why I studied French literature at college, so he could go around here in a beanie? Where does he want to put me now, up in the gallery with the rest of the women? I cannot *stand* that stuff. And the more seriously people take it, the more unattractive it all is. Narrow and constricting and revolting. *And* smug. I will not be trapped into that."

"Be that as it may, if you want to reunite the family, one approach would be to say to him, 'Come back and continue your Hebrew studies here, continue learning Hebrew, studying Torah—'"

"*He* studies *Torah?*"

"At night. Part of becoming an authentic Jew. Authentic's his word—in Israel he can be an authentic Jew and everything about him makes sense. In America being a Jew made him feel artificial."

"Yes? Well, artificial I thought he was just fine. So did all his girlfriends. Look, there are millions of Jews living in New York —are they artificial? That is totally beyond me. I want to live as a human being. The last thing I want to be strapped into is being an authentic Jew. If that's what he wants, then he and I have nothing more to say to each other."

"So simply because your husband wants to be Jewish, you're going to allow the family to dissolve."

"Christ, don't *you* become pious about 'the family.' Or about Being Jewish. No—because my husband, who is an American, who I thought of as my generation, of my era, *free* of all that weight, has taken a giant step back in time, *that's* why I am dissolving the family. As for my kids, their lives are here, their friends are here, their schools are here, their future universities are here. They don't have the pioneer spirit that Henry has, they didn't have the father that Henry had, and they are not going to the biblical homeland for Passover, let alone to a synagogue here. There will be no synagogues in this family! There will be no kosher kitchen in this house! I could not possibly live that life. Fuck him, let him stay there if it's authentic Judaism he wants, let him stay there and find another authentic Jew to live with and the two of them can set up a house with a tabernacle where they can celebrate all their little feasts. But here it is absolutely out of the question—nobody is going around this house blowing the trumpet of Jewish redemption!"

We were halfway to London by the time I was done, and the young fellow beside me was still at his prayer book. Torn wrappers from three or four candy bars were scattered on the seat between us, and perspiration was coursing heavily from beneath his broad-brimmed hat. As there was no turbulence, as the plane was well ventilated and a comfortable temperature, I wondered, like my mother—like *his* mother—if he might not have made himself sick eating all those sweets. Beneath the hat and beard, I thought I could spot a resemblance to somebody I knew; perhaps it was to somebody I'd grown up with in Jersey. But then I'd thought that several times during the last few days about any number of people I'd seen: in the café, watching the passersby on Dizengoff Street, and again outside the hotel while waiting for a taxi, the archetypal Jewish cast of an Israeli face would remind me of somebody back in America who could have been a close relative if not the very same Jew in a new incarnation.

Before putting my notebook back into my briefcase, I reread all I'd written to Henry. Why don't you leave the poor guy alone, I wondered. Another thousand words is just what he needs from you—they'll use it at Agor for target practice. Hadn't I written this for myself anyway, for my own elucidation, trying to make interesting what he could not? I felt, looking back over the last forty-eight hours, that alone with Henry I'd been in the presence of someone shallowly dreaming a very deep dream. I'd tried repeatedly while I was with him to invest this escape he'd made from his life's narrow boundaries with some heightened meaning, but in the end he seemed to me, despite his determination to be something new, just as naïve and uninteresting as he'd always been. Even there, in that Jewish hothouse, he somehow managed to remain perfectly ordinary, while what I'd been hoping—perhaps why I'd even made the trip—was to find that, freed for the first time in his life from the protection of family responsibility, he'd become something less explicable and more original than—than Henry. But that was like expecting the woman next door, whom you suspect of cheating on her husband, to reveal herself to you as Emma Bovary, and, what's more, in Flaubert's French. People don't turn themselves over to writers as full-blown literary characters—generally they give you very little to go on and, after the impact of the initial impression, are barely any help at all. Most people (beginning with the novelist—himself, his family, just about everyone he knows) are absolutely unoriginal, and his job is to make them appear otherwise. It's not easy. If Henry was ever going to turn out to be interesting, I was going to have to do it.

There was another letter for me to write while the events of the last few days were fresh in my mind, and that was an answer to a letter from Shuki that had been hand-delivered to the hotel and was waiting for me at the desk when I'd checked out early that morning. I'd read it first in the taxi to the airport, and now, with the quiet and time to concentrate, I took it out of my briefcase to read again, remembering as I did those few Jews who had crossed my path in my seventy-two hours, how each had presented himself to me—and presented me to himself—and how each had presented the country. I hadn't seen anything really of what Israel was, but I had at least begun to get an idea of what it could be made *into* in the minds of a small number of its residents. I had come to this place more or less cold, to see what my brother was doing there, and what Shuki wanted me to understand was that I was leaving it cold as well—the sparks I'd seen flying at Agor might not mean all I thought. And it was more important than I may yet have realized for me not to be misled. Shuki was reminding me at forty-five—albeit as respectfully and gently as he could—of what I'd been told as a writer (first by my father, as a matter of fact) ever since I began publishing stories at twenty-three: the Jews aren't there for my amusement or for the entertainment of my readers, let alone for their own. I was being reminded to see through to the gravity of the situation before I let my comedy roam and made Jews conspicuous in the wrong way. I was being reminded that every word I write about Jews is potentially a weapon against us, a bomb in the arsenal of our enemies, and that, largely thanks to me, in fact, everyone is now prepared to listen to all kinds of zany, burlesque views of Jews that don't begin to reflect the reality by which we are threatened.

All I could think while slowly rereading Shuki's surprising letter is that there really is no eluding one's fate. I will never lack for those large taboos between whose jawlike pincers I've had to insert my kind of talent. "This rebuke," I thought, "will follow me to my grave. And who knows, if the fellows at the Wailing Wall are right, maybe even beyond."

Ramat Gan
Dec. 10, 1978

Dear Nathan,
I'm sitting at home worrying about you out at Agor. What worries me is that you too are going to become enamored of Mordecai Lippman. What worries me is that you are going to be misled by his vividness and take him to be a far more interesting character than he is. Vivid Jews, after all, haven't been absent from your fiction, nor would Lippman be our first delinquent to delight your imagination. One would have to be blind not to recognize the fascination for you of Jewish self-exaggeration and the hypnotic appeal of a Jew unrestrained, as opposed to your relative indifference as a novelist to our gentle, rational thinkers, our Jewish models of sweetness and light. The people you actually like and admire you find least fascinating, while everything cautious in your own typically ironic and tightly self-disciplined Jewish nature is disproportionately engaged by the spectacle of what morally repels you, of your antithesis, the unimpeded and excessive Jew whose life is anything but a guarded, defended masquerade of clever self-concealment and whose talent runs not toward dialectics like yours but to apocalypse. What worries me is that what you will see in Lippman and his cohorts is an irresistible Jewish circus, a great show, and that what is morally inspiring to one misguided Zuckerman boy will be richly entertaining to the other, a writer with a strong proclivity for exploring serious, even grave, sub-

jects through their comical possibilities. What makes you a normal Jew, Nathan, is how you are riveted by Jewish abnormality.

But if he proves so entertaining to you that you decide you must write about him, I ask you to keep in mind that (a) Lippman is not such an interesting character as a first impression may lead you to think—get half an inch beyond the tirade and he is a fairly uninteresting, if not to say asinine, crackpot, a one-dimensional, repetitious windbag, predictably devious, etc.; (b) Lippman alone is misleading, he is not the society, he is at the fringe of the society; to the outsider, diatribe is the hallmark of our society, and because he's the ultimate diatribalist, one of those here who must give you the whole ideology at one time *every time*, he may even strike you as the very embodiment of Israel. In fact he is a very peripheral paranoid, the most extreme, fanatical voice that this situation engenders, and though potentially he can do even more damage than a Senator Joseph McCarthy, we are talking about a similar kind of phenomenon, a psychopath alienated profoundly from the country's common sense and wholly marginal to its ordinary, everyday life (of which you will have seen nothing, by the way); (c) there is, in short, a little more to this country than what you hear out at Agor from Lippman, or even what you heard in Tel Aviv from me (another peripheral character—the peripheral crank, wasted down to his grievances); remember, if you take as your subject his diatribe—or mine—you will be playing with an argument for which people *die*. Young people do die here for what we are arguing about. My brother died for it, my son can die for it—and may yet—not to speak of other people's children. And they die because they are plugged into something which has a dimension far beyond Lippman's menacing antics.

This is not England, where a stranger can live forever and find out nothing. Even in a matter of hours you pick up vivid impressions in a country like this where everybody is airing his opinion all over the place and out in the open public policy is constantly and feverishly being debated—but don't be misled by them. What is at stake is serious business, and however tedious and unrelenting my disgust may be for much that's been going on here for years, however little I continue to adhere to my father's brand of Zionism, my tantrums are informed by an inescapable identification with Israel's struggle; I feel a certain responsibility to this country, a responsibility which is not inherent to your life, understandably, but is to mine. Disillusionment is a way of caring for one's country too. But what worries me isn't that you'll affront my national pride; it's that if and when you write about your visit to Agor, the average reader of Nathan Zuckerman is going to identify Israel with Lippman. No matter what you write, Lippman will come out stronger than anyone else, and the average reader will remember him better than anyone else and think he is Israel. Lippman is ugly, Lippman is extreme, equals Israel is ugly, the Israeli is extreme—this fanatical voice stands for the state. And this could do much harm.

I don't look upon danger as they do at Agor, but that doesn't mean there *is* no danger. Even if to my mind Agor is itself the greatest danger, there is still the danger from without that is no less real and could be far more horrendous. I don't say this rancorously—I don't accuse all of the Gentiles of being against us, which is the line they take in Lippman's cave, but we do have unrelenting detractors who despise us: you had dinner with some in London the other night, I was interviewed by another on the BBC, they work at newspapers in Fleet Street and all over Europe. You yourself may understand when face-to-face with Lippman that he is a lying, fanatical, right-wing son of a bitch perverting the humane principles on which this state was founded, but to them you would be presenting in Lippman the filthy heart of Zionism, the true face of the Jewish state that they relentlessly represent to the world as chauvinist, militant, aggressive, and power-mad. Moreover, they will be able to say a Jew wrote the bloody thing and he's telling the truth at last. Nathan, this *is* serious business: we have enemies with whom we are continually at war, and though we're much stronger than they are, we are not invincible. These wars in which our kids' lives are at stake are filling us with a sense of death all the time. We live like a person who is being pinpricked so much that it's not our life that's in danger but our sanity. Our sanity and our sons.

Before you sit down to entertain America with Lippman, take a minute to think about this—a vivid story, maybe too vivid, but I'm trying to make a point.

In 1973, had the Arabs attacked on Rosh Hashanah instead of Yom Kippur, we would really have been in a bad way. On Yom Kippur almost everybody is home. You don't drive, you don't travel anywhere, you don't go anywhere—many of us don't like it but still we stay home, it's the easiest way. And so when they attacked that day, even though our defenses were down—because of overconfidence and arrogance, and misreading the other side—when the alarm went out, everybody was home. All you had to do was say goodbye to your family. There was nobody on the roads, you could get to where you had to go, you could get the tanks out to the fronts, and everything was simple. Had they attacked a week earlier, if their Intelligence people had had the intelligence to tell them to strike on Rosh Hashanah, a holy day less solemnly observed, when at least half the country was someplace else—tens of thousands of people all over the Sinai, down in Sharm el Sheikh, people from the south up in Tiberias, and all with their families—had they attacked on that day, and everybody had to get the family home before they joined their unit, and the roads were full, people going in every direction, and the army couldn't get the big trailers with the tanks out to the front, then we would have been in real trouble. They would have run right in, and it would have been utter chaos. I'm not saying they would have conquered us, but we would have been knee-deep in blood, our homes destroyed, children attacked in their shelters—it would have been horrifying. I'm pointing this out to you not to make a case for the Israel's-survival-is-at-stake school of military thinking but to demonstrate that a lot of things are illusory.

Now the next point. Virtually everything we have right now, we have to get from abroad. I'm thinking of those things that, if we didn't have them, the Arab countries wouldn't tolerate us for a minute (and I include plutonium). What keeps them at bay doesn't come from our resources but from somebody else's pocket; as I complained to you the other day, mostly it comes from what Carter appropriates and what his Congress wants to go along with. What we have comes out of the pocket of the fellow from Kansas—part of each of his tax dollars goes to arm Jews. And why should he pay for the Jews? The other side is always trying to undermine us, to erode this support, and their argument is getting better all the time; just a little more help from Begin in the way of stupid policy, and they can indeed foster a situation in which the reluctance to keep shelling out is going to grow until finally nobody in the U.S. feels obligated to fork over three billion a year to keep a lot of Yids in guns. In order to keep doling out the dollars, that American has to believe that the Israeli is more or less the same as himself, the same decent sort of guy after the same sort of decent things. And that is not Mordecai Lippman. If Lippman and his followers are not the Jews they want to pay money for, I won't blame them. He may have a vivid enough point of view to enchant a satirical Jewish writer, but who from

Kansas needs to support that kind of stuff with his hard-earned dough?

By the way, you haven't met Lippman's Arab counterpart yet and been assaulted head-on by the wildness of *his* rhetoric. I'm sure that at Agor you will have heard Lippman talking about the Arabs and how we must rule them, but if you haven't heard the Arabs talk about ruling, if you haven't *seen* them ruling, then as a satirist you're in for an even bigger treat. Jewish ranting and bullshitting there is—but, however entertaining you may find Lippman's, the Arab ranting and bullshitting has a distinction all its own, and the characters spewing it are no less ugly. A week in Syria and you could write satires forever. Don't be misled by Lippman's odiousness—his Arab counterpart is as bad if not worse. Above all, don't mislead the guy in Kansas. It's too damn complicated for that.

I hope that you'll see not only the high comedy of what I'm saying but the gravity as well. The comedy is obvious: Shuki the Patriot and P.R. man—the call for Jewish solidarity, for Jewish responsibility, from your perverse old guide to Yarkon Street. So be it—I am a ridiculously twisted freak, as hopelessly torqued by the demands of this predicament as anybody else in our original history. But then that's a character even more up your alley. Write about an Israeli malcontent like me, politically impotent, morally torn apart, and weary to death of being angry with everyone. But be careful representing Lippman.

Shuki

P.S. I'm not unaware that you've been up against this sort of argument before from Jews in America. I myself always thought that you couldn't write that stuff unless you were more confident about the world you were describing than any of the people who were attacking you. American Jews are tremendously defensive—in a way being defensive *is* American Judaism. It's always seemed to me, from my Israeli perspective, that there's a kind of defensiveness there that's a civil religion. And yet here I am suddenly outdoing your most censorious critic. "How can you think of betraying us like this?" Here we go again. There are endangered Jews on the one hand, vulnerable through misrepresentation to the most dire consequences, and on the other hand there is the dangerous, potentially destructive Jewish writer poised to misrepresent and ruin everything; and that Jewish writer isn't any old Jewish writer, but, because you are inclined to be funny and ironical about things one is supposed to be *for* or *against*—

because, paradoxically, it is your *Jewish* gift to make things look ludicrous, laughable, or absurd, including, alas, even the Jew's vulnerable situation—he frequently turns out to be you. At the symposium here in 1960 you were condemned from the audience by a vociferous American-born Israeli citizen for being unforgivably blind in your fiction to the horror of Hitler's slaughter; nearly twenty years later you finally return only to be warned by me about the three billion dollars in American aid without which we here could find ourselves at a terrible disadvantage. First the six million, now the three billion —no, it *doesn't* end. Cautionary exhortation, political calculation, subliminal fear of a catastrophic outcome—all this Jewish *fraughtness* (if that is English) is something that your Gentile American contemporaries have never had to bother about. Well, that's their tough luck. In a society like yours, where eminent novelists are without serious social impact whatever the honors they accumulate and however much noise or money they make, it may even be exhilarating to find that the consequences of what *you* write are real, whether you like it or not.

Aloft/El Al
Dec. 11, 1978

Dear Shuki,

Stop calling me a normal Jew. There's no such animal, and why should there be? How could the upshot of that history be normalcy? I'm as abnormal as you are. I've just become in my middle years one of the more subtle forms that the abnormality takes. Which brings me to my point—it's entirely debatable as to whether in the halls of Congress it would be Lippman who would get them to scratching their heads over the three billion dollars, or whether it might not actually be you. It's Lippman, after all, who is the unequivocal patriot and devout believer, whose morality is plain and unambiguous, whose rhetoric is righteous and readily accessible, and to whom a nation's ideological agenda is hardly an object for sardonic scrutiny. Guys like Lippman are a great success in America, actually seem quite normal, are even sometimes elected President, whereas the guys like you that we've got are not regularly rewarded with congressional citations. As for the average taxpayer, he might not find a hypercritical, dissident journalist highly attuned to historical paradox and scathing in his judgment of the very country with which he remains deeply identified as sympathetic a figure as I do—nor is he at all likely to find him preferable to a Jewish General Patton whose monomaniac devotion to the narrowest nationalist cause may not be as alien to Kansas as you think. My writing about Shuki Elchanan instead of Mordecai Lippman is not going to do Israel any good in the Congress or among the voters, and you're unrealistic to think so. It may also be unrealistic to think that even if I were inspired to fictionalize Agor, my story, read by my congressman, would thereby alter Jewish history. Fortunately (or unfortunately) for Jewish history, Congress does not depend upon prose narrative to figure out how to divvy up the take; the conception of the world held by 99% of the population, in Congress *and* out, owes a lot more—

Here I noticed that the young man beside me had set his prayer book in his lap and was sitting half crumpled over, seemingly unable to take in enough air, and perspiring even more profusely than when I'd last looked at him. I thought that maybe he was suffering an epileptic seizure or having a heart attack, and so putting aside my answer to Shuki—my halfhearted defense against this crime I hadn't even yet committed—I leaned across and asked him, "You all right? Excuse me, but do you need help?"

"How ya' doin', Nathan?"

"Pardon?"

Pushing his hat brim an inch up from his face, he whispered, "I didn't want to disturb a genius at work."

"My God," I said, "it's you."

"Yeah, it's me all right."

The churning black eyes and the Jersey accent: it was Jimmy.

"Lustig from the West Orange Lustigs. Ben-Joseph," I said, "from the Diaspora Yeshivah."

"Formerly."

"You all right?"

"I'm under a little pressure at the moment," he confided.

He leaned across his briefcase. "Can you keep a secret?" And then whispered directly into my ear, "I'm going to hijack the plane."

"Yes? All on your own?"

"No, with you," he whispered. "You scare the shit out of them with the grenade, I take charge with the pistol."

"Why the get-up, Jim?"

"Because a yeshivah *bucher* they don't check out the same way." Taking my hand, he carried it across to his near coat pocket. Beneath the cloth I felt a hard oval object with a raised, ridged· surface.

Now how could that be? I'd never before seen security measures as thorough as those we'd had to submit to in order to board in Tel Aviv. First, all our luggage had been opened, one bag at a time, by plainclothes guards who were not shy about rummaging through every piece of dirty laundry. Then I was questioned at length by a brusque young woman about where I had been in Israel and where I was off to now, and when what I said seemed to have aroused her suspicion, she'd gone through my bag a second time before calling over a man with a walkie-talkie who interrogated me further and even less politely about the brevity of my stay and the places I'd been. They were so curious about my trip to Hebron and whom I had seen there that I was sorry I'd mentioned it. Only after I repeated for him what I'd told her about Henry and the ulpan at Agor—and explained again how I had got from Jerusalem to Agor and back—and only after the two of them had spoken together in Hebrew while I stood waiting in front of the open suitcase, whose contents had twice been turned upside down, was I allowed to close the bag and proceed the twenty feet to the counter where I was to check the bag directly onto the plane. My briefcase was inspected three times, by her first, a second time by a uniformed guard at the entrance to the departure area, and again as I was entering the lounge designated for the El Al London flight. Along with the other passengers, I was frisked from my armpits to my ankles and asked to pass through an electronic metal detector; and once inside the departure lounge, all the doors were sealed while we waited for the plane to begin loading. It was because of the time required for the meticulously thorough security check that passengers were requested to show up at Tel Aviv airport two hours before the plane's scheduled departure.

Whatever was in Jimmy's pocket had to be a toy. Probably what I'd felt there was some kind of souvenir—a rock, a ball, maybe a piece of folk art. It could have been anything.

"We're in this together, Nathan."

"Are we?"

"Don't be afraid—it won't hurt your image. If there's no hitch and we hit the headlines, it'll be the regeneration of the Jews, and a great shot in the arm to your Jewish standing. People will see how much you really care. It'll turn world opinion completely around on the subject of Israel. Here."

He took a paper out of his pants pocket, unfolded it, and handed me a page raggedly torn from a composition book and covered with words scrawled with a ballpoint pen just about out of ink. Jimmy indicated to me that I should keep the page in my lap while I read it.

FORGET REMEMBERING!

I demand of the Israeli government the immediate closing and dismantling of Yad Vashem, Jerusalem's Museum and Remembrance Hall of the Holocaust. I demand this in the name of the Jewish future. THE JEWISH FUTURE IS NOW. We must put persecution behind us forever. Never must we utter the name "Nazi" again, but instead strike it from our memory forever. No longer are we a people with an agonizing wound and a hideous scar. We have wandered nearly forty years in the wilderness of our great grief. Now is the time to stop paying tribute to that monster's memory with our Halls of Remembrance! Henceforth and forever his name shall cease to be associated with the unscarred and unscarable Land of Israel!

ISRAEL NEEDS NO HITLERS FOR THE RIGHT TO BE
ISRAEL!
JEWS NEED NO NAZIS TO BE THE REMARKABLE
JEWISH PEOPLE!
ZIONISM WITHOUT AUSCHWITZ!
JUDAISM WITHOUT VICTIMS!
THE PAST IS PAST! WE LIVE!

"The statement for the press," he said, "once we're on German soil."

"You know," I said, handing it back to him, "the security people riding these planes probably haven't got a great sense of humor. You could wind up in trouble screwing around like this. They could be anywhere, and they're armed. Why don't you can it?"

"What happens to me doesn't *matter*, Nathan. How can I care about myself when I have penetrated to the core of *the last Jewish problem*? We are torturing ourselves with memories! With masochism! And torturing goyisch mankind! The key to Israel's survival is no more Yad Vashems! No more Remembrance Halls of the Holocaust! Now what we have to suffer *is the loss of our suffering*! Otherwise, Nathan—and here is my prophecy as written in the Five Books of Jimmy—otherwise they will annihilate the State of Israel *in order to annihilate its Jewish conscience*! We have reminded them enough, we have reminded *ourselves* enough—*we must forget*!"

He was no longer whispering, and it was *I* who had to tell *him*, "Not so loud, please." Then I said, very clearly, "I really don't want anything to do with this."

"Israel is their prosecutor, the Jew is their judge! In his heart every goy knows—because every goy in his heart is a little Eichmann. This is why in the papers, at the U.N., everywhere, they all rush to make Israel the villain. This is now the club they use on the Jews—you the prosecutor, you the judge, *you* shall be judged, judged in every infraction to the millionth degree! This is the hatred that we keep alive by commemorating their crime at Yad Vashem. Dismantle Yad Vashem! No more masochism to make Jews crazy—no more sadism to stoke goy hate! Only then, *then*, are we free to run wild with the impunity of everybody else! Free to be as gloriously guilty as they are!"

"Calm down, for Christ's sake. Where'd you get the idea to dress up like this?"

"From none other than Menachem Begin!"

"Yes? You're in touch with Begin too?"

"I wish I could be. If I could only get it into *his* head—

Menachem, Menachem, no more *remembering*! No, I only emulate the great Menachem—this is how he hid from the British in his terrorist days. Disguised as a rabbi in a synagogue! The outfit I got from him, and the big idea itself I owe to you! Forget! Forget! Forget! Every idea I ever had, I got from reading your books!"

I had decided it was about time to change my seat again, when Jimmy, having glanced out the window—as though to see if we were rolling into Times Square—took hold of my arm and announced, "On German soil we abandon the Holocaust! Land in Munich and leave the nightmare where it began! Jews without a Holocaust will be Jews without enemies! Jews who are not judges will be Jews who are not judged—Jews left alone at long last to *live*! Ten minutes more and we rewrite our future! Five more minutes and the Jewish people are saved!"

"You're going to save them on your own—I'm moving to another seat. And my recommendation to you, my friend, is that when we land you get yourself some help."

"Oh, is it really?" He opened the briefcase from which he'd been taking his candy bars and dropped the prayer book inside. He didn't, however, extract his hand. "You ain't going anywhere. Finger's on the trigger, Nathan. That's all the help I need."

"Enough, Jim. You're over the top."

"When I tell you take the grenade, you do just that—*only* that. Very covertly, out of my pocket and into yours. You step into the aisle, nonchalant you walk to where first class begins, I show my pistol, you take out the grenade, and then we both of us start to shout, 'No more Jewish suffering! An end to Jewish victims!'"

"Just Jewish clowning from here on out—making a plaything of history."

"*Undoing* history. Thirty seconds."

I sat quietly back thinking it was best to humor him until the performance was over and *then* to change my seat. Recalling the wording of his "press release," I thought there was obviously a brain there, even some thought; on the other hand, I couldn't quite believe that there was some principle connecting his transformation of the Wailing Wall into deep center field at Jerusalem Giants Stadium with this fervent petition for the demolition of the Jerusalem memorial to the Holocaust. The powerful emotional impulses in this boy to desanctify the holiest shrines of Jewish sorrow—to create a museum of his own that says "Forget!"—finally didn't strike me as having evolved from anything coherent. No, these weren't symbolic acts of cultural iconoclasm challenging the hold on the Jewish heart of its gravest memories so much as a manic excursion into meaningless Dadaism by a wandering, homeless yeshivah yippie, a one-man band high on grass (and his own adrenaline), a character a little like one of those young Americans the Europeans can't believe in, who without the backing of any government, on behalf of no political order old or new, energized instead by comic-book scenarios cooked up in horny solitude, assassinate pop stars and presidents. World War III will be triggered off not by suppressed nationalists seeking political independence, as happened the first time around when the Serbs at Sarajevo shot the heir to the Austrian throne, but by some semiliterate, whacked-out "loner" like Jimmy who lobs a rocket into a nuclear arsenal in order to impress Brooke Shields.

To pass the time I looked around at our neighbors, some of whom had been looking disapprovingly at us. In the aisle beside me, a fellow who must have been a businessman, prosperously dressed in a tan homburg and a pale beige suit with a double-breasted vest and wearing lightly tinted glasses, was leaning over to talk to a bearded young fellow who had been reading his prayer book in the middle row of seats. He wore the long black coat of the pious Jew but had on underneath it a heavy wool sweater and a pair of corduroy pants. In English the businessman was saying to him, "I can't take the jet lag anymore. When I was your age . . ." I had vaguely been expecting to overhear some religious disputation. Both men earlier had been praying in the minyan.

After waiting several more minutes, I finally said to Jimmy, who was now sitting silently, at last out of gas, "What went wrong at the yeshivah?"

"You've got balls, Nathan," and he showed me, in the hand that he withdrew from the briefcase, yet another candy bar. He ripped open the wrapper and offered me a bite before tearing in himself to replenish his energy. "I really had you goin' there. I really had you on the ropes."

"What are you doing dressed like this on the plane? Running away? You in trouble?"

"No, no, no—just following you, if you want the truth. I want to meet your wife. I want you to help me to find a girl like her. The hell with Rabbi Greenspan. I want something old English like Maria."

"How do you know Maria's name?"

"The whole civilized world knows her name. The Virgin Mother of Our Savior. What red-blooded Jewboy could resist? Nathan, I want to live in Christendom and become an aristocrat."

"And what's the rabbi bit about?"

"You guessed it. You would. My Jewish sense of fun. The irrepressible Jewish joker. Laughs are the core of my faith—like yours. All I know about cracking offensive jokes I learned at your great feet."

"Sure. Including this stuff about Yad Vashem."

"Come on, you think I'd be crazy enough to fuck around with the Holocaust? I was just curious, that was all. See what you'd do. How it developed. *You* know. The novelist in me."

"And Israel? Your love of Israel? At the Wailing Wall you told me you were there for life."

"I thought I was till I met you. You changed everything. I want a shiksa just like the shiksa that married dear old Z. Teddibly British. Do like you do—the Yiddische disappearing act with the archgoy, the white priestess. Teach me how, will ya? You're a real father to me, Nathan. And not only to me—to a whole generation of pathetic fuck-ups. We're all satirists *because* of you. You led the fucking way. I went around Israel feeling like your son. That's how I go through *life*. Help me out, Nathan. In England I'm always saying 'sir' to the wrong person—I get my signals mixed. I get nervous there that I'm looking even more ridiculous than I am. I mean the background

173

is so neutral, and we speak the same language, or we think we do, that I wonder if there we don't stand out even more. I always think of England as one of those places where every Jew's shadow has an enormous hooked nose, though I know a lot of American Jews have this fantasy that it's a Wasp paradise where they can just sneak in, passing themselves off as Yanks. Sure, no Jew exists *anywhere* without his shadow, but there it's always seemed to me worse. Isn't it? Can I, Nathan, just ease myself in with the British upper claahhses and wash away the Jewish stain?" Leaning over, he whispered to me, "You really got the inside track on how not to be a Jew. You shed it all. You're about as Jewish as the *National Geographic*."

"You were made for the stage, Jim—a real ham."

"I *was* an actor. I told you. At Lafayette. But the stage, no, the stage inhibited me. Couldn't project. *Without* the stage, that's what I love. Who should I look up in England?"

"Anyone but me."

He liked that. The candy bar had calmed him down and he was laughing now, laughing and mopping his face with his hankie. "But you're my idol. It's you who inspire me to my feats of masterful improvisation. Everything I am I owe to you and Menachem. You're the greatest father figures I ever had in my life. You're two fucking Jews who will say *anything*—Diaspora Abbott and Israeli Costello. They ought to book you boys into the Borscht Belt. I got some bad news from the States, Nathan, some really shitty news from home. You know what happened when the social worker phoned my family long-distance? My old man answered and she told him what had happened and that he would have to wire fare to Jerusalem so I could come home. You know what my old man told her? They ought to book him into the Borscht Belt too. He said, 'It's better if James stays.'"

"What did happen to make him so sanguine about you?"

"I gave my big lecture on the kosher laws to the tourists inside King David's Tomb. Impromptu. 'The Cheeseburger and the Jew.' Rabbi Greenspan didn't like it. Where do I stay in London? With you and Lady Zuckerman?"

"Try the Ritz."

"How do you spell it? I really had Nathan Zuckerman goin', didn't I? Wow. For a few minutes there you really thought, 'Some Jewish pothead from suburban West Orange has got nothing to do better than hijack an El Al 747. As if Israel doesn't have enough troubles with Arafat and that shmatta on his head, now they got Jimmy and his hand grenade.' I know your generous heart. When you thought about the worldwide headlines, you must have felt really sick to your stomach for your fellow Jews."

"What *is* that in your pocket?"

"Oh, that?" He reached in absently to show me. "It's a hand grenade."

The last time I'd seen a live hand grenade was when I'd been taught to throw one in basic training at Fort Dix in August 1954. What Jimmy was holding up looked like the real thing.

"See?" Jimmy said. "The famous pin. Makes people shit-scared, this pin. Pull this pin and everything's just about over on ill-fated Flight 315 from Tel Aviv to London. You really *didn't* believe me, did you? Gee, that's a disappointment. Here, shmuck, I'll show you something else you didn't believe."

It was the pistol, Henry's first-act pistol. This then must be the third act in which it is fired. "Forget Remembering" is the title of the play and the assassin is the self-appointed son who learned all he knows at my great feet. Farce is the genre, climaxing in blood.

But before Jimmy had even drawn the gun half out of his briefcase, someone came leaping up over the back of his seat and had hold of his head. Then from out in the aisle a body hurled across mine—it was the businessman in the tinted glasses and the sharp beige suit who tore from Jimmy's hand the pistol and the hand grenade. Whoever had come upon Jimmy from behind had nearly put him out. Blood was pouring from his nose and he lay tipped over in his seat, his head fallen lifelessly against the side of the plane. Then a hand came down from behind and I heard the thud of an appalling body blow. Jimmy began to vomit just as I, to my astonishment, was lifted bodily from where I sat and a pair of handcuffs snapped around my wrists. As they dragged me up the aisle, people were standing on the seats and some were screaming, "Kill him!"

The three first-class passengers were cleared out of their seats and Jimmy and I were dragged into the empty cabin by the two security guards. After being roughly frisked and having my pockets emptied, I was gagged and slammed into an aisle seat, and then Jimmy was stripped and his clothes torn apart to be searched. Viciously they pulled off his beard, as though they hoped it were real and coming out by the roots. Then they doubled him over a seat, and the man in the beige suit snapped on a plastic glove and drove a finger up his ass, investigating, I suppose, for explosives. When they were sure that he'd been carrying no other weapons, that he wasn't wired up in any way or carrying some hidden device, they dropped him into the seat next to me, where he was handcuffed and shackled. I was then yanked to my feet, able barely to control my terror by thinking that if they believed me to be in any way involved, they would have badly disabled me already. I told myself, "They're simply taking no chances"—though, on the other hand, maybe the sharp kick in the balls was about to come.

The man in the beige suit and the tinted glasses said, "You know what the Russians did last month with a couple of guys who were trying to hijack an Aleutian plane? Two Arabs they were, going out of somewhere in the Middle East. The Russians don't give a shit about Arabs, you know, no more than about anybody else. They emptied the first class," he said, gesturing around the cabin, "took the boys in there, tied towels around their necks, slit their throats, and landed them dead." His accent was American, which I hoped might help.

"My name is Nathan Zuckerman," I said when the gag had been removed, but he gave no sign of absolution. If anything, I'd inspired still more contempt. "I'm an American writer. It's all in my passport."

"Lie to me and I slit you open."

"I understand that," I replied.

His bright, sporty clothes, the tinted glasses, the tough-guy American English all suggested to me an old-time Broadway con artist. The man didn't move, he darted; he didn't speak, he assaulted; and in the highly freckled skin and thinning orangey hair I half sensed something illusionary, as though perhaps he was wigged and completely made-up and underneath was a colorless albino. I was under the impression that it was all a performance and nonetheless was terrified out of my wits.

His bearded sidekick was large and dark and sullen, a very frightening type who didn't speak at all, and so I could not tell if he was American-born too. He was the one who had broken Jimmy's nose and then struck the hammer-blow to his body. Earlier, when we were all still passengers in the economy-class cabin, he'd been wearing the long black coat over the corduroy trousers and heavy wool sweater. He was rid of the coat now and standing a little gigantically directly over me, poring through my notebook. Despite everything to which I was being crudely and needlessly subjected, I was nonetheless grateful to the two of them for how we'd all been saved—in something like fifteen seconds, these brutes had broken up a hijacking and saved hundreds of lives.

The one who'd been about to blow us all up seemed to have less to be thankful for. From the look of the plastic glove lying in the aisle beside the false beard, Jimmy was bleeding not only from the face but internally because of that body blow. I wondered if they intended to land before we got to London in order to get him to a hospital. It didn't occur to me that under instructions from Israeli Security, the plane had circled round and was returning to Tel Aviv.

I was not spared the rectal investigation, though during the eternity that I was made to bend over, handcuffed and totally undefended, nothing that I was dreading happened. Staring into space through my watery eyes, I saw our clothes strewn all over the cabin, my tan suit, Jimmy's black one, his hat, my shoes—and then the gloved finger was withdrawn and I was thrown back into the seat, wearing only my socks.

The silent sidekick took my billfold and my notebook up to the cockpit, and the Broadway hustler removed what looked like a jewelry case from his inside pocket, a long black velvet case which he then laid unopened atop the seat back in front of me. Beside me Jimmy wasn't yet comatose but he wasn't completely alive either. The fabric on which he was sitting was stained with his blood and his smell made me gag. His face by now was badly distorted by the swelling and half of it had turned blue.

"We're going to ask you to give an account of yourself," the Broadway hustler said to me. "An account that we can believe."

"I can do that. I'm on your side."

"Oh, are you? Isn't that nice. How many more of you boys we got on board today?"

"I don't think there's anyone. I don't think he's a terrorist— he's just psychotic."

"But you were with him. So what are you?"

"My name is Nathan Zuckerman. I'm an American, a writer. I was in Israel visiting my brother. Henry Zuckerman. Hanoch. He's at an ulpan in the West Bank."

"The West *what*? If that's the West Bank, where's the East Bank? Why do you speak in Arab political nomenclature about a 'West Bank'?"

"I don't. I was visiting my brother and now I'm going back to London, where I live."

"Why do you live in London? London is like fucking Cairo. In the hotels the Arabs shit in the swimming pools. Why do you live there?"

"I'm married to an English woman."

"I thought you were American."

"I am. I'm a writer. I wrote a book called *Carnovsky*. I'm quite well known, if that's any help."

"If you're so well known, why are you so thick with a psychotic? Give me an account of yourself that I can *believe*. What were you doing with him?"

"I met him once before. I met him in Jerusalem at the Wailing Wall. Coincidentally he turned up on this plane."

"Who helped him get the hardware on board?"

"Not me. Listen—it wasn't me!"

"Then why did you change your seat to be next to him? Why were you talking together so much?"

"He told me he was going to hijack the plane. He showed me the statement for the press. He said he had a grenade and a gun and that he wanted me to help. I thought he was just a crackpot until he held up the grenade. He'd disguised himself as a rabbi. I thought the whole thing was an act. I was wrong."

"You're awfully cool, Nathan."

"I assure you, I'm properly terrified. I don't like this at all. I do know, however, that I have nothing to do with it. Absolutely nothing." I suggested to him then that in order to verify my identity they radio Tel Aviv and have Tel Aviv contact my brother at Agor.

"What's Agor?"

"A settlement," I said, "in Judea."

"Now it's Judea, before it was the West Bank. You think I'm an asshole?"

"Please—contact them. It'll settle everything."

"You settle it for me, fella—who are you?"

This went on for at least an hour: who are you, who is he, what did you talk about, where's he been, why were you in Israel, do you want to get your throat slit, who did you meet, why do you live with the Arabs in London, how many of you bastards are on board today?

When the other security man came back from the cockpit, he was carrying an attaché case out of which he took a hypodermic. At the sight of that I lost control and began shouting, "Check me out! Radio London! Radio Washington! Everybody will tell you who I am!"

"But we know who you are," the hustler said, just as the syringe slid into Jimmy's thigh. "The author. Calm down. You're the author of this," he said, and showed me "FORGET REMEMBERING!"

"I am *not* the author of that! *He* is! I couldn't begin to write that crap! This has nothing to do with what I write!"

"But these are your ideas."

"In no conceivable *way* are those my ideas. He's latched onto me the way he's latched onto Israel—with his fucking craziness! I write fiction!"

Here he touched Jimmy on the shoulder. "Wake up, sweetheart, get up—" and gently shook him until Jimmy opened his eyes.

"Don't hit me," he whimpered.

"Hit you?" said the hustler. "Look around, moron. You're flying first class. We upgraded your ticket."

When Jimmy's head fell my way, he realized for the first time that I was there too. "Poppa," he said weakly.

"Speak up, Jim," the hustler said. "Is this your old man?"

"I was only having fun," Jimmy said.

"With your dad here?" the hustler asked him.

"I am not his father!" I protested. "I have no children!"

But by now Jimmy had begun weeping in earnest. "Nathan said—said to me, 'Take this,' so I did, took it on board. He *is* a father to me—that's *why* I did it."

Quietly as I could, I said, "I am no such thing."

Here the hustler lifted the black velvet case from the seat back in front of me. "See this, Jim? It's what they gave me when I graduated antiterrorist school. A beautiful old Jewish artifact that they award to the first in the class." The reverence with which he opened the box was almost wholly unsatiric. Inside was a knife, a slender amber handle about five inches long ending in a fine steel blade curved like a thumb. "Comes from old Galicia, Jim, a ghetto remnant that's survived the cruel ages. Just like you, me, and Nathan. What they used back then to make little Jews out of our newborn boys. In recognition of his steady hand and his steely nerves, the prize for our class valedictorian. Our best *mohels* today are trained killers—it works out better for us this way. What if we loan this to your dad and see if he's got it in him to make the big biblical sacrifice?"

Jimmy screamed as the hustler sliced the air into bits just above his head.

"Cold steel up against the nuts," he said, "oldest polygraph known to man."

"*I take it back!*"

"Take what back?"

"Everything!"

"Good," the hustler said quietly. He placed the antique scalpel in its velvet case, and laid it carefully atop the seat should it be necessary to show it to Jimmy again. "I'm a very simple guy, Jim, basically uneducated. Worked in gasoline stations in Cleveland before I made aliyah. I never belonged to the country-club set. Shined windows and greased cars and fixed tires. I got the rim off the tire and that kind of stuff. A grease monkey, a garage man. I am a very crude guy with an underdeveloped intellect but a very strong and irrepressible id. You know what that is, you heard of that, the strong and irrepressible id? I don't even bother like Begin to point the accusing finger to justify what I do. *I just do it.* I say, 'That's what I want, I'm entitled,' and I *act*. You wouldn't want to be the first hijacker whose dick I made a souvenir because he handed me a load of shit."

"No!" he howled.

He took Jimmy's press statement out of his pants pocket again and after glancing over it, reading some of it, he said, "Shut down the Holocaust Museum because it upsets the goyim? You really believe that or are you just trying to have a little more fun, Jim? You really think they dislike Jews because the Jew is *judge*? Is that all that's been bothering them? Jim, that's not a hard question—answer me. The hard question is how anybody boarding at Tel Aviv could bring on board with him all this hardware. We're going to swing you by the ears to get the answer to that one, but that's not what I'm asking right now. We're not just going to work on your little pecker, we're going to work on your eyeballs, we're going to work on your gums and your knees, we're going to work you all over the secret parts of your body to get the answer to that, but now all I'm asking, for my own edification, for the education of a Cleveland grease monkey with a strong and irrepressible id, is if these are really things you honestly believe. Don't get tongue-tied—the rough stuff's later, in the lavatory, you and me squeezed up in there, alone with the secret parts of your body. This is just curiosity now. This is me at my most refined. I'll tell you what I think, Jim—I think this is another of those self-delusions you Jews have, thinking you are some kind of judge to them. Isn't that right, Nathan—that you high-minded Jews have serious self-delusions?"

"I would think so," I said.

He smiled benignly. "I do too, Nate. Oh, sure, you may find the occasional masochist Gentile who has meek little thoughts about morally superior Jews, but basically, Jim, I must tell you, they don't really see it that way. Most of them, confronted with the Holocaust, don't really give a shit. We don't have to shut down Yad Vashem to help them forget—they forgot. Frankly, I don't think the Gentiles feel quite as bad about this whole business as you, me, and Nathan would like them to. I think frankly that what they mostly think is not that we are their judge but that we get too much of the cake—we're there too often, we don't stop, and we get too goddamn much of the cake. You put yourselves in the hands of the Jews, with this conspiracy they've got all over the place, and you're finished. That's what they think. The Jewish conspiracy isn't a conspiracy of judges—it's a conspiracy of Begins! He's arrogant, he's ugly, he is uncompromising—he talks in such a way as to shut your mouth all the time. He's Satan. Satan shuts your mouth. Satan won't let the good out, everybody's a Billy Budd, and then there's this guy Begin, who's shutting your mouth all the time and won't even let you *talk*. Because *he's* got the answer! You couldn't ask for anybody who better epitomizes the Jewish duplicity than this Menachem Begin. He's a master of it. He tells the goyim how bad they are, so *he* can turn and be bad! You think it's the Jewish superego they hate? *They hate the Jewish id*! What right do these Jews have to *have* an id? The Holocaust should have taught them never to have an id *again*. That's what got them into trouble in the first place! You think because of the Holocaust they think we're better? I hate to tell you, Jim, but the most they think on that score is that maybe the Germans went a little too far—they think, 'Even if they were Jews, they weren't as bad as all *that*.' The fellows who say to you, 'I expect more of the Jew,' don't believe them. *They expect less*. What they're saying really is,

'Okay, we know you're a bunch of ravenous bastards, and given half the chance you'd eat up half the world, let alone poor Palestine. We know all these things about you, and so we're going to get you now. And how? Every time you make a move, we're going to say, "But we expect *more* of Jews, Jews are supposed to behave *better*." ' Jews are supposed to behave better? After all that's happened? Being only a thick-headed grease monkey, I would have thought that it was the *non-Jews* whose behavior could stand a little improvement. Why are *we* the only people who belong to this wonderful exclusive moral club that's behaving badly? But the truth is that they never thought we were so good, you know, even before we had a Holocaust. Is that what T. S. Eliot thought? I won't even mention Hitler. It didn't just start in Hitler's little brain. Who's the guy in T. S. Eliot's poem, the little Jew with the cigar? Tell us, Nathan —if you wrote a book, if you're 'quite well known' and 'properly terrified,' you ought to be able to answer that one. Who's the little Jew with a cigar in T. S. Eliot's wonderful poem?"

"Bleistein," I said.

"Bleistein! What brilliant poetry that T. S. Eliot came up with! Bleistein—great! T. S. Eliot had higher expectations for Jews, Jim? No! *Lower!* That was what was in the air *all the time*: the Jew with a cigar, stepping on everybody all the time and chomping his Jew lips on an expensive cigar! What they hate? Not the Jewish superego, dummy—not, 'Don't do that, it's wrong!' No, they hate the Jewish *id*, saying 'I want it! I take it,' saying 'I suck away on a fat cigar and just like you I transgress!' Ah, but you *cannot* transgress—you are a Jew and a Jew is supposed to be *better*! But you know what I tell them about being better? I say, 'A bit late for that, don't you think? You put Jewish babies into furnaces, you bashed their heads against the rocks, you threw them like shit into ditches—and the *Jew* is supposed to be better?' What is it they want to know, Jim —how long are these Jews going to go wailing on about their little Holocaust? How long are *they* going to go on about their fucking Crucifixion! Ask T. S. Eliot *that*. This didn't happen to one poor little saint two thousand years ago—*this happened to six million living people only the other day!* Bleistein with a cigar! Oh, Nathan," he said, looking with kindly humor down upon me, "if only we had T. S. Eliot on board today. I'd teach him about cigars. And you'd help, wouldn't you? Wouldn't you, a literary figure like yourself, help me educate the great poet about Jewish cigars?"

"If necessary," I said.

"Study current events, Jim," the hustler told him, satisfied with my tractability and returning to his in-flight educational program for the misguided author of "FORGET REMEMBERING!" "Up to the year 1967 the Jew didn't bother them that much down in his little homeland. Up till then it was all these strange Arabs wanting to wipe away little Israel that everybody had been so magnanimous about. They'd given the Jews this little thing you could hardly find on the map—out of the goodness of their hearts, a little real estate to assuage their guilt—and everybody wanted to destroy it. Everybody thought they were poor helpless shnooks and had to be supported, and that was just fine. The weak little shnook Jew was fine, the Jewish hick with his tractor and his short pants, who could he trick, who could he screw? But suddenly, these duplicitous Jews, these sneaky Jewish fuckers, defeat their three worst enemies, wallop the shit out of them in six fucking days, take over the entire this and the whole of that, and what a shock! Who the hell have they been *kidding* for eighteen years? We were worried about *them*? We were feeling magnanimous about *them*? Oh, my God, they tricked us again! They told us they were weak! We gave them a fucking state! And here they are as powerful as all hell! Trampling over everything! And meanwhile back home, the shnook Jewish general was feeling his oats. The Jewish shnook general was saying to himself, 'Well, now the goyim will accept us because now they see we're as strong as they are.' ONLY THE OPPOSITE WAS TRUE—JUST THE FUCKING OPPOSITE! Because all over the world they said, 'Of course—it's the same old Jew!' *The Jew who is too strong! Who tricks you! Who gets too much of the pie!* He's organized, he takes advantage, he's arrogant, he doesn't respect anything, he's all over the goddamn place, connections *everywhere*. And that's what the whole world cannot forgive, cannot abide, never would, never will—Bleistein! A powerful Jew with a Jewish id, smoking his big fat cigar! *Real Jewish might!*"

But the foe of the Jewish superego was totally out of it now and looked more than likely to be bleeding to death, despite the shot they'd given him. Consequently, as the steep descent into Israel began, it was I alone, returning to the Promised Land with all my clothing peeled away and shackled to God's bird, the El Al plane, who was being lectured on the universal loathing of the Jewish id, and the goy's half-hidden, justifiable fear of wild, belated Jewish justice.

4. Gloucestershire

A YEAR AFTER being put on the drugs, still alive and feeling fit, no longer plagued by cartoon visions of male erections and ejaculations, when I have begun to contain the loss by forcing myself to understand that this is not the worst deprivation, not at my age and after my experience, just as I've begun to accept the only real wisdom—to live without what I no longer have—a temptress appears to test to the utmost this tenuous "adjustment." If for Henry there's Wendy, who is there for me? As I haven't had to endure his marriage or suffer his late sexual start, a vampire-seductress won't really do to lure me to destruction. It can't be for more of what I've tasted that I risk my life, but for what's unknown, a temptation by which I've never before been engulfed, a yearning mysteriously kindled by the wound itself. If the uxorious husband and devoted paterfamilias dies for clandestine erotic fervor, then I shall turn the moral tables: I die for family life, for fatherhood.

I'm over the worst of my fear and bewilderment, able again to engage men and women in ordinary social conversation without thinking bitterly all the while how unfit I am for sexual contention, when into the duplex at the top of the brownstone moves just the woman to do me in. She's twenty-seven, younger than I am by seventeen years. There is a husband and a child. Since the child's birth over a year ago, the husband has grown estranged from his pretty wife and the hours they used to pass in bed they now spend in acrimonious discussion. "The first months after I'd had the baby he was monstrous. So cold. He would come in and ask, 'Where's the baby?' I didn't exist. It's odd that I can't keep his attention any longer, but I can't. I feel quite lonely. My husband, when he even deigns to speak, tells me it's the human condition." "When I found you," I say to her, "you were hanging ripe, ready for plucking." "No," she replies, "I was already on the ground, rotting at the foot of the tree."

She speaks in the most mesmeric tones, and it's the voice that does the seducing, it's the voice that I have to caress me, the voice of the body I can't possess. A tall, charming, physically inaccessible Maria, with curling dark hair, a smallish oval face, elongated dark eyes, and those caressing tones, those gently inflected English ups and downs, a shy Maria who seems to me beautiful but considers herself "at best a near-miss," a Maria I love more each time we meet to speak, until at last the end is ordained and I go to meet my brother's fate. And whether in the service of flagrant unreality, who will ever know?

"Your beauty is dazzling." "No," she says. "It's dazzled me." "It can't, really." "It does." "I don't have admirers anymore, you know." "How can that be?" I ask. "Must you believe that all your women are beautiful?" "You are." "No, no. You're just overwrought." Even more fencing when I tell her I love her. "Stop saying that," she says. "Why?" "It's too alarming. And probably it's not true." "You think I'm deliberately deceiving you?" "It's not me you've deceived. I think you're lonely. I think you're unhappy. You're not in love. You're desperate and want a miracle to happen." "And you?" I say. "Don't ask questions like that." "Why won't you ever call me by my name?" I ask. "Because," she says, "I talk in my sleep." "What are you doing with me?" I ask her, "—would you prefer not to have to come here?" " 'Have to'? I don't have to. I'll carry on as I have." "But you didn't expect after the rush I gave you, for things to develop like this. Right now we should be in a torrid embrace." "There are no shoulds. I expect things to go in all kinds of ways. They usually do. I don't have job-lot expectations." "Well, you have the right expectations at twenty-seven and I have the wrong ones at forty-four. I *want* you." I have only my shirt off while she lies enticingly unclothed on the bed. When the nanny takes the child out in the stroller, and Maria comes down in the elevator to see me, this is the scene that I sometimes ask her to play. I tell my temptress that her breasts are beautiful, and she replies, "You're flattering me again. They were all right before the baby, but no, not now." Invariably she asks if I really want to be doing this, and invariably I don't know. It's true that bringing her to a climax while dressed in my trousers doesn't much alleviate my longing—better than nothing on some afternoons, but on others far worse. The fact is that though we may sneak around the brownstone like a pair of sex criminals, most of our time is passed in my study, where I light a fire and we sit and talk. We drink coffee, we listen to music, and we talk. We never stop talking. How many hundreds of hours of talk will it take to inure us to what's missing? I expose myself to her voice as though it were her body, draining from it my every drop of sensual satisfaction. There's to be no exquisite pleasure here that cannot be derived from words. My carnality is now *really* a fiction and, revenge of revenge, language and only language must provide the means for the release of everything. Maria's voice, her talking tongue, is the sole erotic implement. The one-sidedness of our affair is excruciating.

I say, like Henry, "This is the most difficult thing that I've ever had to face," and she answers, like the hardhearted cardiologist, "You haven't had a difficult life then, have you?" "All I mean," I reply, "is that this is a damn shame."

One Saturday afternoon she comes to visit with the child. Maria's young English nanny, with the weekend off, has gone to see the sights in Washington, D.C., and her husband, the British ambassador's political aide at the U.N., is away at his office finishing a report. "A bit of a bully," she says; "he likes all sorts of people around and a lot of noise." She married him straight from Oxford. "Why so soon?" I ask. "I told you—he's a bit of a bully, and as you may discover, since your powers of observation are not underdeveloped, I am somewhat pliant." "Docile, you mean?" "Let's say adaptable. Docility is frowned upon in women these days. Let's say I have a vital, vigorous gift for forthright submission."

Clever, pretty, charming, young, married most unhappily— and a gift for submission as well. Everything is perfect. She will never utter the no that will save my life. Now bring on the child and close the trap.

Phoebe wears a little knitted wool dress over her diaper and, with her large dark eyes, her tiny oval face, and curling dark hair, looks like Maria exactly. For the first few minutes she is content to lean over the coffee table and quietly draw with crayons in her coloring book. I give her the house keys to play with. "Keys," she says, shaking them at her mother. She comes over, sits in my lap, and identifies for me the animals in her storybook. We give her a cookie to keep her quiet when we want to talk, but wandering alone around the apartment, she loses it. Every time she goes to touch something, she looks first to see if it's permitted by me. "She has a very strict nanny," Maria explains; "there's nothing much I can do about it." "The nanny is strict," I say, "the husband a bit of a bully, and you are somewhat pliant, in the sense of adaptable." "But the baby, as you see, is very happy. Do you know Tolstoy's story," she says, "called, I think, 'Married Love'? After the bliss of the first years wears off, a young wife takes to falling in love with other men, more glamorous to her than her husband, and nearly ruins everything. Only just before it's too late, she sees the wisdom of staying married to him and raising her baby."

I go off to the study, Phoebe running behind me and calling, "Keys." I climb the library ladder to find my collection of Tolstoy's short fiction while the little girl wanders into the bedroom. When I step down from the ladder, I see, inside the room, that she is lying on my bed. I pick her up and carry her and the book to the front of the apartment.

The story Maria remembered as "Married Love" is in fact entitled "Family Happiness." Side by side on the sofa we read the final paragraphs together, while Phoebe, on her knees, crayoning a bit of floorboard, proceeds to fill her diaper. At first, seeing Maria's face flush, I think it's because of popping up and down so often to check on where the child is—then I realize that I've successfully transmitted to her my own inflammatory thoughts.

"You may have a taste for perpetual crisis," she says. "I don't."

I reply softly, as though if Phoebe overheard she'd somehow understand and become frightened for her future. "You've got it wrong. I want to put an end to the crisis."

"If you hadn't met me perhaps you could forget it and lead a quieter life."

"But I have met you."

The Tolstoy story concludes like this:

"It's time for tea, though!" he said, and we went together into the drawing-room. At the door we met again the nurse and Vanya. I took the baby into my arms, covered his bare red little toes, hugged him to me and kissed him, just touching him with my lips. He moved his little hand with outspread wrinkled fingers, as though in his sleep, and opened vague eyes, as though seeking or recalling something. Suddenly those little eyes rested on me, a spark of intelligence flashed in them, the full pouting lips began to work, and parted in a smile. "Mine, mine, mine!" I thought, with a blissful tension in all my limbs, pressing him to my bosom, and with an effort restraining myself from hurting him.

And I began kissing his little cold feet, his little stomach, his hand and his little head, scarcely covered with soft hair. My husband came up to me; I quickly covered the child's face and uncovered it again.

"Ivan Sergeitch!" said my husband, chucking him under the chin. But quickly I hid Ivan Sergeitch again. No one but I was to look at him for long. I glanced at my husband, his eyes laughed as he watched me, and for the first time for a long while it was easy and sweet to me to look into them.

With that day ended my love-story with my husband, the old feeling became a precious memory never to return; but the new feeling of love for my children and the father of my children laid the foundation of another life, happy in quite a different way, which I am still living up to the present moment.

When it's time to give the child her bath, Maria goes around the apartment collecting the toys and the coloring books. Back in the living room, standing beside my chair, she puts her hand on my shoulder. That's all. Phoebe doesn't seem to notice when, furtively, I kiss her mother's fingers. I say, "You could bathe her here." She smiles. "Intelligent people," she says, "mustn't go too far with their games." "What's so special about intelligent people?" I ask, "—in these situations it doesn't really help anything." Outside the door each throws a kiss goodbye—the child first, then, following her example, the mother—and they step into the elevator and go back upstairs, my *deus ex machina* reascending. Inside my apartment I smell the child's stool in the air and see the small handprints on the glass top of the coffee table. The effect of all this is to make me feel incredibly naïve. I want what I've never had as a man, starting with family happiness. And why now? What magic do I expect out of fatherhood? Am I not making of fatherhood a kind of fantasy? How can I be forty-four and *believe* such things?

In bed at night, when the real difficulties begin, I say out loud, "I know all about it! Leave me alone!" I find Phoebe's cookie under my pillow and at 3 a.m. I eat it.

Maria raises all the questions herself the next day, taking up for me the role of challenger. If I wind up enjoying the persistence with which she won't permit me to be swept away, it's because her unillusioned candor is just another argument in my favor—the direct, undupable mind only charms me more. If only I could find this woman just a bit less appealing, I might not wind up dead.

"You cannot risk your life for a delusion," she says. "I cannot leave my husband. I can't deprive my child of her father, and I can't deprive him of her. There's this terrible factor which I guess you don't understand too clearly and that's my daughter. I do try not to think about her interests but I can't help it from time to time. I wouldn't have believed it, but apparently you're another of those Americans who imagine they have only to make a change and the calamity will be over. Everything will always turn out all right. But it's my experience that things don't—all right for a while maybe, but everything has its duration, and in the end things generally don't turn out well at all. Your own marriages seem to have a shelf life of about six or seven years. It wouldn't be any different married to me, if I even wanted to do it. You know something? You wouldn't like it when I was pregnant. It happened to me last time. Pregnant women are taboo."

"Nonsense."

"That's my experience. And probably not only mine. The passion would die out, one way or another. Passion is notorious for its shelf life too. You don't want children. You had three chances and turned them all down. Three fine women and each time you said no. You're really not a good bet, you know."

"Who is? The husband upstairs?"

"*Are* you sensible? I'm not sure. It's a little crazy to spend your life writing."

"It is. But I no longer want to spend it just writing. There was a time when everything seemed subordinate to making up stories. When I was younger I thought it was a disgrace for a writer to care about anything else. Well, since then I've come to admire conventional life much more and wouldn't mind getting besmirched by a little. As it is, I feel I've practically written myself *out* of life."

"And now you want to write yourself back in? I don't believe any of this. You have a defiant intelligence: you like turning resistance to your own advantage. Opposition determines your direction. You would probably never have written those books about Jews if Jews hadn't insisted on telling you not to. You only want a child now because you can't."

"I can only assure you that I believe I want a child for reasons no more perverse than anyone else's."

"Why pick on me for this experiment?"

"Because I love you."

"That terrible word again. You 'loved' your wives before you married them. What makes this any different? And it needn't be me you 'love' of course. I'm terribly conventional and I'm flattered, but, you know, there might well be someone else with you right now."

"Who would she be? Tell me about her."

"She'd be rather like me, probably. My age. My marriage. My child."

"She'd *be* you then."

"No, you're not following my faultless logic. She'd be just like me, performing my function, but she wouldn't be me."

"But maybe you *are* she, since you're so very like her."

"Why *am* I here? Answer that. You can't. Intellectually I'm not your style and I'm certainly not a bohemian. Oh, I tried the Left Bank. At university I used to go with people who walked around with issues of *Tel Quel* under their arms. I know all that rubbish. You can't even read it. Between the Left Bank and the green lawns, I chose the green lawns. I'd think, 'Do I have to hear this French nonsense?' and eventually I'd just go away. Sexually too I'm rather shy, you know—a very predictable product of a polite, genteel upbringing among the landless gentry. I've never done anything lewd in my life. As for base desires, I seem never to have had one. I'm not greatly talented. If I were cruel enough to wait until the wedding to show you what I've published, you'd rue the day you made this proposal. I'm a hackette. I write fluent clichés and fluffy ephemera for silly magazines. The short stories I try writing are about all the wrong things. I want to write about my childhood, that's how original I am—about the mists, the meadows, the decaying gentlefolk I grew up with. If you seriously want to risk your life to vulgarly marry yet another woman, if you really want a child to drive you crazy for the next twenty years—and after all that solitude and silent work, you would be driven quite mad—you really ought to find somebody more appropriate. Somebody befitting a man like you. We can have a friendship, but if you're going to go on with these domestic fantasies, and think of me that way, then I can't come down here to see you. It's too hard on you and almost as hard on me. I get childishly disorientated hearing that stuff. Look, I'm unsuitable."

I am in the easy chair in the living room, and she is sitting facing me, straddling my knees. "Tell me something," I ask, "do you ever say fuck?"

"Yes, I say it quite a lot, I'm afraid. My husband does too, in our marital discussions. But not down here."

"Why not?"

"I'm on my best behavior when I come to see an intellectual."

"A mistake. Maria, I'm too old to have to find somebody suitable. I adore you."

"You can't. You can't possibly. If anything, it's the illness I've captivated, not you."

" 'And as for my long sickness, do I not owe it indescribably more than I owe my health?' "

"I would have thought you were more hardheaded," she says. "Those portraits you paint of the men in those books didn't prepare me for this."

"My books aren't intended as a character reference. I'm not looking for a job."

"There's quite an age gap between us," she says.

"Nice, isn't it?"

She agrees, inclining her head to acknowledge that yes, it is indeed, and that our affinity is just about all she could ask for. Though you'd think a man who has been himself a husband on three occasions might know the answer, I cannot understand, when I see her like that, looking so wooable and so content, how to the husband upstairs practically nothing she does is right. As far as I can tell there's nothing she can do that's wrong. What I can't figure out is why every man in the *world* hasn't found her as enchanting as I do. That is how undefended I am.

"I had a very bumpy ride last night," she says. "A terrible scene. Howls of rage and disappointment."

"About what?"

"You continually ask questions and I keep answering them. That's really out of bounds. It feels like such a betrayal of him. I shouldn't tell you all of this because I know you're not to be trusted. *Are* you writing a book?"

"Yes, it's all for a book, even the disease."

"I half believe that. You're not, at any rate, to write about me. Notes are okay, because I know I can't stop you taking notes. But you're not to go all the way."

"Would that really bother you?"

"Yes. Because this is our *private* life."

"And this is a very boring subject about which, over these many years, I have already heard too much from too many people."

"It's not so boring if you happen to be on the wrong end of it. It's not so boring if you find your private life spread all over somebody's potboiler. 'Twere profanation of our joys to tell the laity our love.' Donne."

"I'll change your name."

"Terrific."

"No one would know it was you anyway, except me."

"You don't know what people will recognize. You *won't* write about me, will you?"

"I can't write 'about' anyone. Even when I try it comes out someone else."

"I doubt that."

"It's true. It's one of my limitations."

"I haven't begun to list all of mine. You have an easily excited imagination—you ought to take a moment and ask yourself if you're not inventing a woman who doesn't exist, making me somebody else already. Just as you want to make *this* something else. Things don't have to reach a peak. They can just go on. You *do* want to make a narrative out of it, with progress and momentum and dramatic peaks and then a resolution. You seem to see life as having a beginning, a middle, an ending, all of them linked together with something bearing your name. But it isn't necessary to give things a shape. You can yield to them too. No goals—just letting things take their own course. You must begin to see it as it is: there are insoluble problems in life, and this is one. As for me, I'm just the housewife who moved in upstairs. You'd be risking too much for far too little. There's much that's missing in me."

"You've been underappreciated so long upstairs that that's all you can think about. But as a matter of fact you're looking very expensive today. You have a very expensive face and long, expensive limbs and the voice is positively sumptuous. You look very well, you know; much better than when I met you."

"That's because I'm happier than when I met you. I would never have pulled myself together if I hadn't met you. It did a lot for me. To put it in reductive country English, it cheered me up. You too, I think. You look eighteen."

"Eighteen? That's very sweet of you."

"Like a bright boy."

"You're trembling."

"I'm frightened. Happier but very frightened. My husband's going away."

"Is he? When?"

"Tomorrow."

"You should have told me. You English do keep things to yourself. How many years is he going away for?"

"He's only going away for two weeks."

"Can you get rid of the nanny?"

"I've already seen to it."

We play house for two weeks. Every night we eat dinner upstairs after the baby has gone to sleep. She tells me about her parents' divorce. I see girlhood snapshots of her in Gloucestershire, a middle child, fatherless, all bones and dark braids, clinging to the jeans of two sisters. I see the desk where she sits when she phones each morning minutes after her husband has left for work. On the desk is a framed Polaroid shot of them at university, a seemingly solemn young man, towering even over her and wearing round wire-rimmed sixties spectacles. That recently they were at college, and thinking that, I feel entirely shut out. "Laid-back establishment," she says, when I hold up the photo and ask about his background; "the difficulty is that in worldly terms, you see, it's quite a suitable marriage." In the elevator, when he and I happen to meet, we each pass ourselves off as men without mood or passion. Large-boned and ruddy-complexioned, at thirty successful, vigorous, and on his way, he gives no outward sign, other than his size, of being a bit of a bully who likes all sorts of people around and a lot of noise—he presents to me only his Etonian opacity, and I pretend that I've never met his wife. If this were Restoration drama the audience would be in stitches, since it's the husband, after all, who is cuckolding the impotent paramour.

After she has drunk lots of wine at dinner, she is less inclined to be so doggedly sensible, though I still find myself thinking that the husband who is known to throw the dishes when crossed and then not to speak to her for days at a time is still more appropriate and satisfactory a mate than I, unable to enact my love. There are insoluble problems in life and this is one.

"I never had a Jewish boyfriend before. Or have I said that?"

"No."

"At university I did have a protracted meeting of mouths with a Nigerian Marxist, but it was only mouths that met. He was the same year as me. The boyfriends I had in darkest Gloucestershire were all sort of landed-gentry types and absolutely thick. You tell me when you have to go—I'm drunk."

"I don't have to go." Yet I should, must—she seduces me with every word into risking my life.

"There wasn't just repressiveness in my background, you know—there was an extraordinary mixture of that *and* freedom."

"Yes? Freedom emanating from what?"

"The freedom emanated from the horse. Because you could go long distances with all sorts at any time of the day, and you met a lot of people that way. If I'd actually been remotely sexually aware, which I wasn't, I could have just been screwing all the time from the age of twelve on. It would have been no problem. Not many really did but an awful lot of people spent an awful lot of time getting quite close."

"But not you."

Wryly, sadly: "No, never me. Would you like to look at one of my stories? It's about people messing about in the English mud, and dogs, and it's full of hunting slang, and there's no reason why it should mean anything to anyone born in the twentieth century. Do you really want to see it?"

"Yes. Though don't expect a brilliant reading. At college I

gave up on Victorian literature because I could never figure out the difference between a vicar and a rector."

"I shouldn't show you this," she says. "Remember, I don't really aspire to newness of perception," and hands me the typescript. The story begins, *Hunting people swear like fury, their language is quite blue. When I was a child people used to hunt sidesaddle* . . .

As I finish the last page, she says, "I told you we'd heard it all before."

"Not from you."

"If you don't like it you're free to say so."

"The fact is that you're a much better writer than I am."

"Oh, nonsense."

"You're much more fluent than I am."

"That," she replies, mildly indignant, "has *nothing* to do with it. There are plenty of literate people who can write fluent, good English. No, this isn't anything really. It's embarrassingly beside the point. It's just that the combination of this extraordinary nineteenth-century carry-on and the way they swore outrageously . . . well, that's it. I'm afraid that's all. There is fiction that is fired noisily into the air, wildly into the crowd, and there is the fiction that misfires, explosives that fail to ignite, and there is fiction that turns out to be aimed into the skull of the writer himself. Mine's none of those. I don't write with ferocious energy. Nobody could ever use what I write as a club. Mine is fiction displaying all the English virtues of tact, good sense, irony, and restraint—*fatally* retrograde. It all comes very naturally, unfortunately. Even if I found the nerve to 'tell all' and write about you, you'd just come out as a rather pleasant chap. I should sign these stories 'By a throwback.' "

"And what if you are?"

"Not very suitable for you."

Two days before her husband is to return:

"I had a dream last night," she says.

"What about?"

"Well, it's difficult to explain the geography of the place I was in. A shipyard, something like that, the open sea, a harbor. I don't know the terms for those places, but I've seen them. The open sea is on my left, and then there are all those jetties and wharves and landings and things. It's actually a harbor, yes. I was swimming from one jetty to another one, which was some distance away. I was fully dressed. I had a bundle under my coat, a baby—it wasn't my daughter, it was another child, I don't know who it was. I was swimming toward this other jetty. I was escaping from something. There were all these boys jumping up and down, gesticulating on the far jetty. They were encouraging me— 'Come on, come on!' Then they started directing me to turn right. And when I looked right, and started to swim toward the right, there was, on the right-hand side, another inlet, water, which was a little tiny boatyard. And it was under a great big— like a railway station, a great big roof. They were suggesting that I should get a boat and, instead of swimming, I could row. Out to sea, of course. They were all gesticulating and shouting at me, 'Judea! Judea!' But when I got there and was about to take a boat—and there were several moored up, you know, tied together —and I was still half in the water—I realized that my husband was there, in charge of the boats, and waiting to take me home. And he had a green tweed suit on. That was the dream."

"Does he own a green tweed suit?"

"No. Of course not."

" 'Of course not'? Why, isn't that 'done'?"

"No. Sorry. I mean 'of course not' in private terms. But green and tweed represent all kinds of *blatantly* obvious English things. The whole dream is so grotesquely obvious, Freud needn't have bothered. Anybody could understand that dream—couldn't they? It's childishly simple."

"Simple how?"

"Well, green, straightaway, as soon as you wake up, you know that green means country, lots of trees and countryside—green means Gloucestershire. Gloucestershire is the land where the grass couldn't be greener. And tweed means something the same, but with the air of formality and—well, one wears tweeds, one has a tweed suit as a woman because one is grown-up and conventional. I don't go in for that myself, but the point is that tweeds arise from the country, they take the colors from the countryside, the heather and the stones, and even when they're beautiful they make of them something terribly repressive, with a slight hint of snobbishness. That's what tweeds are used for anyway—they're 'frightfully English' and," she said, laughing, "I don't like it."

"And the boatyard?"

"Boatyards, railway stations. Points of departure."

"And Judea?" I ask. "The preferred English term is West Bank."

"I wasn't reading headlines. I was asleep."

"And whose baby was it, Maria, under your coat?"

Shyly: "No idea. It didn't feature."

"It's the one we're going to have."

"Is it?" she asks helplessly. "It's a sad dream, isn't it?"

"And getting sadder."

"Yes." Then she bursts out, "It drives me absolutely wild that he cannot appreciate what is under his nose unless I start behaving like a prima donna. It just makes me feel so terribly cross that you get put through all this for nothing, really. It's just heartbreaking that if you're nice to people, if you're reasonable, if you're modest, they tread all over you. It just drives me absolutely insane. Don't you think it's a cruel thing that all the virtues that we've been brought up with are nothing, absolutely nothing, in marriage, at work, everywhere? It was the same at the magazine in London. What a load of bullies there are in the world! I find it absolutely outrageous." Then, characteristically: "Never mind. I shouldn't really simplify like that. The frenzy I get into invariably disperses, and I slide into my usual Slough of Despond. I really don't know why, but it goes and I lose the impetus to move."

"Judea, Judea."

"Yes. Isn't that strange?"

"The Promised Land versus the Green Tweed Suit."

The night before her husband comes back I conduct an investigation lasting to dawn. The transcript here, heavily abridged, omits to mention those demi-intimacies that disrupted the questioning, and the attendant despair that's transformed everything.

I imagine that the more I ask her, the less likely I will be to make a terrible mistake, as though misfortune can be contained by *knowing*.

"Why do you stay in this?" I begin. "With me in this condition."

"Do you think that women only stay in relationships for sex? It usually comes to be the last thing. Why do I stay? Because you're intelligent, because you're kind, because you seem to love me (to use the terrible word), because you tell me I'm beautiful, whether I am or not—because you're an escape. Of course I'd like to have the other as well, but we don't."

"How frustrated are you?"

"It's frustrating . . . but not dangerous."

"What do you mean by that? It's under control?"

"Yes, yes, I do. I mean that without the physical commitment somehow a woman like me feels stronger. I suppose most women feel stronger once they think they've got you physically addicted to them. But that's when I begin to feel most vulnerable. This way I still in a way have the upper hand. I have the control and the choice. Or feel I have. It's even *I* that am refusing *you* marriage. It *is* frustrating, but it gives me a power that in an ordinary relationship I would never have, because you'd have power over me. I find it somehow exciting. You want me to be candid, I am."

"He still sleeps with you, your husband."

"I take back what I said about candor. This is the point where I retire into polite discretion."

"You can't. How often? Not at all, infrequently, sometimes, or often."

"Often."

"Very often?"

"Very often."

"Nightly?"

"Not quite. But nearly."

201

"You fight over everything, you don't speak for days, he throws the crockery, and yet he wants you that much."

"I don't know what that much is."

"I mean all this cruelty obviously turns him on. I mean his sexual enthusiasm, if nothing else, appears to be undiminished."

"He's very highly sexed. He'd happily boff me all day and all night. He doesn't particularly want me for anything more."

"Do you get satisfaction yourself?"

"It's all complicated by my being so furious and resentful. We go to bed negotiating all sorts of degrees of hostility. In any case, it's very impersonal. As though it isn't happening. He never thinks of me."

"Why don't you tell him no then?"

"I don't want that kind of trouble. Sexual tension like that is all we need to make it completely impossible to live together."

"So you remain sexually available to a very nasty man."

"You could put it that way if you like."

"And still you see me every afternoon. Why do you continue to show up?"

"Because I wouldn't be anywhere else. Because I'm welcome. Because if I don't see you I miss you. Up here it's cold and we're always fighting and jarring each other's nerves. Either we're saying rather polite, friendly, icy things to each other, which each finds rather dull, and secretly thinking about someone else or something else, or we're not saying anything, or we're fighting. But when I come downstairs, I come into a lovely room with books and the fireplace and the music and the coffee and your affection. Who wouldn't go there, if they're given that? I don't think you give that to everybody, but you give it to me. I think that for *you* it's a vast frustration that you don't have the other as well and so I wish you had it. But for me it's almost enough."

"But if everything were all right up here, you wouldn't be down there."

"That goes without saying. We would have been acquaintances in the lift, that's all. There's always something wrong, otherwise why should one want to create such complications?"

"Do you have erotic fantasies about me?"

"Yes, I do, but I probably would have more had we had sex. As it is, I push them away. Because they would make me edgy and dissatisfied."

"Is what we have at all exciting for you?"

"I told you—I think it's unusual and strange. When I lie on the bed naked, when you touch me—some women are deeply satisfied by that."

"Are you?"

"Not always. Look, you're not a hopelessly unattractive man. We've had a few quite interesting conversations during the course of our acquaintance, we've talked so much, but I'm sure all this talk is quite secondary—one's sexual perceptions are still the most important thing about someone, however things may turn out. Even if we never get to bed together, there's some essential sexual tension that we've had. Whether at the moment you're able to fuck or not is not the point. Virility hasn't only to do with that. You're very different from my husband, which is really the background I've always wanted to get away from anyway."

"If that's true, why did you marry him?"

"Well, we were young and he looked very manly. I'm very tall—well, he's even taller. He was so big physically—I equated that with masculinity. I've refined my ideas since, but then it was something I knew nothing about. We were three sisters and my father had left. How would you know what a man is, if you've never seen a grown one in action? I thought that this was the masculine force. He was my monument to the Unknown Man. He had that kind of athletic exterior, and he was very funny, very clever, and once we both had jobs in London, he *wanted* marriage so much. I don't think I'd have married so early if I had any sense that the world had a place for me. This was a time when marriage was right out, everybody was living together, but I was just so damn frightened, I thought it was sensible to get married. I've got over so many fears, and am so much less frightened now that it's really hard to recognize myself. But at nineteen and twenty I was pathologically frightened—ever since my father had walked out, I had felt my life on this huge, huge slide.

You think I'm 'sweet,' but, really, it's only the worst kind of weakness. I didn't find it easy to make friends. I had masses and masses of acquaintances and an awful lot of admirers then, but there were very few people I could express my real feelings to. That was not so stupid because everybody I knew was completely hung up on idiotic jargon in that period. People were just carried away with a wave of sixties sentiment that turned their brains to custard. They were very intolerant. If you dared to question some piety or dogma, they would give you a monstrous time that could reduce you to tears. Not that I would cry, but I was frightened of expressing anything I really felt intellectually. It seems to me so awful in retrospect—perfectly ghastly. And my husband was somebody who reacted very like me. He was extremely clever, he came from the same kind of background. Everybody else we knew, they were either philistines or intellectuals. If they were intellectuals they came from lower social backgrounds and they gave us hell for it. You cannot imagine the persecution. I was supposed to be privileged. If I had any guts I would have told them, 'Do *you* have a father? Does he have a job? Are you going to be given any money this summer?' But then, even though they were rich and I was poor, because of my accent they would patronize me in the most awful way. So it was such a relief to find somebody who was intellectually very bright, and engaged with interesting things, and entertaining. Who's still entertaining when he wants to talk. And he came from my background, so there was no need to apologize. He had enormous charm and style and taste, and loved all kinds of things that I did, so it was a really tempting refuge. And I shouldn't have taken it. But sexually it was wonderful, and socially it was very suitable because it took all of that awful sixties heat off of everything, all this business about privileged-underprivileged, dropping your accents and all that crap. He was a refuge, a real one—and just so damn suitable. He's my age, my contemporary in every way, where you're a different race, a different generation, a different nationality—but he's not even a brother to me any longer. You're more of a brother—*and* a lover, really. He's not a friend. You're the adventure now and he's the known."

"Judea, Judea."

"I told you it was an obvious dream."

"But you're going to stay with him."

"Oh yes. All that's happened has been a classic tale that happens to a lot of women. I suited his needs, he suited mine—and after x years it's ceased to be true. We have done a lot of damage to each other, and I've become withdrawn and resentful and no fun, but divorce is still to be avoided. Divorce is a disaster. I'm not neurotic but I *am* fragile. The best thing is just to give up trying and give up fighting and go back to the real old-fashioned stuff. Separate bedrooms, a pleasant 'Good morning,' and you don't cross him—you're as nice as you can be. Every man's dream is as follows: she is fantastically good-looking, she does not age, she's fun and lively and interesting, but above all, *she doesn't give a fellow a hard time.* I may be able to get by on that."

"But you are only twenty-seven. Don't you think I'd be kind to your child?"

"I do. But I think if you had this operation for me and a family and all those dreams, you'd be putting such a weight on our relationship that nothing could ever, ever live up to your expectations. Particularly me."

"But a year after, the operation would be forgotten and we'd be just like everybody else. You think I won't want you any longer then?"

"That's possible. More than likely. Who knows?"

"Why won't I?"

"Because it *is* a dream. I don't know, I can't see into a man's mind, but it is a dream, I know: everything will be made right, and the right woman is waiting. No, things don't ever pan out like that. I don't want you to have that operation for me."

"But I am."

"No, you're not. You're having it, if you have it, for you, for your own masculinity, for your life. But to make all of it contingent on whether I will marry you or not, whether you can fuck me or not—that's putting a weight on me *and* fucking that I don't think either could bear. I wasn't brought up to take chances. I wish I were more independent, but I can sort of see

205

why I'm not. My whole experience growing up was clinging, clinging, clinging. This is what happens when you grow up as an intelligent child with only a mother. Careful, careful, careful—that was the message. It's unjust to put all this on me. Nobody, I don't think, in *history* has been asked to make a decision like this. Why can't we just go on as we are?" .

"Because I want to have a child with you."

"I think maybe you ought to go and speak to a psychiatrist."

"Everything I'm saying is perfectly reasonable."

"You're *not* reasonable. Because you *don't* have an operation that could kill you unless there's no choice. I have this vision sometimes when I wake up at night of you on the altar and the priest plunging this—is it obsidian, what did the Aztecs use, is that the word?—into your breast and tearing out your heart, for me and family happiness. It's one thing to say you lose your heart to somebody but another actually to do it."

"So what you're suggesting is that we just continue like this."

"Absolutely. I'm rather enjoying it."

"But you'll go away someday, Maria. Your husband will be made boy ambassador to Senegal. What then?"

"If he's posted to Senegal I'll put the child in school and say I can't join him. I'll stay here. That I promise you, if you promise not to have the operation."

"And what if he's called back to England? What if he goes into politics? That's bound to happen sometime."

"Then you'll come to England too, take a flat, and write your books there. What difference does it make where you are?"

"And we carry on this odd triangle forever."

"Well, until medical science bails us out."

"And you think I'll like that. Each day you leave me and go back to him, and every night, not because he particularly likes you but because he's so powerfully oversexed, he comes home from the House of Commons and fucks you. How do you think I'll like that all by myself in my London flat?"

"I don't know. Not much."

The next day, like the best of wives, she goes out to the airport to pick him up, and I go to the cardiologist to tell him my decision. There is nothing bizarre about my goals. This is the choice not of a desperate adulterer crazed by a drastic sexual blow, but of a rational man drawn to an eminently sane woman with whom he plans to lead a calm, conventionally placid, conventionally satisfying life. And yet I feel in the taxi as though I've become a child, given myself up to the whole innocent side of my being, and just when circumstances demand a ruthless coming to terms with my impairment. I have taken a fresh romance, with all those charming pleasures that anyone even half my age understands to be evanescent, and turned it into my *salto mortale*. To be doing this for an insane passion might actually begin to make some sense, but because I've been hopelessly charmed by the quiet virtues that she shares with her fiction is hardly sufficient reason to be taking such a chance. Can I really have been overcome by the wistful tones of the landless gentry? Is what's there so powerfully enticing, or *is* her allurement my disease's invention? Who is she anyway but, by her own description, the unhappy housewife who's moved in upstairs, continually cautioning me how unsuitable she is? Had we met and had a heated affair back before my illness, chances are we would never have had to do all this talking and it would more than likely be over now, another adultery safely contained by the ordinary impediments. Why suddenly do I want so passionately to become a father? Is it entirely unlikely that far from the latent paterfamilias coming to the fore, it's the feminized part of me, exacerbated by the impotence, that's produced this belated yearning for a baby of my own? I just don't know! What is driving me on toward fatherhood, despite the enormous danger it poses to my life? Suppose all I have fallen in love with is that voice deliciously phrasing its English sentences? The man who died for the soothing sound of a finely calibrated relative clause.

I tell the cardiologist that I want to marry and have a child. I understand the risks, but I want the operation. *If I can have this wonderfully bruised, supercivilized woman, I can be recovered from my affliction fully.* A truly mythological pursuit!

Maria is beside herself. "You may not feel this way about me once you're well. Nor will I hold you to it. Nor can I hold myself to it. Nor do I want to do it."

"It wouldn't have been strange a hundred years ago, our being both in love and chaste, but by now the farce is even more intolerable than the frustration. We can't see anything about anything without the operation first."

"It's too rash a thing to be doing! There's too much uncertainty about everything! *You can die*."

"People make decisions like this every day. If you seriously want to renew your life, there's no way around taking a serious risk. A time comes when you just have to forget what frightens you most. Besides, it'll be a rash thing to do no matter how long I wait. Someday it'll be done anyway—out of necessity. All I gain by waiting is the strong probability of losing you. I *will* lose you. Without a sexual bond these things don't last."

"Oh, this *is* awful. An ordinary afternoon soap opera and we've magnified it into *Tristan and Isolde*! *That's* the farce. It's all become so hopelessly tender just because we *don't* make love—because everything is always trembling just on this edge we can't cross over. This endless talk that never reaches a climax has caused two supremely rational people to entertain the most irrational fantasy until finally it's come to seem absurdly *tangible*. The paradox is that we've so overexamined this dream that we've lost sight of the fact that *it's an utterly irresponsible illusion*. This disease has distorted *everything*!"

"When it's gone, my disease, we can, if you like, conduct a very thorough investigation of our feelings. We can overexamine *those*, and if it *has* been nothing more than some overheated verbal infatuation—"

"Oh, no—no! I couldn't let you go ahead if everything were to dissolve when the worst is over. I will. I'll do it. I'll marry you."

"Now my name. *Say it*."

At last she submits. There is the climax to all our talk—Maria speaking my name. I have hammered and hammered—at her scruples, at her fears, at her sense of duty, at her thralldom to husband, background, child—and finally Maria gives in. The rest is up to me. Caught up entirely in what has come to feel like a purely mythic endeavor, a defiant, dreamlike quest for the self-emancipating act, possessed by an intractable idea of how my existence is to be fulfilled, I now must move beyond the words to the concrete violence of surgery.

So long as Nathan was alive, Henry couldn't write anything unself-consciously, not even a letter to a friend. His book reports back in grade school had been composed with no more difficulty than anyone else's, and in college he'd got through English with B's and had even done a brief stint as a sports reporter with the student weekly before settling into a predental program, but when Nathan began publishing those stories that hardly went unnoticed, and after them the books, it was as though Henry had been condemned to silence. There are few younger brothers, Henry thought, who had to put up with that too. But then all the blood relatives of an articulate artist are in a very strange bind, not only because they find that they are "material," but because their own material is always articulated for them by someone else who, in his voracious, voyeuristic using-up of all their lives, gets there first but doesn't always get it right.

Whenever he sat down to read one of the dutifully inscribed books that used to arrive in the mail just before publication, Henry would immediately begin to sketch in his head a kind of counterbook to redeem from distortion the lives that were recognizably, to him, Nathan's starting point—reading Nathan's books always exhausted him, as though he were having a very long argument with someone who wouldn't go away. Strictly speaking there could be no distortion or falsification in a work not intended as journalism or history, nor could you charge with incorrect representation writing under no obligation to represent its sources "correctly." Henry understood all that. His argument wasn't with the imaginative nature of fiction or the license taken by novelists with actual persons and events—it was with the imagination unmistakably his brother's, the comic hyperbole insidiously undermining everything it chose to touch. It was just this sort of underhanded attack, deviously legitimizing itself as "literature," and directed most injuriously at their parents in the caricatured Carnovskys, that had led to their long estrangement. When their mother succumbed to a brain tumor only a year after the death of their father, Henry was no less willing than Nathan to let the break become final, and they had never seen each other or spoken again. Nathan had died without even telling Henry that he had a heart problem or was going in for surgery, and then, unfortunately, Nathan's eulogist praised just those exploitative aspects of *Carnovsky* that Henry had never been able to forgive and wanted least to hear about at a time like this.

He had come over to New York by himself, ready and eager to be a mourner, and then had to sit there listening to that book described as, of all things, "a classic of irresponsible exaggeration," as though irresponsibility, in the right literary form, were a virtuous achievement and the selfish, heedless disregard for another's privacy were a mark of courage. "Nathan was not too noble," the mourners were told, "to exploit the home." And not overly sympathetic, you can be sure, for the home that had been exploited. "Plundering his own history like a thief," Nathan had become a hero to his serious literary friends, if not necessarily to those who'd been robbed.

The eulogist, Nathan's young editor, spoke charmingly, without a trace of sadness, almost as though he were preparing to present the corpse in the casket with a large check rather than to usher it on to the crematorium. Henry had expected praise, but, naïvely perhaps, not in that vein or so remorselessly on that subject. Focusing entirely on *Carnovsky*, the eulogy seemed deliberately to be mocking their rift. The thing that drove our family apart, thought Henry, is here being enshrined—that was *designed* to destroy our family, no matter how much they say about "art." Here they all sit, thinking, "Wasn't it brave of Nathan, wasn't it daring to be so madly aggressive and undress and vandalize a Jewish family in public," but none of them, for that "daring," had to pay a goddamn dime. All their pieties about saying the unsayable! Well, you ought to see your old parents down in Florida dealing with their bewilderment, with their friends, with their memories—they paid all right, they lost a *son* to the unsayable! I lost a *brother*! Somebody paid dearly for his saying the unsayable and it wasn't that effete boy making that pretentious speech, it was *me*. The bond, the intimacy, all we'd had during childhood, lost because of that fucking book and then the fucking fight. Who needed it? Why *did* we fight—what was *that* all about? You give my brother to this over-educated dandy, this boy who knows everything and nothing, whose literary talk makes so neat and clean what cost my family so much, and now just *listen* to him—memorializing the mess right out of existence!

The person speaking should have been Henry himself. *He* by all rights should have been the intimate of his brother to whom everyone was listening. Who was closer? But the night before, when he'd been asked on the phone by the publisher if he'd speak at the funeral, he knew he couldn't, knew he would never be able to find the words to make all those happy memories—of the father-and-son softball games, of the two of them skating on the Weequahic Park lake, of those summers with the folks down at the shore—mean anything to anyone other than himself. He spent two hours trying to write at his desk, remembering all the while the big, inspiring older brother he'd trailed behind as a child, the truly heroic figure Nathan had been until at sixteen he'd gone off to college to become remote and critical; yet all he was able to put down on his pad was "1933–1978." It was as though Nathan were still alive, rendering him speechless.

Henry wasn't speaking the eulogy because Henry didn't have the words, and the reason he didn't have the words wasn't because he was stupid or uneducated but because if he had chosen to contend, he would have been obliterated; he who wasn't at all inarticulate, with his patients, with his wife, with his friends —certainly not with his mistresses—certainly not in his *mind*—had taken on, within the family, the role of the boy good with his hands, good at sports, decent, reliable, easy to get along with, while Nathan had got the monopoly on words, and the power and prestige that went with it. In every family somebody has to do it—you can't *all* line up to turn on Dad and clobber him to death—and so Henry had become loyal Defender of Father, while Nathan had turned into the family assassin, murdering their parents under the guise of art.

How he wished, listening to that eulogy, that he was a person who could just jump up and shout, "Lies! All lies! That is what drove us *apart*!," the kind of person who could seize the moment and, standing on his feet, say anything. But Henry's fate was to have no language—that was what had saved him from having to compete with somebody who had been *made* out of words . . . made himself *out* of words.

Here is the eulogy that drove him nuts:

"I was lying on the beach of a resort in the Bahamas yesterday, of all things rereading *Carnovsky* for the first time since it was published, when I received a phone call telling me that Nathan was dead. As there was no flight off the island till late afternoon, I went back to the beach to finish the book, which is what Nathan would have told me to do. I remembered an astonishing amount of the novel—it's one of those books that stain your memory—although I had also distorted scenes in a revealing (to me) way. It's still diabolically funny, but what was new to me was a sense of how sad the book is, and emotionally exhausting. Nathan does nothing better than to reproduce for the reader, in his style, the hysterical claustrophobia of Carnovsky's childhood. Perhaps that's one reason why people kept asking, 'Is it fiction?' Some novelists use style to define the distance between them, the reader, and the material. In *Carnovsky* Nathan used it to collapse the distance. At the same time, inasmuch as he 'used' his life, he used it as if it belonged to someone else, plundering his history and his verbal memory like a vicious thief.

"Religious analogies—ludicrous analogies, he would be the first to tell me—kept recurring to me as I sat on the beach, knowing he was dead and thinking about him and his work. The meticulous verisimilitude of *Carnovsky* made me think of those medieval monks who flagellated themselves with their own perfectionism, carving infinitely detailed sacred images on bits of ivory. Nathan's is the profane vision, of course, but how he must have whipped himself for that detail! The parents are marvelous works of the grotesque, maniacally embodied in every particular, as Carnovsky is as well, the eternal son holding to the belief that he was loved by them, holding to it first with his rage and, when that subsides, with tender reminiscence.

"The book, which I, like most people, believed to be about rebellion is actually a lot more Old Testament than that: at the core is a primitive drama of compliance versus retribution. The real ethical life has, for all its sacrifices, its authentic spiritual rewards. Carnovsky never tastes them and Carnovsky yearns for them. Judaism at a higher level than he has access to does offer real ethical rewards to its students, and I think that's part of what so upset believing Jews as opposed to mere prigs. Carnovsky is always complying more than rebelling, complying not out of ethical motives, as perhaps even Nathan believed, but with profound unwillingness and in the face of fear. What is scandalous isn't the man's phallicism but, what's not entirely unrelated, yet far more censurable, the betrayal of mother love.

"So much is about debasement. I hadn't realized that before. He is so clear on the various forms it can take, so accurate about the caveman mentality of those urban peasant Jews, whom I happen to know a thing or two about myself, sacrificing their fruits on the altar of a vengeful god and partaking of his omnipotence —through the conviction of Jewish superiority—without understanding the exchange. On the evidence of *Carnovsky*, he would have made a good anthropologist; perhaps that's what he was. He lets the experience of the little tribe, the suffering, isolated, primitive but warmhearted savages that he is studying, emerge in the description of their rituals and their artifacts and their conversations, and he manages, at the same time, to put his own 'civilization,' his own bias as a reporter—and his readers'—into relief against them.

"Why, reading *Carnovsky*, did so many people keep wanting to know, 'Is it fiction?' I have my hunches, and let me run them past you.

"First, as I've said, because he camouflages his writerliness and the style reproduces accurately the emotional distress. Second, he breaks fresh ground in the territory of transgression by writing so explicitly about the sexuality of family life; the illicit erotic affair that we all are born to get enmeshed in is not elevated to another sphere, it is undisguised and has the shocking impact of confession. Not only that—it reads as though the confessor's having fun.

"Now *Sentimental Education* doesn't read as if Flaubert was having fun; *Letter to His Father* doesn't read as if Kafka was having fun; *The Sorrows of Young Werther* sure as hell doesn't read as if Goethe was having fun. Sure, Henry Miller seems like he's having fun, but he had to cross three thousand miles of Atlantic before saying 'cunt.' Until *Carnovsky*, most everybody I can think of who had tackled 'cunt' and that particular mess of feelings it excites had done it exogamously, as the Freudians would say, at a safe distance, metaphorically or geographically, from the domestic scene. Not Nathan—he was not too noble to exploit the home and to have a good time while doing it. People wondered if it was not guts but madness that propelled him. In short, they thought it was about him and that he had to be crazy—because for *them* to have done it *they* would have had to be crazy.

"What people envy in the novelist aren't the things that the novelists think are so enviable but the performing selves that the author indulges, the slipping irresponsibly in and out of his skin, the reveling not in 'I' but in escaping 'I,' even if it involves— *especially* if it involves—piling imaginary afflictions upon himself. What's envied is the gift for theatrical self-transformation, the way they are able to loosen and make ambiguous their connection to a real life through the imposition of talent. The exhibitionism of the superior artist is connected to his imagination; fiction is for him at once playful hypothesis and serious supposition, an imaginative form of inquiry—everything that exhibitionism is not. It is, if anything, closet exhibitionism, exhibitionism in hiding. Isn't it true that, contrary to the general belief, it is the *distance* between the writer's life and his novel that is the most intriguing aspect of his imagination?

"As I say, these are just a few hunches, clues to answering the question that has to be answered since it's the question that hounded Nathan at every turn. He could never figure out why people were so eager to prove that he couldn't write fiction. To his embarrassment, the furor over the novel seemed to have as much to do with 'Is it fiction?' as with the question asked by those still struggling to separate from mothers, fathers, or both, or from the stream of mothers and fathers projected onto sexual partners, and that is, 'Is this *my* fiction?' But the less attached one is to that umbilicus, the less horrible fascination the novel has, at which point it is just what it seemed to me yesterday, and what it is: a classic of irresponsible exaggeration, reckless comedy on a strangely human scale, animated by the impudence of a writer exaggerating his faults and proposing for himself the most hilarious sense of wrongdoing—conjecture run wild.

"I've talked about *Carnovsky* and not about Nathan, and that's all I intend to do. If there were time and we had the whole day to be here together, I'd talk about the books in turn, each at great length, because that's the kind of funeral oration Nathan would have enjoyed—or that would have least displeased him. It would have seemed to him the best safeguard against too much transient, eulogistic cant. *The book*—I could almost hear him telling me this on that beach—*talk about the book, because that is least likely to make asses of us both*. For all the seeming self-exposure of the novels, he was a great defender of his solitude, not because he particularly liked or valued solitude but because swarming emotional anarchy and self-exposure were possible for him only in isolation. That's where he lived an unlimited life. Nathan as an artist, as the author paradoxically of the most reckless comedy, tried, in fact, to lead the ethical life, and he both reaped its rewards and paid its price. But not Carnovsky, who is to some degree his author's brutish, beastly shadow, a de-idealized, travestied apparition of himself and, as Nathan would be the first to agree, the most suitable subject for the entertainment of his friends, especially in our grief."

When the service was over, the mourners filed into the street, where groups of them lingered together, seemingly reluctant to return too soon to the ordinary business of an October Tuesday. Occasionally somebody laughed, not raucously, just from the kind of joking that goes on after a funeral. At a funeral you can see a lot of someone's life, but Henry wasn't looking. People who had noticed his strong resemblance to the late novelist looked *his* way from time to time, but he chose not to look back. He had no desire to hear yet more from the young editor about *Carnovsky*'s wizardry, and it unnerved him to contemplate meeting and talking with Nathan's publisher, who he believed to have been the elderly bald man looking so sad in the first row just beside the casket. He wanted simply to disappear without having to speak to anyone, to return to real society, where physicians are admired, where dentists are admired, where, if the truth be known, no one gives a fuck about a writer like his brother. What these people didn't seem to understand was that when most people think of a writer, it isn't for the reasons that the editor suggested but because of how many bucks he made on his paperback rights. *That*, and not the gift for "theatrical self-transformation," was what was really enviable: what prize has he won, who's he fucking, and how much money did the "superior artist" make in his little workshop. Period. End of eulogy.

But instead of leaving he stood glancing down at his watch and pretending that he was expecting to be met by someone. If he left now, then nothing that he'd wanted would have happened. Shutting down the office and making this trip hadn't to do with doing "the right thing"—it wasn't a matter of what others thought he should feel, it was what he himself wanted to feel, despite that seven-year estrangement. *My older brother, my only brother*, and yet he'd realized the day before that it was entirely possible for him, after he'd learned from the publisher of Nathan's death, to hang up the office phone and go back to work. It had been alarming to discover just how easy it would have been to wait and read the obituary in the next day's paper, professing to the family that he had not been told or invited to the funeral, let alone asked if he wanted to speak. Yet he couldn't do it—he might not be able to make the speech, he might not be able to feel the feelings, but out of love for his parents and what they would have wished, out of all those memories of what he and Nathan had shared as youngsters, he could at least be there and, in the presence of the body, effect something like a reconciliation.

Henry had been more than prepared to shed his hatred and forgive, but as a result of that eulogy, the bitterest feelings had been reactivated instead: the elevation of *Carnovsky* to the status of a *classic*—a classic of *irresponsible exaggeration*—made him glad that Nathan was dead and that he was there to be sure it was true.

I should have been the speaker—the cottage at the shore, the Memorial Day picnics, the Scout outings, the car trips, I should have told them all I remember and the hell with whether they thought it was badly written, sentimental crap. I would have given the eulogy and our reconciliation would have been *that*. I was intimidated, intimidated by all those people, as though they were an extension of him. So, he thought, today is just more of the same goddamn thing. It was never going to work, because I was *always* intimidated. And with that quarrel I only reinforced it—quarreling just because I couldn't stand any *more* of his intimidation! How did I get stuck there, when it wasn't ever what I wanted?

It was an awful day, but for all the wrong reasons. Here he wanted to be able to mourn his brother like everyone else and was having instead to contend with the stinkiness of the worst feelings.

When he heard his name called, he felt like a criminal, not from guilt but for having allowed himself to be trapped. It was as though outside a bank he'd just robbed, he'd committed some humane and utterly gratuitous act, like helping a blind man across the street, thereby delaying his getaway and allowing the police to close in. He felt ridiculously caught.

Coming toward him was the last of the three wives Nathan had left, Laura, looking not a day older or any less amiable than when they'd all been in-laws eight years back. Laura had been Nathan's "proper" wife, plainly pretty, if pretty at all, reliable, good-hearted, studiously without flair, back in the sixties a young lawyer with high ideals about justice for the poor and oppressed. Nathan had left her at about the time that *Carnovsky* was published and celebrity seemed to promise more tantalizing rewards. That, at any rate, was what Carol had surmised when they first heard about the separation. Henry wasn't so sure that success was the only motive: he saw what was admirable about Laura, but that may have been more or less all there was—her colorless Wasp uprightness, whose appeal for Nathan Henry could never fathom, was all *too* unmistakable. Ever since adolescence, he had been expecting Nathan to marry someone both very smart and very sultry, a kind of intellectual bar girl, and Nathan never came close. Neither of them did. Even the two women with whom Henry had had his most torrid affairs turned out to be as temperate as his wife, and no less trustworthy and decent. In the end it was like *having* an affair with his wife, for him if not for Carol.

While they embraced he tried to think of something to say that wouldn't immediately reveal to Laura that he was not deeply grieving. "Where did you come from?"—the wrong words entirely. "Where do you live? New York?"

"Same place," she said, stepping back but holding on momentarily to his hand.

"Still in the Village? By yourself?"

"Not by myself—no. I'm married. Two children. Oh, Henry, what a terrible day. How long did he know he was going to have this operation?"

"I don't know. We had a falling-out. Over that book. I didn't know anything either. I'm as stunned as you are."

She gave no indication that it was apparent to everyone that he wasn't stunned at all. "But who was with him?" she asked. "Was he living with someone?"

"Is there a woman? I don't know."

"You literally know nothing about your brother?"

"Well, maybe it's shameful," he said, hoping to make it less so by saying it.

"I don't know," Laura said, "but I can't bear to think that he was alone when he went in to have that operation."

"That editor who gave the eulogy—he seems to have been close to him."

"Yes, but he just got back last night—he was in the Bahamas. Mind you, he always had girls around. Nathan was never alone for long. I'll bet there's some poor girl at this moment—she may even have been inside. There were a lot of people there. I hope so, for his sake. The thought of him alone . . . Oh, it's so sad. For you too."

He couldn't bring himself to lie outright and agree.

"He had a lot more books to write," Laura said. "Still, he'd accomplished a lot of what he wanted to do. It wasn't a wasted life. But he had much more coming."

"As I say, I don't know what to make of it myself. But we had a serious quarrel, a falling-out—it was probably stupid on both sides." Everything he was saying sounded senseless. More than likely their falling-out was what was meant to be, the result of irreconcilable differences for which he, for one, had no need to apologize. He had spoken his mind about that book as he had every right to, and what ensued ensued. Why should writers alone get to say the unsayable?

"Because of *Carnovsky*?" Laura asked. "Yes, well, when I read it, I thought this was not going to go down very well with you or your folks. I understand it, but of course he had to use the life around him, the people he knew best."

It wasn't the "using," it was the *distortion*, the *deliberate* distortion—couldn't these people understand that? "Which sexes are your children?" he asked, again sounding to himself as insipid as he felt, as though he were speaking a language he barely knew. The ex-wife, Henry thought, so obviously distraught over Nathan's death, was utterly in control, while the brother who was not distressed was unable to say anything right.

"A boy and a girl," she said. "Perfect arrangement."

"Who is your husband?" That didn't come out like English spoken by an English-speaking person, either. He was speaking no known language. Perhaps the only English that would have sounded right was the truth. He's dead and I don't give a shit. I wish I did but I don't.

"What does he do?" Laura said, seemingly translating his question into her own tongue. "He's a lawyer too. We don't work together, it's a bad idea, but we're on the same wavelength. This time I married a man like myself. I'm not on the creative wavelength, I never was. I thought I was, in college, and even had remnants of it when I first met Nathan. Putting the idea of being a writer ahead of everything else is something I know a little about. I read those books too, and had those thoughts once, and, at a certain expense, even carried on like that in my early twenties. But I was lucky and wound up in law school. Now I'm mostly on the practical wavelength. I only have a real life, I'm afraid. It turns out I don't need any other."

"He never wrote about you, did he?"

She smiled for the first time, and Henry saw that, if anything, she'd become even plainer, even *sweeter*. She didn't seem to hold a single thing against his brother. "I wasn't interesting enough to write about," Laura said. "He was too bored with me to write about me. Maybe he wasn't bored enough. One or the other."

"And now what?"

"For *me*?" she asked.

That wasn't what he meant though he replied, "Yes." He'd meant something awful—something he *didn't* mean—like, "Now that this is over and my office is shut, what do I do with the rest of the day?" It had just slipped out, as though something internal that seemed as if it was external was trying to sabotage him.

"Well, I'm quite content," she said. "I'll just go on with what I have. And you? How's Carol? Is she here?"

"I wanted to come by myself." He should have said that Carol was getting the car and that he had to join her. He'd missed his opportunity to end the conversation before whatever wished to sabotage him went all the way.

"But didn't she want to come?"

His immediate impulse was to set the record straight—the record that Nathan was always distorting—to point out to her, in Carol's defense, that it was she who had been most perplexed and exasperated by Nathan's tossing Laura over. But Laura wouldn't care—she'd forgiven him. "He never wrote about you," he said, "you don't know what that's like."

"But he never wrote about Carol, he never wrote about you. Did he?"

"After I had the argument with him, one of the reasons we decided to stay out of his way was so that he wouldn't be tempted."

She showed no emotion, though he knew what she was thinking—and suddenly he understood everything that Nathan must have come to despise in her. Cold. Bland and upright and blameless and cold.

"And what do you think today?" Laura asked him in her very quiet, even voice. "Was it worth it?"

"To be truthful?" Henry said, and it *felt* truthful as he was about to say it, the first entirely truthful statement he'd been able to make to her. "To be truthful, it wasn't a bad idea."

She displayed nothing, nothing at all, just turned and calmly, coldly walked away, her place immediately taken, before Henry could even move, by a bearded man of about fifty, a tall, thin man wearing gold-rimmed bifocals and a gray hat, looking from the conservative cut of his clothes as though he might be a broker—or perhaps even a rabbi. Henry did, after a moment, think he recognized him as another writer, some literary friend of Nathan's whose picture Henry had seen in the papers but whose name he'd forgotten—someone who was now going to be as affronted as Laura not to find Henry and his entire family standing on the sidewalk knee-deep in tears.

He should never have closed the office. He should have stayed in Jersey, seen to his patients, and left it to time to deal with his feelings—a funeral was the last place ever to find what he and Nathan had lost.

The bearded man didn't bother with introductions and Henry still couldn't recall who he was.

"Well," he said to Henry, "he did in death what he could never do in life. He made it easy for them. Just went in there and died. This is a death we can all feel good about. Not like cancer.

With cancer they go on forever. They try all our patience. After the initial surge, the first sickness, when everybody comes around with the coffee cakes and the casseroles, they don't die right then, they hang on, usually for six months, sometimes for a year. Not Zuckerman. No dying, no decay—just death. All very thoughtful. Quite a performance. Did you know him?"

He knows, Henry thought, sees the resemblance—*his* is the performance. He knows exactly who I am and what I don't feel. What else is this about? "No," Henry said, "I didn't."

"Just a fan."

"I suppose."

"The bereaved editor. He reminds me of an overprivileged kid—only instead of money it's intellectuals. He's the only person in the world I can imagine reading a thing like that and thinking it's a eulogy. That wasn't a eulogy, it was a book review! Know what he was really thinking when he got the news? I lost my star. For him it's a career setback. Maybe not a disaster, but for a young editor on the make, who's already cultivated the grand style, to lose his star—*that's* grief. Which book is your favorite?"

Henry heard himself saying "*Carnovsky*."

"Not *Carnovsky* as bowdlerized in that book review. The editor's revenge—editing the real writer right out of existence."

Henry stood there on the street corner as though it were all a dream, as though Nathan hadn't died other than in a dream; he was over in New York at a funeral in a dream, and why the eulogy had celebrated the very thing that had driven him and his brother apart, why he had himself been speechless, why the ex-wife showed up to feel more grief than he did and to silently condemn Carol for not being present, was because that is what happens in a terrible dream. There's an insult everywhere, one is oneself the loneliest imaginable form of life, and people like this suddenly materialize, as unidentifiable as a force of nature.

"The deballing of Zuckerman is now complete," the bearded man informed Henry. "A sanitized death, a travesty of a eulogy, and no ceremony at all—completely secular, having nothing to do with the way Jews bury people. At least a good cry around the hole, a little remorse as they lower the coffin, but no, no one even allowed to go off with the body. Burn it. There is no body. The satirist of the clamoring body—without a body. All backwards and sterile and stupid. The cancer deaths are horrifying. That's what I would have figured him for. Wouldn't you? Where was the rawness and the mess? Where was the embarrassment and the shame? Shame in this guy operated *always*. Here is a writer who broke taboos, fucked around, indiscreet, stepped outside that stuff deliberately, and they bury him like Neil Simon— Simonize our filthy, self-afflicted Zuck! Hegel's unhappy consciousness out under the guise of sentiment and love! This unsatisfiable, suspect, quarrelsome novelist, this ego driven to its furthest extremes, ups and presents them with a palatable death —and the feeling-police, the grammar-police, they give him a palatable funeral with all the horseshit and mythmaking! The only way to have a funeral is to invite everyone who ever knew the person and just wait for the accident to happen—somebody who comes in out of the blue and says the truth. Everything else is table manners. I can't get over it. He's not even going to rot in the ground, this guy who was *made* for it. This insidious, unregenerate defiler, this irritant in the Jewish bloodstream, making people uncomfortable and angry by looking with a mirror up his own asshole, really despised by a lot of smart people, offensive to every possible lobby, and they put him away, decontaminated, deloused—suddenly he's Abe Lincoln and Chaim Weizmann in one! Could this be what he *wanted*, this kosherization, this stenchlessness? I really had him down for cancer. The works. The catastrophe-extravaganza, the seventy-eight-pound death, with the stops all pulled out. A handful of hairless pain howling for the needle, even while begging the nurse's aide to have a heart and touch his prick—one last blow job for the innocent victim. Instead, the dripping hard-on gets out clean as a whistle. All dignity. A big person. These writers are great—real fakes. Want it *all*. Madly aggressive, shit on the page, shoot on the page, show off their every last fart on the page—and for that they expect medals. Shameless. You gotta love 'em."

And what's this mouth want me to say—you're a mind reader and I agree? I had him down for cancer too? Henry said absolutely nothing.

"You're the brother," the bearded one whispered, speaking from behind his hand.

"I am not."

"You are—*you're* Henry."

"Fuck off, you!" Henry told him, making a fist, and then, stepping rapidly from the curb, he was nearly knocked down by a truck.

Next he was in the entryway to Nathan's brownstone, explaining to an elderly Italian woman with a very dour face and what looked like a killer tumor swelling out of her scalp, that he'd left the keys to his brother's apartment over in Jersey. She was the one who had come to the door when he'd pushed the superintendent's bell. "It's been a helluva day," he told her. "If my head wasn't screwed on, I would have forgotten that."

What with that growth of hers he should never have said "head." That was probably *why* he'd said it. He was still not entirely in control. Something else was.

"I can't let no one in," she told him.

"Don't I look like his brother?"

"You sure do, you look like twins. You gave me a shock. I thought it was Mr. Zuckerman."

"I've just come from the funeral."

"They buried him, huh?"

"Cremating him." Just about now, he thought. Nothing now left of Nathan that you couldn't pour into a baking-soda box.

"It'll make it easier," he explained, his heart pounding away, "if I don't have to drive back tomorrow with the keys," and he slipped her the two twenties he'd rolled up in his hand before entering the building.

Following her to the elevator, he tried to think what pretext he'd offer if anybody came upon him while he was inside

Nathan's apartment but instead began to harangue himself for failing to pay this visit long ago—if only he had, today would have been nothing like today. But the truth was that since their fight, Henry really had not thought about his brother that much, and was kind of amazed that he had got stuck in his resentment and it had all worked out this way. He had certainly never prepared himself for Nathan's dying or even imagined Nathan *capable* of dying, not so long as he was himself alive; in front of the funeral parlor, defending against the assault of that overbearing clown, he had even momentarily imagined him to *be* Nathan—Nathan's spirit giving it to him, just like Laura, for his heartlessness.

Suppose he's tailed me and shows up here.

There were two locks to be opened, and then he was inside the little hallway alone, thinking how even as an adult one continues, like a child, to believe that when someone dies it's some kind of trick, that death isn't entirely death, that they are in the box and not in the box, that they are somehow capable of jumping out from behind the door and crying, "Had you fooled!" or turning up on the street to follow you around. He tiptoed to the wide doorway opening onto the living room and stood at the edge of the Oriental carpet as though the floor were mined. The shutters were closed and the long curtains drawn. Nathan might have been away on a vacation, if he weren't dead. Next week, he thought, it would be thirty years since he'd taken that Halloween walk in his sleep. Another recollection for his undelivered eulogy—Nathan holding his hand and shepherding him around the neighborhood earlier that night in his pirate costume.

The furniture looked substantial and the room impressive, the home of a successful and important man, the kind of success with which Henry could never compete, he who had himself been phenomenally successful. It had to do not primarily with money but with some irrational protection accorded the anointed, some invulnerability Nathan had always seemed to possess. It had sometimes driven him crazy when he thought of how Nathan had achieved it, though he knew there was something petty and awful—tragic even—in allowing yourself the minutest perception of wanting to be your brother's equal. That was why it had been better not to think of him at all.

Why, asked Henry, is being a good son and husband such a big joke to that society of intellectual elite? What's so wrong with a straightforward life? Is duty necessarily such a cheap idea, is the decent and the dutiful really shit, while "irresponsible exaggeration" produces "classics"? In the game as played by those literary aristocrats, the rules are somehow completely reversed . . . But he hadn't come all the way here so as to stand staring morbidly off into space, summoning up yet again his most rancorous feelings, mesmerized in some sort of regressive freeze while waiting for Nathan to jump out of the box and tell him it was all a joke—he was here because there was a nasty job to be done.

Inside a deep closet along a wall of the passageway separating the rear of the apartment—Nathan's study and the bedroom—from the living room, kitchen, and foyer at the front, were four filing cabinets containing his papers. Finding the journals took only seconds—they were stacked up, four columns of them, in chronological sequence, right on top of the filing cabinets: twenty black three-ring binders, each one plump with loose-leaf pages and held round with a stout red rubber band. Though the brain cells might have been burned to cinders, there was still this memory bank to worry about.

Thanks to Nathan's orderliness, Henry was able, with none of the difficulties he'd foreseen, to locate a volume identified on the spine with the year of his first adulterous affair—and, sure enough, he had been absolutely right to heed his paranoia and not to reproach himself about that too, for there it all was, every intimate detail, recorded for posterity. Not only were the entries as plentiful as he'd been imagining since the news had reached him of Nathan's death, but it was all more compromising than he'd remembered.

To think that he could have been in such hot pursuit, only ten years back, of Nathan's admiration! The lengths to which I went to gain his attention! Nearly thirty, a father of three, yet my needs with him the needs of a blabbing adolescent boy! And, he thought, reading through the pages, the adolescent with her as well. From the look of it no greater asshole lives than the husband and father fleeing the domestic scene—there could be no sorrier, shallower, more ridiculous spectacle than himself as revealed in those notes. He was stunned to see how little it had taken to bring him so close to squandering everything. For a fuck, according to Nathan—and depend on him to get that right—for a fuck in the ass with a Swiss-German blonde, he had been ready to give up Carol, Leslie, Ruthie, Ellen, the practice, the house . . . *I am a virgin there no longer, Henry. They all think I'm so good and responsible. Nobody knows!*

But had he failed to get into the apartment and to get his hands on these pages, had he really believed he'd been followed, had he turned back to Jersey like a man in a dream fearful of being apprehended, *everyone* would have known. Because they publish these journals when writers die—biographers plunder them for biographies, and then everyone would have known everything.

Leaning against the wall in the narrow passageway, he read twice through the journal covering the crucial months, and when he was certain that he had tracked down every entry bearing his or her name, neatly, with a sharp tug, he tore out those pages, and then carefully returned the notebook to its chronological place atop the filing cabinet. From the volumes and volumes of words dating back to when Nathan had been discharged from the army and had moved to Manhattan to become a writer, he had extracted a mere twenty-two pages. He'd bribed his way into the apartment, he was there unlawfully, but by removing fewer than two dozen pages from the five or six thousand closely covered with Nathan's handwriting, he could not believe that he had committed a flagrant outrage against his brother's property; he had certainly done nothing to damage Nathan's reputation or diminish the value of his papers. Henry had merely intervened to prevent a dangerous encroachment upon his own privacy— for were these notes to become public, there was no telling what difficulties they could cause, professionally as well as at home.

And if by removing those few pages he was doing his old mistress a favor too, well, why shouldn't he? Theirs had been quite a fling: a brief, regressive, adolescent interlude from which he had mercifully escaped without committing a really stupendous blunder, yet he'd been absolutely mad for her at the time. He remembered watching her kneel in the black silk camisole to pick up the money off the motel floor. He remembered dancing with her in his own dark house, dancing like kids to Mel Tormé after having spent all afternoon in the bedroom. He remembered slapping her face and pulling her hair and how, when he'd asked what it was like coming again and again, she had answered, "Paradise." He remembered how it had excited him to see her face flush when he made her talk dirty to him in Swiss-German. He remembered hiding the black silk camisole in his office safe when he'd found himself unable to throw it away. The thought of her in that underwear caused him, even now, to press his hand against his cock. But it was illicit enough rummaging through the papers in his dead brother's apartment—it would have been simply too obscene there in the passageway to jerk himself off because of what he was remembering from ten years back, thanks to Nathan's notes.

He looked at his watch—he'd better call Carol. The phone was in the bedroom at the back of the flat. Sitting at the edge of Nathan's bed, he dialed his home number, prepared for his brother to pop up grinning from beneath the box springs, to leap fully alive out of the clothes closet, telling him, "Tricked you, Henry, had you fooled—put the pages back, kid, you're not my editor."

But I am. He may have given the eulogy, but I can now edit out whatever I like.

While the phone rang he was astonished by an amazing smell from the courtyard back of the building. It took a while before he realized that the smell was coming from him. It was as though in a nightmare his shirt had been soaked in something more than mere perspiration.

"Where are you?" Carol asked when she answered the phone. "Are you all right?"

"I'm fine. I'm in a coffee shop. There's no burial service—he's being cremated. There was just the eulogy at the funeral home. The casket was there. And that was it. I ran into Laura. She's remarried. She seemed pretty shaken."

"How do *you* feel?"

He lied, or maybe he was telling the precise truth. "I feel as though my brother died."

"Who gave the eulogy?"

"Some pompous ass. His editor. I probably should have said something myself. I wish I had."

"You said it yesterday, you said it all to me. Henry, don't wander around New York feeling guilty. He could have called you when he was ill. Nobody has to be alone if he doesn't want it. He died without anyone because that's how he lived. It's how he *wanted* to live."

"There was probably a woman around," said Henry, parroting Laura.

"Yes? Was she there?"

"I didn't look, but he always had girls around. He was never alone for long."

"You've done all you can. There's nothing more to do. Henry, come home—you sound awful."

But there *was* more to do, and it was another three hours before he left for Jersey. In the study, at the center of Nathan's desk, otherwise tidy and clear of papers, was a cardboard stationery box marked "Draft #2." In it were several hundred pages of typewritten manuscript. This second draft of a book, if that's what it was, appeared to be untitled. Not the chapters themselves, however—each, at the top of the first page, had as a title the name of a place. He sat down at the desk and began to read. The first chapter, "Basel," was purportedly about him.

Despite everything he thought he knew about his brother, he couldn't believe that what he was reading could have been written even by Nathan. All day long he had been distrusting his resentment, chastising himself for that resentment, feeling wretched for feeling nothing and lacerating himself for his incapacity to forgive, and here were these pages in which he was not only exposed to the worst sort of ridicule but identified by his own real name. Everyone was identified by name, Carol, the children, even Wendy Casselman, the little blonde who before she'd married had briefly worked as his assistant; even Nathan, who had never before written about himself *as* himself, appeared as Nathan, as "Zuckerman," though nearly everything in the story was either an outright lie or a ridiculous travesty of the facts. Of all the classics of irresponsible exaggeration, this was the filthiest, most recklessly irresponsible of all.

"Basel" was about his, Henry's, death from a bypass operation; about his, Henry's, adulterous love affairs; about his, Henry's, heart problem—not Nathan's, *his*. All the while Nathan had been ill, his diversion, his distraction, his entertainment, his amusement, his *art*, had been the violent disfiguring of *me*. Writing *my* eulogy! This was even worse than *Carnovsky*. At least there he'd had the decency, if that was the word, to shake up a little the lives of real people and change a few things around (for all the camouflage that had provided the family), but this exceeded everything, the worst imaginable abuse of "artistic" liberty.

In the midst of all that was sheer sadistic, punitive, spiteful invention, sheer sadistic sorcery, there, copied verbatim from the notebooks, were half the journal entries that Henry had torn out to destroy.

He was a man utterly without a sense of consequence. Forget morality, forget ethics, forget feelings—didn't he know the law? Didn't he know that I could sue for libel and invasion of privacy? Or was that precisely what he wanted, a legal battle with his bourgeois brother over "censorship"? What is most disgusting, Henry thought, the greatest infringement and violation, is that this is *not* me, not in any way. I am *not* a dentist who seduces his assistants—there is a line of separation that I do *not* cross. My job isn't fucking my assistants—my job is getting my patients to trust me, making them comfortable, completing my work as painlessly and cheaply as possible for them, and just as well as it can be done. What *I* do in my office is *that*. His Henry is, if anyone, *him* —it's Nathan, using me to conceal himself while simultaneously disguising himself *as* himself, as *responsible*, as *sane*, disguising himself as a reasonable man while I am revealed as the absolute dope. The son of a bitch seemingly abandons the disguise *at the very moment he's lying most!* Here is Nathan who knows everything and here is Henry with his little life; here is Henry who just wanted to be accepted and to get away with his little tawdry affairs, Henry the shlub who buys his potency with his death as a way of trying to free himself from being a good husband, and here am I, Nathan the artist, seeing through him completely! Even here, thought Henry, ill with heart disease and facing serious surgery, he continued to persist with the lifelong domination, forcing me into his sexual obsessions, his family obsessions, controlling and manipulating my freedom, seeking to overpower me with satirical words, making of *everyone* a completely manageable adversary for Nathan. Yet all the while it was *he* still hallucinating about the very things that are laughed at in this strawbrother who's supposed to be me! I was right: the driving force of his imagination was revenge, domination and revenge. Nathan always wins. Fratricide without pain—a free ride.

He must have been made impotent by heart medication and then chosen, like "Henry," to have an operation that killed him. *He*, not me, would never accept the limits—*he*, not me, was the fool who died for a fuck. Not the dopey dentist but the allseeing artist was the ridiculous Zuckerman who died the idiotic death of a fifteen-year-old, trying to get laid. *Dying* to get laid. There's his eulogy, shmuck: *Carnovsky* wasn't fiction, it was *never* fiction—the fiction and the man were one! Calling it fiction was the biggest fiction of all!

The second chapter he'd titled "Judea." Me again, back from the dead for a second drubbing. Once around was never enough for Nathan. He could not wish upon me enough misfortune.

He read—he who had never gone to Israel or had any desire to visit the place, a Jew who didn't think twice about Israel or about being a Jew, who simply took it for granted that Jews were what he and his wife and children were and then went on about his business—he read of himself learning Hebrew in Israel, on some kind of Jewish settlement, under the tutelage of some political hothead, and of course in unthinking flight from the banal strictures of his conventional life . . . Yet another troubled, volatile "Henry," again in need of rescue, again behaving like a boy—and as unlike him as a man could be—and yet another superior "Nathan," detached and wise, who sees right through to "Henry's" middle-class dissatisfaction. Well, I see right through *his* cliché of domestic claustrophobia! Another dream of domination, fastening upon me another obsession from which *he* was the one who could never be rescued. The poor bastard had Jew on the brain. Why can't Jews with their Jewish problems be human beings with their human problems? Why is it always Jews after shiksas, or Jewish sons with their Jewish fathers? Why can't it ever be sons and fathers, men and women? He protests ad nauseam that I'm the son strangling on his father's prohibitions and succumbing helplessly to his father's preferences, while he's the one unable ever to grasp that I behaved as I did *not* because I was bugged by our father but because I *chose* to. Not everyone is fighting his father or fighting his life—the one unnaturally bugged by our father was *him*. What's proven here in every word, what's crying out from every line, is that the father's son who never grew up to make a family of his own, who no matter how far he traveled and how many stars he fucked and how much money he made could never escape the Newark house and the Newark family and the Newark neighborhood, the father's clone who went to his death with JewJewJew on his brain, was *him*, the superior artist! You'd have to be *blind* not to see it.

The last chapter, called "Christendom," appeared to be his dream of escape from all that, a pure magical dream of flight—from the father, the fatherland, the disease, flight from the pathetically uninhabited world of his inescapable character. Except for two pages—which Henry removed—nowhere was there any mention of a childish younger brother. Here Nathan was dreaming about only himself—*another* self—and once Henry had realized that, he didn't take the time to examine every paragraph. He'd taken too much time already—outside the study window the courtyard was growing dark.

"Christendom" 's "Nathan" lived in London with a pretty, pregnant young Gentile wife. *He'd given her Maria's name!* Yet when Henry double-checked, looking quickly back and then ahead, he found that none of it had anything to do with his Swiss mistress. Nathan called all shiksas Maria—the explanation seemed as ludicrously simple as that. As far as Henry could tell, reading now like an examination student racing to beat the clock, it was a dream of everything that an isolate like his brother could never hope to achieve, a dream fueled by deprivations that went far beyond the story—a story about becoming a daddy, of all things. How delicious—a daddy with enough money, enough social connections to amuse him, a lovely place to live, a wonderful intelligent wife to live with, all the paraphernalia to make it like *not* having a child. So full of meaning and thought, this fatherhood of his—and missing the point completely! Entirely failing to understand that a child isn't an ideological convenience but what yóu have when you are young and stupid, when you're struggling to forge an identity and make a career—having babies is tied up with all *that*! But, no, Nathan was utterly unable to involve himself in anything not entirely of his own making. The closest Nathan could ever come to life's real confusion was in these fictions he created about it—otherwise he'd lived as he died, died as he'd lived, constructing fantasies of loved ones, fantasies of adversaries, fantasies of conflict and disorder, alone day after day in this peopleless room, continuously seeking through solitary literary contrivance to dominate what, in real life, he was too fearful to confront. Namely: the past, the present, and the future.

It was not Henry's intention to take away with him any more than what he had to, yet he wondered if leaving the box half full and the manuscript beginning on page 255 might not arouse suspicion, especially if the superintendent were to mention his visit to the executors when they arrived to assume custody of Nathan's estate. Taking it all, however, would have seemed like thievery, if not something even more gravely offensive to his sense of himself. What he'd already done was indecent enough—totally necessary, deeply in his interest, but hardly to his liking.

Despite the sadism of Nathan's "Basel," he refused to be gratuitously vengeful—except for two pages, "Christendom" had nothing to do with him or his family, and so he left it where it was. Culling from the manuscript only what could be compromising, he removed in their entirety the chapters "Basel" and "Judea" and the opening of a chapter about an attempted skyjacking, with Nathan on board as the innocent victim and, on the evidence of a cursory reading, having as little relation to the real world as everything else in the book. These pages consisted of a letter about Jews from Nathan to Henry, and then a phone conversation about Jews between Nathan and a woman bearing no relationship to Henry's wife and of course called "Carol"— fifteen Jew-engrossed, Jew-engorged pages mirroring, purportedly, *Henry's* obsessions. Reading through them, it occurred to Henry that Nathan's deepest satisfaction as a writer must have derived from just these perverse distortions of the truth, as though he wrote *to* distort, for that pleasure primarily, and only incidentally to malign. No mind on earth could have been more alien than the mind revealed to him by this book.

I'd tried repeatedly while I was with him to invest this escape he'd made from his life's narrow boundaries with some heightened meaning, but in the end he had seemed to me, despite his determination to be something new, just as naïve and uninteresting as he'd always been.

He had to be supreme always, unquenchably superior, and I, thought Henry, was the perpetual inferior, the boy upon whom he learned to sharpen his sense of supremacy, the live-in subordinate, the junior conveniently there from the day of my birth to be overshadowed and outperformed. Why did he have to belittle me and show me up even here? Was it just gratuitous enmity, the behavior of an antisocial delinquent who chooses anybody, like a plaything, to shove in front of the subway car? Or was I simply the last in the family left to attack and betray? That he had to outrival me right to the end! As if the world didn't know already which was the incomparable Zuckerman boy!

If Henry was ever going to turn out to be interesting, I was going to have to do it.

Thank you, thank you, Nathan, for redeeming me from my pathological ordinariness, for assisting in my escape from my life's narrow boundaries. What the hell was wrong with him, why did he have to go on like this, why, even at the end of his life, could he leave nothing and no one alone!

Eager though he was to be gone, he spent yet another hour in search of copies of "Draft #2" and looking to locate a "Draft #1." All he came up with, in a drawer of one of the file cabinets, was a diary Nathan had kept during a lecture stint in Jerusalem two years before and a packet of clippings from a tabloid called *The Jewish Press*. The diary looked to be so much unembellished reporting—scribbled impressions of people and places, snippets of conversation, names of streets and lists of names; as far as Henry could tell, all of it fact, with himself nowhere to be seen. In a file folder in the drawer below, he found a yellow pad whose first pages were covered with fragments of sentences that sounded oddly familiar. *More Old Testament than that—compliance vs. retribution. The betrayal of mother love. Conjecture run wild.* It was the notes for the eulogy that he'd heard delivered that morning. Inside the pad were three successive revisions of the eulogy itself; in each version were marginal emendations and insertions, lines crossed out and rewritten, and all of it, text and corrections, in no one's hand but Nathan's.

He had written his eulogy himself. For delivery in the event he didn't survive the surgery, his own appraisal of himself, disguised as someone else's!

For all the seeming self-exposure of the novels, he was a great defender of his solitude, not because he particularly liked or valued solitude but because swarming emotional anarchy and self-exposure were possible for him only in isolation—

Swarming all right—*his* version, *his* interpretation, *his* picture refuting and impugning everyone else's and *swarming* over *everything*! And where was his authority? *Where*? If I couldn't breathe around him, it's no wonder—lashing out from behind a fortress of fiction, exerting his mind-control right down to the end over every ego-threatening challenge! Could not even entrust his *eulogy* to somebody else, couldn't extend that much trust to a faithful friend, but intrigued to contrive even his own memorial, secretly supervising those sentiments too, controlling exactly how he was to be judged! Everyone speaking that bastard's words, everyone a dummy up on his knee ventriloquizing his mouthful! My life dedicated to repairing mouths, his spent stopping them up—his spent thrusting those words down everybody's throat! In his words was our fate—*in our mouths were his words*! Everyone buried and mummified in that verbal lava, including finally himself—nothing straightforward, unvarnished, directly alive, nothing faced up to as it actually is. In his mind it never mattered what *actually* happened or what anyone *actually* was—instead everything important distorted, disguised, wrenched ridiculously out of proportion, determined by those endless, calculated illusions cunningly cooked up in this terrible solitude, everything self-calculation, deliberate deception, always this unremittingly dreadful conversion of the facts into something else . . .

It was the funeral oration that Henry had been unable to compose the night before, the unsayable at last dredged up out of his unlived existence and ready now to be delivered over the file cabinets and the folders and the notepads and the composition books and the stacks of three-ring binders. Unheard but eloquent, Henry at last recited his uncensored assessment of a life spent *hiding* from the flux of disorderly life, from its trials, its judgments, its assailability, a life lived out behind a life-proof shield of well-prepared discourse—of cunningly selected, self-protecting words.

"Thanks for letting me in," he told the superintendent when he knocked to say he was going. "You saved me a trip over tomorrow."

She kept the door of her street-floor apartment three-quarters shut on its little chain, showing through the opening only a narrow slice of face.

"Do yourself a favor," he said, "don't tell anyone I was here. They might try making trouble for you."

"Yeah?"

"The lawyers. With lawyers every little thing's a production.

You know lawyers." He opened his wallet and offered her two more twenties, this time very calmly, with no palpitations of the heart.

"I got troubles enough," she said, and with two fingers plucked the money from his hand.

"Then forget you ever saw me." But she had already shut the door and was turning the lock as though he had been forgotten long ago. He probably hadn't even had to ice the cake and indeed he wondered, out in the street, if the forty bucks more might not lead her to suspect that something was up. But as far as she knew he'd done nothing wrong. The large manila envelope he had carried away with him was nicely concealed beneath an old raincoat of Nathan's that he'd found in the hall closet on the way out. Before opening the closet door, he'd once again been overtaken by the utterly ridiculous fear that Nathan would be hiding there among the coats. He wasn't, and in the elevator Henry just casually draped the raincoat over his arm—and over the envelope stuffed with Nathan's papers—as though it were his own. It could have been. The minds may have been alien but the men were pretty much the same size.

All the way up Madison Avenue there were city trash baskets into which he could easily have dispatched the envelope, but drop these pages into the Manhattan trash, he thought, and they'll wind up serialized in the *New York Post*. He had no intention, however, of bringing this stuff home for Carol to read or for her to come upon inadvertently among his papers; the objective was to spare Carol no less than himself. Ten years, even five years back, he had indeed done what married men do and tried to fuck his way out of his life. Young men fuck their way into their lives with the girls who become their wives, then they are married and someone new comes along and they try to fuck their way out. And then, like Henry, if they haven't already ruined everything, they discover that if they're sensible and discreet, they can manage to be both in and out at the same time. A lot of the emptiness that he had once attempted to fill fucking other women no longer panicked him; he'd discovered that if you're not afraid of it or angry with it, and don't overvalue it, that emptiness passes. If you just sit tight—even alone with someone you are supposed to love, feeling utterly empty with her—it goes away; if you don't fight it or rush off to fuck somebody else, and if you both have something else important to do, it does go away and you can recover some of the old meaning and substance, even for a time the vitality. Then that goes too, of course, but if you will just sit tight, it comes back again . . . and so it goes and comes, comes and goes, and that's more or less what had happened with Carol and how they had preserved, without ugly warfare or unbearable frustration, their marriage, the children's happiness, and the orderly satisfactions of a stable home.

Sure he was still tempted, and even managed taking care of himself from time to time. Who can bear a marriage of single-minded devotion? He was experienced enough and old enough to understand that affairs, adultery, whatever you call it, take a lot of the built-in pressure out of marriage and teach even the least imaginative that this idea of exclusivity isn't God-given but a social creation rigorously honored at this point only by people too pathetic to challenge it. He no longer dreamed of "other wives." A law of life he seemed finally to have learned is that the women you want most to fuck aren't necessarily the women you want to spend all that much time with, anyway. Fucking yes, but not as a way out of his life or as an escape from the facts. Unlike Nathan's, what Henry's life had come to represent was *living* with the facts—instead of trying to alter the facts, taking the facts and letting them inundate him. He no longer permitted himself to be carried heedlessly off in a sexual whirlwind—and certainly not in the office, where his concentration was entirely on the technical stuff and achieving the ultimate degree of professional perfection. He never let a patient leave his office if he thought to himself, "I could have done it better . . . it could have fit better . . . the color wasn't right . . ." No, his imperative was perfection—not just the degree of perfection needed for the patient to get through his life, not even the degree of perfection you could realistically hope for, but the degree of perfection that might just be possible, humanly and technically, if you pushed yourself to the limit. If you look at the results with bare eyes it's one thing, but if you look with loupes it's another, and it was by the minutest microscopic standards that Henry measured success. He had the highest re-do rate of anybody he knew—if he didn't like something he'd tell the patient, "Look, I'll put it in as a temporary, but I'm going to re-do it for you," and never so as to charge for it but to assuage that exacting, insistent, perfectionist injunction with which he had successfully solidified life by siphoning off the fantasy. Fantasy is speculation that is characteristically you, the you with your dream of self-overpowering, the you perennially bonded to your prize wish, your pet fear, and distorted by a kind of childish thinking that he'd annihilated from his mental processes. Anybody can run away and survive, the trick was to stay and survive, and this was how Henry had done it, not through chasing erotic daydreams, not by fleeing or through adventurous defiance, but by sounding the minutely taxing demands of his profession. Nathan had got everything backwards, overestimating —as was *his* fantasy—immoderation's appeal and the virtues of sweeping away the limits on life. The renunciation of Maria had signaled the beginning of a life that, if not quite a "classic," might be eulogized at *his* funeral as a damn good stab at equanimity. And equanimity was enough for Henry, even if to his late brother, student and connoisseur of intemperate behavior, it didn't measure up to the selfless promotion of the great human cause of irresponsible exaggeration.

Exaggeration. Exaggeration, falsification, rampant caricature —everything, thought Henry, about my vocation, to which precision, accuracy, and mechanical exactness are absolutely essential, overstated, overdrawn, and vulgarly enlarged. Witness the galling misrepresentation of my relations with Wendy. Sure when the patient is in the chair, and he's got the hygienist or assistant working on him, and she's playing with his mouth with her delicate hands and everything is hanging all over him, sure there is a part of it that stimulates, in the *patient*, sexual fantasy. But when I am doing an implant, and the whole mouth is torn open, and the tissue detached from the bone, and the teeth, the roots, all exposed, and the assistant's hands are in there with mine, when I've got four, even six, hands working on the patient, the *last* thing I'm thinking about is sex. You stop concentrating, you let that enter, and you fuck up—and I'm not a dentist who fucks up. I am a success, Nathan. I don't live all day vicariously in my head—I live with saliva, blood, bone, teeth, my hands in mouths as raw and real as the meat in the butcher's window!

Home. That was where he was finally headed, through the rush-hour traffic, with Nathan's raincoat and the envelope back in the trunk. He'd shoved them down in the well beside the spare so as to try to forget for a while disposing of the papers. Now that he was on his way, undetected, he felt as wrung out as a man who'd been ransacking, not his brother's files, but his brother's grave, while at the same time increasingly unsettled by the fear that he had been insufficiently thorough. If he'd had to stay till 3 a.m. to be sure nothing compromising in those files had been overlooked, that's what he should have done. But once it turned dark outside, he could go no further—he'd again begun to sense Nathan's presence, to feel himself disoriented inside a dream, and desperately wanted to be home with his children and for the strain and the ugliness to be over. If only he'd had it in him to empty the files and light a match—if he could only have been sure that when they saw the ashes in the fireplace they'd assume that Nathan had burned it all, destroyed everything personal before entering the hospital . . . Stalled in the smelly back-up of commuter cars and heavy trucks outside the Lincoln Tunnel, he was seething suddenly with remorse, because of having done what he'd done and because he hadn't done more. Seething with outrage too, about "Basel" more than anything—as outraged by what Nathan had got right there as by what he'd got wrong, as much by what he'd been making up as by what he was reporting. It was the two in combination that were particularly galling, especially where the line was thin and everything was given the most distorted meaning.

By the time he got over to Jersey and had pulled off the turnpike to telephone Carol from a Howard Johnson's, he was thinking that it might be enough for now to store the pages in his safe, to stop at his office before going home and leave the envelope there. Seal it, lock it away, and then bequeath it in his will to some library to open fifty years hence, if anyone should even be interested by then. Keeping it in the safe, he could at least think everything through again in six months. Far less likely then to do the wrong thing—the thing that Nathan would expect him to do, were Nathan waiting to see what became of the manuscript. Already once this week—while writing that eulogy —he had pretended to be dead . . . suppose he were at it again, waiting to see me confirm his imaginings. The thought was absurd and yet he couldn't stop thinking it—his brother was provoking him to enact the role that he had assigned him, the role of a mediocrity. As though that word could *begin* to describe the structure he had built himself!

Long ago, before their parents had sold the Newark house and moved to Florida, back before *Carnovsky*, when everything had been different for everyone, Henry, with Carol, had driven his mother and father down to Princeton to hear Nathan deliver a public lecture. While dialing home from the restaurant, Henry remembered that after the lecture, during the question period, Nathan had been asked by a student if he wrote "in quest of immortality." He could hear Nathan laughing and giving the answer—it was as close to his dead brother as he'd come all day. "If you're from New Jersey," Nathan had said, "and you write thirty books, and you win the Nobel Prize, and you live to be white-haired and ninety-five, it's highly unlikely but not impossible that after your death they'll decide to name a rest stop for you on the Jersey Turnpike. And so, long after you're gone, you may indeed be remembered, but mostly by small children, in the backs of cars, when they lean forward and tell their parents, 'Stop, please, stop at Zuckerman—I have to make a pee.' For a New Jersey novelist that's as much immortality as it's realistic to hope for."

Ruthie answered the phone, the very child whom Nathan had pictured playing her violin over Henry's coffin, whom he had placed in tears beside her father's grave, bravely proclaiming, "He was the best, the best . . ."

He had never loved his middle child more than when he heard her ask, "Are you okay? Mom was worried that one of us should have gone with you. So was I. Where *are* you?"

She was the best, the best daughter ever. He had only to hear that kindly, thoughtful child's grown-up voice to know that he had done the only thing there was to do. My brother was a Zulu, or whoever the people are who wear bones in their noses; he was our Zulu, and ours were the heads he shrunk and stuck up on the post for everyone to gape at. The man was a cannibal.

"I wish you'd called—" Carol began, and he felt like someone who survives a harrowing ordeal and only afterwards begins to weaken and appreciate how precarious it all had been. He felt as though he'd survived a murder attempt by himself disarming the murderer. Then, beneath what he recognized as the thinking of someone utterly exhausted, he saw with clarity all the ugliness that lay behind what Nathan had written: *he was out to murder my whole family the way he'd murdered our parents, murder us with contempt for what we are. How he must have loathed my success, loathed our happiness and the way we live. How he must have loathed the way he lived to want to see us squirm like that.*

Only minutes later, within sight of the headlights of the cars streaking homeward along the turnpike, Henry stood at the dark edge of the parking area down from the restaurant and, pushing open the metal flap at the top of a tall brown trash can, let the papers pour out into the garbage. He dropped the envelope in too, once it was empty, then pushed Nathan's raincoat in on top of that. He was a Zulu, he thought, a pure cannibal, murdering people, eating people, without ever quite having to pay the price. Then something putrid was stinging his nostrils and it was Henry who was leaning over and violently beginning to retch, Henry vomiting as though *he* had broken the primal taboo and eaten human flesh—Henry, like a cannibal who out of respect for his victim, to gain whatever history and power is there, eats the brain and learns that raw it tastes like poison. This was no squeezing out of those tears of grief he'd hoped to shed the day before, nor was it the forgiveness that he had expected to overtake him at the funeral home, nor was it like that surge of hatred when he'd first seen his name recklessly typed across the pages of "Basel"—this was a realm of emotion unlike any he had known or would wish to know again, this quaking before the savagery of what he'd finally done and had wanted to do most of his life, to his brother's lawless, mocking brain.

How did you find out that he was dead?

The doctor called around noon. And told me just like that. "It didn't work, and I don't know what to say. There was every chance that it would, and it just didn't." He was strong and relatively young, and the doctor didn't even know why it failed. It was just the wrong decision to take. And it wasn't even necessary. The doctor just called and said, "I don't know what to tell you, I don't know what to say . . ."

Were you tempted to go to the funeral?

No. No, there was no point. It was over. I didn't want to go to the funeral. It would have been a false situation.

Do you feel responsible for his death?

I feel responsible in that if he hadn't met me it wouldn't have happened. He met me and suddenly he felt this horrible urge to quit his life and be another person. But he was so driven that perhaps if it hadn't been me it would have been somebody else. I tried to tell him not to do it, I thought it was my duty to warn him beforehand, but I also didn't think he could live as he was— he was too unhappy. He couldn't bear to live as he was. And for me to have refused him would really have meant the continuation of that. I was probably only the catalyst but of course I was deeply involved. Of course I feel responsible. If only I had fought it! I knew it was a major operation, and I knew there was a risk, but you hear of people having it all the time, seventy-year-old men have it and go bouncing about. He was so healthy, I never imagined that this could happen. But nonetheless I was deeply involved—you feel guilty if you haven't given somebody a new pair of shoelaces and they die. You always feel when somebody dies that you didn't do something that you should have done. In this case, I should have stopped him from dying.

Shouldn't you just have called it quits and stopped seeing him?

I suppose I should have, yes, when I saw the way that it was going. Every instinct *told* me to stop. I'm a very ordinary woman in my way; I suppose it was all much too intense for me. It certainly was a drama of the sort I'm not accustomed to. I had never been through all those hoops before. Even if he had lived, I don't know if I could have kept up with the intensity. He very quickly gets bored—got bored. I'm convinced that if he'd had the operation and come back and was free to move as he wanted in the world, he would have been bored with me in three or four years and moved on to somebody else. I would have left my husband, taken our child, and perhaps have had a couple of years of what one calls happiness, and then been worse off than I was before and have had to go back and live with my family in England, alone.

But what you had with him wasn't boring.

Oh, no—we were both of us too far in over our heads for that, but it could have *become* boring to him. After a certain age people do have a pattern that's theirs, and there's little that can be done about it. It needn't have been boring, but it very well might have been.

And what did you do when they were having the funeral?

I took the child for a walk in the park. I didn't want to be alone. There was nobody I could talk to. Thank goodness it was in the morning and my beloved husband wasn't coming back until the evening and I had time to pull myself together. I had no one to share it with, but I couldn't have shared it with anyone if I had gone there. It would have been his family, his friends, his ex-girlfriends, a Jewish funeral, which I don't think he really wanted. Which I know he didn't want.

It wasn't.

I was afraid it was going to be, and I knew that was what he didn't want. Of course nobody told me about the funeral arrangements. He'd confided about me only to the surgeon.

What happened was that his editor read a eulogy. That was it.

Well, that's what he would have wanted. A flattering eulogy, I hope.

Flattering enough. And then in the evening, you went down there to the apartment.

Yes.

Why?

My husband was with the ambassador, at a meeting. I didn't know he was going to be gone. Not that I wanted him with me. It's always a dreadful business trying to keep one's expression in order. I sat upstairs by myself. I didn't know what to do with myself. I didn't go down there looking for what he'd written—I went to see the apartment. As I couldn't go to the hospital, couldn't go to the funeral, it was the nearest I could come to saying goodbye. I went down to see the apartment. When I went into the study there was the box on his desk—it had "Draft #2" written on it. It was what he'd been working on during the time he was with me. His last thoughts, it turned out. I always said, "Don't write about me," but I knew he always used everybody else and I didn't see why he shouldn't use me. I wanted to see—well, I suppose I thought there might be a message in it, in some way.

You went downstairs "to say goodbye." What does that mean?

I just wanted to sit alone in the apartment. Nobody knew I had a key. I just wanted to sit there for a while.

And what was it like?

It was dark.

Did it frighten you?

Yes and no. Secretly I've always believed in ghosts. And been afraid of them. Yes, I was frightened. But I sat there, and I thought, "If he's here . . . then he'll come." I started to laugh. I had a kind of conversation with him—one-sided. "Of course you wouldn't, how could you come back when you have no belief in these totally idiotic things?" I started to wander about like Garbo in *Queen Christina*, touching all the furniture. Then I saw the cardboard box on his desk, with "Draft #2" on it and the date he'd gone into the hospital. I used to say to him when I went into his study, "Be careful what you leave out, because anything that's on that desk, upside down or anywhere, I will read. If it's there. I don't go snooping, but I'll read anything that's left out. I can't help it." We joked about it. He'd say, "Mankind divides into two groups, those who will read other people's correspondence and those who won't, and you and I, Maria, fall on the wrong side of the line. We are people who open medicine cabinets to look at other people's prescription drugs." There was the box, and I was drawn to it, as they say, like a magnet. I thought, "There may be some message in it."

Was there?

There sure was. Something called "Christendom." A section, a chapter, a novella—I couldn't be certain. And I thought, "That's a little threatening. Is 'Christendom' the enemy? Is it me?" And I picked it up and I started to read it. And perhaps a lot of the love I had felt for him went at that moment. Well, not a lot of it, not when I read it again, but some of it, the first time round. The second time what touched me more than anything was his longing just to shed it all and have another life, his longing to be a father and a husband, things the poor man never was. I suppose he realized that he had missed that. However much one hates the sentimentality, it's a big thing to have missed in your life, not to have had a child. And he was so touching about Phoebe. Whereas everybody else in "Christendom" he changes, Phoebe alone he perceives as she is, as just a child, a little girl.

But what about the first time round?

I saw the other side of him, the irrational, the violent side of him. I don't mean physically, I mean how he would turn everything that wasn't familiar to him into the outsider—that I had been used in that way too, and that my family had been maligned most terribly. Of course, like all English families *they* thought of the outsider as the outsider, but it doesn't mean that they have those feelings that he had given them, of superiority and loathing —of apartheid, so to speak. My sister, perhaps not the best character in the world, is nonetheless only a poor, pathetic girl who never found her place anywhere, who's never been able to do anything, but to her he ascribed these terrible feelings about Jews and a disgusting sense of superiority that, if you knew Sarah, was ludicrous. You see, he had met my sister Sarah once, when she came to visit—I'd introduced them, as though he were just a neighbor. But what he had taken from my sister was so far from what she was that I thought there was something deeply twisted in him that he couldn't help. Because he had been brought up as he was, ringed round by all that Jewish paranoia, there was something in him that twisted everything. It seemed to me that *he* was my sister—*he* was the one who thought of "the other" as the other in that derogatory sense. He'd put all his feelings, actually, onto her—his Jewish feelings about Christian women turned into a Christian woman's feelings about a Jewish man. I thought that the great verbal violence, that "hymn of hate" he ascribed to Sarah, was in *him*.

But what about love for you in "Christendom"?

Oh, the subject is his love for, in quotations, me. But you can see at the end of it, when they have this quarrel, what the chances are for that love. Even though you know he goes back to her, and they pick up their lives, their lives are going to be tremendously difficult. You know that absolutely. Because he had tremendous ambivalence about a Christian woman. I was a Christian woman.

But you're talking about what "Christendom" is like, not about what Nathan was like. This never came up between you, did it?

It never came up because we never lived together. We had a romantic affair. Never before had I been so romantically involved with anyone. Nothing came up between us, except that operation. We met as if in a time capsule, imprisoned by my fear of discovery, like something one reads about in a nineteenth-century novel. There's a sense in which it's completely fictitious. I could believe I made the whole thing up. And that's not just because it's now gone—it was the same when it was in the very active present. I don't know what our life would have been like had we been able to live together. I saw no violent feelings—because of the drug there wasn't even a chance for good old-fashioned genital aggression. I saw only tenderness. The drug had done that as well—overtenderized him. That was what he secretly couldn't stand. It was the aggression he wanted to recover too.

But his imaginative life might have remained quite separate from your real life. Your sister would have been your sister to him, not the sister he imagined.

I've never lived with a novelist, you know. On first reading I took it all rather literally, as a bad critic would take it—I took it as *People* magazine would take it. After all, he used our names, he used people who were recognizably themselves and yet radically different. I think he might have changed the names later on. I'm sure he would have changed them. Of course I can see how Mariolatry appealed to him; in the circumstances he invented, Maria is the perfect name. And if it *was* the perfect name, he might *not* have changed it. But surely he would have changed Sarah's name.

And his name, would he have changed that?

I'm not so sure—maybe in a later draft. But if he wanted to, he would have used it. I'm not a writer, so I don't know how far these people will go for the desired effect.

But you are a writer.

Oh, only in a very minor risk-free league. That's *all* he was. Anyway, I read this story, or chapter, or fragment, whatever it was to be, this draft, and I didn't know what to do. All my life I despised Lady Byron, and Lady Burton, all those people who destroyed their husbands' memoirs, and letters, and erotic writings. It's always seemed to me the most incredible crime that we'll never know what those letters of Byron's contained. I thought of these women quite deliberately, quite consciously— I thought, "I think I am going to do with this what they have done that I've despised all my life." It's the first time that I understood why they did it.

But you didn't do it.

I cannot destroy the only thing he cared about, the only thing he had left. He had no children, he had no wife, he had no family: the only thing left was these pages. Into this went his unconsumed potency as a man. This imaginary life is our off-spring. This is *really* the child he wanted. It's simple—I couldn't commit infanticide. I knew that if it was published, unfinished, in this form, all the characters would be quite identifiable, but I thought the only thing I could do, with my husband, was to lie my way out of it. I thought, "I'm going to say, 'Yes, it's me—he met my sister, he used everybody, he used us. I knew the man very slightly. I knew him a little more than you thought I did, we had a coffee together, we went for a walk in the park, but I know how jealous you are and I never told you.' " I would say that he had been impotent and we never had an affair, but we were good friends, and that this is fantasy. And it is. I'll lie my way out and I'll also be telling the truth. I thought of tearing it up and throwing it down the incinerator chute, but in the end I couldn't. I'm not taking part in destroying a book just because the author isn't here to protect it. I left it on the desk, where it was when I came in.

You're in a lot of hot water, aren't you?

Why? If my marriage breaks up because of that, then it does. I think it'll take at least a year before it's published. I'll have a year to pull myself together, to think up fairy stories, and perhaps even to leave my husband. But I'm not going to destroy Nathan's last words for a marriage that I'm unhappy in.

Perhaps this is the way out of that marriage.

Perhaps. It's true, I would never have the courage to say, "I want a divorce"—this is certainly much easier for me than saying, "I have a lover and I want a divorce." Let him find it out, if he wants to. He's not a great reader, by the way, not anymore.

I think it'll be brought to his attention.

If I want to disguise myself, the only chance I have is to go to his editor and to say, "Look, I know, because he showed it to me, what he was writing. I know that he used characters very close to me and my family. He used our names. But he had said to me that this is only a draft, and if the book is published I'm going to change the names." I'll say to his editor, "If the book is published the names have to be changed. I have no threat to make—I'm only saying that otherwise it'll destroy my life." I don't think he'll do it, I don't think he can do it, but it's probably what I shall do.

But its publication won't destroy your life.

No, no, it won't—it *is* my way out.

And that's why you didn't destroy the manuscript.

Is it?

If you had a good marriage you certainly would have.

If I had a good marriage I wouldn't have been down there in the first place.

You two had an interesting time, didn't you?

It was interesting, all right. But I will not take responsibility for his death . . . to go back to that. It's very hard to step *away* from that, isn't it? I don't believe that he did it only for me. As I said, he would have done it anyway—he would have done it for somebody else. He would have done it for *himself*. Being the man he was, he didn't see that to women like me the impotence was of secondary importance. He couldn't understand it. He said to me, "A time comes when you have to forget what frightens you most." But I don't think it was dying that most frightened him—it was facing the impotence for the rest of his life. That *is* frightening, and that he couldn't forget, certainly not so long as my presence was there to remind him. I was the one who was there at the time, of course—he was in love with me, but at the time. If it wasn't me, it would have been somebody else later.

That you'll never know. You may have been desired more than you can bear to believe right now—no less loved in life than you are in "Christendom."

Oh, yes, the dream life that we had together in that fictional house-to-be. The way it sort of vaguely might have been. He didn't know Strand on the Green in Chiswick. I told him about it and how, when I'd first got married, I'd dreamed of living there and having a house there. I suppose I gave him that idea. I showed him a picture postcard of it once, the towpath protecting the houses from the Thames, and the willows leaning over the water.

Did you tell him about the incident at the restaurant?

No, no. In the sixties he'd spent a summer in London with one of his wives, and he told me what had happened to them in a restaurant there and what he has in the story happening with me. It certainly wasn't like him to make a scene in a restaurant. Though I really wouldn't know—we were never in a restaurant. How does one know what is real or false with a writer like that? These people aren't fantasists, they're imaginers—it's the difference between a flasher and a stripper. Making you believe what he wanted you to believe was his very reason for being. Maybe his only reason. I was intrigued by the way he'd turned events, or hints I *had* given him about people, into reality—that is, *his* kind of reality. This obsessive reinvention of the real never stopped, what-could-be having always to top what-is. For instance, my mother is not a woman like the mother in "Christendom" who's written outstanding books but an extremely ordinary English woman, living in the country, who's never done anything of interest in her life and never set pen to paper. However, the only thing I ever told him about her, once, was that like most provincial English women of her class, she has a touch of anti-Semitism. This of course has been built into something gigantic and awful. Look at *me*. After reading "Christendom" twice I went upstairs, and when my husband came home, I began to wonder which was real, the woman in the book or the one I was pretending to be upstairs. Neither of them was particularly "me." I was acting just as much upstairs; I was not myself just as much as Maria in the book was not myself. Perhaps she was. I began not to know which was true and which was not, like a writer when he comes to believe that he's imagined what he hasn't. When I saw my sister, I resented the things she said to Nathan in the church—*in the book*. I was confused, deeply confused. It was obviously a very strong experience to read it. The book began living in me all the time, more than my everyday life.

So now what?

I'm going to sit back and see what happens. The one thing he did get about me in that story, the fact of my character, is that

I'm deeply passive. And yet inside there is some mechanism that ticks away and tells me what is the right thing to do. I always seem to preserve myself in some way. But in a very circular manner. I think I shall be rescued.

By what he wrote.

It's begun to look that way, hasn't it? I think that my husband will read it, that he will ask me about it, that I will lie, that he will not believe me. My husband will have to come to grips with what has been going on in our lives for some time now. He's not such a hypocrite as to find this utterly surprising. I do think he has another life. I think he has a mistress; I'm sure of it. I think he's as deeply unhappy as I am. He and I are caught up in a terrible, neurotic symbiosis that both of us are rather ashamed of. But what he'll do because of "Christendom" I don't know. He's, on the one hand, very *comme il faut*, he wants to rise quickly in the diplomatic service, he wants to run for Parliament, he wants quite a bit—but he is also sexually very competitive, and if this looks to him like an affront to his manhood, he does have it in him to do dreadful things. I don't know what exactly, but his spitefulness can be quite inventive, and, in a very modest way, he could make sort of what used to be called a scandal. He'd have no *real* motive for kicking up a horrible fuss, other than to make my life unpleasant. But people do that all the time. Especially if they think they can put you in a position of wrong. You know: thou art more treacherous than me. I just don't know what he'll do, but what I want, above all, is finally to go home. Nathan's story has made me terribly homesick. I don't want to live in New York any more. I dread going back to my family. They're not so disagreeable as Nathan described, but neither are they very intelligent, by any means. He both heightened their intelligence and lowered their conscience and their moral tone. They're just deeply boring people who sit and watch television, and that was too boring for him—to put into a book, I mean. I don't think I'll be able to bear that for long either, but I don't really have the money to set up by myself, and I don't want to ask my husband for anything. I'll have to get a job. But after all I speak several languages, I'm still only twenty-eight, I have only one child, and there's no reason why I can't pick my life up. Even a well-bred penniless girl can get a job cleaning houses. I'll just have to get up and go out hawking myself like everybody else.

What do you think he loved so about you?

Drop the "so" and I'll answer. I was pretty, I was young, I was intelligent, I was very needy. I had tremendous wooability—I was there. Very much there—just upstairs. Upstairs downstairs. He called the lift our *deus ex machina.* I was foreign enough for him, but not so foreign as to make it taboo-foreign or bizarre-foreign. I was touchable-foreign, less boring to him than the equivalent American woman he was partial to. I wasn't that different in class from the women he'd married; as far as class and interests go, we were really very much the same kind of women, fairly refined, intelligent, amenable, educated, Nathanly coherent, but I was English and that made it less familiar. He liked my sentences. He said to me before he went into the hospital, "I'm the man who fell in love with a relative clause." He liked my speech, my English archaisms and my schoolgirl slang. Oddly, those American women were *really* "the shiksa," but because I was English I think there was even a difference in that. I was surprised in "Christendom" by his rather romantic idea of me. Maybe that's what one always feels when one reads about oneself—if you're written about, if you're turned into a character in a book, unless it is really crushingly derogatory, the very fact of being focused on like that is somehow curiously romanticizing. He certainly exaggerated my beauty.

But not your age. It didn't hurt that you were twenty-eight. He liked that.

All men like that you're twenty-eight. The twenty-two-year-old men like it, and the forty-five-year-old men like it, and even the twenty-eight-year-old men don't seem to be bothered too much. Yes, it's a very good age. It's probably a very good age to stay.

Well, you will, in the book.

Yes, and I'll have that dress, the dress that I wear at the restaurant. This perfectly ordinary dress I had, he made into something so voluptuous and beautiful. That pleasant, old-fashioned night out he gave us, such an old-fashioned fifties idea he had about having a night out at an expensive restaurant with the woman who's having your baby and has the hormonal glow. How romantically extravagant, and how innocent, the bracelet he gives me for my birthday. What a surprise. The wish-fulfillment aspect is very touching. It's too late to say I was moved, but I was, to put it mildly. The romantic life we might have had, in the Chiswick home . . . I don't think he really wanted any of these things, mind you. I'm not even sure he wanted me. He may well have wanted me as copy. Yet I do think, however much he romanticized my desirability, he saw me in an extremely cruel and clear way. Because with all the affection, he still does see her—my—passivity. I *am* all talk. And, yes, I do like money, I do like good things, I do like much more of a frivolous life, I presume, than he would have liked. The carol service, for instance. I actually wasn't there with him, in the church, as he has it in the story—that was in New York, that carol service, with a *real* Christian wife—but the point is that people go to carol service for fun, not because they believe in Jesus Christ or the Holy Virgin or whatever but just to have a good time. I think he never understood that side of me. I like to passively enjoy my life. I never wanted to be anything or to do anything. A lot of people do things not for the deep Jewish or religious reasons that he thinks they do, but they just do them—there are no questions to be asked. He asked so many questions, all of them interesting, but not always from the other person's point of view. I'm like everything else in the story: he elevated and intensified everything. That's what made the operation inevitable—he intensified and heightened his illness too, as though it were taking place in a novel. The writer's refusal to accept things as they are—everything reinvented, even himself. Maybe he wanted that operation for copy too, to see what that drama was like. That's not impossible. He was always, I believe the expression is, upping the ante —"Christendom" is just that. Well, he upped it once too far, and it killed him. He did with his life exactly what he did in his fiction, and finally paid for it. He finally confused the two—just what he was always warning everybody against. So did I momentarily confuse things, I suppose—began to collaborate with him on a far more interesting drama than the one I had going up-stairs. That, upstairs, was just another conventional domestic farce, so every afternoon, I took the *deus ex machina* down to the oldest romantic drama in the world. "Go ahead, save me, risk your life and save me—and I'll save you." Vitality together. Vitality at any price, the nature of all heroism. Life as an act. What could be more un-English? I yielded too. Only I survived and he hasn't.

Have you? What if your husband uses this to try to get Phoebe away from you?

No, no. You really can't use a work of fiction in a court of law, not even to expose a treacherous, double-dealing woman like me. No, I really don't think he could do that, however hurtful he may try to be. I'll take care of Phoebe and I'll have the day-to-day responsibilities, and he'll see her from time to time, and that's how it will end, I'm sure. My mother of course is going to be very upset. As for Sarah, it's so far from anything she could ever say or do, I don't think she'll take it seriously. She'll realize that if he had lived, he would have changed the names before he'd finished, and that'll be that.

And you will be, at least among his readers, the Maria of "Christendom."

I will, won't I? Oh, I won't suffer. I think relics are always rather fascinating. I remember when I was at university there was a woman pointed out to me as H. G. Wells's mistress, one of the many. I was fascinated. She was ninety. It hadn't seemed to have done her any harm. Even women like me have some extrovert fantasy.

So it's all worked for you, really. This is how you free yourself from the bullying husband. This is the happy ending. Saved, free to cultivate your child and your sense of yourself as the woman you are, without having to do the loony thing of running off with another man. Without having to do anything.

Except that the poor other man I was to run off with died, remember. Suddenly there is death. Life goes on but he's not here. There are certain recurrent shocks in life, which you can just steady yourself for—you can take a deep breath and it passes by and it doesn't hurt so much. But this is different. He was such a support for me in my head for so long. And now he's not here even to be there. I've managed, however. Actually I've been so heroic I wouldn't recognize myself.

And what will it have meant to you?

Oh, the great experience of my life, I think. Yes, without question. A footnote in an American writer's life. Who would have thought that would happen?

Who would have thought you'd be the angel of death?

No, the footnote's more me, but yes, I can see how somebody might see it that way. Like in a Buñuel film—the dark young woman that Buñuel has in those films, one of those mysterious creatures, totally innocent of it, but yes, the role assigned her is angel of death. Somewhat more devastating than my role in "Christendom." I did nothing to instigate it, and yet through my weakness it happened. I think a stronger woman would have had more humor than I did, would have got less caught up, and would have known how to deal with the situation better. But, as I say, I think he would have done it with the next one anyway. Like Mayerling—like the Archduke Rudolf and Maria Vetsera. She wasn't the first woman that he'd asked to commit suicide with him, she was just the first who agreed to do it. He'd tried with many women. It came out afterwards that he'd had it in his mind for a long time to commit a double suicide.

Are you suggesting that Nathan was trying to commit suicide?

I think he succeeded, but no, he didn't want that. I think that was the joke, that was exactly the kind of humiliating irony, the kind of self-inflicted brutal life-fact that he admired so: someone wants to be given back his masculine life, and instead he dies. But, no, that wasn't what he wanted. He wanted health and strength and freedom. He wanted virility again, and the force that drives it. I was instrumental, as who isn't? That *is* love.

And now, are there any questions you want to ask me?

I can answer questions but I can't ask them. You ask them.

The smart woman who's learned not to ask smart questions. You know who I am, don't you?

No. Well, yes. Yes, I know who you are, and I know, so to speak, why you've come back.

Why?

To learn what happened. What it's like now. What I did. You have the rest of the story to tell. You need the hard evidence, the details, the clues. You want an ending. Yes, I know who you are—the same restless soul.

You look tired.

No, just slightly pale, and unkempt. I'll be all right. I didn't sleep well last night. I'm in a marital low. My burdens, fallen from my shoulders, are gathering around my ankles. Resignation's a hard thing, isn't it? Especially if you're not sure it's the right thing. Anyway, I was lying in my bed and I suddenly woke up, and there was this presence. Just out there. It was your prick. By itself. Where's the rest of his body, where's everything else? And it was as if I could touch it. And then it sort of went into a shadow, and then the rest of you assembled itself around it. And I knew it was just a thought. But for a little while it was just there. Last night.

So what is it like now? Right now.

My life began again when I absolutely gave up on him, and started writing again, and met you—all sorts of things happened that were really wonderful. And I felt much better. But living again in such a cold way fills me with, not horror, but terrible pain. Sometimes I feel it so acutely I can't even sit still. Saturday, as people always do, he supplied some unreasonable behavior, just enough to make me feel in a bit of a rage, and I said to him, I can't put up with any more of being the outdated, extraneous wife. Unfortunately I said it once before, and of course did nothing, and these things have a diminishing impact. Getting ready not to do things is most exhausting. On the other hand, things one says repeatedly do sometimes happen. But frankly what it is, since you ask, is boring now. I'm the one who's bored, because you're not here. Now I think, "I can't spend the whole rest of my life being so bored, apart from everything else." You brought such clandestine excitement. And the talk. The intensity of all that lovely talk. Most people have sex cut off from love, and maybe it appears that we had the opposite, love cut off from sex. I don't know. That endless, issueless, intimate talk— sometimes it must have seemed to you like the conversation of two people in jail, but to me it was the purest form of eros. It was clearly different and less fulfilling for a man who'd spent his whole life getting to the solace of sex so very quickly and was far more compelled to consummation. But for me it had its power. For me those times were tremendous.

But of course—you're the great talker, Maria.

Am I? Well, you've got to have someone to talk *to*. I could certainly talk to you. You listened. I can never talk to Michael. I try, and I see the glassy look in his eye, and I get out my book.

Keep talking to me then.

I will. I will. I know now what a ghost is. It is the person you talk to. That's a ghost. Someone who's still so alive that you talk to them and talk to them and never stop. A ghost is the ghost of a ghost. It's my turn now to invent you.

And how's your little girl?

Very well. She can speak so well now. "I want a piece of paper." "I want a pencil." "I'm going outside."

How old is she?

She's not quite two.

5. Christendom

AT SIX in the evening, only a few hours after leaving Henry at Agor and arriving in London with the notes I'd amassed on the quiet flight up from Tel Aviv, my mind suffused still with all those implacable, dissident, warring voices and the anxieties stirring up their fear and resolve—in under five hours back from that unharmonious country where it appears that nothing, from the controversy to the weather, is ever blurred or underdone —I was seated in a church in London's West End. With me were Maria, Phoebe, and some three or four hundred others, many of whom had rushed from work to be in time for the carol service. It was just two weeks before Christmas; in the Strand the heavy traffic was at a standstill and the streets leading out of the West End were clogged with cars and shoppers. After a mild afternoon, the evening had turned cold, and a light fog diffused the beams of the cars. Phoebe was so excited by the traffic and the traffic lights and the Christmas lights and the jostling crowds that she had to be taken to the bathroom in the crypt while I found our seats in the reserved pew, just down the row from Georgina and Sarah, Maria's sisters. As a longtime member of the board of the charity for whom the collection would be taken, Maria's mother, Mrs. Freshfield, was to read one of the lessons.

Maria led Phoebe around to her grandmother, who was sitting with the other readers in the first row, and then to see her two aunts. They rejoined me in our seats just as the choir was filing in, the bigger boys first, in blue school blazers, striped ties, and gray trousers, then the smaller boys, in their short pants. The choirmaster, a neatly attired young man with prematurely gray hair and wearing horn-rimmed glasses, seemed to me a composite of kindly schoolteacher and circus lion-tamer—when, with the tiniest inclination of his head, he directed the boys to be seated, even the smallest responded as though the whip had cracked dangerously nearby. Maria pointed out to Phoebe the Christmas tree off to one side of the nave; though impressively tall, it was rather sparsely decorated with red, white, and blue tinsel, and pinned to the top was a lopsided silver star that looked like the handiwork of a Sunday School class. In front of us, directly beneath the pulpit, was a large circular arrangement of white chrysanthemums and carnations embedded in evergreen and holly branches. "See the flowers?" Maria said, and a little confused but utterly enthralled, Phoebe replied, "Grandma story." "Soon," Maria whispered, straightening the pleats in the child's plaid dress, and then the organ solo began and with it the mild undercurrent of antipathy in me.

It never fails. I am never more of a Jew than I am in a church when the organ begins. I may be estranged at the Wailing Wall but without being a stranger—I stand outside but not shut out, and even the most ludicrous or hopeless encounter serves to gauge, rather than to sever, my affiliation with people I couldn't be less like. But between me and church devotion there is an unbridgeable world of feeling, a natural and thoroughgoing incompatibility—I have the emotions of a spy in the adversary's camp and feel I'm overseeing the very rites that embody the ideology that's been responsible for the persecution and mistreatment of Jews. I'm not repelled by Christians at prayer, I just find the religion foreign in the most far-reaching ways—inexplicable, misguided, profoundly *inappropriate*, and never more so than when the congregants are observing the highest standards of liturgical decorum and the cleric most beautifully enunciating the doctrine of love. And yet there I was, behaving as every well-trained spy aspires to do, looking quite at ease, I thought, agreeable, untrammeled, while squeezed up against my shoulder sat my pregnant Christian-born English wife, whose mother was to read the lesson from St. Luke.

By conventional standards Maria and I must certainly have seemed, because of the dissimilar backgrounds and the difference in age, to be a strangely incongruous couple. Whenever our union seemed incongruous even to me, I wondered if it wasn't a mutual *taste* for incongruity—for assimilating a slightly untenable arrangement, a shared inclination for the sort of unlikeness that doesn't, however, topple into absurdity—that accounted for our underlying harmony. It was still beguiling for people raised in such alien circumstances to discover in themselves interests so strikingly similar—and, of course, the differences continued to be pretty exhilarating too. Maria was keen, for instance, to pin my professional "seriousness" to my class origins. "This artistic dedication of yours is slightly provincial, you know. It's far more metropolitan to have a slightly anarchic view of life. Yours only seems anarchic and isn't at all. About standards you're something of a hick. Thinking things *matter*." "It's the hicks who think things matter who seem to get things done." "Like books written, yes," she said, "that is so. That's why there are so few upper-class artists and writers—they haven't got the seriousness. Or the standards. Or the irritation. Or the ire." "And the values?" "Well," she said, "we certainly haven't got that. That really *is* over the top. One used to expect the upper classes at least to pay for it all, but they won't even do that anymore. On that score, I was a renegade, at least as a child. I'm over it now, but when I was little I used terribly to want to be remembered after my death for something I had *achieved*." "I wanted to be remembered," I said, "before my death." "Well, that is also important," Maria said, "—in fact, slightly more important. Slightly provincial, unsophisticated, and hickish, but I must say, attractive in you. The famous Jewish intensity." "Counterbalanced in you by the famous English insouciance." "And that," she said, "is a gentle way of describing my fear of failure."

After the organ solo, we rose and everyone began to sing the first carol, except me and children like Phoebe who were too small to know the words and couldn't read them from the program. The assemblage sang with tremendous zest, an eruption of good clean vehemence that I hadn't anticipated from the chastening authority of the choirmaster or the genteel solemnity of the minister who was to make the blessing. The men with briefcases, the shoppers with their parcels and bundles and bags, those who at the worst of the rush hour had come all the way into the West End with overexcited little children or with their elderly relatives —no longer were they unattached and on their own, but merely by opening their mouths and singing out, this crowd of disparate Londoners had turned into a battalion of Christmas-savoring Christians, relishing every syllable of Christian praise with enormous sincerity and gusto. It sounded to me as though they'd been hungering for weeks for the pleasure of affirming that enduring, subterranean association. They weren't rapturous or in a delirium—to use the appropriately old-fashioned word, they seemed *gladdened*. It may well be a little hickish to find the consolations of Christianity a surprise, but I was struck nonetheless to hear from their voices just how delightful it was—in Zionist argot, how very *normal* they felt—to be the tiniest component of something immense whose indispensable presence had been beyond Western society's serious challenge for a hundred generations. It was as though they were symbolically feasting upon, communally devouring, a massive spiritual baked potato.

Yet, Jewishly, I still thought, what *do* they need all this stuff for? Why do they need these wise men and all these choruses of angels? Isn't the birth of a child wonderful enough, *more* mysterious, for *lacking* all this stuff? Though frankly I've always felt that the place where Christianity gets dangerously, vulgarly obsessed with the miraculous is Easter, the Nativity has always struck me as a close second to the Resurrection in nakedly addressing the most childish need. Holy shepherds and starry skies, blessed angels and a virgin's womb, being materializing on this planet without the heaving and the squirting, the smells and the excretions, without the plundering satisfaction of the orgasmic shudder—what sublime, offensive kitsch, with its fundamental abhorrence of sex.

Certainly the elaboration of the story of the Virgin Birth had never before struck me as quite so childish and spinsterishly unacceptable as it did that evening, fresh from my Sabbath at Agor. When I heard them singing about that Disneyland Bethlehem, in whose dark streets shineth the everlasting light, I thought of Lippman distributing his leaflets in the marketplace there and consoling, with his *Realpolitik*, the defiant Arab enemy: "Don't give up your dream, dream of Jaffa, go ahead; and someday, if you have the power, even if there are a *hundred* pieces of paper, you will take it from me by force."

When her turn came, Maria's mother ascended to the pulpit lectern and, in that tone of simplicity with which you induce first gullibility and then sleep in children to whom you're telling a bedtime story, charmingly read from St. Luke the fifth lesson, "The Angel Gabriel salutes the Blessed Virgin Mary." Her own writing disclosed a stronger affinity to a lowly, more corporeal existence: three books—*The Interior of the Georgian Manor House, The Smaller Georgian Country House,* and *Georgians at Home*—as well as numerous articles over the years in *Country Life*, had earned for her a solid reputation among students of Georgian interior design and furnishings, and she was regularly asked to speak to local Georgian societies all over England. A woman who took her work "dead seriously," according to Maria —"a very reliable source of information"—though on this occasion looking less like someone who spent her London days in the V & A archives and the British Library than like the perfect hostess, a short, pretty woman some fifteen years older than I, with a soft round face that reminded me of a porcelain plate and that very fine hair that turns from a mousy blond to snowy white with very little difference of effect, hair that's been done for thirty years by the same very good, old-fashioned hairdresser. Mrs. Freshfield had the air of someone who never put a foot wrong— which Maria claimed had nearly been so: her big mistake had been her husband, but she'd made that only once, and after her marriage to Maria's father had never again been distracted from Georgian interiors by the inexplicable yearning for an attractive man.

"She was the beauty of the Sixth," Maria explained to me, "the Queen of Hockey—she carried off all the prizes. He was academically rather stupid, but terribly athletic, and he had enormous glamour. The black Celt. He stood out a mile. Elegant and, even before he arrived at university, quite stuck up about his glamour. Nobody could understand what it was that made him so famous. There were all these other boys wanting to be judges, or cabinet ministers, or soldiers, and this stupid twit was turning on the girls. Mother hadn't been turned on before. After, she never wanted to be again. And she wasn't—from all the evidence, never so much as touched again. She did everything to give us a solid world, a good and solid, traditional English upbringing—that became the entire meaning of her life. He had always behaved beautifully to us; no man could have enjoyed three little girls more. We enjoyed him too. He behaved beautifully to everyone, except her. But if you're convinced that your wife is fundamentally uninterested in what interests you, which is your erotic power, and if the history of your relationship is that you can hardly communicate with her at all, and there's nothing really but resentment between you in the end, and however sterling a character she may have, she doesn't really *come across*— I think that's the expression—and you yourself have lots of vitality and are rather highly sexed, as he was—and like all you boys, he seemed to find it a great torture, you just want it *so much*— then you have no choice, really, do you? First you devote lots of hours to the humiliation of your wife, with her best friends ideally, and then with the obliging neighbors, until having exhausted every possibility for betrayal in the immediate hundred square miles, you vanish, and there's an acrimonious divorce, and after there's never enough money, and your little girls are forever susceptible to dark men with beautiful manners."

Until her grandmother had taken her place in the pulpit, Phoebe had been mostly intrigued by the tiny trebles in their short pants, some of whom, not halfway through the hour, were looking as though they wouldn't have minded being home in bed. But when Grandmother stepped into the pulpit to read, the child suddenly found everything amusing—tugging at Maria's hand, she began to laugh and get excited, and could be quieted only by climbing onto Mummy's lap, where she was gently rocked into a semi-stupor.

A solo followed, sung by a slender boy of about eleven whose untainted charm reminded me of a doctor with too much bedside manner. After he concluded his part and the entire choir had seraphically joined in, he brazenly focused a coquettish smile upon the choirmaster, who in turn acknowledged how remarkable a boy the beautiful soloist was with a half-suppressed but lingering smile of his own. Still not about to be taken in by all this Christian heartiness, I was relieved to think that I'd caught a little whiff of homoerotic pedophilia. I wondered if in fact my skepticism hadn't already prompted the rector to single me out as someone privately making unseasonal observations. On the other hand, as we were seated in pews reserved for the readers' families, it may have been that he had simply recognized Maria as her mother's daughter and that alone explained the scrutinizing appraisal of the gentleman next to the Freshfield girl who appeared to have come to the carol service determined not to sing.

We stood for the carols and sat for the lessons and remained seated when the choir sang "The Seven Joys of Mary" and "Silent Night." When the program directed "All kneel" for the blessing, which came after the collection, I remained obstinately upright, fairly sure I was the only one in all the church failing to assume a posture of devout submission. Maria leaned forward just enough so as not to affront the rector—or her mother, should she turn out to have eyes in the back of her skull—and I was thinking that if my grandparents had disembarked at Liverpool instead of continuing on in steerage for New York, if family fate had consigned me to schools here rather than to the municipal education system of Newark, New Jersey, my head would always have been sticking up like this when everyone else's was bowed in prayer. Either that, or I would have tried to keep my origins to myself, and to avoid seeming a little boy inexplicably bent on making himself strange, I too would have kneeled, however well I understood that Jesus was a gift to neither me nor my family.

After the rector's blessing everyone rose for the final carol, "Hark, the Herald Angels Sing." Inclining her head conspiratorially toward me, Maria whispered, "You are a very forbearing anthropologist," and holding Phoebe so as to keep her from slumping over with fatigue, she proceeded to sing out rousingly, along with everyone else, "Christ, by highest heaven adored / Christ, the everlasting Lord," while I remembered how shortly after our arrival in England her ex-husband had referred to me on the phone as "the aging Jewish writer." When I'd asked how she'd responded, she slipped her arms around me and said, "I told him that I liked all three."

Following the organ finale we took a stairway by the porch of the church down into a spacious, low-ceilinged, whitewashed crypt, where mulled wine and mince pie were being served. It took some time to navigate little Phoebe through all of the people heading down the stairs for refreshment. The child was to spend the night with her grandmother, a treat for both, while I took Maria out to celebrate her birthday. Everyone said how lovely the singing had been and told Mrs. Freshfield how wonderfully she had read. An elderly gentleman whose name I couldn't catch, a friend of the family who had also read one of the lessons, explained to me the purpose of the charity for which the collection had been taken—"Been going on for a hundred years," he said, "—there are so many poor and lonely people."

Fortunately there was our new house to give us all something to talk about, and there were Polaroid snapshots to look at, taken by Maria when she had driven over the day before to check on the construction. The house was to be renovated over the next six months while we stayed in a rented mews house in Kensington. Actually it was two connecting, smallish brick houses, on the site of an old boatyard in Chiswick, that we were converting into one large enough for the family and the nanny and for studios for Maria and me.

We talked about how Chiswick wasn't as far out as it seemed

and yet with the gate closed on the stone wall to the street it had the seclusion of a remote rural village—the quiet Nathan needed for his work, Maria told everyone. On the rear-street side there was the wall and a paved garden with daffodils and irises and a small apple tree; at the front of the house, beyond a raised terrace where we could sit on warm evenings, there was a wide towpath and the river. Maria said that it looked as though most of the people who walked along the towpath were either lovers having assignations or women with small children—"one way or another," she said, "people in a very good mood." There were people fishing for trout now that the river was cleaned up, and early in the morning, when you opened the shutters on what was to be our bedroom, you could see rowing eights out to practice. In the summer there were small boats going up for holidays on the river and the steamers carrying sightseers from Charing Cross to Kew Gardens. In late autumn the fog came down and in winter barges went by with their cargo covered, and often in the morning there was mist. And there were always gulls—ducks as well, that walked up the terrace steps to be fed, if you fed them, and, occasionally, there were swans. Twice a day at high tide the river rose over the towpath and lapped at the terrace wall. The elderly gentleman said that it sounded as though for Maria it would be like living in Gloucestershire again while only fifteen minutes by the Underground from Leicester Square. She said, no, no, it wasn't the country *or* London, and it wasn't the suburbs either, it was living on the river . . . on and on, amiably, amicably, aimlessly.

And nobody asked about Israel. Either Maria hadn't mentioned my being there or they weren't interested. And probably just as well: I wasn't sure how much Agor ideology I could manage to get across to Mrs. Freshfield.

To Maria, however, I'd talked all afternoon about my trip. "Your journey," she'd called it, after hearing about Lippman and reading my letter to Henry, "to the Jewish heart of darkness." A good description, that, of my eastward progress and I delineated it further in my notes—from the Tel Aviv café and the acid dolefulness of disheartened Shuki, inland to the

Jerusalem Wailing Wall and my prickly intermingling there with the pious Jews, and then on to the desert hills, the plunge into the heart, if not of darkness, of demonic Jewish ardor. The militant zealotry of Henry's settlement didn't, to my mind, make their obdurate leader the Kurtz of Judea, however; the book suggested to me by the settlers' fanatical pursuit of God-promised deliverance was a Jewish *Moby-Dick*, with Lippman as the Zionist Ahab. My brother, without realizing, could well have signed onto a ship destined for destruction, and there was nothing to be done about it, certainly not by me. I hadn't mailed the letter and wouldn't—Henry, I was sure, could only see it as more domination, an attempt to drown him in still more of my words. Instead I copied it into my notes, into that ever-enlarging storage plant for my narrative factory, where there is no clear demarcation dividing actual happenings eventually consigned to the imagination from imaginings that are treated as having actually occurred—memory as entwined with fantasy as it is in the brain.

Georgina, younger by a year than Maria, and Sarah, three years older, were not tall and dark-haired like the middle sister and their father but resembled the mother more, slight, shortish women, with straight fair hair that they didn't much bother about and the same soft, round, agreeable faces that had probably been prettiest when they were girls of fifteen living in Gloucestershire. Georgina had a job with a London public relations firm and Sarah had recently become an editor with a company specializing in medical texts, her fourth publishing job in as many years and work having little to do with anything she cared about. Yet Sarah was the sister who was supposed to have been the genius. She had spent her childhood mastering dancing, mastering riding, mastering just about everything as though, if she didn't, terrible tragedy and chaos would ensue. But now she was constantly changing jobs and losing men and, in Maria's words, "fucking up, absolutely, any opportunity that's presented to her, throwing it away in the most monumental way." Sarah spoke to people with an almost alarming rapidity, when she spoke at all; in conversation she pounced and then abruptly withdrew, making no use whatsoever of the enigmatic smile that was her mother's first line of defense and that even sedate-looking Maria, uneasy upon entering a room full of strangers, would shield herself with until the initial social timidity subsided. Unlike Georgina, whose awful shyness was a kind of trampoline to catapult her overeagerly into every minute and meaningless exchange, Sarah held herself aloof from all courteous pleasantries, leading me to think that when the time came, we two might actually be able to talk.

I'd as yet had no success at breaking through to Mrs. Freshfield, though our first encounter a few weeks earlier hadn't been quite the disaster that Maria and I had begun to imagine on the drive to Gloucestershire with Phoebe. We had our presents to ease the way—Maria's was a piece of china for her mother's collection that she'd found in a Third Avenue antique shop before we'd left New York, and I had, of all things, a cheese. From London, the day before we left, Maria had phoned to ask if there was anything we could bring with us, and her mother had told her, "What I'd like more than anything is a decent piece of Stilton. You can't get proper Stilton down here anymore." Maria immediately rushed to Harrods for the Stilton, which I was to present at the door.

"And what do I talk about after the cheese?" I asked as we were turning off the motorway onto the country road to Chadleigh.

"Jane Austen is always good," Maria said.

"And after Jane Austen?"

"She has excellent furniture—what's known as 'good pieces.' Very unostentatious, really nice eighteenth-century English furniture. You can ask about that."

"And then?"

"You're counting on some very ghastly silences."

"Is that impossible?"

"Not at all," Maria said.

"Are you nervous?" She didn't look nervous so much as a little too still.

"I'm properly apprehensive. You *are* a homewrecker, you know. And she was very keen on your predecessor—socially speaking he was very acceptable. She's not very good with men, anyway. And I believe she still thinks Americans are upstarts and brash."

"What's the worst that can happen?"

"The worst? The worst would be that she will be so ill at ease that she will put you down after every sentence. The worst would be that whatever effort either of us makes, she will say one very clipped put-down remark, and then there will indeed be a frightful silence, and then another topic will be taken up and put down again in the same way. But that is not going to happen, because, one, there is Phoebe, whom she adores and who will distract us, and, two, there is you, a renowned wit of prodigious sophistication who is quite expert at these things. Isn't that so?"

"You'll find out."

Before swinging through the hilly country lanes to get to her mother's house in Chadleigh, we took a short detour in order for Maria to show me her school. As we passed the fields close by, Maria held Phoebe up so she could look at the horses—"Horses around here," she said to me, "as far as the eye can see."

The school was a long way from any human habitation, set in a vast, immaculately kept, old deer park shaded by large cedar trees. The playing fields and the tennis courts were empty when we arrived—the girls were in class and there was no one at all to be seen outside the grand Elizabethan-looking stone building where Maria had lived as a boarder until she went off to Oxford. "Looks to me like a palace," I said, rolling down the window to take in the view. "The joke was that the boys used to be brought up in laundry baskets at night," she said. "And were they?" I asked. "Certainly not. No sex at all. Girls would get crushes on the hockey mistress, that sort of thing. We'd write our boyfriends pages of letters in various colored inks on pink paper sprayed with scent. But otherwise, as you see, a place of extreme innocence."

Chadleigh, less grand but more innocent-looking even than the school, was thirty minutes on, set halfway up a very steep, very lonely Gloucestershire valley. Years ago, before the wool industry moved off, it had been a village of poor weavers. "In the old days," said Maria as we turned into the narrow main road, "these were just hovels of tuberculosis—thirteen children and no TV." Now Chadleigh was a picturesque cluster of streets and lanes, situated dramatically across the valley from a hanging beech woods—a muddle of monochromatic stone houses, grayish and austere under the clouds, and a long triangular village green where some dogs were playing. Just beyond the houses and their kitchen gardens, the farms on the rising hillside were parceled off like New England fields with old dry stone walls, meticulously laid layers of tilelike rock the color of the houses. Maria said that the first sight of the stone walls and the irregular pattern of the fields was always very emotional for her if she hadn't been back for a while.

Holly Tree Cottage seemed from the road a sizable house, though nothing like as impressive, Maria told me, as The Barton, where the family had lived before her father had taken flight. His family had been rich, but he was a second son and had got the family name with nothing to go with it. After university he'd been a banker in the City, only weekending with his family, but he hadn't much liked work and eventually skipped to Leicestershire with a very famous, horsy woman of the fifties, who had worn a top hat with a veil and ridden sidesaddle and had been known maliciously, for witty and (to me) obscure English reasons, as "Keep Death Off the Road." To put himself beyond the financial edicts of the divorce court he'd wound up only a few years later in Canada, married to a rich Vancouver girl and occupied mainly with sailing around the Sound and playing golf. The Barton proved to be too big and—after the support payments stopped coming in—beyond maintaining on Mrs. Freshfield's income. She had been left only her mother's modest capital and, thanks to the help of her stockbroker and some very stern economical management of her own, the small sum had proved to be just sufficient to get the girls through school. But this had meant selling The Barton, which lay in the open country, and renting Holly Tree Cottage, at the edge of Chadleigh village.

There was a log fire in the drawing room when we arrived and, after the presents were opened and admired and Phoebe had been allowed a wild run around the garden and given a glass of milk, we sat there having a drink before lunch. It was a pleasant room with worn Oriental carpets on the dark wood floors and on the walls a lot of family portraits along with several portraits of horses. Everything was a little worn and all in very discreet taste—chintz curtains with birds and flowers and lots of polished wood.

Following the advice garnered on the drive down, I said, "That's a very nice desk."

"Oh, it's just a copy of Sheraton," Mrs. Freshfield replied.

"And that's a beautiful bookcase."

"Oh, well, Charley Rhys-Mill was here the other day," she said, looking while she spoke at neither Maria nor me, "and he said he thought that it might well be a Chippendale design, but I'm certain it's a country piece. If you look there," she said, momentarily acknowledging my presence, "you can see the way the locks are put in, it's very rural. I think it's taken from the pattern book but I don't think it's Chippendale."

I decided that if she was going to belittle everything I admired, I had better stop here.

I said nothing more and just sipped my gin until Mrs. Freshfield took it upon herself to try to make me feel at home.

"Where are you from exactly, Mr. Zuckerman?"

"Newark. In New Jersey."

"I'm not very good at American geography."

"It's across the river from New York."

"I didn't know New York was *on* a river."

"Yes. Two."

"What was your father's profession?"

"He was a chiropodist."

There was a great silence while I drank, Maria drank, and Phoebe crayoned; we could *hear* Phoebe crayoning.

"Do you have brothers and sisters?"

"I have a younger brother," I said.

"What does he do?"

"He's a dentist."

Either these were all the wrong answers or else she knew by then all she needed to know, for the conversation about my background lasted all of half a minute. The chiropodist father and the dentist brother seemed to have summed me up instantly. I wondered if perhaps these were occupations that were simply too useful.

She had cooked the lunch herself—very English, perfectly nice, and rather bland. "There is no garlic in the lamb." She said this with what seemed to me a most ambiguous smile.

"Fine," I said amiably, but still uncertain as to whether there might not be lurking in her remark some dire ethnic implication. Perhaps this was as close as she would come to mentioning my strange religion. I couldn't imagine that was any less difficult for her than my being American. I clearly had everything going for me.

The vegetables were from the garden, Brussels sprouts, potatoes, and carrots. Maria asked about Mr. Blackett, a retired agricultural laborer who had supplemented his meager pension by working for them one day a week, mowing, hauling wood, and doing the vegetable garden. Was he still living? Yes, he was, but Ethel had recently died and he was alone in his council flat, where, said Mrs. Freshfield, she was afraid he existed just this side of hypothermia.

Maria said to me, "Ethel was Mrs. Blackett. Our cleaning lady. A very thorough cleaner. Always washed the doorstep on her knees. Terrible problems when we were teenage girls about giving Ethel a Christmas present. He'd get a bottle of whiskey from Mother, and Ethel invariably wound up with hankies from us. Mr. Blackett speaks a dialect that's almost incomprehensible. I wish you could hear it. He's a quite surprisingly nineteenth-century figure, isn't he, Mother?"

"It's going, that, the very strong rural accent," Mrs. Freshfield said, and then, Maria's effort to make the Blacketts of interest seemingly having fizzled out, we fell into a spell of doing nothing but cutting and chewing our food that I was afraid might last till we left for London.

"Maria says you're a great reader of Jane Austen," I said.

"Well, I've read her all my life. I began with *Pride and Prejudice* when I was thirteen and I've been reading her ever since."

"Why is that?"

This evinced a very wintry smile. "When did you last read Jane Austen, Mr. Zuckerman?"

"Not since college."

"Read her again and then you'll see why."

"I will, but what I was asking is what *you* get out of Jane Austen."

"She simply records life truthfully, and what she has to say about life is very profound. She amuses me so much. The characters are so very good. I'm very fond of Mr. Woodhouse in *Emma*. And Mr. Bennet, in *Pride and Prejudice*, I'm very fond of too. I'm very fond of Fanny Price, in *Mansfield Park*. When she goes back to Portsmouth after living down with the Bertrams in great style and grandeur, and she finds her own family and is so shocked by the squalor—people are very critical of her for that and say she's a snob, and maybe it's because I'm a snob myself— I suppose I am—but I find it very sympathetic. I think that's how one would behave, if one went back to a much lower standard of living."

"Which book is your favorite?" I asked.

"Well, I suppose whichever I'm reading is my favorite at the time. I read them all every year. But in the end, it's *Pride and Prejudice*. Mr. Darcy is very attractive. And then I like Lydia. I think Lydia is so foolish and silly. She's beautifully portrayed. I know so many people like that, you see. And of course I do sympathize with Mr. and Mrs. Bennet, having all these daughters of my own to marry off."

I could not tell if this was intended as some kind of blow— whether the woman was dangerous or being perfectly benign.

"I'm sorry I haven't read your books," she said to me. "I don't read very much American literature. I find it very difficult to understand the people. I don't find them very attractive or very sympathetic, I'm afraid. I don't really like violence. There's so much violence in American books, I find. Of course not in Henry James, whom I do like very much. Though I suppose he hardly counts as an American. He really is an observer of the English scene, and I think he really is very good. But I prefer him on television, I think, now. The style *is* rather long-winded. When you see them on television, they get to the point so much more quickly. They've done *The Spoils of Poynton* recently, and of course I was particularly interested in that, with my interest in furniture. They did it awfully well, I thought. They did *The Golden Bowl*. I enjoyed that very much. It *is* a rather long book. Your books are published over here, are they?"

"Yes."

"Well, I don't know why Maria hasn't sent them to me."

"Oh, I don't think you'd like them, Mother," Maria said.

Here a decision was unanimously reached to be distracted by Phoebe, who in fact was harmlessly fiddling with the vegetables on her plate and being a perfect little girl. "Maria, she's dribbling, dear," said Mrs. Freshfield, "—see to her, will you?" and for the remainder of the meal everyone's remarks had to do with the child.

During coffee in the drawing room, I asked if I might see the rest of the rooms. Just as she had disparaged the furniture when I admired it, now she disparaged the house. "It's nothing very special," she said. "It was just a bailiff's house, you know. Of course they did themselves much better in those days." I understood from this that she was herself used to far better and said no more on the subject. However, when the coffee was finished, I found I was to get the tour after all—Mrs. Freshfield rose, we followed, and this seemed to me such a good sign that I launched into a new line of inquiry that I thought might finally be appropriate.

"Maria tells me that your family has lived around here for a long time."

The reply came back at me like a hard little pellet. It could have struck my chest and gone out between my shoulder blades. "Three hundred years."

"What did they do here?"

"Sheep," like a second shot. "Everyone was in sheep then."

She pushed open the door to a large bedroom whose windows looked out to a field where some cows were grazing. "This was the nursery. Where Maria and her sisters grew up. Sarah was the oldest and she got to have a bedroom first, and Maria had to go on sleeping here with Georgina. This was a great source of bitterness. So was inheriting Sarah's clothes. When Sarah grew out of them, Maria was made to wear them, and by the time she was finished they weren't worth passing on to Georgina. So the oldest got new clothes and the youngest got new clothes, and Maria, in the middle, never did. Another source of bitterness. We were awfully hard-up for a bit, you know. Maria never quite understood that, I don't think."

"But of course I did," Maria said.

"But you resented things, I think. Perfectly naturally, quite naturally. We couldn't afford ponies, and your friends could, and you seemed to think it was my fault. Which it wasn't."

And was recalling Maria's resentment meant to suggest something about her choosing me? I couldn't really tell from Mrs. Freshfield's tone. Maybe this was affectionate banter, even if it didn't sound that way to me. Maybe it was just straight historical reporting—fact, without implication or subtle significance. Maybe this was just how these people talked.

Out in the hallway I decided to make a last effort. Pointing to a bureau at the head of the stairs, I said lightly, as if to no one, "A lovely piece."

"That's from my husband's family. My mother-in-law bought that. She found it in Worcester one day. Yes, it's a very nice piece. The handles are right too."

Success. Stop there.

While Phoebe napped, Maria and I walked down the road to the little church where she'd been taken to worship as a child.

"Well," she said, after we had left the house, "that wasn't too bad, was it?"

"I have no idea. Was it? Wasn't it?"

"She made a real effort. She doesn't do treacle tart unless it's a special occasion. Because you're a man there was wine at lunch. She obviously thought about your coming for a week."

"That I didn't get, quite."

"She went to Mr. Tims, the butcher, and asked him for a

specially nice joint. Mr. Tims made a real effort—the whole village made a real effort."

"Yes? Well, I made a real effort too. I felt as though I were crossing a mine field. I didn't have much luck with the furniture."

"You admired it too much." Maria laughed. "I must teach you never to praise someone's possessions to his face quite that way. But that's my mother, anyway. You praise it and, if it's hers, she runs it down. You made a hit with the Stilton. She cooed in ecstasies when we were alone in the kitchen."

"I can't see her in ecstasies."

"Over a Stilton, oh yes."

There was a dark patch of ancient yews outside the tiny church, a nice old building, surrounded by tombstones. "You do know the name of this tree," she said to me. "From Thomas Gray," I said, "yes, I do." "You had a very good education in Newark." "To prepare me for you, I had to." Maria opened the door to the church, whose earliest stones, she told me, had been laid by the Normans. "The smell," she said when we stepped inside, and sounded just a little stunned, as people do when their past comes wafting powerfully back, "—the smell of the damp in these places." We looked at the effigies of the noble dead and the wood carving on the bench ends until she couldn't stand the chill anymore. "There used to be six people in here for evensong on a winter Sunday. The damp *still* gets right through to my knees. Come, I'll show you my lonely places."

We walked up the hill through the village again—Maria explaining who lived in each of the houses—and then got into the car and drove out to her old hideaways, the "lonely places" that she would always revisit, whenever she came home from school, to be sure they were still there. One was a beech woods where she used to go for walks—"very haunting," she called it— and the other lay beyond the village at the bottom of the valley, a ruined mill beside a stream so small you could hop across it. She'd come there with her horse, or, after her mother had decided that she was having a hard enough time paying for the children and their schools without ponies to be fed and looked after, she'd ride out on her bicycle. "This is where I'd have my visionary feelings of the world being one. Exactly what Wordsworth describes —the real nature mysticism, moments of extreme contentment. You know, looking at the sun setting and suddenly thinking that the universe all makes sense. For an adolescent there is no better place for these little visions than a ruined mill by a trickling stream."

From there we drove to The Barton, which was quite isolated, behind a high ivy-covered wall on a dirt road several miles outside of Chadleigh. It was getting dark and, as there were dogs, we hung back by the gate looking to where the lights were burning throughout the house. It was built of the same grayish-yellow stone as Holly Tree Cottage and most every other house we'd seen, though from its size and the impressive gables it couldn't have been mistaken for the home of a poor local weaver or even of a bailiff. There was a strip of garden beyond the wall leading to the French windows downstairs. Maria said that the house had no central heating when she was a child, and so there were log fires in all the rooms, burning from September through May; electricity they'd made themselves, using an old diesel engine that pumped away most of the time. At the back, she said, were the stables, the barn, and a walled kitchen garden with rose patches; beyond was a duck pond where they had fished and learned to skate, and beyond that a nut woods, another haunted place full of glades and birds, wildflowers and bracken, where she and her sisters used to run up and down the green paths frightening each other to death. Her earliest memories were all poetic and associated with that woods.

"Servants?"

"Just two," she said. "A nanny for the children and one maid, an old parlor maid left over from before the war. My grandmother's parlor maid, called by her surname, Burton, who did all the cooking and stayed with us until she was pensioned off at the end."

"So moving into the village," I said, "was a comedown."

"We were just children, not so much for us. But my mother never recovered. Her family hasn't given up an inch of land in Gloucestershire since the seventeenth century. But her brother

278

has the estate of three thousand acres and she has nothing. Just the few stocks and shares inherited from her mother, the furniture you admired so, and those portraits of horses you failed to overpraise—kind of sub-Stubbs."

"It is all extremely foreign to me, Maria."

"I thought I sensed that at lunch."

While Phoebe, buoyed up by the mince pie, entertained Georgina, and Maria continued talking to her mother about the Chiswick house, I edged into a corner of the church crypt, away from the crush of the hungry carolers juggling wine cups and bits of pastry, and found myself across from Maria's older sister, Sarah.

"I think you like to play the moral guinea pig," Sarah said in that gun-burst style she was noted for.

"How does a moral guinea pig play?"

"He experiments with himself. Puts himself, if he's a Jew, into a church at Christmastime, to see how it feels and what it's like."

"Oh, everybody does that," I said amiably, but to let her know that I hadn't missed anything, I added, slowly, "not just Jews."

"It's easier if one's a success like you."

"What is easier?" I asked.

"Everything, without question. But I meant the moral guinea pig bit. You've achieved the freedom to knock around a lot, to go from one estate to the other and see what it's all about. Tell me about success. Do you enjoy it, all that strutting?"

"Not enough—I'm not a sufficiently shameless exhibitionist."

"But that's another matter."

"I can only exhibit myself in disguise. All my audacity derives from masks."

"I think this is getting a bit intellectual. What's your disguise tonight?"

"Tonight? Maria's husband."

"Well, I think if one's successful one should show off a bit—to encourage everybody else. Georgina's our extrovert—that says everything about this family. She still works hard at being Mummy's good girl. I, as you must have heard, am not entirely

279

stable, and Maria is utterly defenseless and a little spoiled. Her whole life has been aimed at doing nothing. She manages to do it very well."

"I hadn't noticed."

"Oh, there's nothing in the world that makes Maria so happy as a big, big check."

"Well, that's easy then. I'll give her a big one every day."

"Are you good at choosing clothes? Maria loves to have men help to choose her clothes. Men have to help Maria with everything. I hope you're prepared. Do you like to sit in that chair in the store while some lady twirls around and says, 'What do you think of this?' "

"It depends on the store."

"Yes? What store do you like? Selfridge's? Georgina keeps a horse down in Gloucestershire. She's something else entirely. All this English carry-on. Yesterday she had a big one-day event down there. Do you know what a one-day event is like? Of course you don't. It's physically terrifying. These huge, huge fences. Real English lunacy. At any moment a horse might fall and crash your brains."

"Such as they are."

"Yes, just mad," Sarah said. "But Georgina likes that."

"And what do you like?"

"What I'd like most to do? Well, what I'd most like to do and would be hard for me, which is why I really don't aspire to it in the near future, is what you do—and my mother does. But it's the hardest life I can imagine."

"There are harder."

"Don't be modest. You think it's the suffering that makes it so admirable. They say if you meet a writer it's sometimes more difficult to hate his work than if you just get the book and open it up and throw it across the room."

"Not for everyone. Some find it much easier to hate you having met you."

"My whole childhood was spent vomiting away all over the place whenever I had to perform or deliver. As I was then still in hot contention for Mummy's good girl, I had to perform and deliver *all the time*. And now I have this terribly agonizing relationship with any piece of work that I'm doing. I've never been able to function, really, in work. Neither can Maria—she can't work at all. I don't know that she's done anything for years, except to tinker with those one and a half short stories she's been writing since school. But then she's beautiful and spoiled and gets all these people to marry her instead. I'm not prepared to stay at home and be so hellishly dependent."

"Is it 'dependence'? Is it really hell?"

"What does a woman do who is intelligent and brings a lot of energy and enthusiasm to all that domestic carry-on, and in the end, for all very natural reasons, the husband disappears, either right out of the house or, like our dear father, with sixty-two girls on the side? I think the good reason that this option has disappeared is that intelligent women are not prepared to be so dependent."

"Maria's an intelligent woman."

"And didn't have such a hot time of it, did she, the first time round."

"He was a prick," I said.

"He wasn't at all. Have you met him? He actually has some wonderful qualities. I enjoy him enormously. At times he can be infinitely charming."

"I'm sure. But if you remove yourself emotionally from somebody's life, as he did, their sense of connection will eventually be eroded."

"If you're helplessly dependent."

"No, if you require some human connection from the person to whom you are married."

"I think you are leading an impostor's life," Sarah said.

"Do you?"

"With Maria, yes. There's a word for it, actually."

"Do tell me."

"Hypergamy. Do you know what it is?"

"Never heard of it."

"Bedding women of a superior social class. Desire based on a superior social class."

"So I, putting it politely, am a hypergamist; and Maria, taking revenge against the rejecting father by marrying beneath herself, is helplessly dependent. A spoiled, dependent woman of a superior social class who likes big checks with her bedside bonbons and whose life has been aimed at doing nothing. And what are you, Sarah, aside from envious, bitter, and weak?"

"I don't like Maria."

"So what? Who cares?"

"She's spoiled, she's indolent, she's soft, she's 'sensitive,' she's vain—but then so are you vain. You surely have to be quite vain in your profession. How could you take seriously what you think about otherwise? You must still be very much in love with the drama of your life."

"I am. That's why I married a beauty like your sister and give her those big checks every day."

"Our mother's terribly anti-Semitic, you know."

"Is she? No one told me."

"I'm telling you. I think you may find that in experimenting with Maria you've gone a bit over the top."

"I like to go over the top."

"Yes, you do. I've read your famous ghetto comedy. Positively Jacobean. What's it called again?"

"*My Darling Self-Image.*"

"Well, if you are, as your work suggests, fascinated with the consequences of transgression, you've come to the right family. Our mother can be hellishly unpleasant when it comes to transgression. She can be hard like a mineral—an Anglo-Saxon mineral. I don't think she really likes the idea of her languid, helpless Maria submitting to anal domination by a Jew. I imagine that she believes that like most virile sadists you fancy anal penetration."

"Tell her I take a crack at it from time to time."

"Our mother won't like that at all."

"I don't know a mother who would. That sounds typical enough to me."

"I think you're filled with rage, resentment, and vanity, all of which you cloak beneath this urbane and civilized exterior."

"That sounds rather typical too. Though there are clearly those who don't even bother with the civilized exterior."

"Do you understand everything I'm saying to you?" she asked.

"Well, I hear what you're saying to me."

Suddenly she thrust at me the half of the mince pie still in her hand. I thought momentarily that she was going to push it into my face.

"Smell this," she said.

"Why should I do that?"

"Because it smells good. Don't be so defensive because you're in a church. Smell it. It smells like Christmas. I'll bet you have no smells associated with Chanukah."

"Shekels," I said.

"I'll bet you'd like to do away with Christmas."

"Be a good Marxist, Sarah. The dialectic tells us that the Jews will never do away with Christmas—they make too much money off of it."

"You laugh very quietly, I notice. You don't want to show too much. Is that because you're in England and not in New York? Is that because you don't want to be confused with the amusing Jews you depict in fiction? Why don't you just go ahead and show some teeth? Your books do—they're all teeth. You, however, keep very well hidden the Jewish paranoia which produces vituperation and the need to strike out—if only, of course, with all the Jewish 'jokes.' Why so refined in England and so coarse in *Carnovsky*? The English broadcast on such low frequencies—Maria particularly emits *such* soft sounds, the voice of the hedgerows, isn't it?—that it must be terribly worrying whether you're going suddenly to forget yourself, bare your teeth, and cut loose with the ethnic squawk. Don't worry about what the English will think, the English are too polite for pogroms—you have fine American teeth, show them when you laugh. You look Jewish, unmistakably. You can't possibly hide that by not showing your teeth."

"I don't have to act like a Jew—I am one."

283

"Quite clever."

"Not as clever as you. You're too clever and too stupid all at the same time."

"I don't much like myself, either," she said. "Nonetheless, I do think Maria ought to have told you that she is from the sort of people who, if you knew anything about English society, you would have *expected* to be anti-Semitic. If you ever read any English novels—have you?"

I didn't bother to answer, but I didn't walk away either. I waited to see just how far my new sister-in-law actually intended to go.

"I recommend beginning your education with a novel by Trollope," she said. "It may knock some of the stuffing from your pathetic yearning to partake of English civility. It will tell you all about people like us. Read *The Way We Live Now*. It may help to explode those myths that fuel the pathetic Jewish Anglophilia Maria's cashing in on. The book is rather like a soap opera, but the main meat of it from your point of view is a little subplot, an account of Miss Longestaffe, an English young lady from an upper-class home, sort of country gentry, a bit over the hill, and she's furious that nobody's married her, and she's failed to sell herself on the marriage markets, and because she's determined to have a rich social life in London, she's going to demean herself by marrying a middle-aged Jew. The interesting bit is all her feelings, her family's feelings about this comedown, and the behavior of the Jew in question. I won't spoil it by going on. It will be quite an education, and coming, I think, not a moment too soon. Oh, you're going to go slightly ape about this stuff, I'm sure. Poor Miss Longestaffe reckons she's doing the Jew a big favor, you see, by marrying him, even if her sole motive is to get hold of his money, and to have as little to do with him as possible. And she has no thought really of what's in it for him. In fact, she feels she's conferring a social favor."

"It seems awfully fresh in your mind."

"As I was seeing you today, I got it down to look at. Are you interested?"

"Go on. How does her family take the Jew?"

"Yes, her family *is* the point, isn't it? They're thunderstruck. 'A Jew,' everyone cries, 'an old fat Jew?' She's so upset by their reaction that her defiance turns to doubt, and she has a correspondence with him—he's called Mr. Brehgert. He's actually, as it happens, though rather colorless, a thoroughly decent, responsible man, a very successful businessman. However, he is described frequently, as indeed other Jews in the book are, in terms which will set your teeth on edge. What will be particularly instructive to you is their correspondence—what it reveals about the attitudes of a large number of people to Jews, attitudes that only *appear* to be a hundred years old."

"And is that it?" I asked. "Is that all?"

"Of course not. Do you know John Buchan? He sort of flourished around the First World War. Oh, you'll like him too. You'll learn a lot. I would recommend him just on the strength of a few astonishing asides. He's terribly famous in England, enormously famous, a boy's adventure-thriller writer. His stories are all about how blond Aryan gentlemen go forth against the forces of evil, which are always amassed in Europe and have huge conspiracies, not unconnected with Jewish financiers, to somehow bring an evil cloud over the world. And of course the blond Aryans win in the end and get back to their manor houses. That's the usual story. And the Jews are usually at the bottom of it, lurking there somewhere. I really don't suggest you actually read him—it's a bit of a labor. Have a friend do it for you. Have Maria do it—she has plenty of time. She can just read out the good bits, for the sake of your education. The thing is that once in every fifty pages you get some overtly anti-Semitic remark which is simply an aside, simply the shared consciousness of all the readers and the writer. It's not like in Trollope, a developed idea. Trollope is actually interested in the predicament—this is evidence of *a shared consciousness*. And it wasn't written in 1870—this sort of mystique is still very much around, even if Maria has failed to inform you. Maria is a child in many ways. You know how children understand to stay off certain subjects. Of course talking her way into a man's pants is one of Maria's specialties, I don't mean to say she can't do that. In bed she makes it virginal again, I'm sure, with all her natural English delicacy—in bed with Maria we're back to Wordsworth. I'm sure she even made adultery virginal. Where the orgy is with Maria is in the talk. She mind-fucks a man to death, doesn't she, Nathan? You should have seen her at Oxford. For her poor tutors it was an agony. But still she doesn't say it all, you know. There are certain things you don't tell a man, and certain things, clearly, haven't been told you. Maria lies in the good way—to maintain peace. However, you ought not, because of her lies and her lapses of memory, to be grievously misled—or unprepared."

"For what? Enough of the glories of the English novel—and quite enough about Maria. Unprepared for what from whom?"

"From our mother. You will be making a mistake if, when this infant arrives, you try to stand in the way of a christening."

In the taxi, I chose not to ask Maria whether she knew how little her sister cared for her, or how profoundly Sarah resented me, or if what had been suggested about their mother's expectations for our child was, in fact, true. I was too stunned—and then we were on our way to celebrate Maria's twenty-eighth birthday at her favorite restaurant, and once I'd begun on her sister's barrage of abuse, that lovingly articulated hymn of hate, I knew there'd be no celebration. What mystified me was that all I'd ever heard about Maria's relations with Sarah was the unastonishing news that they were no longer anything like as close as they'd been as schoolgirls. She'd said something once about psychiatric problems, but only in passing, while describing the aftereffects of Sarah's lurid ninety-day marriage to a scion of the Anglo-Irish aristocracy, and not to account for her sister's feelings toward her or Buchanite view of people like me. Maria had certainly never characterized her mother as "terribly anti-Semitic," though of course I suspected that there could well be more than a trace of it in the layers and layers of social snobbery and the generalized xenophobia that I'd felt at Holly Tree Cottage. What I didn't know was whether the specter of the baptismal font was only an irresistible finale to a nasty little joke, a hilarious punch line that Sarah figured couldn't fail to arouse the ire of her sister's rich middle-aged Jew, or whether the christening of baby Zuckerman, however laughably absurd to contemplate, was something Maria and I would actually have to oppose in an ugly struggle with her mother. What if while resisting the mother who never put a foot wrong, the unfortified daughter obediently collapsed? What if Maria couldn't even *bring* herself to fight against what seemed to me, the more I thought about it, not only a more-than-symbolic attempt to kidnap the child but an effort to annul her marriage to the kike?

I began only then to realize how naïve I'd been not to have seen something like this coming, and to wonder if it hadn't been me, not Maria, who had been childishly "staying off certain subjects." I seemed to have almost deliberately blinded myself to the ideology that, of course, might underlie her proper upbringing among the country gentry, and to have failed as well to appreciate the obvious family implications of the unprecedented defiance Maria had dared to display by returning to England divorced from the well-connected young First Secretary at the U.K. mission to the U.N. and married instead to me, the Moor—in their eyes—to her Desdemona. More disturbing even than the ugly encounter with Sarah was the likelihood that I had allowed myself to be beguiled mostly by fantasy, that everything up until now had been largely a dream in which I had served as a mindless co-conspirator, spinning a superficial unreality out of those "charming" differences that had at last broken upon us with their full—if fossilized—social meaning. Living on the river indeed. The swans, the mists, the tides gently lapping at the garden wall—how could that idyll possibly be a real life? And how poisonous and painful would this conflict be? It suddenly looked as though all these months two rational and hardheaded realists had been moonily and romantically circumventing a very real and tricky predicament.

Yet in New York I'd been so eager to be rejuvenated that I simply hadn't thought it through. As a writer I'd mined my past to its limits, exhausted my private culture and personal memories, and could no longer even warm to squabbling over my work, having finally tired of my detractors rather the way you fall out of love with someone. I was sick of old crises, bored with old issues, and wanted only to undo the habits with which I had chained myself to my desk, implicated three wives in my seclusion, and, for years on end, lived in the nutshell of self-scrutiny. I wanted to hear a new voice, to make a new tie, to be enlivened by a new and original partner—to break away and take upon myself a responsibility unlike any bound up with writing or with the writer's tedious burden of being his own cause. I wanted Maria and I wanted a child, and not only had I failed to think it through, I had done so intentionally, thinking-it-through being another old habit for which I had no nostalgia. What could suit me more than a woman protesting how unsuitable she was? As by this time I was wholly unsuitable for myself, *ipso facto*, we were the perfect pair.

Five months into pregnancy the rush of hormones must do something to the skin, because Maria's had a visible radiance. It was a great moment for her. There was no movement of the baby yet, but the early sickness was well over and the discomfort of being huge and cumbersome hadn't begun, and she said that all she felt was coddled and protected and special. Over her dress she was wearing a long black wool cape with a hood that had a tassel dangling from the point; it was soft and warm and I could hold her arm as it emerged from the opening in the side. Her dress was dark green and flowing, a silk jersey dress with a deep round collar and long sleeves that closed around her wrists. That dress looked to me like all you could ask for, plain and sexy and faultless.

We were seated side by side near the end of a plush banquette, facing the paneled dining room. It was after eight and most of the tables were already occupied. I ordered champagne while Maria found in her purse the Polaroid snapshots of the house—I still hadn't had a chance to look at them closely and there were lots of things she wanted me to see. Meanwhile, I had taken out of my pocket a long black velvet box. Inside was the bracelet that I'd bought for her the week before just off Bond Street, at a shop specializing in the sort of Victorian and Georgian jewelry that she liked to wear. "It's light but not flimsy," the clerk had assured me, "delicate enough for the lady's small wrists." Sounded like handcuffs, the price was shocking, but I took it. I could have taken ten. It was a great moment, really, for both of us. Whether it qualified as "real life" remained to be seen.

"Oh, this is nice," she said, fixing the clip and then holding her arm out to admire the present. "Opals. Diamonds. The river house. Champagne. You. You," she repeated, musingly this time, "—so much rock for this moss to adhere to." She kissed my cheek and was, incarnate, in that moment, the delectability of the female. "I find being married to you a tremendous experiment in pleasure. Isn't this the best way to be fed?"

"You look lovely in that dress."

"It's really very ancient."

"I remember it from New York."

"That was the idea."

"I missed you, Maria."

"Did you?"

"I appreciate you, you know."

"That's a very strong card, that one."

"Well, it's so."

"I missed *you*. I tried very hard not to think of you all the time. When will I begin to get on your nerves?" she asked.

"I don't think you have to worry tonight."

"The bracelet is perfect, so perfect that it's hard to believe it was your own idea. If a man does something very appropriate it's usually not. It's lovely, but you know what else I want, what I want most when we move? Flowers in the house. Isn't that middle class of me? Mind you, I have a very long list of material desires, but that's what I thought when I saw the builders there today."

After that, it simply wasn't in me to yield to the impulse pressing me to blurt it out, to say to her, outright, without embellishment, "Look, your mother's a terrific anti-Semite who expects us to have our child baptized—true or false? And if true, why pretend you're oblivious to it? That's more disturbing than anything else." Instead, as though I felt no urgency about what she knew or was pretending not to know and expected to hear nothing to dismay me, as though I weren't disturbed about anything at all, I said in a voice as softly civilized as hers, "I'm afraid breaking through to your mother is still beyond me. When she regroups her forces back of that smile, I really don't know where to look. She was nothing tonight if not glacially correct, but what precisely *does* she think of us? Can you figure it out?"

"Oh, what everybody seems to be thinking, more or less. That we've 'traversed enormous differences.'"

" 'Traversed'? She said that to you?"

"She did."

"And what did you say to her?"

"I said, 'What's so tremendously different? Of course I know that in one sense we could hardly be more different. But think of all the things we've read in common, think of all the things we know in common, we speak the same language—I know far more about him than you think.' I told her I've read masses of American fiction, I've seen masses and masses of American films—"

"But she's not talking about my Americanness."

"Not solely. That's true. She's thinking about our 'associations.' She says all that's been obscured by the way we met—a secret liaison in New York. We never met among friends, we never met in public places, we never met to do things, so that we could never exasperate each other with visible signs of all of our differences. Her point is that we got married there without ever really allowing ourselves to be tested. She's concerned about our life in England. Part of these things, she tells me, is how one's group perceives one."

"And how *do* they perceive us?"

"I don't think people are terribly interested, really. Oh, I think that if they bother at all the first thing everybody thinks, when they hear about a thing like this, is that you're interested in a young woman to recharge your batteries, and maybe you're interested in English culture, that might be possible, and the shiksa syndrome, of course—that would all be obvious to them. On my side, equally obvious, they'd say, 'Well, he may be quite a lot older, and he may be Jewish, but my goodness, he's a literary star and he has got lots of money.' They'd think I was after you purely for your status and money."

"Despite my being Jewish."

"I don't think many people bother much about that. Certainly not literary types. Along the road where my mother lives, yes, there might be one or two mutters. Lots of people will be quite cynical, outrightly, of course, but then that would be true in New York as well."

"What does Georgina think?"

"Georgina is very conventional. Georgina probably thinks that I have sort of slightly given up on what I had really wanted in life, and this is a frightfully good second best and has much to recommend it."

"What have you given up on?"

"Something more obvious. More obviously the sort of thing that sorts like me are after."

"Which is?"

"Well, I think that would be . . . oh, I don't know."

"My advanced years."

"Yes, I think someone my own age, more or less. Ordinary people are profoundly disturbed by these age differences. Look, is this a good thing, this kind of talk?"

"Sure. It gives me a foothold in a foreign land."

"Why do you need that? Is something wrong?"

"Tell me about Sarah. What does she think?"

"Did something happen between you two?"

"What could happen?"

"Sarah is a little ropey sometimes. She sometimes speaks so quickly—it's like icicles breaking. Snapping. Bu-bu-bu-*bup*. You know what she said tonight, about my wearing pearls? She said, 'Pearls are a tremendous emblem of a conventional, privileged, uneducated, unthinking, complacent, unaesthetic, unfashionable, middle-class woman. They're absolute death, pearls. The only way you can wear them is masses and masses of very large ones, or something that's different.' She said, 'How can *you* be wearing pearls?' "

"And what did you tell her?"

"I said, 'Oh, because I like them.' That's the way you deal with Sarah. One just doesn't make too much of a fuss, and she eventually clams up and goes away. She knows lots of peculiar people and she can be very peculiar herself. She's always been completely fucked-up about sex."

"That puts her in good company, doesn't it?"

"What did she say to you, Nathan?"

"What *could* she say?"

"It *was* about sex. She's read you. She thinks sexual nomadism is your bag."

" 'And I upped my tent and I went.' "

"That's the idea. She thinks no man is a good bet, but a lover as a husband is worst of all."

"Is Sarah generalizing off of vast experience?"

"I wouldn't think so. I think that anybody in his right mind wouldn't try to have a sexual relationship with her. She goes through long periods of just disliking men in principle. It isn't even feminist ranting—it's all her very own, all these internal battles she's got going on. I would think that the experience she's generalizing off of has been very meager and sad. So was mine meager and sad till not long ago. I got very angry, you know, when my husband didn't speak to me for a year. And when I spoke he insisted on stopping me, smashing me all the time whenever I tried to say anything. Always. I thought about that when you were away."

"I actually enjoy listening to you speak."

"Do you, really?"

"I'm listening to you now."

"But why? That's what nobody can figure out. Girls raised like us don't ordinarily marry men interested in books. They say to me, 'But *you* don't have intellectual conversations, do you?' "

"Intellectual enough for me."

"Yes, I talk intellectual? Do I really? Like Kierkegaard?"

"Better."

"They all think I'd make a marvelous housewife—one of the last terrific ones around. Frankly, I've often thought that maybe that is my métier. I see my two sisters going out to work, and I think, I'm now twenty-eight, nearly thirty, and since university I've achieved absolutely nothing, aside from Phoebe. And then I think, What's wrong with that? I have a delightful daughter, I now have a delightful husband who does not smash me all the time whenever I try to speak, and I'll soon have a second child and a lovely house by the river. And I'm writing my little stories about the meadows, the mists, and the English mud that no one will ever read, and that no one *will* ever read them doesn't matter to me at all. There is also a school of thought in the family that says I married you because ever since our father walked out I was always going around looking for him."

"According to this school, I am your father."

"Only you're not. Though you do have fatherly qualities here and there, *you* are definitely not my father. Sarah is the one who sees us as three grossly fatherless women. It's a cherished preoccupation of hers. She says the father's body is like Gulliver—something you can rest your feet on, snuggle up in, walk around on top of, thinking, 'This is mine.' Rest your feet on it and step off from there."

"Is she right?"

"To a degree. She's clever, Sarah. Once he was gone we never saw him that often—a day at Christmas, a weekend in the summer, but not much more. And for years now not at all. So, yes, there probably was a sense of the world being very thin at the edges. The mother can be as competent and responsible as ours, but in our world the value was entirely defined by the father's activity. Somehow we were always out of the run of ordinary life. I didn't realize until I was older some of the jobs that women might do. I still don't."

"You regret that?"

"I told you, I have never been happier than being this preposterous, atavistic woman who does not care to assert herself.

Sarah is working at it all the time, trying so hard to be assertive, and every time an opportunity is presented to her, a serious opportunity and not just badgering Georgina or me, she goes into a terrible gloom or a terrible panic."

"Because she's a daughter whose father vanished."

"When we were at home, she used to go around every March eleventh like the character at the beginning of *Three Sisters*. 'It's a year ago today that Father pissed off.' She always felt that there was nobody behind us. And there *was* something uneasy-making about Mother having the ambition for us. Wanting us to be well-educated, putting us through university, wanting us to get good jobs—that was all quite unusual in Mother's world, it had something vicarious and compensatory written all over it, something desperate, at least for Sarah."

It was while we were eating our dessert that I heard a woman loudly announcing, in exaggeratedly English tones, "Isn't that perfectly disgusting." When I turned to see who'd spoken, I found it was a large, white-haired, elderly woman at the end of our banquette, no more than ten feet away, who was finishing her dinner beside a skeletal old gentleman I took to be her husband. He didn't seem to be disgusted by anything, nor did he seem quite to be dining with the woman who was, but silently sat contemplating his port. I took them at a glance to be very well-heeled.

Addressing the room at large, but looking now directly at Maria and me, the woman said, "Isn't it, though—simply disgusting," while the husband, who was both present and absent, gave no indication that her observation might be relevant to anything he knew or cared about.

A moment earlier, convinced by Maria's customary candidness that it was not she who'd been trying to delude or mislead me but "ropey" Sarah all on her own, reassured by all she'd said that between us nothing was other than as I'd always assumed, I had reached out to touch her, the back of two fingers lightly brushing her cheek. Nothing bold, no alarmingly public display of carnality, and yet when I turned and saw that we were still pointedly being stared down, I realized what had aroused this naked rebuke: not so much that a man had tendered his wife a tiny caress in a restaurant but that the young woman *was* the wife to this man.

As though a low-voltage shock were being administered beneath the table, or she had bitten into something awful, the elderly white-haired woman began making odd, convulsive little facial movements, seemingly in some kind of sequence; as though flashing coded signals to an accomplice, she drew in her cheeks, she pursed her lips, she lengthened her mouth—until unable apparently to endure any further provocation, she called out sharply for the headwaiter. He came virtually on the run to see what the trouble was.

"Open a window," she told him, again in a voice that no one in the restaurant could fail to hear. "You must open a window immediatcly—there's a terrible smell in here."

"Is there, madam?" he courteously replied.

"Absolutely. The stink in here is abominable."

"I'm terribly sorry, madam. I don't notice anything."

"I don't wish to discuss it—please do as I say!"

Turning to Maria, I quietly told her, "I am that stink."

She was puzzled, even at first a little amused. "You think that this has to do with you?"

"Me *with* you."

"Either that woman is crazy," she whispered, "or she's drunk. Or maybe you are."

"If she were one, or the other, or both, it might have to do with me and it might not have to do with me. But inasmuch as she continues looking at me, or me with you, I have to assume that I am that stink."

"Darling, she is mad. She is just a ridiculous woman who thinks someone has on too much scent."

"It is a racial insult, it is intended to be that, and if she keeps it up, I am not going to remain silent, and you should be prepared."

"*Where* is the insult?" Maria said.

"The emanations of Jews. She is hypersensitive to Jewish emanations. Don't be dense."

"Oh, this is ridiculous. You are being absurd."

From down the banquette, I heard the woman saying, "They smell so funny, don't they?" whereupon I raised my hand to get the headwaiter's attention.

"Sir." He was a serious, gray-haired, soft-spoken Frenchman who weighed what was said to him as carefully and objectively as an old-fashioned analyst. Earlier, after he'd taken our order, I'd remarked to Maria on the Freudian rigorousness with which he'd done nothing to influence our choice from among the evening's several specialties whose preparation he'd laconically described.

I said to him, "My wife and I have had a very nice dinner and we'd like our coffee now, but it's extremely unpleasant with someone in the restaurant intent upon making a disturbance."

"I understand, sir."

"A window!" she called imperiously, snapping her fingers high in the air. "A window, before we are overcome!"

Here I stood and, for good or bad, even as I heard Maria entreating me—"Please, she's quite mad"—made my way out from behind the table and walked to where I could stand facing the woman and her husband, who were seated side by side. He didn't pay any more attention to me than he did to her—simply continued working on his port.

"Can I help you with your problem?" I asked.

"Pardon me?" she replied, but without the flicker of an upward glance, as though I were not even there. "Please, leave us alone."

"You find Jews repellent, do you?"

"Jews?" She repeated the word as though she'd not come upon it before. "*Jews*? Did you hear that?" she asked her husband.

"You are most objectionable, madam, grotesquely objectionable, and if you continue shouting about the stink, I am going to request that the management have you expelled."

"You will do *what*?"

"*Have—you—thrown—out.*"

Her twitching face went suddenly motionless, momentarily at least she appeared to have been silenced, and so rather than stand there threatening her any longer, I took that for a victory and started back to our table. My face was boiling hot and had obviously turned red.

"I'm not good at these things," I said, slipping back into the seat. "Gregory Peck did it better in *Gentleman's Agreement*."

Maria did not speak.

This time when I waved for service, a waiter *and* the head-waiter came hurrying over. "Two coffees," I said. "Would you like anything else?" I asked Maria.

She pretended not even to hear me.

We'd finished the champagne and all but a little of the bottle of wine, and though I really didn't want any more to drink, I ordered a brandy, so as to make it known to the surrounding tables and to the woman herself—*and* to Maria—that we had no intention of curtailing our evening in any way. The birthday celebration would go on.

I waited until after the coffee and brandy were set down, and then I said, "Why aren't you speaking? Maria, speak to me. Don't act as though I was the one who committed the offense. If I had done nothing, I assure you it would have been even less tolerable to you than my telling her to shut up."

"You went quite crazy."

"Did I? Failed to observe British rules of dignified restraint, did I? Well, that stuff she was pulling is very trying for us people —even more trying than Christmas."

"It isn't necessary now to go for *me*. All I'm saying is that if she meant that about the window, literally, to you, about you, then she is clearly *mad*. I don't believe any sane English person would allow themselves to go so far. Even drunk."

"But they might think it," I said.

"No. I don't even think they think it."

"They wouldn't associate stink with Jews."

"No. I do not think so. There is no general interest in this occurrence," Maria said firmly. "I don't believe you can—if that is what you want to do—extrapolate anything about England or the English, and you mustn't. Especially as you cannot even be sure, much as you seem to want to be, that your being Jewish had anything even to do with it."

"There you are wrong—there you are either innocent or blind in both eyes. She looks over here and what does she see? Miscegenation incarnate. A Jew defiling an English rose. A Jew putting on airs with a knife and a fork and a French menu. A Jew who is injurious to her country, her class, and her sense of fitness. I shouldn't, inside her mind, *be* at this restaurant. Inside her mind, this place isn't for Jews, least of all Jews defiling upper-class girls."

"What has come over you? The place is full of Jews. Every New York publisher who comes to London stays at this hotel and eats in this restaurant."

"Yes, but she's probably slow on the uptake, this old babe. In the old days it wasn't like that, and clearly there are still people who object to Jews in such places. She meant it, that woman. She did. Tell me, where do they get these exquisite sensibilities? What exactly do they smell when they smell a Jew? We're going to have to sit down and talk about these people and their aversions so that I'm not caught off guard next time we go out to eat. I mean, this isn't the West Bank—this isn't the land of the shoot-out, this is the land of the carol service. In Israel I found that everything comes bursting out of everyone all the time, and so probably means half as much as you think. But because on the surface, at least, they don't seem to be like that here, their little English outbursts are rather shocking—perhaps revealing too. Don't you agree?"

"That woman was *mad*. Why are you suddenly indicting *me*?"

"I don't mean to—I'm overheated. And surprised. Sarah, you see, tried to make clear to me, back in the church, something else that I didn't know—that your mother, as she put it, is 'terribly anti-Semitic.' So much so that I'm mystified I wasn't told about it long ago so as to know what to expect when I got here. Not terribly anti-American, terribly anti-*Semitic*. *Is* it true?"

"Sarah said that? To you?"

"Is it true?"

"It doesn't have to do with us."

"But it's true. Nor is Sarah England's greatest Jew-lover—or didn't you know that either?"

"That has nothing to do with us. None of it does."

"But why didn't you *tell* me? I do not understand. You've told me everything, why not that? We tell each other the truth. Honesty is one of the things we have. Why did it have to be hidden?"

She stood up. "Please stop this attack."

The bill was paid and in only minutes, leaving the restaurant, we were passing the table of my enemy. She now seemed as innocuous as her husband—once we'd faced off, she hadn't dared to go on about the smell. However, just as Maria and I stepped into the passageway joining the dining room to the hotel lobby, I heard her Edwardian stage-accent rising above the restaurant murmur. "What a disgusting couple!" she announced, summarily.

It turned out that Maria had been embarrassed ever since her adolescence by Mrs. Freshfield's anti-Semitism, but as she'd never known it to affect anything other than her own equanimity she'd simply endured it as a terrible flaw in someone who was otherwise an exemplary protector. Maria described her mother's family as "all crazy—a life of drink and boredom, total prejudice overlaid with good manners and silly talk"; anti-Semitism was just *one* of the stupid attitudes by which her mother could hardly have been uncontaminated. It had more to do with the imprint of her times, her class, and her impossible family than with her character—and if that seemed to me a specious distinction, it wasn't one that Maria cared to defend, since she herself knew the argument against it.

What mattered, she said, what explained everything—more or less—was that so long as it had looked as though we'd be living in America, in a house in the country with Phoebe and the new baby, there'd been no need to bring any of this up. Maria admired her mother's strength, her courage, loved her still for the full life she'd worked so hard to make for her children when there was virtually no one around who would seriously help her out, and she couldn't bear me despising her for something that wasn't going to do us any harm and to which I couldn't have been expected to bring, from my background, even the simplest sort of social understanding. If we had been able to make America our home, her mother would have come for a couple of weeks each summer to visit the children and that would have been all we ever saw of her; even if she had wanted to interfere, she would have been too clever to risk her prestige in a struggle she could only lose, opposing me from such a distance.

And then once we were legally pledged to live in London, the problem was too big for Maria to confront. She felt that by adapting to the stringent custody guarantees extracted by her ex-husband, I had already taken on more than I'd bargained for; she couldn't bring herself to announce that in addition there was waiting to pounce upon me in England an anti-Semitic mother-in-law waving a burning cross. What's more, she hoped that if I weren't prematurely antagonized, I could probably dislodge her mother's prejudice just by being myself. Was that so unrealistic? And had she been proved wrong? Though Mrs. Freshfield might seem to me inexplicably aloof, so far she had said nothing to Maria even remotely disparaging about marrying a Jew, nor had she so much as hinted that she expected our infant to be chris-tened. That might please her, Maria had no doubt that it would, but she was hardly deluded enough to expect it, or so fanatical as to be unable to survive without it. Maria was desolated about Sarah; she still had trouble believing that Sarah could have gone so far. But Sarah, whom everyone accepted as peculiar—who had been known all her life for her "petulant little outbursts," for being "cross and mean," who never was, as Maria put it, "a purely likable person"—was not her mother. However perturbed her mother might be about the implausible match her daughter had made in New York, she was being positively heroic in sup-pressing her chagrin. And that wasn't only the best we could have hoped for—for a beginning it was extraordinary. In fact, if it hadn't been for that woman turning up at the other end of our banquette, a rather tender evening would have taken most of the sting out of Sarah's misbehavior down in the crypt, leaving relations between Maria's anti-Semitic mother and her Jewish husband just as respectful, if remote, as they'd been since our arrival in England.

"That dreadful woman," Maria said. "And that *husband*."

With Phoebe at Mrs. Freshfield's sister's London flat and the nanny off till the following noon, with just the two of us alone together in the living room of the rented house, I was reminded of Maria lying on the sofa of my New York apartment the year before, trying to convince me how unsuitable she was. Unsuitability—what could be more suitable for a man like me?

"Yes," I said, "the old guy really let her go."

"I've seen a lot of that where I come from," Maria said. "Women of a certain class and disposition behaving terribly, talking very loudly, and they allow them to get away with absolutely every last comma."

"Because the men agree."

"Could be, needn't be. No, it's their generation—you simply never contradict a lady, a lady is not wrong, and so on. They're all misogynist anyway, those men. Their way to behave to women like that one is to be civil toward her and just let her rave. They don't even hear them."

"And she meant what I thought she meant."

"Yes," and just when it seemed that the restaurant incident had been completely defused, Maria began to cry.

"What is it?" I asked.

"I shouldn't tell you."

"The moral of this evening is that you should tell me everything."

"No, I shouldn't." She dried her eyes and did her best to smile. "That was exhaustion, really. Relief. I'm delighted we're home, I'm delighted by this bracelet, I was delighted by the shade of crimson you turned while telling that woman off, and now I have to go up to bed because I just can't take any more pleasure."

"What shouldn't you tell me?"

"Don't—don't pump me. You know why it may be that I

never explained about my mother? Not because I thought it would antagonize you, but because I was afraid it would be too intriguing. Because I do not want my mother in a book. Bad enough that's my fate, but I do not want my mother in a book because of something that, shameful as it is, is doing no one any harm. Except herself, of course—isolating her from people like you whom she has every reason to admire and enjoy."

"What made you cry?"

She closed her eyes, too exhausted to resist. "It was—well, when that woman was raving on, I had the most awful memory."

"Of?"

"This is terrible," she said. "It's shameful. It really is. There was a girl in our office when I was at the magazine—before Phoebe was born. She was a girl I liked, a colleague, my age, a very nice girl, not a close friend but a very pleasant acquaintance. We were out in Gloucestershire working on a picture story, and I said, 'Joanna, come and stay with us,' because Chadleigh isn't far from the village we were photographing. So she stayed at the house for a couple of nights. And my mother said to me, and I think Joanna may even have been in the house at the time, though she was certainly out of earshot—and I should add that Joanna is Jewish—"

"Like me—with the unmistakable genetic markings."

"My mother wouldn't miss it, I wouldn't think. Anyway, she said to me exactly, but exactly what that woman said in the restaurant. They were her very words. I had forgotten this incident entirely, just put it completely out of my mind, until I heard that woman say, 'They smell so funny, don't they?' Because I think my mother had, I don't know, got into Joanna's bedroom, or in some perfectly normal way—oh, I don't know what, this is all very difficult to go into, and I just wish to hell I hadn't remembered it and it would all go away."

"So it wasn't entirely accurate to tell me at dinner that no one would say that unless they were mad. Since your mother is clearly not mad."

Softly, she said, "I was wrong . . . and wrong despite my knowledge . . . I told you, I'm ashamed of that. She thought it and she meant it—is it mad to say it? I don't know. Must we go on about this? I'm so tired."

"Is this why the night before I left, when all those well-brought-up English liberals were loathing Zionism and attacking Israel, you jumped in and started swinging?"

"No, not at all—I said what I believe."

"But with all this baggage, what did you think would happen when you married me?"

"With all your baggage, what did you think when you married me? Please, we can't start having one of those discussions. Not only is it beneath us, it doesn't matter. You simply cannot start putting everything in a Jewish context. Or is this what comes of a weekend in Judea?"

"More likely it comes of never before having lived in Christendom."

"What's the United States, a strictly Jewish preserve?"

"I didn't run into this stuff there—never."

"Well, then you have led a very protected life. I heard plenty of it in New York."

"Yes? What?"

"Oh, 'stranglehold on the cultural life, on the economy,' and so on—all the usual stuff. I think there's more in America, actually, just because there are more Jews, and because they're not so diffident as English Jews. English Jews are beleaguered, there are so few of them. On the whole they find the thing rather an embarrassment. But in the U.S. they speak up, they speak out, they're visible everywhere—and the consequence, I can assure you, is that some people don't like it, and say as much when Jews aren't around."

"But what about here, where I now live? What do you folks really think of us folks?"

"Are you trying to upset me," she asked, "to bait me after what's happened tonight to both of us?"

"I'm just trying to find out what I don't know."

"But this is all being blown out of proportion. No, I'm not telling you, because whatever I say you're going to resent and you're only going to go at me. Again."

"What do the folks think here, Maria?"

"They think," she said sharply, " 'Why do Jews make such a bloody fuss about being Jewish?' That's what they think."

"Oh? And is that what you think?"

"It's something I've felt at times, yes."

"I didn't realize that."

"It's an extremely common feeling—and thought."

"What is meant exactly by 'fuss'?"

"Depends on what your starting point is. If you don't actually like Jews at all, practically everything a Jew does you'll perceive as Jewish. As something they ought to have dropped because it's very boring they're being so Jewish about it."

"For instance?"

"This is a bad idea," she said. "Don't you see that this is a bad idea?"

"Go on."

"I won't. No. I am incapable of protecting myself against people when they start on me like this."

"What is so boring about Jews being Jews?"

"It's all or nothing, isn't it? Our conversation doesn't seem to have any middle road. Tonight it's either sweetness or thunder."

"I am not thundering—I am dismayed, and the reason, as I told you, is that I have never run into this stuff before."

"I am not Nathan Zuckerman's first Gentile wife. I am the fourth."

"True enough. Yet never have I run into this 'mixed marriage' crap. You're the fourth, but the first from a country about which, in matters relevant to my personal well-being, I seem to be totally ignorant. Boring? That's a stigma that I would think attaches more readily to the English upper classes. Boring Jews? You must explain this to me. In my experience it's usually boring *without* the Jews. Tell me, what is so boring to the English about Jews being Jews?"

"I will tell you, but only if we can have a discussion and not the useless, destructive, and painful clash that you want to instigate regardless of *what* I say."

"What is so boring about Jews being Jews?"

"Well, I object to people—this is a feeling only, this is not a thought-out position; I might have to discipline it if you insist on keeping us up much longer, after the chablis and all that champagne—I object to people clinging to an identity just for the sake of it. I don't think there's anything admirable about it at all. All this talk about 'identities'—your 'identity' is just where you decide to stop thinking, as far as I can see. I think all these ethnic groups—whether they are Jewish, whether they're West Indian and think they must keep this Caribbean thing going— simply make life more difficult in a society where we're trying to just live amicably, like London, and where we are now very very diverse."

"You know, true as some of that may sound, the 'we-ness' here is starting to get me down. These people with their dream of the perfect, undiluted, unpolluted, unsmelly 'we.' Talk about *Jewish* tribalism. What is this insistence on homogeneity but a not very subtle form of *English* tribalism? What's so intolerable about tolerating a few differences? *You* cling to *your* 'identity,' 'just for the sake of it'—from the sound of it, no less than your mother does!"

"Please, I cannot be shouted at and keep talking. It's not intolerable and that's not what I said. I certainly do tolerate differences when I feel they're genuine. When people are being anti-Semitic or anti-black or anti-anything *because* of differences, I despise it, as you know. All I have been saying is that I don't feel that these differences are always entirely genuine."

"And you don't like that."

"All right, I'll tell you a thing I don't like, since that's what you are dying to push me to say—I don't like going to north London, to Hampstead or Highgate, and finding it like a foreign country, which it really does seem to me."

"Now we're getting down to it."

"I'm not getting *down* to anything. It's the truth, which you wanted—if it happens to make you unreasonable, that's not my fault. If you want to leave me as a result, that's not my fault either. If the upshot of my malicious sister trying to destroy this marriage is that she actually succeeds, well, that'll be her first great triumph. But it won't be ours!"

"It's pleasing to hear you raise your voice to make a point like those of us who smell."

"Oh, that is not fair. Not at all."

"I want to learn about Hampstead and Highgate being a foreign country. Because they're heavily Jewish? Can't there be a Jewish variety of Englishman? There is an English variety of human being, and we all manage to tolerate that somehow."

"If I may *stick* to the point—there are many Jews who live there, yes. People there who are my generation, who are my peers—they have the same sort of responses, they probably went to the same sort of schools, generally they'd have similar kinds of education, forgetting religious education, but they all have a different style from me, and I am *not* saying that's distasteful—"

"Just boring."

"Nor boring. Only that I do feel alien among them—being there makes me feel left out and it makes me feel that I'm better off somewhere I feel more normal."

"The net of the Establishment draws ever tighter. How is the style different?"

All this time she'd been lying across the sofa, her head propped on a pillow, looking toward the fire and the chair where I was sitting. Suddenly she sat straight up and hurled the pillow onto the floor. The catch must have come undone on the bracelet, because it came flying off and fell to the floor too. She picked it up and, leaning forward, laid it between us on the glass top of the coffee table. "Of course nothing is understood! Nothing is ever understood! Not even with you! Why won't you stop? Why don't you save your nettle-grasping for your writing?"

"Why don't you just go on and tell me all the things you shouldn't tell me? Certainly *not* telling them to me hasn't worked."

"All right. All *right*. Now that we have overestimated the meaning of everything and are assured that whatever I say will come back to haunt me—all I was going to tell you, which was no more than an anthropological aside, is that it is common parlance—though it is not necessarily anti-Semitic—for people to say, 'Oh, such-and-such is frightfully Jewish.' "

"I would have thought such sentiments were more subtly coded here. In England, they say that outright? Really?"

"Indeed they do. You betcha."

"Give me examples, please."

"Why not? Why not, Nathan? *Why* stop? An example. You go for drinks somewhere in Hampstead, and you're plied by an active hostess with an overabundance of little things to eat and sort of assaulted with extra drinks and, generally speaking, made to feel uncomfortable by a superabundance of hospitality and introductions and energy—well, then one is liable to say, 'That's very Jewish.' There is no anti-Semitic feeling behind the statement, it is merely drawing-room sociology, a universal phenomenon—everybody does it everywhere. I'm sure there have been times when even a tolerant and enlightened citizen of the world like you has been at least *tempted* to say, 'That's very goyish'—maybe even about something that *I* have done. Oh, look," she said, coming to her feet in that perfect green dress, "why don't you go back to America where they do 'mixed marriages' right? This is absurd. This was all a great mistake, and I'm sure the fault is entirely mine. Stick to American shiksas. I should never have made you come back here with me. I should never have tried to paper over things about my family that it would be impossible for you to understand or accept—though that's exactly why I did it. I shouldn't have done anything I've done, beginning with letting you invite me into your apartment for that one cup of tea. Probably I should just have let him go on shutting me up for the rest of my life—what difference does it make who shuts me up, at least that way I would have kept my little family together. Oh, it just makes me feel terribly cross that I went through all this to wind up with yet another man who cannot stand the things I say! It's been such an extended education—and for *nothing*, endless preparation for just *nothing*! I stayed with him for my daughter, stayed with him because Phoebe went around with a sign on her head saying, 'One father in residence—and it's a lot of fun.' Then stupidly, after you and I met, I said, 'But what about me? Instead of an enemy for a husband, what about a soul mate—that unattainable impossibility!' I've gone through hell, really, to marry you—you're the most daring thing I've ever done. And now it turns out that you actually think that there is an International Gentile Conspiracy of which I am a paid-up member! Inside your head, it now turns out, there is really no great difference between you and that Mordecai Lippman! Your brother's off his rocker? *You are your brother!* Do you know what I should have done, despite his generally outrageous behavior to me? True to the tradition of my school, I should have laced my shoes up tighter and got on with it. Only you feel so dishonest and so cowardly—compromising, compromising—but maybe the compromising is just being grown-up and looking for soul mates is so much idiocy. I certainly didn't find a soul mate, that's for sure. I found a Jew. Well, you certainly never struck me as very Jewish, but that's where I was wrong again. Clearly I never began to understand the depths of this thing. You disguise yourself as rational and moderate when *you* are the wild nut! *You are Mordecai Lippman!* Oh, this is a disaster. I'd have an abortion if you could have an abortion after five months. I don't know what to do about that. The house we can sell, and as for me, I'd rather be on my own if this is going to go on all our lives. I just can't face it. I don't have that kind of emotional reserves. How terribly unfair for you to turn on me—*I* didn't plant that woman next to us! And my mother really isn't my fault, you know, nor are the attitudes with which she was raised. You think I don't know about people in this country and how petty and vicious they can be? I don't say this to excuse her, but in her family, you know, if you weren't a dog or didn't have a penis, you weren't likely to get much attention—so she's had to put up with her shit too! And quite on her own has come a very long way. As have we all! I did not choose to have a malicious sister and I didn't choose to have an anti-Semitic mother—no more than you chose to have a brother in Judea toting a gun, or a father who, from all you say, was not extremely rational about

Gentiles, either. Nor, I remind you, has my mother said a single thing to offend you, or, privately, to offend me. When she first saw your picture, when I showed her a photograph, she did say, rather quietly, 'Very Mediterranean-looking, isn't he?' And I said, just as quietly, 'You know, Mummy, I think, taking a global view, that blue eyes and blond hair may be on the way out.' She nearly wet herself, she was so astonished to hear such a sentiment from the lips of her amiable child. But, you see, like many of us, the illusion she's come to is the one she wants. However, she was quite smooth about it, really, didn't rise to it in any way—and otherwise, though you are a homewrecker, as I've explained to you, and *any* new man of mine, Gentile as well as Jew, would be clouded by that, she said nothing more and was actually quite nice, wildly so, really, for someone who, as we know, is not all that keen on Jews. If this evening she was 'glacial,' it's because that's how she is, but she has also been as affable as she can, and probably that is because she is very anxious not to see *us* now go off in different directions. You really think she wants me to have a *second* divorce? The irony is, of course, that she's the one who's turned out to be right—not you and me with our enlightened blather but my bigoted mother. Because it's obvious that you *can't* have people from such different starting points understand each other about *anything*. Not even we, who seemed to understand each other so marvelously. Oh, the irony of everything! Life always something other than what you expect! But I just cannot take this subject as the center of my life. And you, to my astonishment, want suddenly to take it as the center of yours! You, who in New York hit the ceiling when I called the Jews a 'race,' are now going to tell me that you're genetically unique? Do you really think that your Jewish beliefs, which I can't see on you anywhere, frankly, make you incompatible with me? God, Nathan, you're a human being—I don't care if you're a Jew. You ask me to tell you what 'us folks' think about you folks, and then when I try to, as truthfully as I can, without fudging things, you resent what I say, *as predicted*. Like a narrow-minded fart! Well, I can't stand it. I won't! I already have a narrow-minded mother! I already have a crazy sister! I'm not married to Mr. Rosenbloom in North Finchley, I'm married to *you*! I don't think of you, I don't go around thinking of you as being a Jew or a non-Jew, I think of you as yourself. When I go down to see how the house is coming along, do you think I ask myself, 'Is the Jew going to be happy here? Can a Jew find happiness in a house in Chiswick?' *You're* the one who's mad. Maybe on this subject *all* Jews are mad. I can understand how they might be, I can see why Jews feel so touchy and strange and rejected, and certainly misused, to put it mildly, but if we are going to go on misunderstanding each other about this, quarreling all the time and putting this subject at the center of our lives, then I don't want to live with you, I *can't* live with you, and as for our baby—oh, God only knows, now I'll have *two* children without fathers. Just what I wanted! Two children without fathers in residence, but even that is better than this, because this is just *too stupid*. Go back to America, please, where everybody loves Jews—you think!"

Imagine. Because of how I'd been provoked by Sarah in the church and then affronted in the restaurant, it was conceivable that my marriage was about to break up. Maria had said it was just too stupid, but stupidity happens unfortunately to be real, and no less capable of governing the mind than fear, lust, or anything else. The burden isn't either/or, consciously choosing from possibilities equally difficult and regrettable—it's and/and/and/and/and as well. Life *is* and: the accidental and the immutable, the elusive and the graspable, the bizarre and the predictable, the actual and the potential, all the multiplying realities, entangled, overlapping, colliding, conjoined—plus the multiplying illusions! This times this times this times this . . . Is an intelligent human being likely to be much more than a large-scale manufacturer of misunderstanding? I didn't think so when I left the house.

That there were people in England who, even after Hitler might have been thought to have somewhat tarnished the Jew-hater's pride, still harbored a profound distaste for Jews hadn't come as a surprise. The surprise wasn't even that Maria should extend as much tolerance as she did to her mother, or that, so improbably, she should have been naïve enough to believe that she was averting a disaster by pretending that there wasn't that kind of poison around. The unpredictable development was how furious it all made me. But then I had been wholly unprepared —usually it was the Semites, and not the anti-Semites, who assaulted me for being the Jew I was. Here in England I was all at once experiencing first-hand something I had never personally been bruised by in America. I felt as though gentlest England had suddenly reared up and bit me on the neck—there was a kind of irrational scream in me saying, "She's not on my side—she's on their side!" I'd considered very deeply and felt vicariously the wounds that Jews have had to endure, and, contrary to the charges by my detractors of literary adventurism, my writing had hardly been born of recklessness or naïveté about the Jewish history of pain; I had written my fiction in the knowledge of it, and even in consequence of it, and yet the fact remained that, down to tonight, the experience of it had been negligible in my personal life. Crossing back to Christian Europe nearly a hundred years after my grandparents' westward escape, I was finally feeling up against my skin that outer reality which I'd mostly come to know in America as an "abnormal" inner preoccupation permeating nearly everything within the Jewish world.

All this being so, I still had to wonder if I wasn't suffering from the classic psychosemitic ailment rather than the serious clinical disease, if I wasn't perhaps a paranoid Jew attaching false significance to a manageable problem requiring no more than common sense to defuse—if I wasn't making them all stand for far too much and overimagining everything; if I wasn't wanting the anti-Semitism to be there, and in a big way. When Maria had implored me not to pursue it, why hadn't I listened? Talking about it, going on about it, mercilessly prolonging that discussion, it was inevitable that we would reach the burning sore. But then it wasn't as though I had been unprovoked or that separating us from all this vile stuff was wholly within my power. Of course resisting provocation is always an option, but can you really have your sister-in-law calling you a dirty Jew bastard, and someone else saying that you're stinking up the place, and then someone you love saying why do you make such a production of these things, without your head starting to explode, no matter what sort of peaceable person you've tried turning yourself into? It was even possible that far from making them stand for too much, I had come upon a deep, insidious Establishment anti-Semitism that is latent and pervasive but that, among the mild, well-brought-up, generally self-concealing English, only the occasional misfit like a madwoman or a fucked-up sister actually comes out with. Otherwise by and large it's subliminal, one can't hear it, no rampant signs anywhere you look, except perhaps in the peculiarly immoderate, un-English-like Israel-loathing that the young people at that dinner party had seemed to go in for.

In America, I thought, where people claim and disown "identities" as easily as they slap on bumper stickers—where even though there are people sitting in clubs who think it's still the land of Aryans, it just don't happen to be so—I could act like a reasonable fellow when she'd distinguished Jews from Caucasians. But here, where you were swathed permanently in what you were born with, encased for life with where you began, here in a *real* land of Aryans, with a wife whose sister, if not her mother as well, appeared to be the pointwoman for some pure-blooded phalanx out to let me know that I was not welcome and had better not come in, I couldn't let the insult pass. Our affinity was strong and real, but however much complicity we'd felt at the carol service, Maria and I were *not* anthropologists in Somaliland, nor were we orphans in a storm: she came from somewhere and so did I, and those differences we talked so much about could begin to have a corrosive effect once the charm began wearing thin. We couldn't just be "us" and say the hell with "them" any more than we could say to hell with the twentieth century when it intruded upon our idyll. Here's the problem, I thought: even if her mother is a completely entrenched and bigoted upper-class snob, Maria loves her and is trapped by that —she doesn't really want her mother referring to her pagan grandchild and yet she doesn't want to fight me either, while I, for my part, don't intend to lose—not the woman, the baby, or the argument. How do I salvage what I want out of this clash of atavistic wills?

God, how enraging to blunder smilingly into people who want no part of you—and how awful to compromise, even for love. When asked to accede, whether by Gentile or Jew, I discover that all my efforts seem to go against it.

The past, the unevadable past, had gained control and was about to vandalize our future unless I did something to stop it. We could digest each other so easily, but not the history clinging to the clan that each of us brought along into our life. Is it really possible that I will go around with the sense that, however subtly, she is buying into their anti-Semitism, that I will hear echoes of the anti-Semite in her, and that she will see in me a Jew who can't do otherwise than let being a Jew eclipse everything else? Is it possible that neither of us can control this old, old stuff? What if there's no extracting her from a world I don't wish to enter even if I were welcome there?

What I did was to hail a taxi to take me to Chiswick, to the house on the river that we had bought and were remodeling to encapsulate what we had imagined we had, the house that was being transformed into ours and that represented my own transformation—the house that represented the rational way, the warm human enclosure that would shelter and protect something more than my narrative mania. It seemed at that moment that everything was imaginatively possible for me except the mundane concreteness of a home and a family.

Because walls were coming down and not every floorboard was in place, I didn't wander around inside, even though when I tried the front door I found it unlocked. A lonely midnight visit to the unfinished haven was sufficiently symbolic of my predicament without overwriting the scene entirely by stumbling around in the dark and breaking my neck. Instead, I wandered from window to window, peering in as though I were casing the joint, and then I sat on the sill of the French doors to the terrace, staring out at the Thames. There was nothing gliding by but water. I could see the lights of some of the houses through the branches of the trees on the far side of the river. They seemed tiny and far away. It was like looking across to a foreign country —from one foreign country to another.

I sat for nearly an hour like somebody who's lost his key, all alone, feeling pretty forlorn and rather cold, but gradually I quieted down and was breathing more evenly again. Even if it wasn't yet snug and glowing above the water, the tangibility of the house helped to remind me of all that I had worked so hard to suppress in order to make contact with these ordinary, temporal satisfactions. The tangibility of that half-rebuilt, unoccupied house made me reconsider very seriously whether what had happened warranted this drama, if the evidence was adequate for what my feelings had concluded. When I looked back over the last year and recalled the obstinacy and resilience with which we had successfully combated whatever had blocked our way, I felt ridiculous for being so easily overwhelmed and feeling so innocently victimized. You do not go from being a conventionally unhappy married mother and a thrice-divorced, childless literary anchorite to being partners in a flourishing domestic life as father-to-be and pregnant wife, you do not proceed in fourteen months to thoroughly rearrange nearly everything important to you by being two helpless weaklings together.

What had happened? Nothing particularly original. We had a fight, our first, nothing more or less annihilating than that. What had overcharged the rhetoric and ignited the resentment was of course her role of mother's daughter rubbing against mine of father's son—our first fight hadn't even been ours. But then the battle initially rocking most marriages is usually just that— fought by surrogates for real antagonists whose conflict is never rooted in the here and now but sometimes originates so far back that all that remains of the grandparents' values are the newly-weds' ugly words. Virginal they may wish to be, but the worm in the dream is always the past, that impediment to all renewal.

So what do I say when I get home? What do I do now, now that I know all this? Do I run up the stairs and kiss her as though everything's fine, do I wake her to tell her all I've been thinking—or isn't it better to come quietly and unobtrusively into the house and leave the damage to be repaired by the mundane glue of the round of life? Only what if she isn't there, if upstairs is dark and the house still because she's gone to share Phoebe's divan at her aunt's flat? What if the interminable day that began at dawn Middle Eastern Time in a taxi from Jerusalem to the airport security check ends with Maria fleeing Kensington from a militant Jew? From Israel, to the crypt, to the banquette, to the divorce court. In this world, I'm the terrorist.

If she isn't there.

Sitting and staring across the dark river, I envision a return of the life I'd fought free of by anchoring myself to Maria. This woman of profound forbearance and moral courage, this woman of seductive fluency whose core is reticence and discretion, this woman whose emotional knowledge is extraordinary, whose intellect is so clear and touching, who, even though she favors one sexual position, is hardly innocent of what love and desire are about, a bruised, deliciously civilized woman, articulate, intelligent, coherent, with a lucid understanding of the terms of life and that marvelous gift for recitative—*what if she isn't there?* Imagine Maria gone, my life *without* all that, imagine no outer life of any meaning, myself completely otherless and reabsorbed within—all the voices once again only mine ventriloquizing, all the conflicts germinated by the tedious old clashing of contradictions within. Imagine—instead of a life inside something other than a skull, only the isolating unnaturalness of self-battling. No, no—nò, no, no, this chance may be my last and I've disfigured myself enough already. When I return, let me find in the bed, beneath our blanket, all those beautiful undulations that are not syntactical, hips that are not words, soft living buttocks that are not my invention—let me find sleeping there what I've worked for and what I want, a woman with whom I'm content, pregnant with our future, her lungs quietly billowing with life's real air. For if she should be gone, should there be only a letter beside my pillow . . .

But forgo the lament (which everyone who's ever been locked out of anything knows by heart)—what exactly is in that letter? Being Maria's, it could be interesting. This is a woman who could *teach* me things. *How* have I lost her—if I've lost her—this contact, this connection to a full and actual outer existence, to a potent, peaceful, happy life? Imagine that.

I'm leaving.

I've left.

I'm leaving you.

I'm leaving the book.

That's it. Of course. The book! She conceives of herself as my fabrication, brands herself a fantasy and cleverly absconds, leaving not just me but a promising novel of cultural warfare barely written but for the happy beginning.

Dear Nathan,

I'm leaving. I've left. I'm leaving you and I'm leaving the book and I'm taking Phoebe away before anything dreadful happens to her. I know characters rebelling against their author has been done before, but as my choice of a first husband should have made clear—at least to me—I have no desire to be original and never did. I loved you and it was kind of thrilling to live totally as somebody else's invention, since, alas, that is how I am bent anyway, but even my terrible tameness has its limits, and I will be better off with Phoebe back where we began, living upstairs with him. Sure it's lovely being listened to as opposed to being shut up, but it's also quite creepy to think that I am monitored closely only to be even more manipulated and exploited than I was when you extracted me (for artistic purposes) from my situation upstairs. This stuff isn't for me, and I warned you as much in the beginning. When I begged you not to write about me, you assured me that you can't write "about" anyone, that even when you try to, it comes out someone else. Well, insufficiently someone else to suit me. I recognize that radical change is the law of life and that if everything quietens down on one front, it invariably gets noisy on another; I recognize that to be born, to live, and to die is to change form, but you overdo it. It was not fair to put me through your illness and the operation and your death. "Wake up, wake up, Maria—it was all only a dream!" But that gets wearing after a while. I can't take a lifetime of never knowing if you're fooling. I can't be toyed with forever. At least with my English tyrant I knew where I stood and could behave accordingly. With you that'll never be.

And how do I know what's to happen to Phoebe? That terrifies me. You weren't beyond killing your brother, you weren't beyond killing yourself, or grandiosely amusing yourself on the plane up from Israel by staging a lunatic hijack attempt—what if you decide everything will be more interesting if my daughter steps off the towpath into the river? When I think about literary surgery being performed experimentally upon those I love, I understand what drives the antivivisectionists nuts. You had no right to make Sarah, in that crypt, say words she would never have spoken if it weren't for your Jewish hang-up. Not only was it unnecessary, it was cruelly provocative. Since I had already confided to you that Jews seem to me too quick finding fault with Gentiles, condemning things as horrendously anti-Semitic, or even mildly so, when they aren't, you made sure to provide me with a sister who is anti-Semitic in spades. And then that creature at the restaurant, planted there by *you*, and just when everything was so perfect, the loveliest evening I'd had in years. Why do these things always happen when you're all set up for a wonderful time? Why isn't it okay for us to be happy? Can't you imagine *that*? Try for a change confining your fantasies to satisfaction and pleasure. That shouldn't be so hard—most people do it as a matter of course. You are forty-five years old and something of a success—it's high time you imagined life *working out*. Why this preoccupation with irresolvable conflict? Don't you want a new mental life? I was once foolish enough to think that's what this was all about and why you wanted me, not to reenact the dead past but to strike out happily on a new course, to rise in exuberant rebellion against *your* author and remake your life. I had the temerity to think that I was having a tremendous effect. Why did you have to ruin everything with this anti-Semitic outburst against which you now must rage like a zealot from Agor? New York you made into a horror by perversely playing *Carnovsky* out in reverse with that ghastly experiment in impotence. I for one would rather have taken the part of Marvelous Maria the porn-queen fellator in some interminable priapic romp—even all the choking would have been preferable to the terrible sadness of seeing you crushed in that way. And now, in London, the Jews. When everything was going so beautifully, the Jews. Can't you ever forget your Jews? How can that turn out to be—particularly in someone who's been around as much as you—your irreducible core? It *is* boring, boring and regressive and crazy to continue on about your connection to a group into which you simply happened to have been born, and a very long time ago at that. Disgusting as you've discovered my Englishness to be, I'm really *not* wedded to it, or to any label, in the way that most of you Jews do persist in being Jewish. Hasn't the man who has led your life been a loyal child long enough?

You know what it's like being with a Jew when the subject of Jews arises? It's like when you're with people who are on the verge of insanity. Half the time you're with them they're absolutely fine, and some of the time they're completely barking. But there are curious moments when they're hovering, you can see them tipping over the edge. Actually what they are saying is no less reasonable than what they were saying five minutes before, but you know that they have just stepped over that little magic line.

What I'm saying is that all the way back on page 73 I saw where you were preparing to take us, and should have got myself up and out before your plane even landed, let along rushing to the airport to catch you sky-high still on the Holy Land. It works this way (your enveloping mind, I mean): inasmuch as it has been established by my sister that my mother is determined to make an issue of having our child symbolically sprinkled with the purifying waters of the church, you are now determined to counterattack by demanding that the child, if a boy, shall make his covenant with Yahweh through the ritual sacrifice of his foreskin. Oh, I do see through to your contrary core! We would have argued again—*we who never argue*. I would have said, "I think it's a barbaric mutilation. I think it's physically harmless in a million cases out of a million and one, so that I can't produce any medical arguments against it, except the general one that one would rather not intervene in anyone's body unless it's necessary. But I nonetheless think it's terrible, circumcising boys *or* girls. I just think it's wrong." And you would have said, "But I would find it very hard having a son who isn't circumcised," or something even more subtly menacing. And so it would go. And who would win? Guess. It *is* a barbaric mutilation, but, being reasonable and completely your creature, I would of course have given in. I'd say, "I think a child should be like a father in that way. I mean, if the father is *not* circumcised, then I think the child should be like *his* father, because I think it would puzzle a child to be different from his father and would cause all sorts of problems for him." I'd say—be made to say is nearer the truth—"I think it's better not to interfere with these customs when they cause so much feeling. If you are going to be incensed about anybody interfering with this link between you and your son, I don't care if it looks to me as though an intellectual agnostic is being irrationally Jewish, I now understand the feeling and don't propose to stand in its way. If it's this that establishes for you the truth of your paternity—that regains for you the truth of your *own* paternity—so be it." And *you* would have said, "And what about *your* paternity—what about your mother, Maria?" and then we would *never* have got to sleep, not for years, because the issue would have been joined and you would have been having the time of your life what with our intercontinental marriage having become so much more INTERESTING.

No, I won't do it. I will not be locked into your head in this way. I will not participate in this primitive drama, not even for the sake of your fiction. Oh, darling, the hell with your fiction. I remember how back in New York, when I let you read one of my stories, you immediately ran out and bought me that thick leather-bound notebook. "I've got something for you to write in," you told me. "Thank you," I replied, "but do you think I have that much to say?" You didn't seem to realize that writing for me isn't everything about my existence wrestling to be born but just some stories about the mists and the Gloucestershire meadows. And I didn't realize that even a woman as passive as I has to know when to run for her life. Well, I would be just too stupid if I didn't know by now. Admittedly, it's no return to Paradise, but since he and I do have a great deal in common, have a deep bond of class and generation and nationality and background, when we fight like cats and dogs it really has little to do with anything, and afterwards everything goes on just as before, which is how I like it. It's too intense, all this talk that *means* something. You and I argue, and twentieth-century history comes looming up, and at its most infernal. I feel pressed on every side, and it takes the stuffing out of me—but for you, it's your métier, really. All our short-lived serenity and harmony, all our hope and happiness, was a bore to you, admit it. So was the idea of altering your ways in middle age by becoming a calmly detached observer, a bit more of a percipient spy on the agony of others, rather than, as of old, being tossed and torn apart yourself.

You do want to be opposed again, don't you? You may have had your fill of fighting Jews and fighting fathers and fighting literary inquisitors—the harder you fight that sort of local opposition, the more your inner conflict grows. But fighting the goyim it's *clear*, there's no uncertainty or doubt—a good, righteous, guilt-free punch-up! To be resisted, to be caught, to find yourself in the midst of a battle puts a spring in your heel. You're just dying, after all my mildness, for a collision, a clash—anything as long as there's enough antagonism to get the story smoking and everything exploding in the wrathful philippics you adore. To be a Jew at Grossinger's is obviously a bit of a bore—but in England being Jewish turns out to be difficult and just what you consider fun. People tell you, *There are restrictions,* and you're in your element again. You *revel* in restrictions. But the fact is that as far as the English are concerned, being Jewish is something you very occasionally apologize for and that's it. It is hardly my perspective, it strikes me as coarse and insipid, but it still is nothing like the horror you have imagined. But a life without horrible difficulties (which by the way a number of Jews do manage to enjoy here—just ask Disraeli or Lord Weidenfeld) is inimical to the writer you are. You actually *like* to take things hard. You can't weave your stories otherwise.

Well, not me, I like it amiable, the amiable drift of it, the mists, the meadows, and not to reproach each other for things outside our control, and not every last thing invested with urgent meaning. I don't usually give in to strange temptation and now I remember why. When I told you about that scene at Holly Tree Cottage when my mother said, about my Jewish friend, "They smell so funny, don't they?" I saw exactly what you were thinking—not "How awful for someone to say such a thing!" but "Why does she write about those stupid meadows when she can sink her teeth into *that*? Now *there's* a subject!" Perfectly true, but not a subject for me. The last thing I would ever want are the consequences of writing about *that*. For one thing, if I did, I wouldn't really be telling the English anything they didn't know but simply exposing my mother and me to incalculable distress in order to come up with something "strong." Well, better to keep the peace by writing something weak. I don't entirely share your superstitions about art and its strength. I take my stand for something far less important than axing everything open—it's called tranquillity.

But tranquillity is disquieting to you, Nathan, in writing particularly—it's bad art to you, far too comfortable for the reader and certainly for yourself. The last thing you want is to make readers happy, with everything cozy and strifeless, and desire simply fulfilled. The pastoral is not your genre, and Zuckerman Domesticus now seems to you just that, too easy a solution, an idyll of the kind you hate, a fantasy of innocence in the perfect house in the perfect landscape on the banks of the perfect stretch of river. So long as you were winning me, getting me away from him, and we were struggling with the custody issue, so long as there was that wrestling for rights and possessions, you were engrossed, but now it begins to look to me that you're afraid of peace, afraid of Maria and Nathan alone and quiet with their happy family in a settled life. To you, in that, there's a suggestion of Zuckerman unburdened, too on top of it, that's not earned—or worse, insufficiently INTERESTING. To you to live as an innocent is to live as a laughable monster. Your chosen fate, as you see it, is to be innocent of innocence at all costs, certainly not to let me, with my pastoral origins, cunningly transform you into a pastoralized Jew. I think you are embarrassed to find that even you were tempted to have a dream of simplicity as foolish and naïve as anyone's. Scandalous. How can that be? Nothing, but nothing, is simple for Zuckerman. You constitutionally distrust anything that appears to you to be effortlessly gained. As if it were effortless to achieve what we had.

Yet when I'm gone don't think I didn't appreciate you. Shall I tell you what I'm going to miss, despite my shyness and well-known lack of sexual assertiveness? It's feeling your hips between my thighs. It's not very erotic by today's standards, and probably you don't even know what I'm talking about. "My hips between your thighs?" you ask, dumbly rubbing your whiskers. Yes, position A. You'd hardly ever done anything so ordinary in your life before I came along, but for me that was just lovely and I won't forget for a long time what it was like. I will also remember an afternoon down in your apartment before my enemy came home for dinner; there was an old song on the radio, you said it was a song you used to dance to in high school with your little girl-friend Linda Mandel, and so for the first and only time, there in your study, we danced the fox-trot like adolescent kids out of the forties, danced the fox-trot glued loin to loin. When I look back on all this fifteen years from now, you know what I'll think? I'll think, "Lucky old me." I'll think what we all think fifteen years later: "Wasn't that nice." But at twenty-eight this is no life, especially if you are going to be Maupassant and milk the irony for all its worth. You want to play reality-shift? Get yourself another girl. I'm leaving. When I see you now in the lift or down in the foyer collecting your mail, I will pretend, though it may only be the two of us who are there, that we have never been anything other than neighbors, and if we meet in public, at a party or a restaurant, and I am with my husband and our friends, I will blush, I do blush, not as much as I used to, but I always blush at a very revealing moment, I blush at the most extraordinary things, though perhaps I can get out of it by coming boldly up to you and saying, "I'd just like to tell you how profoundly I identify with the women characters in your argumentative books," and nobody will guess, despite my blushing, that I was almost one of them.

P.S. I think Maria is a nice enough name for other people, but not for me.

P.P.S. At the point where "Maria" appears to be most her own woman, most resisting you, most saying I cannot live the life you have imposed upon me, not if it's going to be a life of us quarreling about your Jewishness in England, that is impossible—at this point of greatest strength, she is least real, which is to say *least* her own woman, because she has become again your "character," just one of a series of fictive propositions. This is diabolical of you.

P.P.P.S. If this letter sounds terribly rational, I assure you it's the last thing I feel.

My Maria,

When Balzac died he called out for his characters from his deathbed. Do we have to wait for that terrible hour? Besides, you are not merely a character, or even a character, but the real living tissue of my life. I understand the terror of being tyrannically suppressed, but don't you see how it's led to excesses of imagination that are yours and not mine? I suppose it can be said that I do sometimes desire, or even require, a certain role to be rather clearly played that other people aren't always interested enough to want to perform. I can only say in my defense that I ask no less of myself. Being Zuckerman is one long performance and the very opposite of what is thought of as *being oneself*. In fact, those who most seem to be themselves appear to me people impersonating what they think they might like to be, believe they ought to be, or wish to be taken to be by whoever is setting standards. So in earnest are they that they don't even recognize that being in earnest *is the act*. For certain self-aware people, however, this is not possible: to imagine themselves being themselves, living their own real, authentic, or genuine life, has for them all the aspects of a hallucination.

I realize that what I am describing, people divided in themselves, is said to characterize mental illness and is the absolute opposite of our idea of emotional integration. The whole Western idea of mental health runs in precisely the opposite direction: what is desirable is congruity between your self-consciousness and your natural being. But there are those whose sanity flows from the conscious *separation* of those two things. If there even *is* a natural being, an irreducible self, it is rather small, I think, and may even be the root of all impersonation—the natural being may be the skill itself, the innate capacity to impersonate. I'm talking about recognizing that one is acutely a performer, rather than swallowing whole the guise of naturalness and pretending that it isn't a performance but you.

There is no you, Maria, any more than there's a me. There is only this way that we have established over the months of performing together, and what it is congruent with isn't "ourselves" but past performances—we're has-beens at heart, routinely trotting out the old, old act. What is the role I demand of you? I couldn't describe it, but I don't have to—you are such a great intuitive actress you *do* it, almost with no direction at all, an extraordinarily controlled and seductive performance. Is it a role that's foreign to you? Only if you wish to pretend that it is. It's *all* impersonation—in the absence of a self, one impersonates selves, and after a while impersonates best the self that best gets one through. If you were to tell me that there are people, like the man upstairs to whom you now threaten to turn yourself in, who actually do have *a strong sense of themselves*, I would have to tell you that they are only impersonating people with a strong sense of themselves—to which you could correctly reply that since there is no way of proving whether I'm right or not, this is a circular argument from which there is no escape.

All I can tell you with certainty is that I, for one, have no self, and that I am unwilling or unable to perpetrate upon myself the joke of a self. It certainly does strike me as a joke about *my* self.

What I have instead is a variety of impersonations I can do, and not only of myself—a troupe of players that I have internalized, a permanent company of actors that I can call upon when a self is required, an ever-evolving stock of pieces and parts that forms my repertoire. But I certainly have no self independent of my imposturing, artistic efforts to have one. Nor would I want one. I am a theater and nothing more than a theater.

Now probably this is all true only to a point and I am characteristically trying to take it too far, "tipping over the edge," as you say of Jews, "like people who are on the verge of insanity." I could be altogether wrong. Obviously the whole idea of what is a self philosophers have gone on about at extraordinary lengths, and, if only from the evidence here, it is a very slippery subject. But it *is* INTERESTING trying to get a handle on one's own subjectivity—something to think about, to play around with, and what's more fun than that? Come back and we'll play with it together. We could have great times as Homo Ludens and wife, inventing the imperfect future. We can pretend to be anything we want. All it takes is impersonation. That is like saying that it takes only courage, I know. I am saying just that. I am willing to go on impersonating a Jewish man who still adores you, if only you will return pretending to be the pregnant Gentile woman carrying our minuscule unbaptized baby-to-be. You cannot choose a man you can't stand against the person that you love just because the unhappy life with him is easy by comparison to the paradoxically more difficult happy life with me. Or is that what all the aging husbands say when their young wives disappear in the middle of the night?

I just can't believe that you are serious about living upstairs. I hate to have to be the one to make the perfectly crude, predictable, feminist point, but even if you weren't going to live with me, couldn't you think of something else to do rather than going back to him? It seems so self-reductive of you, unless I'm reading you too literally, and the point you're hammering home is that *anything's* better than me.

Now to what you say about pastoralization. Do you remember the Swedish film we watched on television, that microphotography of ejaculation, conception, and all that? It was quite wonderful. First was the whole sexual act leading to conception, from the point of view of the innards of the woman. They had a camera or something up the vas deferens. I still don't know how they did it—does the guy have the camera on his prick? Anyway, you saw the sperm in huge color, coming down, getting ready, and going out into the beyond, and then finding its end up somewhere else—*quite* beautiful. The pastoral landscape par excellence. According to one school, it's where the pastoral genre that you speak of begins, those irrepressible yearnings by people beyond simplicity to be taken off to the perfectly safe, charmingly simple and satisfying environment that is desire's homeland. How moving and pathetic these pastorals are that cannot admit contradiction or conflict! That that is the womb and this is the world is not as easy to grasp as one might imagine. As I discovered at Agor, not even Jews, who are to history what Eskimos are to snow, seem able, despite the arduous education to the contrary, to protect themselves against the pastoral myth of life before Cain and Abel, of life before the split began. Fleeing now, and back to day zero and the first untainted settlement—breaking history's mold and casting off the dirty, disfiguring reality of the piled-up years: this is what Judea means to, of all people, that belligerent, unillusioned little band of Jews . . . also what Basel meant to claustrophobic Henry lustlessly boxed-in back in Jersey . . . also—let's face it—something like what you and Gloucestershire once meant to me. Each has its own configuration, but whether set in the cratered moonscape of the Pentateuch, or the charming medieval byways of orderly old Schweiz, or the mists and the meadows of Constable's England, at the core is the idyllic scenario of redemption through the recovery of a sanitized, confusionless life. In dead seriousness, we all create imagined worlds, often green and breastlike, where we may finally be "ourselves." Yet another of our mythological pursuits. Think of all those Christians, hearty enough to know better, piping out their virginal vision of Momma and invoking that boring old Mother Goose manger. What's our unborn offspring meant to me, right up to tonight in fact, but something per-

326

fectly programmed to be my little redeemer? What you say is true: the pastoral is not my genre (no more than you would think of it as Mordecai Lippman's); it isn't complicated enough to provide a real solution, and yet haven't I been fueled by the most innocent (and comical) vision of fatherhood with the imagined child as the therapeutic pastoral of the middle-aged man?

Well, that's over. The pastoral stops here and it stops with circumcision. That delicate surgery should be performed upon the penis of a brand-new boy seems to you the very cornerstone of human irrationality, and maybe it is. And that the custom should be unbreakable even by the author of my somewhat skeptical books proves to you just how much my skepticism is worth up against a tribal taboo. But why not look at it another way? I know that touting circumcision is entirely anti-Lamaze and the thinking these days that wants to debrutalize birth and culminates in delivering the child in water in order not even to startle him. Circumcision is startling, all right, particularly when performed by a garlicked old man upon the glory of a newborn body, but then maybe that's what the Jews had in mind and what makes the act seem quintessentially Jewish and the mark of their reality. Circumcision makes it clear as can be that you are here and not there, that you are out and not in—also that you're mine and not theirs. There is no way around it: you enter history through my history and me. Circumcision is everything that the pastoral is not and, to my mind, reinforces what the world is about, which isn't strifeless unity. Quite convincingly, circumcision gives the lie to the womb-dream of life in the beautiful state of innocent prehistory, the appealing idyll of living "naturally," unencumbered by man-made ritual. To be born is to lose all that. The heavy hand of human values falls upon you right at the start, marking your genitals as its own. Inasmuch as one invents one's meanings, along with impersonating one's selves, this is the meaning I propose for that rite. I'm not one of those Jews who want to hook themselves up to the patriarchs or even to the modern state; the relationship of my Jewish "I" to their Jewish "we" is nothing like so direct and unstrained as Henry now wishes his to be, nor is it my intention to simplify that connection by flying the flag of our child's foreskin. Only a few hours ago, I went so far as to tell Shuki Elchanan that the custom of circumcision was probably irrelevant to my "I." Well, it turns out to be easier to take that line on Dizengoff Street than sitting here beside the Thames. A Jew among Gentiles and a Gentile among Jews. Here it turns out, by my emotional logic, to be the number-one priority. Aided by your sister, your mother, and even by you, I find myself in a situation that has reactivated the strong sense of difference that had all but atrophied in New York, and, what's more, that has drained the domestic idyll of its few remaining drops of fantasy. Circumcision confirms that there is an us, and an us that isn't solely him and me. England's made a Jew of me in only eight weeks, which, on reflection, might be the least painful method. A Jew without Jews, without Judaism, without Zionism, without Jewishness, without a temple or an army or even a pistol, a Jew clearly without a home, just the object itself, like a glass or an apple.

I think in the context of our adventures—*and* Henry's—that it's fitting to conclude with my erection, the circumcised erection of the Jewish father, reminding you of what you said when you first had occasion to hold it. I wasn't so chagrined by your virginal diffidence as by the amusement that came in its wake. Uncertainly I asked, "Isn't it to your liking?" "Oh, yes, it's fine," you said, delicately weighing it in the scale of your hand, "but it's the phenomenon itself: it just seems a rather rapid transition." I'd like those words to stand as the coda to that book you so foolishly tell me you wish to escape. To escape into what, Marietta? It may be as you say that this is no life, but use your enchanting, enrapturing brains: this life is as close to life as you, and I, and our child can ever hope to come.

Also available in Vintage

Philip Roth

THE ANATOMY LESSON

'*The Anatomy Lesson* is a ferocious, heartfelt book…lavish with laughs and flamboyant inventions'
John Updike

At forty, the writer Nathan Zuckerman comes down with a mysterious affliction – pure pain, beginning in his neck and shoulders, invading his torso, and taking possession of his spirit. Zuckerman, whose work was his life, is unable to write a line. Now his work is trekking from one doctor to another, but none can find a cause for the pain and nobody can assuage it. Zuckerman himself wonders if the pain can have been caused by his own books. And while he is wondering, his dependence on painkillers extends to an addiction to vodka and marijuana.

The third volume of the trilogy and epilogue *Zuckerman Bound, The Anatomy Lesson* is a great comedy of illness and provides some of the funniest scenes in all of Roth's fiction as well as some of the fiercest.

'Roth has a genius for the comedy of entrapment…He writes America's most raucously funny novels'
Time

VINTAGE

Philip Roth

THE PRAGUE ORGY

'Scabrous, gutsy and scathing'
The Times

In quest of the unpublished manuscript of a martyred
Yiddish writer, the American novelist Nathan Zuckerman
travels to Soviet-occupied Prague in the mid-1970s. There,
in a nation straitjacketed by totalitarian Communism, he
discovers a literary predicament, marked by institutional-
ised oppression, that is rather different from his own. He
also discovers, among the oppressed writers with whom
he quickly becomes embroiled in a series of bizarre and
poignant adventures, an appealingly perverse kind of
heroism.

The Prague Orgy, consisting of entries from Zuckerman's
notebooks recording his sojourn among these outcast
artists, completes the trilogy and epilogue *Zuckerman
Bound*. It provides a startling ending to Roth's intricately
designed magnum opus on the unforeseen consequences of
art.

'A black fable about the lies and fictions which are the life
blood of both politics and literature'
Sunday Times

VINTAGE

BY PHILIP ROTH
ALSO AVAILABLE IN VINTAGE